"W
YOU WON . . . ?"

she said with a small knot of apprehension growing in her breast.

"You, my pet." He regarded her coldly.

She gasped and the world grew black in front of her eyes; she thought she might faint. "I am not a slave to be disposed of on a turn of a card. You have no control over me."

"You are mine now, my haughty vixen."

"So you will force me to become . . ." her voice broke and she could not finish.

"A farmer's whore . . . you are my property now," he supplied cruelly. "We will spend the night in the countess' house."

"Together?" Her voice quivered.

"Most assuredly together," he added as he lifted her in his arms and started down the road with her.

DESIRE'S COMMAND

Marlene Suson

PUBLISHED BY POCKET BOOKS NEW YORK

A POCKET BOOKS/RICHARD GALLEN *Original* publication

POCKET BOOKS, a Simon & Schuster division of
GULF & WESTERN CORPORATION
1230 Avenue of the Americas, New York, N.Y. 10020

ISBN: 0-671-41786-X

First Pocket Books printing January, 1981

10 9 8 7 6 5 4 3 2 1

POCKET and colophon are trademarks of Simon & Schuster.

Printed in the U.S.A.

Part One

Chapter 1

The long-case clock in the lower hall was striking eleven as Chandra Taylor came down the polished oak staircase at Northlands, but the winter morning was so gray that twilight seemed to have already descended. At the foot of the stairs, a candle had been lit in a brass wall sconce. The defective taper flickered, its light pale and uncertain, as uncertain as Chandra's future. The past week's shattering events had altered everything.

As she passed the door of the library, her cousin, Sir Henry Taylor, called curtly from within, "Come here, Chandra. I want a word with you."

It was the summons that Chandra had been dreading since Sir Henry's arrival at Northlands the previous day. Reluctantly, she turned toward the library. It contained so many reminders of her father: his neatly shelved books, his prized miniature of her mother—his late wife—his winged easy chair in which no one but he ever sat.

As Chandra entered the library, she stiffened at the sight of Sir Henry sprawled carelessly in her father's chair as though he owned it. She wanted to protest, but she stopped herself in time. The chair did indeed belong to Sir Henry now. It was his to dispose of as he saw fit, as was everything at Northlands—even herself.

Sir Henry did not rise to greet her. This deliberate rudeness was not half so distressing to Chandra, however, as his lascivious perusal of her that seemed to strip her modest black wool gown from her body. She felt naked before him. Determined that he should not suspect the apprehension welling up in her, she forced herself to meet his insulting gaze with a cool hauteur that she did not feel.

The elegant tailoring of Sir Henry's embroidered cream satin waistcoat and black silk jersey breeches could not hide the flabbiness of his body. He was a man of eight and thirty years with a hairline that had greatly receded only on the left side, giving his head a curious lopsided appearance. His face was florid and puffy; his protruding eyes were as gray and cold as the day. He was toying with a gold and enameled snuffbox as she entered the room.

"What a lazy miss you are, Chandra." His rasping, voice was scornful. " 'Tis nearly noon and you are just arising."

His unjust accusation brought a wave of color to her face. She had been awake with her grief until the early hours of the morning and then, exhausted, had fallen into the first deep and lengthy sleep she had had since her father's death a se'enight ago. His gig had hit a patch of ice on a curve and overturned. The vehicle had landed atop him, crushing the strong body that Chandra had always imagined as indestructible.

Somehow Philip Taylor had managed to cling to life for three days after the accident, and Chandra did not leave his side until he died. Even then she could snatch no more than short, fitful naps between storms of grief. The most terrible moment had come yesterday as she had watched the coffin containing the body of the man who had been both her father and her idol consigned to the grave.

Sir Henry's voice brought her back to the present. "You will not sleep so late at Blackstone Abbey," he said with a smirk. "I do not permit such sloth in my household."

"What?" she stammered, unable for a second to comprehend. Blackstone was Sir Henry's country estate near London.

"We leave for there at dawn tomorrow," he told her.

"I fear a storm is coming, and I have no desire to be snowbound in the north of England."

"But what of Northlands?"

"I am closing it. I have already dismissed the servants, and I shall sell it to the first fool I can find who is stupid enough to buy it."

Chandra had been born and reared at Northlands and had never known another home. She swallowed hard at the news. The house had been owned originally by her uncle, Sir James Taylor, and since his death by his son, Sir Henry.

Sir Henry snapped open the lid of his oval snuffbox. "My father would have gotten rid of Northlands years ago had he not had to use it to hide your parents." An odor of camphor wafted from the box in Sir Henry's hand. "And had his will not prevented me, I would have sold it years ago."

His aggrieved tone told Chandra just how bitter was his resentment. Sir James's will had stipulated that Northlands was to remain her father's home and could not be sold so long as he lived. But now Northlands was, at last, Sir Henry's in fact as well as title.

He ran his finger along the edge of the box. "But now I do have that legal right and can begin to manage things effectively. And not only in the matter of houses and estates." He gave Chandra an appraising look. "I am surprised a girl of your beauty has failed to capture a husband. Your father neglected your marital interests shamefully."

Chandra bridled at this criticism of her father, whose paramount concern had been to find her a worthy husband. She had had suitors, of course, some of them of respectable fortune, but they had not found favor with either her or her father, although for different reasons. He had high ambitions for the man who would become her husband and would accept nothing less than a scion of prestigious family. She, on the other hand, had dreamed of finding a love as great as the one that her mama had borne for her father.

Sir Henry took a pinch of snuff from his box. "Blackstone Abbey will be your home, Chandra, only until I can find you a husband."

Her sea blue eyes flared with defiance. "And I am to have no say in the matter?"

The snuff fell from his fingers. "You wretched ingrate," he snapped. "You should be thankful for my kindness in making a penniless orphan my ward." He glared at her. "You are your father's daughter—as proud and willful and haughty as ever he was. Not that he had any reason to be. Any man who would run off as he did with the Duke of Warfolk's betrothed and destroy himself with his silly passion is an idiot, pure and simple. But never doubt it, Chandra. You will marry the man I choose for you."

Her blue eyes turned as stormy as the sea in a gale. "What if I do not like him?"

"Only fools marry for love."

"My parents married for love, and they were not fools!"

"Weren't they?" Sir Henry's voice was heavy with contempt. "Look at the price they paid. Your father might have had a brilliant political career, but he threw it away. Only a week before your perfidious mother was to marry the most powerful duke in England, they eloped! Extraordinary fools!"

"Her betrothal was forced upon her. She wanted none of it."

"So she brought misery to us all instead." His face tightened with anger. "When your parents fled, it was their families who bore the brunt of the duke's rage. His insatiable thirst for revenge dogged us for years."

Sir Henry looked down at the miniature portrait of Chandra's mother, now five years dead, on the little table beside her father's chair. "She was a great beauty—that cannot be denied. You strongly resemble her, you know." He studied Chandra critically. "The same striking blue eyes and flawless complexion. The same upward tilt of the nose. And it appears you have inherited her foolishness as well as her beauty. She had the world at her feet, and she threw it away for your father, a dreamer who squandered his fortune."

"He did not." Chandra was rigid with anger. "He was robbed of it by that treasonous American pirate, Captain Devil."

"Nonsense. The American colonies were warring for their independence. Everyone knew about their privateer, the one they called Captain Devil, and the destruction he was inflicting on our shipping. Only a bloody idiot like your father would have gambled all his money on a convoy bound for the West Indies in the midst of a war."

Sir Henry dipped into his little snuffbox and, placing a pinch on his thumbnail, he lifted it awkwardly to his nose. Chandra silently seethed at his indictment of her father. Philip Taylor had only done what he felt he had to do in order to multiply his modest fortune so that he and her mother would be able to elope to a comfortable life abroad. His audacious gamble had almost succeeded. The convoy in which he had invested every penny he could scrape together had reached the West Indies safely, and its cargo of guns, furniture, and porcelain had been sold to the rich planters at a handsome profit. The ships had taken on an even more lucrative load of rum, molasses and sugar, and sailed for home. It was then that Captain Devil himself, a legend of the seas, descended upon the convoy during a storm and seized the ships one by one. This was another stunning triumph for the rebel pirate. Everything was taken, including the profits from the outward voyage.

The loss ruined Chandra's father. When word of it reached England a week before her mother's scheduled wedding to the duke, her parents had no choice. They eloped to Italy and to a life of poverty that claimed the life of their firstborn when the boy was but a year old. For the rest of his life, Philip Taylor had blamed Americans for the death of his adored son. He despised them with a white-hot fury.

How often Chandra had heard him say, "Never was

a man more fittingly named than Captain Devil. He consigned your mama and me to a life of hell in Italy."

Her father and her mother—then pregnant with Chandra—had finally been rescued by Sir Henry's father, who smuggled them back into England and concealed them at Northlands, his remote estate in the north of England. Sir James passed her parents off to the local people as impoverished distant cousins whom he had hired to manage the estate. Only his family and Chandra's mother's two brothers knew that the fugitive couple had returned. Had the vengeful duke learned of it, there was no telling what he might have done to her parents and their benefactor. The man was reputed to be terrifying in his rages.

Chandra still remembered how, when she was small, her mother would pale at the sight of a stranger and turn away so that she could not be recognized. But very few strangers and no member of the London ton who might have known her parents visited this remote and barren spot, and they remained undetected.

Sir Henry, having finished his snuff ritual, set the enameled case down on the table beside the miniature of Chandra's mother. He gestured at the portrait. "I shall not permit you to waste yourself as she did. Although it may be difficult to find a husband for a dowerless orphan, I am determined to have you married off before the year is out."

Chandra gave him a murderous look. "You will never force from my lips vows binding me to a man I do not choose to wed!"

Her cousin jumped to his feet. "You are my chattel. You will do as I wish." His expression turned sly. "Surely your spinsterhood concerns you."

"Nineteen is hardly an age to be considered long in the tooth," she answered tartly. "Besides, spinsterhood is infinitely preferable to marrying a man I cannot bear."

"How would you support yourself if you had no husband? You cannot presume upon my generosity for the rest of your life."

"Nor would I accept it even if it were offered." She

raised her head regally. Philip Taylor's legacy to her had been in pride and determination instead of pounds and pence. "I shall become a teacher. My father gave me a fine education."

"Which only proves again what a fool he was," her cousin scoffed. "Education is wasted on women. There is only one place for a morsel like you—in a man's bed." He gave her slender but voluptuous figure another lascivious examination. "I suspect that once introduced to lovemaking you will like it very much, indeed. Your body is built for it. I cannot deny that I should like a taste of you myself."

Before Chandra realized what he was about, he reached up and cupped one of her full round breasts in his hand and squeezed it roughly. It was, for a moment, as if she had been turned to stone, so great was her shock. Never before had any man dared to touch her so intimately. Then her shock gave way to fury. She tried to slap his hand away and flee.

But he was too quick for her. He grabbed her wrist and yanked her around, pulling her against him. She struggled to free herself from his hateful embrace. But for a man so lacking in physical tone, he had surprising strength, and Chandra could not break his grip.

A scream rose in her throat but it died there as he forced his lips over hers in a brutal kiss that smothered her protest. His mouth was sour and bruising on her tender, virgin lips, and he filled her with revulsion. He strove to penetrate her soft mouth with his tongue and she clinched her teeth tightly against this invasion. The odor of the snuff was overpowering on his breath.

He seized her hair, freeing the long, luxurious mass from its fastenings, and it fell in shimmering sable waves to her waist.

He increased his pressure against her, arching her backward farther and farther until she feared her spine would snap. She was completely off balance and so could offer no resistance when he shoved her down. She was suddenly, mercifully freed from the hateful assault of his mouth upon hers. But her relief lasted only an instant. To her horror, she found herself next to him, crushed down upon the settee.

Sir Henry sat on its edge, pinning her shoulders to the seat, and he bent to claim her lips once again. She rolled her head from side to side in a frantic effort to avoid his mouth and probing tongue. The rough upholstery of the settee chafed the delicate skin of her face. Although her shoulders were trapped against the seat, he had let go of her hands, and she fought to extricate herself from his grasp.

With an oath, Sir Henry straightened above her and grabbed her wrists. As he did, he was distracted on sighting another part of her anatomy. As he had pushed her down upon the settee, the full skirt of her gown had caught beneath her, leaving bare a long expanse of shapely legs. He held her wrists together in his left hand and pinned them down upon her breast. With his free hand, he tugged her skirt still higher and then pushed beneath it, groping along her thighs toward her most private place.

Terror filled her. Here in her father's favorite room among his beloved mementos, beneath the miniature portrait of her mother, would she be cruelly raped? Would this dreadful cousin she despised rob her of the only dowry she had to give a husband? Her fear and revulsion gave new strength to her limbs, and with a mighty effort, she managed to free her wrists from Sir Henry's grasp. She shoved him from the edge of the settee.

As he crashed to the floor, Chandra scrambled up and tried to flee. Sir Henry grabbed for her skirt as she dashed by him, catching the hem and yanking it. Chandra tripped and stumbled against the chair, but quickly she regained her balance and resumed her interrupted flight toward the library door.

But the brief delay had given her cousin the opportunity to get to his feet and give chase. She was but three feet from the door when he caught her hair, which was streaming out behind her. Using it as he would have a rope, he hauled her back to him.

Tears sprang to her eyes from the pain. Sir Henry forced her around to face him, leering at her with evil triumph. Then his hands shot up to the high neck of her black mourning gown and he seized it, ripping it open to her waist. Her full swelling breasts were exposed, the pink tips thrusting against the light, almost translucent material of her shift, which quickly suffered the same fate in his hands that her dress had.

Sir Henry stared down at the firm, beautifully formed globes that lay before him. "What beautiful breasts you have," he murmured thickly. Sweat was trickling down his face, and his fingers bit bruisingly into her arms. He gave a low, cruel laugh as she tried in vain to conceal her nakedness with her hands. He thrust his face close to hers, and the strong odor of camphor on his breath stung her nostrils.

"Perhaps," he said, "I shall not find this brief time until I can get you a husband so unrewarding after all."

A wave of nausea swept over Chandra, generated partly by the revulsion she felt for this man and partly by the bleakness of the future for which she was destined. Even if somehow she managed to fend him off now, the reprieve would be only temporary. He would take her against her will whenever he pleased, and she had no recourse against him. She was, as he had pronounced it, his chattel, and he could inflict his will—and himself—upon her as he wished. She had no weapon to protect herself. None, save her wits and her tongue. Desperately, she searched for some reason that would impress him.

"If you rob me of my virtue now," she began slowly, "you may find it impossible to peddle me to another man. And I promise you that I shall proclaim to every prospective husband you find how you have raped and maltreated your helpless ward!"

The color faded from her cousin's face, and the bulge of his desire softened and sank. He turned angrily away from her, and she knew she had won—temporarily.

Chandra grabbed the wreckage of her bodice and, holding it together, hastened for the door. As she reached the portal, he called to her in a low, spiteful voice, "You will marry whomever I find for you and do so quickly, or you shall pay your debt to me in another currency."

Chandra fled into the back hall where she grabbed her plain wool cloak from its peg by the side door and wrapped it tightly around herself to conceal her torn dress.

She was so shocked and shamed by the events of the past few minutes that she scarcely knew what she was doing. The dreadful odor of camphor seemed to cling to her, and she longed for a deep breath of clean air. She opened the side door, stepped out into the cold, pale day, and gulped the fresh, frigid air into her lungs. She longed to cry but somehow she felt as if her tears had been frozen within her.

Chandra stared out across the bleak, snow-scattered landscape of the high moors. On the path leading up from the stable, she saw the figure of a man as sturdy and gnarled as the stunted oak that grew in the corner of the garden. He wore an old black cloak and carried a small canvas bundle. His face, weathered by long years of summer sun and winter storms, was as brown and wrinkled as a prune. George O'Rourke had cared for her father's horses since Chandra was a baby. As he drew nearer, she saw the deep sadness in his faded blue eyes, but his wrinkled face lit up with joy when he saw her.

"Me heart was nigh to bursting with fear I should not see yourself again, Miss Chandra," he said in a worried tone.

"George," she cried, forgetting her own troubles as her heart went out to this loyal servant. He was being turned out without so much as an extra farthing in reward for his long years of faithful service. "What will you do?"

He grinned bravely, the folds around his eyes crinkling up as he smiled.

"Now, then, don't you be worrying none about meself," he told her. "Me brother, he be a coachman for a fine lord in London. Many's the time he's offered me a position, too. It's there I'll be going."

Chandra looked down at the small canvas bundle that he carried and realized that it contained all his worldly possessions. What a pitiful result of such a life of hard work. She thought of the tiny cache of pounds that her father had been saving to finance a London season for her. He had given it to her as he lay dying. Things might not be so easy for George as he hoped, after all.

Chandra took George's chapped and calloused hand in hers. "Papa left a few pounds. 'Tis not much, but let me share them with you."

George squeezed her hand affectionately. "I'll not be taking what little you have. It's not likely above half what you'll be needing to keep you for a month."

"I won't need it," she lied. "Sir Henry is taking me to live at Blackstone Abbey."

George took in her disheveled appearance. "Sure and if that be the case, 'tis *you* that *I* be worried about," he told her bluntly.

Meeting his gaze, she drew her cloak more tightly about her as if she feared his eyes could penetrate it and see the ruins of her gown.

"That Sir Henry, he be a cruel man," George went on. "Don't be going with him."

"I have nowhere else to go."

The sorrow in George's eyes told Chandra that he recognized the truth of her statement. Reluctantly, he took his leave of her and started down the path that would lead him away from Northlands forever.

He had gone several yards when he stopped, turned, and called back to her. "What of your uncle, Lord Lunt? Perhaps he would take you . . ." But then he shrugged as he himself recognized the futility of Chandra's applying to her mother's older brother for aid. He shook his head sadly and resumed his journey.

As Chandra watched him go, she waved and tried to smile, but now she could not keep her thoughts from her uncle, Lord John Lunt, and the enmity he bore her parents. The Duke of Warfolk's vengeance against the

Taylors had been nothing compared with that which he had inflicted on her mother's family. When Lord Lunt's only son, upon whom he doted, had obtained a commission in the army, the duke had used his power to see that the boy was sent to India to join the command of Marquess Cornwallis, who was then attempting to subdue Tipu Sultan, the ruler of Mysore. Warfolk so arranged it that young Lunt was assigned to lead the first troops into battle. There was little doubt that he would be killed. And he was.

Chandra had seen Lord Lunt only once. She had been ten years old that day he had come to Northlands. Although it had been four months since his son's death, his face was still ravaged with grief. Chandra would never forget the bitter hatred in Lord Lunt's eyes as he looked at her, and in his voice as he said to her mother, "You have your beautiful child, my sister, but in marrying and begetting her, you have cost me my beloved son."

Nor would Chandra ever forget the agony on her mother's face when her brother spoke those words of accusation. No, Chandra thought, Lord Lunt would give her no refuge.

The only reason he had come to Northlands that day so long ago was to make Chandra's sixteen-year-old cousin Percy his heir, since his own son—and only child—was dead.

Percy, whom Chandra's mother had taken in two years earlier, was the child of a disastrous union between Lord Lunt's younger brother and an Irish actress. When Percy was fourteen, his father had succeeded in drinking himself to death after losing all his money at the gaming tables. By that time, the boy's mother had vanished with a traveling theatrical troupe. On his deathbed, Percy's father had written his sister, begging her to give the boy a home. She had agreed instantly. Chandra was only eight when Percy arrived and she quickly came to love him as a brother.

How much more terrible, then, when Lord Lunt offered to make Percy his heir, because there was a condition attached: the boy must swear that he would have nothing more to do with Chandra's parents, whom his lordship blamed for the death of his son. Percy, who had long dreamed of London and the company of the ton to which he felt he rightfully belonged, had eagerly accepted and agreed to the condition. There was a brief, tearful goodbye, and that was all. Chandra had not seen Percy since. If only she knew where he was now. He might be in a position to help her.

Chandra shivered. The cold, penetrating blasts known as the "thin wind" had begun to blow off the moors, and her worn wool cloak was little protection against it. She looked up at the barren hills rising above her. Most people hated these moors, finding them bleak and lonely and unfriendly, but Chandra loved them. Her long rides with her father across them had afforded her some of her happiest hours.

On this day, however, with the sky a gray slate roof that no sunlight could penetrate, the treeless moors looked dismal even to her. They were clad in a ragged sheet of dirty, crusted snow, through which gray clumps of gorse and masses of heather poked like beggars' elbows through tattered sleeves.

The burbling calls of the curlews, the melodious song of the ring ouzels, and the silly squeaks of the meadow pipits were silenced by the winter's solemnity, and only the thin, eerie cry of the wind as it sped across the moors pierced the gloomy quiet.

But Chandra knew these moors better—they harbored beauty as well as bleakness: lovely gills—the hidden glens that sheltered mountain ash; swift, rocky creeks; and in some places, at some times, even tumbling waterfalls. How she longed to saddle Zeus, the brown stallion her father had given her as a foal, and vanish with him forever into one of those secret gills.

Never again, she realized with sudden pain, was she likely to see the moors at those moments that she loved them most: in April when the daffodils heralded the coming of spring with their yellow trumpets, in May when that prickly nuisance, gorse, was transformed into masses of golden flowers that looked like splashes of earthbound sunlight, or in August when the heather spread its honey-scented carpet of purple. She had lost her father who had promised her such a glorious life, and now she was losing the only home she had ever known. And her future seemed as bleak as the moors on this gray winter day.

Choking back tears, she turned and reluctantly dragged herself toward Northlands. She swore to herself as she went that somehow she would outwit Sir Henry.

As Chandra ascended the oak staircase to her room, Sir Henry came to the drawing room door. He watched her with his protruding eyes. His lips were drawn into a cruel, thin line.

What pleasure it would give him to turn the proud, haughty wench out, leaving her alone and penniless, forcing her to fend for herself. In fact, he had planned to do just that until he had arrived at Northlands the previous day. When he discovered what a rare beauty she had become, he realized he had a prize for which some fool would pay well, and Sir Henry was not a man to overlook the possibility of a handsome return on any of his assets. And much as it galled him, he recognized the wisdom of her warning earlier that morning. He could not afford to diminish her value by taking her virginity, nor could he afford to embroil himself in a scandal over his treatment of her. Not only would that jeopardize his social ambitions, but also his marriage. He dreaded to think of the vituperation his shrewish wife would heap upon him. She would give him no peace for the rest of his life with her vitriolic tirades.

Still, watching the proud tilt of Chandra's head and the sensuous sway of her hips as she ascended the stairs, he hungered to sample her. What delight it would be, he thought, to feel that fine body of hers fighting beneath him until he had forced her into submission, taking her swiftly and brutally, without mercy.

Somehow, he swore to himself, he would find a way to have his moment with her. The damned, impudent wench was as stubborn as her father had been. Sir Henry had not had the power to work his will upon the father but, by God, he would see the daughter humbled.

And then an idea of how to accomplish this came suddenly to him. He pondered the thought. Could he possibly . . . ? Yes, of course—it was a magnificent plot. Long after Chandra had disappeared upstairs, he stood in the doorway turning it over in his mind and weighing the possible risks and rewards. He would have to organize it carefully; he could afford no misstep. But properly executed, the plan could bring him a very rich bounty. It would not only humble this proud vixen, but would reap a posthumous revenge upon her father, who had caused Sir Henry and the rest of the Taylor family so much trouble.

Sir Henry's narrow lips twisted in an evil little smile, and he congratulated himself on his brilliant scheme.

Chapter 2

The first pink promise of dawn colored the eastern sky as Chandra crept past the bedchambers of Sir Henry and his wife and started down the winding staircase of Blackstone Abbey. She clutched her riding boots in her hand. A step creaked beneath her foot and she paused in terror, holding her breath. But the sound, although it had seemed as loud as a gunshot to her ears, apparently had aroused no one.

She shuddered at the thought of Sir Henry's rage should he find her sneaking from his house at dawn dressed in men's pants and shirt with only a spencer to ward off the morning chill. Her strange riding costume had been a habit with her for many years—in her father's disappointment that he had no son, he had encouraged her in a variety of unfeminine activities. He had raised her more as a boy than a girl and taught her to ride astride, to hunt, and to shoot. Although he demanded from her all the obedient demureness of a gently born lady when she grew to young womanhood, he still permitted her to wear her peculiar riding outfit when they were alone. If he knew they would not be seen on their long gallops together across the lonely moors, he would allow her to dress as a boy.

Now, as Chandra slipped out the door of Blackstone Abbey, she threw a nervous glance over her shoulder at the silent Gothic monstrosity, a gray castellated pile of stone with parapets and arches piercing the heavy morning mist. The month she had lived there had been the most miserable of her life. Lady Taylor, a thin, dyspeptic woman, made it abundantly clear that she disliked Chandra and suffered her in the household only with the greatest reluctance. She obviously trusted her husband no more than Chandra did herself and kept a close eye upon him. Lady Amelia Taylor was a thin stalk of a woman, and no amount of the rouges and other artifices that she so liberally employed could disguise her plainness. Her father had been one of the richest merchants in England and had tried desperately to marry her to an earl at least, but even his great wealth had been able to buy her only Sir Henry. It was clear that Lady Taylor still harbored great ambitions, and while her husband had been born a mere baronet, she was determined that he would die with a more impressive title.

To Chandra's relief, Sir Henry was careful not to fuel his wife's suspicion. Still she had the uneasy feeling that he was only biding his time, waiting for the proper moment to force himself upon her. He was gone frequently to London on what he implied were husband-hunting expeditions. When he was at home, he contented himself with demonstrating his total authority over Chandra, even forbidding her to ride Zeus, who had been brought to Blackstone Abbey for stud.

Chandra ran toward the stables with the express intent of breaking Sir Henry's ban and of escaping the oppression of his house for at least an hour or so. The flowers of early spring had begun to bloom: bright yellow celandine, lovely white cinquefoil, and white and blue periwinkle on their trailing vines, but she scarcely noticed their delicate display in her eagerness to escape.

The stables were a long way from the house, and when Chandra reached Zeus's stall, she was panting from the run. As she stroked him lovingly, she noted his deep brown coat was not so well tended as it had been when George O'Rourke had cared for him. A lump rose in Chandra's throat at the thought of George, and she prayed that he had fared well in London.

She hastily saddled Zeus and led him from the stable, walking him stealthily past a holly bush where a thrush sang from its nest amid the shining green leaves. A sudden cloak of fog rolled over her, and she took advantage of its protection to mount Zeus and push him to a gallop. She raced him over long stone fences in the green fields through the mist that was slowly lifting. They kept up their frantic pace long after they were out of sight of Blackstone Abbey.

In her haste to escape, Chandra had failed to fasten her long hair securely, and now the wind whipped it from its restraints. Her waist-length tresses streamed out behind her as she rode, but she cared not a whit. There would be no one about this early to see her.

Miles Carrington pushed his horse along the road toward London, cursing the poor animal roundly as he rode through the misty dawn light. This mount had been the best he had been able to obtain on short notice, but he was a connoisseur of horses and was offended by having to make do with this inferior animal.

He longed to be done with this ill-starred affair and home again across the sea in Virginia. All Tom's considerable powers of persuasion had been required to persuade Miles to undertake this mission, but, through no fault of either Tom or himself, it had been foredoomed. Even on that cold February day before Miles had set sail when the presidential election had finally been decided, the mission could never have succeeded.

No one in America had known it then, but William Pitt had already resigned as prime minister over the Irish question and King George III had again sunk into madness, unable even to transfer power formally to his new chief minister, Henry Addington. The British government was in confusion and disarray when Miles arrived in England.

He had held his secret meeting with Pitt, although it was fraught with political risk for Tom if word of it leaked out at home. But Pitt was now a man without power, and the conference was doomed to failure.

Miles had thought of contacting Addington, but he did not dare do so without first consulting Tom. The letters he carried were very personal ones, designed only for Pitt's eyes.

So there was nothing for Miles to do now but contemplate the failure of his mission. He had three days to idle away before the *Golden Drake,* the ship on which he had booked passage home, would sail. At least his sweet Ninon would help him pass the time.

As Miles reached the top of a small, bowl-shaped hill, he was slapped by a strong gust of wind. Reining his horse to a stop, he drew his cloak more tightly around him and yearned for the warmth of his luxurious carrick. He had not dared to wear it, however, knowing such a fine coat would attract attention. He had dressed plainly, as a yeoman might, and had risen before dawn to return to London. No one, except perhaps a farmer or two, would be upon the road to see him so early. Should word get out about Miles's mission, it would cause acute embarrassment, or worse, for Tom. The embittered and defeated Federalists would spread scurrilous slanders if they were to learn that Tom had sent a secret envoy to Britain outside of regular diplomatic channels.

Miles looked about him. The fog was lifting rapidly now, revealing the crooked fields enclosed by hedgerows and low stone fences. A movement to his left caught his eye. Grabbing his glass, he examined the figure it revealed and gasped in surprise. The rider he saw streaking across the fields on a powerful brown stallion wore pants, rode astride like a man, and was a superb equestrian, but there could be no doubt it was a woman. Her long hair flowed behind her like a shimmering brown stream on the wind. Never had Miles seen such an excellent seat on a woman.

The woman urged her mount over a stone fence and rode into a coppice almost directly below the hill from which Miles watched. The stubby oaks were still leafless, and he could see her plainly through the barren branches as she dismounted and sat down upon a fallen tree. Her spencer was inexpensive, but then no lady of gentle birth would be riding dressed like that and alone at dawn besides.

Her riding skill piqued his curiosity, and her attire aroused another kind of interest. A woman who dressed and rode as she did most certainly was a free-living, rebellious spirit who might not be averse, after a bit of persuasion, to an amorous adventure with a stranger. Miles was not a man to pass up the opportunity—nor the challenge. If she were reluctant, he shrugged to himself, at least his curiosity would be assuaged.

Miles dismounted and, with the noiseless stealth he had learned from the Indians of his native land, he slipped through the trees into the copse where she sat.

As he approached her, he stopped, catching his breath at the sight of her exquisite face. Her eyes, framed by thick curling fringes of dark lashes, were as blue as the sea on a sunny day. Her skin was as white and translucent as fine porcelain, and her wild cascade of sable hair was as soft and luxurious as that fur. Her perfectly molded body had full breasts, a tiny waist, and a tantalizing curve to the hips. Miles realized that she was much younger than he had thought, probably not yet twenty. But her beauty was stunning, and he felt a pressure rising in his loins at such splendid provocation.

So engrossed was Chandra in her unhappy thoughts that she did not notice the stranger watching her. The joy she had first felt in riding Zeus had faded as she thought of her untenable position in Sir Henry's household. He was determined to marry her to the first man who would take her off his hands. Her cheeks reddened in humiliation as she thought of it.

Her father had been determined that she should make a brilliant marriage worthy of her distinguished ancestors. A great-grandfather on her mother's side had been a duke. Papa's father might have been a mere baronet, but he was descended from some of the best blood in England. There were an earl and a viscount among the branches, although those titles were held now by distant cousins. So while papa had had no title himself, he was descended from several. He had taken great pride in his breeding and ancestry, in his "impeccable blood-lines" as he had called them.

Despite his long years of banishment, Philip Taylor still had believed firmly that he rightfully belonged to the first ranks of society, and so did his daughter. Of course, no brilliant matches were to be made at remote Northlands, and her father could persuade no one to sponsor Chandra for a London season since no one dared to test the Duke of Warfolk's thirst for vengeance.

But this did not discourage her father's firm faith that Chandra would eventually make a great marriage. In his most high-flown and unrealistic dreams for her, he had favored the progeny of three great houses—the Leighs, the Rodwells, and the Brainerds—as prospective husbands. Of these, the House of Leigh was, on balance, the most distinguished, for it was an ancient line, noted for its courage.

It most certainly would have been his first choice, except that one of its members, the ninth Marquess of Pelham's younger brother, Lord Scott Leigh, had been a black sheep. After a particularly disgraceful scrape, Lord Scott had been disowned and had fled to America, where he later became a leader in the colonies' struggle for independence. The fact that any member of a family, even a disowned member, could have supported the hated Americans was enough to taint the entire house in her father's eyes, and so he leaned toward the Rod-wells.

His were foolish dreams for the daughter of a social outcast, especially one without a dowry. But Chandra, who knew nothing of the mercenary London marriage market, never doubted her father's dreams for her, although she did once question him about her lack of dowry.

He had dismissed the qualm with a shrug of his hand, saying, "You have your virtue and your great beauty. That will be enough."

As she sat in the coppice upon the log, tears welled up in Chandra's eyes. She remembered her vow to her father just before he died. He had lain on his big tester bed at Northlands, fighting for each breath of air, drawing it into his crushed body in great gasps. Staring up at her, his handsome face ravaged by pain and approaching death, he had rasped, "Chandra, you know the kind of man I wish you to marry—a man of family that would have made me proud to have his blood flow in my grandsons' veins. You must swear to me that you will not squander yourself on one who is beneath you. Do not betray me and my faith in you."

His hands had grasped feebly at hers as he had pleaded, "Give me your vow, Chandra . . . so that I may die in peace."

She could not deny him his dying request and so she had vowed. A tiny smile had flickered on his face before he slipped into a coma. Two hours later he was dead.

Now Sir Henry would force her to break her vow, force her to marry the first man he could find for her, or he would take her himself for his own pleasure. Her tears grew to wrenching sobs as she thought of the hopelessness of her situation. She threw herself down on the rough bark of the tree and cried as though her heart would break.

" 'Griefs, when they wound in solitude, wound more deeply.' "

These words came from a rich male voice, soft and comforting, and very near to her. She started and jumped to her feet, staring at the tall, tanned stranger in black cloak and polished Hessian boots. Her heart gave a strange leap as she examined him. He was as handsome a man as she had ever seen, with searching hazel eyes beneath straight thick brows, a patrician nose, sensitive lips and a firm jaw. His hair was dark and unruly, and his cloak did not entirely mask his strong, well-muscled body. He had a small mole to the side of his right brow that drew the viewer's attention to those intelligent eyes.

"What do you want?" Chandra demanded nervously, holding back fresh tears.

The stranger gave her a reassuring smile and another quotation. " 'Fellowship in woe doth woe assuage.' "

His fingers gently touched her chin and tilted her tear-streaked face up toward his, as the hazel eyes studied her with curiosity and compassion. "I want to offer you comfort in your sorrow."

There was a clean, scrubbed scent about him, and his nearness inexplicably caused Chandra's heart to beat faster. His voice had a soft, strange accent that she could not identify, and his touch was as gentle as his eyes, which seemed to hold genuine concern for her.

Chandra knew that she should be terrified and furious at being approached like this by a stranger, but she was totally disarmed. How often did one meet a man who quoted so easily from the classics, as if they were old friends? Certainly he must be a gentleman of manners and education. His compassion and kindness also reassured her, and she found that she felt quite safe with him.

He smiled again at her. This was the first time since her father's death that anyone had exhibited tenderness toward her, and it had an alarming effect. Coping with the cruelty of Sir Henry and the hostility of his wife, Chandra had hidden deep within her body her grief and her anxiety over the future. But now, tasting this first sip of compassion after so long a drought, her interrupted tears began anew, swelling to a torrent, accompanied by sobs that rose from the very depths of her soul.

Miles put his arms around her as a father would a child. His hands stroked her sable hair, so soft beneath his fingers, as he murmured soothing words of consolation. Chandra's cheek rested against his shoulder, and she felt completely protected within the circle of his strong arms.

And so they remained for some moments. Although this was hardly the reception that Miles had anticipated, the girl's grief was so overwhelming that he was filled with compassion for her and quite forgot his original intention. This girl was such a mass of contradictions. She dressed like a free spirit, and yet the modulation of her soft, low voice indicated she was well born. He wondered what terrible sorrow generated such despairing sobs. She looked so young and vulnerable that he suddenly felt like a cad for his initial designs upon her. He longed to be able to protect her from whatever it was that was causing her such pain. The depth of her grief and the many different qualities she possessed were sufficiently provocative to raise his curiosity and his interest to new heights.

When the storm of her sorrow had spent itself, he cradled her head with one hand and dabbed at the tears that glistened on her cheeks with his handkerchief. As he finished his delicate chore, he stared down into her eyes. How blue they were behind the thick, dark lashes. The bluest and the most beautiful he had ever seen. And that pert, slightly upturned nose was a delight. God, but she was exquisite—irresistible.

As he stared down at her, her beauty quite overwhelmed his good sense and, almost without realizing what he was doing, he bent and kissed her tenderly, ever so tenderly, his fingertips caressing her face.

The compassion in the stranger's eyes had warmed and comforted Chandra, and now, strangely, his kiss did the same. It was totally different from Sir Henry's sour kiss, as different as bliss from pain, and so was her reaction to it. Her lips responded to his almost as if they were out of her control, and she felt suddenly intoxicated. Slowly his kiss grew more demanding. Deep within her, she felt strange stirrings. In some inner core never before touched, pleasurable sensations bloomed like the first tender flowers of spring.

His fingers moved from her face to her hair, then followed its lustrous waves slowly down her back to her waist. His hands caressed the curves of her hips, then fastened behind her and drew her close. His muscular body was strong and exciting against hers. His tongue parted her lips and gently explored the tender recess beyond.

For a moment she was lost, entranced in a strange euphoria. She had never experienced anything like this before. Then his hand moved up and stole beneath her spencer to the curve of her breast. His touch was as light and tantalizing as a butterfly's. When his fingers moved to the top button of her blouse, reality suddenly penetrated the enchantment in which his kiss and caresses had enveloped her. Even then, despite her horror at her own shocking wantonness, she could scarcely summon the will to rebuff him.

Nevertheless, she pulled away. With hurt in her eyes and reproach in her voice, she murmured, "How cruel of you to take advantage of my unhappiness."

His handsome face looked confused. "Yes, I suppose it was," he said contritely. "But I swear you are so irresistible that you robbed me of my good sense." He looked at her quizzically. "Still, I have no doubt you found our embrace as enjoyable as I did."

Chandra's eyes blazed with anger, fueled as much by the truth of his statement as by his boldness. Her voice ringing with contempt, she retorted, "And I mistook you for a gentleman."

His gentle eyes hardened at her accusatory tone. He examined her carefully, then said, "But I did not mistake you for a lady."

She blushed with indignation. "I am, and I pray that you treat me like one."

"For a lady, you wear peculiar dress." His hazel eyes boldly explored the slender curves of her body, which were more revealed than concealed by her unusual attire. Raising one eyebrow mockingly, he commented, "Your costume cannot but lead me to other conclusions. Where I come from, ladies do not ride great brown stallions like a man, and in men's clothing as well."

Her flushed cheeks grew even redder with embarrassment, and she quickly changed the subject. "Where do you come from?" she demanded, picking the most innocuous topic she could think of.

"The United States."

She gasped in horror. Although Chandra had never before laid eyes on an American, she shared her adored father's hatred of that inferior, depraved species.

"A Yankee," she spit out.

He shook his head at her vehement reaction, and his voice held a hint of amusement as he replied, "Not a Yankee. I am from Virginia."

The distinction was lost upon Chandra. "You are a rebel," she rejoined.

He laughed a low, rich laugh. "Come now, the Treaty of Paris giving us our independence was signed eighteen years ago."

"You are all traitors to the king."

"Quite to the contrary," he said, his amusement fading in the face of her stubborn persistence. "I am a patriot who would die for my country. In the United States, we pledge our loyalty to our ideals and our nation, not to one man placed by divine right upon a throne, and especially not to one who is mad in the bargain."

"Mad?" She could not fathom his meaning. "How dare you speak of the king like that!" She glared at him. "You Americans are sons of convicts. Even your mothers were nothing but Newgate thieves and whores."

"You seem well versed in our genealogy," he said testily. "How is it you are so familiar with it?"

"I read *Moll Flanders*."

The American stared at her in blank astonishment for an instant, then threw back his head in a laugh so hearty that the rough bark of the tree behind him caught at his dark hair. "How silly you are! And I took you to be intelligent."

"I am no longer shocked by your behavior," she said haughtily, "knowing that you are a savage from a savage land."

Miles gave her a contemptuous bow. "I apologize for having offended your virtue, milady. I suggest that you be more careful in the future when strange men come upon you in your trousers, your hair streaming about you like a courtesan's after a night's romp."

She sputtered with rage. "You rebel devil. You are the lowest scum on this earth."

He raked her with a look, at once angry and devouring, and came at her. Before she realized what he was

about, his arms encircled her in a steel grip. He bent
her back, capturing her lips in a long, passionate kiss.

She struggled futilely against the power of his arms
as his tongue breached her lips. But those sensations he
had awakened in her before once against throbbed within her and seemed to sap the will from her limbs. Gradually her resistance faded beneath the ardor of his kiss.
Her fight died within her, and she moaned softly. She
could not understand the power this man—a hated
American at that—had over her. Instead of filling her
with revulsion and loathing as had Sir Henry, he coaxed
her body into a traitorous betrayal and made her tremble
with pleasure at his touch.

When at last he let her loose, she was limp and breathless.

His hazel eyes and tart voice mocked her. "I detest
women who insist upon playing games with men. You
pretend coldness to hide the heat of your own fires."

Before she could spit out an angry retort, he turned
and strode with long purposeful steps up the hill to his
horse and galloped off.

Chapter 3

As the hoofbeats of the stranger's horse faded, Chandra sank weakly to the ground, shaken to her very soul. His searing kiss had stoked fires never before kindled in her by a man. She was shocked by the man's bold behavior but even more shocked by her own. It was some moments before her confusion subsided sufficiently. Then she remounted Zeus and headed back to Blackstone Abbey.

She did not even know the name of this handsome American who had caused her heart to beat as no other man had ever done. After she had returned Zeus to the stable, she slipped quietly into the house and upstairs, unnoticed by the servants who were busy at their chores in the kitchen. The other members of the household were still in their rooms, and she managed to reenter hers without detection. But once there, she was haunted by the rebel's mocking face and the fire of his kiss.

"Bold, crude jackanapes," she railed furiously to the four walls. Yet she knew much of the blame was hers. She had let him take her in his arms and comfort her as if he had been her husband instead of a stranger. Her heart fluttered at the memory of the sweet tenderness of his first kiss. But how foolish she had been to trust him. If only she had known he was an American, she would have been immediately on her guard.

Yet while she condemned him for his origins and detested him for the liberties he had taken, she was sufficiently honest with herself to realize that part of her ire was directed inwardly. She was disgusted with herself for her inexplicable reaction. Had the stranger's parting insult about pretending coldness been so wide off the mark? He had, in fact, kindled an unsuspected blaze within her that startled her and yet made her yearn for a deeper taste of the forbidden fruit that she had scarcely sampled in his arms.

Her own wantonness shocked her. And how it would have horrified her father! He had impressed upon her time and again that any misstep in manners or morals would ruin any chance of a desirable marriage.

Nourished by her father's dreams for her, Chandra had set her own high moral standards for herself. Her fantasies about her future had run to a titled husband, perhaps even an earl. When she had been small, she had been awed that her mother had rejected a powerful duke. But oddly, her gentle mother had seemed to care nothing for titles. Once, when Chandra was about ten, she said to her mama, "But think, you might have been a duchess."

Her mother had smiled at Chandra's reverent tone. "I loved your father, Chandra. That was what was important. Besides, if you knew the duke, you would not be so impressed. His only recommendation was his title."

"Why?" Chandra asked in disappointment. "Was he ugly?"

"Not in physical appearance—at least not then—although I understand from your Uncle James that he is much changed now. What is important is the man himself, not a label he wears by virtue of his fortunate birth," she concluded.

And that was all Chandra had ever managed to pry out of her mother about the jilted duke.

A hard knock on her door drew Chandra from her reverie. Before she could inquire who was there, the door was flung open, and Sir Henry entered, wearing a banyan of heavy purple brocade lined with lavender velvet. Chandra was reminded of some vain, plump potentate. *The caliph of Blackstone Abbey,* she thought derisively.

"The dressmaker is here with a new gown that you

are to wear tonight," he announced without preamble. "We are having important guests. When I was in London yesterday, a lord of great influence expressed a desire to see Blackstone Abbey. He had heard it was one of the most impressive examples of Gothic revival in all England."

Chandra wondered with amusement who had so misinformed the influential lord on the architectural merits of Blackstone Abbey.

"Entertaining him," her cousin continued, "offered an excellent excuse to invite two bachelors to peruse you."

Chandra swallowed her curiosity, refusing to give Sir Henry the satisfaction of asking the identity of either the influential lord or her prospective suitors.

A noise in the corridor heralded the arrival of Lady Amelia Taylor followed by the dressmaker, a wan, elderly woman who carried a gown of blue silk.

"I cannot wear a gown of that color when I am in mourning for papa," Chandra protested firmly.

Sir Henry, who was about to step into the hall to leave the women alone, stopped abruptly, turned, and said sharply, "You will wear what you are told. Stop your ungrateful whining and try it on." He whirled and stalked into the hall, slamming the door behind him.

Chandra slipped out of her modest black cotton dress, and the seamstress helped her into the gown. While it clasped her tiny waist tightly, it hardly held her full breasts at all. Looking into the mirror, Chandra was shocked at how much the gown revealed.

When Sir Henry returned to inspect it, she told him emphatically, "I cannot possibly wear this. I feel naked."

"But you will wear it," he countered in a tone of iron. "You have nothing but your beauty to offset your lack of dowry, and we must emphasize the only assets you have." He glanced down significantly at her bosom, caught so lightly by the blue silk.

Her eyes flared defiantly. "I will not be displayed like a brood mare on the auction block."

Sir Henry slapped her hard across the face, bringing

tears to her eyes and a gasp of shock and pain to her lips.

"If that does not convince you that you will wear this gown, I have a whip that will. Your father spoiled you, but I shall be happy to apply a little discipline." He turned on his heel, beckoning to his wife, who followed sullenly after him.

Still stunned from his blow, Chandra watched them depart. They made such a strange couple. She doubted that there was any affection between them, only shared overriding ambition. As the door closed behind them, she heard Lady Taylor complain, "I want that creature out of my home."

"She will be out very soon now."

Sir Henry's words filled Chandra with anxiety, and she sank down weakly on her narrow bed. Its thread-bare russet hangings smelled faintly of dust and mildew. Time was running out for her. Her thoughts turned again, as they had so often recently, to her cousin, Percy Lunt. He was her only hope—she was convinced now. If she could manage to locate him, he surely would aid her, take her in until he could assist her in finding a suitable position as a teacher or a governess. After all, her parents had given Percy a home when he needed one.

Chandra suspected that part of the reason her mother had been so eager to take Percy in had been her hope that papa might find in the boy a replacement for the son he had lost and still grieved for.

But Percy had been a strange lad of delicate constitution who did not like to ride or shoot or hunt, and papa was unsympathetic toward Percy's sensibilities. He found the boy's defects little short of disgusting. Nor had Percy been much of a scholar, which had further displeased papa. Instead he had preferred to laze about in the garden spinning grandiose daydreams or entertaining Chandra with thrilling stories of kings and castles and faraway lands. Although Percy had little industry or talent, he had great charm.

Chandra's certainty that Percy would help her

stemmed from more than their happy times together as children and the debt that he owed her parents, however. It sprang from the promise he had made to her when they had parted at Northlands nine years ago.

Chandra lay back on the musty bed covering and closed her eyes, replaying in her mind that farewell scene as she and Percy stood in the shade of an old yew tree.

She had been heartbroken at his leaving. "How can you reject us like this?" she demanded through her tears.

"My dearest Chandra," Percy had said soothingly, holding her little hands tightly in his. "This is the only opportunity I shall ever have. I would be a fool not to take it."

He had placed his finger over her lips to silence her protest and given her his most irresistible smile. "I am not rejecting you, believe me. Now I must play my uncle's game, but once he is dead and I am Lord Lunt, I shall make it up to you, I promise."

Percy had lifted her hands to his lips and kissed them. "If ever you need help, I shall be at your command, Chandra, I swear."

Now, Chandra thought grimly, opening her eyes and staring up at the ceiling, Percy would have a chance to redeem that vow. Perhaps one of Sir Henry's guests tonight might know Percy and might be able to tell her whether he was at Lord Lunt's estate in Essex or in London.

London. Suddenly the figure of another flashed through her mind. London was where the handsome American had been headed. Was he there now? Chandra wondered what sort of lodging he would take in London. No doubt a mean inn in one of the poorer sections was all that he could afford, she thought, recalling his plain cloak and barely adequate horse. But still, she thought, London might be her destination—just as it had been Percy's and the American's, not that it really mattered where *he* was.

*   *   *

On the outskirts of London, a small, gray-haired butler opened the door of an elegant mansion, its entry flanked by four fluted columns and arched Venetian windows. He welcomed Miles Carrington in French and took his wet hat and cloak, which dripped on the marble floor of the hall.

A cold driving rain mixed with sleet had made the final hour of Miles's journey back to London miserable. His body ached with cold and weariness from the long, wet ride. His Hessian boots, which had been polished to a high gloss when he had set out that morning, were splattered with mud, and his damp hair was curled in unruly confusion.

When the butler told Miles that Ninon was awaiting him in her apartment, Miles had to suppress a groan. He desperately longed for a hot bath to soak the cold from his tired body and would have preferred forestalling their meeting until he was properly rested. Ninon took a lot out of a man. Slowly, he climbed the stairs.

As he approached Ninon's door, it opened. She must have been listening for his footsteps. To his dismay, he saw that she was wearing only a robe of emerald green velvet bound with green satin, and he well knew what she expected of him. The robe was fitted to fully reveal the contours of her mature ripe body, so skilled at giving a man pleasure. Her mass of copper hair was piled high on her head above the heart-shaped face with its dark, almond eyes and generous mouth.

Despite the dampness of his clothes, she drew him to her, her mouth seeking his. After a long kiss, she drew back, shaking her head. "You are freezing and wet besides," she commented in her musical accent. "I shall have hot water brought at once for a bath."

A tiny smile of appreciation pulled at the corners of Miles's mouth. Ninon would, of course, divine immediately what would most please a man.

A tub and pails of steaming water were brought to his dressing room. He stripped off his damp clothing and slid gratefully into the warm water. He eased down in the tub to enjoy a long, leisurely soak.

As he lay in the soothing water, he could not thrust from his mind the woman he had met that morning on the road to London. Her lovely oval face set with sea blue eyes and framed by tumbling waves of sable hair were vivid in his imagination. At first, when he had angrily stalked away from her and ridden off, he had been certain that she had been pretending with him, that her outraged dignity merely covered her own passion. As he had told her, he detested a woman who led a man on and then denied him. He preferred those like Ninon, who recognized their own sensuous depths and reveled in them. As Miles's anger had cooled, however, he had been less certain of the strange woman's motives, and his curiosity about her had mounted with his doubts.

The door to his dressing room opened, disturbing his thoughts, and Ninon came in.

"I thought you might like help with your bath," she said, walking toward him, her hips undulating provocatively beneath the green velvet of her robe. It was cut low in front to reveal the upper curve of her voluptuous breasts, which swung forward and very nearly escaped the material altogether as she bent over the tub to scoop up the soap. The view brought a quickening to Miles's loins.

"I will wash your back," she announced, her eyes traveling appreciatively over his tight, muscular body. He was broad-chested, slim-hipped, and his physique was impressively defined. She spoke in French, preferring her native tongue to that of the country in which she had been forced to find refuge.

As she ran the soap over his body, Miles asked her idly, "What would your husband say if he came home to find you washing a strange man's back?"

"You are not a stranger to me. I have known you for more years than I have known my husband."

True enough, Miles thought. It had been fifteen years ago, when he was with Tom in Paris, that he had first met Ninon. How young they had all been. Yet even then Ninon displayed the talents that were to make her the preeminent courtesan of the French court. Her career, however, was cut short at its zenith by the French Revolution, which had been responsible for the execution of most of her titled lovers. Ninon had managed to flee across the channel to England, where she had met and hastily married a middle-aged widower of enormous wealth, who could keep her in the grand style to which she had become accustomed.

"You need not worry," she answered Miles. "My husband will not return from Ireland for another fortnight." Her fingers expertly massaged the weariness and tension from the back of his neck and his shoulders.

"And what will you do if, when he does return, one of the servants tells him of the guest you entertained in his absence?"

Ninon's fingers momentarily ceased their massaging. "Both the butler and the housekeeper fled with me from France. They are utterly loyal, and they make sure the others keep their thoughts to themselves. Besides," she shrugged, and her fingers resumed their ministrations, "my husband is a very tolerant man."

This was a tolerance Miles could not understand. Although he was not averse to sampling other men's wives when the ladies signified their desire for such attentions, he would never permit his wife such freedom. Were he ever to marry, he would demand of his mate absolute fidelity.

"If I were your husband," he told Ninon, "I would allow you no lover but myself."

Ninon brushed her lips against his cheek and whispered, "If I were your wife, I would want no one but you. I am not so fortunate, however. But at least I am discreet."

Miles gave a hoot of laughter. "Is *this* discretion? To install your lover of the moment in the apartment next to your own?"

"But I do not flaunt you in public nor in front of him," she protested. "Besides, you are an old friend."

She finished with his back, but not with her attentions, which she turned to another section of his anatomy that sprang to rigid life beneath her touch. She

knelt at the side of the tub to better reach her quarry.
Her breast nearly grazed his nose, and he reached up,
lightly brushing its pink tip with his finger, and it stiffened in response. Ninon's practiced fingers caressed his
manhood until he groaned with pleasure.

She smiled and handed him a towel. "Come," she
said invitingly, heading toward the connecting door into
her own apartment. "Our time together is too short as
it is."

Obediently, Miles dried himself and grabbed his
banyan of cream brocade lined with an intricately quilted
cream silk. He started to put it on, but deciding this was
a waste of time in light of what had transpired in the
tub, he merely draped it over his arm and entered
Ninon's bedroom.

She was standing by her wide bed, which had been set
in a curtained alcove hung with heavy gold damask. She
pulled back the damask cover that matched the hangings and turned to face him, her eyes avidly caressing
his body.

He dropped his banyan and bent to kiss her full
mouth, his tongue parting her lightly rouged lips as his
hand quickly removed the pins that bound her copper
hair. It fell free about her shoulders. His fingers moved
down and deftly managed the row of tiny buttons that
held her velvet robe. As he reached the last button, he
lowered his lips to the curve of her neck. Her robe
opened and his mouth sought one of the twin peaks now
bared to him.

But Ninon, impatient, shrugged the heavy velvet from
her shoulders. As the robe dropped to the floor, she
wrapped Miles in her arms and tugged so that they
tumbled together onto her bed. She needed no other preliminaries, and they swiftly joined in a surge of hot desire almost savage in its intensity. They moved in unison
with a passion that became quicker and more frenzied
as they climbed toward their ultimate summit. Miles felt
her stiffen and thrust herself against him as if she wanted
to swallow him within her. Together they reached an

exalted height and were held for a moment in a powerful, magnetic grip that gave way to blissful release.

When it was over, they lay in each other's arms, their bodies damp and drained and satisfied.

Miles looked down at Ninon's face. How much she reminded him of Kitty Keating, his mistress back home in Virginia. Their hair was nearly the same shade, and both were women of lusty physical appetites. He closed his eyes then, weary from his long ride and recent exertion, and he dozed.

When he awoke, Ninon was asleep, her body pressed close against his, her luxuriant hair half covering his face. He reached up and smoothed the tangled copper mass gently. Then he lay quietly beside her.

He had dreamed of the woman he had met on the road, and once again he was consumed with curiosity about her. Who could she have been? What tragedy had prompted her grief? There was no question in his mind that it had not been feigned merely to gain a stranger's sympathy.

If only he had bided his time and learned more about her before insisting upon kissing her. He had acted too quickly, and had only succeeded in repelling her. But her extraordinary beauty had dulled his good sense. Now he was furious with himself: he had not even had the wit to find out her name.

Ninon's hand brushed his cheek. "What are you thinking of?" she asked softly.

He started and turned to her. "Nothing," he lied, assailed by guilt for lying beside a creature as satisfying as Ninon and dreaming of another woman.

In reparation, he sought to pleasure her with all of his considerable skill. Slowly he caressed her voluptuous body, exploring every recess. He covered her with kisses, his mouth moving over her entire body. Like Ninon, Miles reveled in giving pleasure as well as in taking it. He had made careful note of what delighted her the most, and now he lavished his attention on her most vulnerable spots until she writhed beneath his touch and his tongue and begged him to prolong the blissful agony no longer. He slipped within her, and they were soon swept on a wave of passion through a sea of delight.

Then it was Ninon's turn. She excited him with every technique in her extensive repertoire, repaying him in rich and sensuous coin for the rapture he had given her. They came together again and again until they lay exhausted and satiated.

Ninon nuzzled his ear. "Don't sail for home so soon," she pleaded. "Wait another week or two."

"It's not so simple as that," he said, thinking of Tom, who was impatiently awaiting his return and results of his mission. Unhappy as Miles's tidings would be, he owed it to Tom to return at once.

"The *Golden Drake* is the only ship sailing to my part of the United States for weeks. I must be on it, for I have urgent business."

Seeing the acute disappointment his words brought to her face, so close beside his own on the pillows, Miles teased her. "Come now. You were not so anxious to keep me fifteen years ago when I left Paris."

He recalled their night of intense lovemaking just prior to his return to America, when he had tried to persuade her to accompany him. He was just nineteen then, and infatuated. But her protector was the wily old Duc d'Abbé, the king's most influential adviser, and the ambitious Ninon had preferred the old man's power to the young man's passion.

"You were but a student of love then; now you are a master," she complimented him. She ran her fingers through the dark hair curling on his chest. "A rare master. I have had enough experience to know."

Miles smiled at the accolade and closed his eyes.

"Tell me about your mistress in America," Ninon said, testing him.

Miles's eyes flew open. "I never said I had one."

"But you do. A man as handsome and virile as you is never without a woman. What is she like?"

"As a matter of fact, much like you," Miles replied, deciding that honesty was his best course. "Same copper hair, same lusty enjoyment of love. Even the same practical side. A few years ago, after she was left an impoverished widow with a small son to support, she married the richest planter she could trap. He was an old man, twice a widower, and the only satisfaction he could offer her was material. So, like you, she seeks her pleasure elsewhere."

"Why have you never married?"

Miles wondered if Ninon expected him to say it was because of her. Actually he had realized within a month of leaving Paris fifteen years earlier that he had mistaken infatuation for love and that it would have been a disaster if Ninon had accepted his offer. She pleasured his body but not his intellect. No woman had ever done both, and that was the reason he had not married.

"I never found the right woman," he said after a pause.

"Perhaps you are too particular. You cannot have wanted for eager candidates."

"No," he admitted, his honesty devoid of conceit. There had been plenty of them; some had been a damned nuisance. Like Sally Humphreys, his neighbor's daughter, blonde and petite and brimming with empty-headed talk. Although Sally had managed to bring many of the eligible young men of Virginia to their knees with her flirtatious wiles, it was Carrington she was determined to capture.

But Miles appreciated a woman of fire, intelligence and loyalty. His mother and his sister, Ondine, had possessed these qualities in abundance. His mother, now dead, had been as strong and determined as many men. And his sister was so like her. Beautiful but sure of herself; confident of her mind and soul.

Perhaps if Miles had met a woman like Ondine or his mother—companions in life as well as in the home—he might have been willing to accept the shackle of marriage. But none of the women he had ever encountered —and there had been many, for he was an accomplished lover—had ever tempted him to the altar.

Ninon chuckled beside him on the pillow. "You are just too particular, my dear."

"Yes," he agreed. And perhaps, Miles thought to himself, at four and thirty he was too old to ever submit to the bonds of matrimony. It would have to be an astounding woman who could ever persuade him to make that commitment.

Chapter 4

When Chandra entered the drawing room of Blackstone Abbey that night, wearing the blue silk gown as she had been ordered, Sir Henry's neighbor Sylvester Simms and his wife and two daughters were already there. The Misses Mary and Eliza Simms were both fat and nearing thirty, with small, darting eyes, noses like eagles' beaks, and thin, disapproving mouths. No doubt Sir Henry had invited them to make his plotting less obvious, knowing that their surpassing ugliness would guarantee they would, by comparison, make Chandra shine. Surely they were no competition for the attention of the two bachelors who had not yet made their appearance.

The Misses Simms, garbed in modest, high-necked gowns of sprigged muslin, stared pointedly at Chandra's décolletage as they greeted her, and a light blush rose to her cheeks. But her moment of embarrassment passed quickly. The sisters were too brimming with gossip, their favorite pastime, to be distracted by anything for long.

Their tongues ran endlessly with the latest scandals: which lady was having an affair with a lord who was not her husband, or the Prince of Wales's latest extravagance at Carleton House.

"Have you heard?" Mary asked Chandra, her knowing tone betraying that she was about to divulge a particularly choice bit of scandal. " 'Tis said Lady Hamilton has given birth to Lord Nelson's daughter. Lest anyone mistake it for her husband's progeny, the brazen hussy has had the gall to name her Horatia Nelson."

"You would think," Eliza sniffed, "that she would want to hide her sins instead of flaunt them."

Having disposed of Lady Hamilton, Mary moved on briskly to the next target. "Poor Fanny Chidwell's husband has demanded an annulment because she was not a virgin on their wedding night."

The Misses Simms' speculation on the identity of poor Fanny's seducer gave way to chatter about how one beauty was rejected by a young lord because her dowry was inadequate, while another was dropped in favor of a duke's daughter. As Chandra listened, much as she disliked the bent of the conversation, she began to suspect the folly of her father's marital expectations for her. He had never really been aware of the cut-throat nature of the marriage market, she was now certain.

The first of the two bachelors arrived, and Sir Henry hastened to deposit him at Chandra's side. Paul Addington was more pretty than he was handsome, with a slender, hipless body. He was clad in white silk breeches, a red velvet coat, and more lace than Chandra had ever seen on one person—male or female—before. Lace cascaded down from his neck and his wrists, and a long lace handkerchief trailed from his fingers. He was, she judged, not much older than herself—nineteen, perhaps. From her cousin's introduction, she gathered that young Addington was a relative of the king's new chief minister.

Addington's arrival was followed closely by that of the second bachelor, the younger son of Lord Call, one of the parvenu barons who had been raised to the peerage by Pitt's political machinations. The son was about eight and twenty with huge buck teeth, slightly crossed eyes and, it became quickly apparent, a deficient intelligence.

Still, the mysterious guest of honor, the influential lord Sir Henry had mentioned, had not arrived. As they waited, Chandra decided to take the opportunity she had hoped for. She asked Paul Addington if he were acquainted with her cousin Percy.

"But, of course," Paul replied. "I have not seen Percy since he was packed off to America."

"America?" she echoed, astonished. Of all the places on earth she would have least expected her comfort-loving cousin to be, it was that wild, uncivilized land. She shook her head in disbelief. "I cannot imagine Percy there."

"Neither could he, but he had no choice in the matter," Paul said with a swish of his lace handkerchief. "His uncle got him out of England just in the nick, before he lost all his inheritance at the faro tables."

"Percy, a gambler?" Chandra was shocked. Could this man really be discussing her beloved cousin?

Young Addington laughed. "One of London's most dedicated and unlucky gamblers."

"But what is he doing in America?"

"His uncle secured him a post in the diplomatic service."

"This news is most amazing," Chandra murmured, her heart heavy with despair. Percy had been her one hope to escape Sir Henry. What would she do now?

"I hear he's living in that new capital of theirs—not even a halfway civilized town like Boston. I believe the place is now called Washington after their rebel general."

A loud, commanding knock was heard. The influential lord had arrived, and Sir Henry hastened to the door.

Through the open door of the drawing room, Chandra heard snatches of Sir Henry's effusive greeting: ". . . so honored, Your Grace . . . may I . . . Your Grace?"

Your Grace, Chandra thought with rising excitement. So Sir Henry's mysterious guest was a duke. She was suddenly wildly curious. She had never before seen one of these fabled creatures whom her father had so lauded, and she turned quickly toward the door so that she would not miss the entrance of the august noble.

Many seconds went by before her cousin reappeared at the drawing room door. He was accompanied by the most monstrous mountain of human flesh that Chandra had ever seen. Her excitement turned to distaste, tinged with incredulity, at the sight of him.

The newcomer was supported on each side by two straining footmen, whose maroon and gold livery was so rich and beautifully ornamented that Chandra suspected it cost their wheezing master more than did their annual pay. His Grace, however, was a far less impressive sight. His great belly and thighs bulged against his silk breeches, and his costly coat of green velvet and his waistcoat of embroidered white satin gaped untidily over the rolls of fat. His teeth were rotted and his left foot was bandaged, signifying that he suffered from the gout. It was difficult to ascertain his age or even his features, which were all but drowned in his bloated face.

Chandra gaped at this revolting hulk, finding it virtually impossible to believe such a wretched creature could actually be a duke. This horrifying spectacle flew in the face of all her cherished fantasies about the nobility.

Sir Henry, a strange little smirk playing on his lips, announced, "The Duke of Warfolk."

At first Chandra's stunned mind simply refused to comprehend her cousin's words. Sudden fear stabbed at her belly, and she had a wild urge to run from the room and hide.

Surely this could not be . . . No, it was not possible. . . . It was unthinkable.

But gradually the realization sank in. This repulsive creature before her was the duke to whom her mother had once been betrothed. The very duke she had jilted to elope with Chandra's father. As Chandra stared at this obscene mockery of the distinguished figure she had always imagined, she fully comprehended what a terrible man he must be. She thought of Lord Lunt's son dead upon the Mysore battlefield, a blood sacrifice to this awful creature's insatiable thirst for revenge.

Chandra's limbs turned to jelly as terror rose within her. What if he should recognize her as the daughter of the woman who had spurned him? Even Sir Henry had remarked on Chandra's resemblance to her mother. What insanity had prompted her cousin to allow the duke to dine with the daughter of the couple who had so humiliated him?

Chandra felt as though she had been plunged into a nightmare from which there was no waking. She longed to flee from the room before her turn came to be introduced to Warfolk. But that would only call more attention to herself.

With legs trembling so beneath her blue gown that they could scarcely support her and with face lowered, she bowed as she was presented to the duke. She prayed more fervently than she had ever prayed before in her life that he would not guess who she was.

Warfolk's breath was so fetid that she thought for a moment she would gag. His eyes lingered on her face, and she held her breath, certain that he was searching his memory for a reason that she seemed familiar to him.

Finally, after what seemed like an eternity, he acknowledged her only with a bored nod and turned to Mary Simms, who was next in the reception line. Chandra was so shaken she could scarcely make her way into the dining room.

At dinner, Chandra was delighted to find that she was seated well down the table from the duke, whose presence seemed to cast a pall over the entire party. The other guests talked in subdued tones, and their snatches of conversation were interspersed with awkward silences.

The duke contributed not a word, but tore at his food as though he had been denied it for a week. Wine and gravy dribbled down onto the embroidered satin of his waistcoat. Chandra, who was seated next to Paul Addington, more than once caught the fastidious young man staring with disgust at the duke. She herself could barely manage a bite, and kept her eyes on her plate as much as possible.

In the drawing room after dinner, Chandra and Addington drifted to the opposite end of the room from the duke. He was settled by his two footmen into a chair beside the pianoforte and sat wheezing at the effort it had cost him to make the trip from the dining room.

Addington whispered with an audible sniff and a disdainful swish of his long lace handkerchief, "What a disgusting specimen. And to think he is one of the most powerful men in England! Especially now that his great friend Prinny, who shares his vulgar appetites, may become regent. You have heard the rumors, I assume, that the king has gone insane again."

Chandra started. That American. He had told her this morning that the king was mad. How could he have known?

Addington watched the duke thoughtfully. "Warfolk was rather handsome once, you know. I have seen a portrait that Gainsborough did of him many years ago, shortly before he was jilted by his betrothed, and you would not recognize this as the same man. They say he was besotted by the woman, insanely in love with her, and when she ran off with someone else, he was never the same afterward. Both his heart and his pride were sorely wounded, and he became consumed with a desire to revenge his loss and his humiliation. It's said he has hated women ever since, and uses them most cruelly."

"Did he ever marry?" Chandra asked, consumed with morbid curiosity.

"Eventually, for he wanted a son. But by that time he was in fearsome shape. It's said his bride suffered horribly at his hands. The poor creature killed herself a few months after the wedding without producing an heir."

Chandra choked back her nausea. How thankful she was that her mother had escaped this revolting creature.

"Chandra." Sir Henry summoned her sharply from across the room. "You must entertain my guests with a few songs."

She bridled at his transparent ploy to put her on display for the prospective suitors, but she dared not openly defy him. Reluctantly she crossed to the pianoforte and seated herself gracefully. She sat for a moment, choosing a selection, and then began.

Her voice was pure and pleasing, and her first song was greeted with compliments from all the guests except the duke, who sat stolidly and breathed heavily, his face hidden by the shadows. As the other guests called out suggestions for her second song, he struggled to his feet with the aid of his footmen and departed.

Chandra sang two more songs, then begged for a respite.

"A lovely performance," young Addington complimented her. "You have a special talent for music—that is evident."

Poor Lord Call's son merely grinned his idiot's smile.

After the door closed behind the last of Sir Henry's guests, he said to Chandra with a smirk, "I think it was a profitable evening. Lord Call's son was dazzled by you."

She choked in dismay. "That poor sad creature," she cried. "Were his father not a lord, he would be only the village idiot."

Her cousin gave her an evil grin. "Some say only an idiot would marry a woman without a dowry."

Chandra stared at him in shock. Surely he did not mean to marry her to a moron. Did this man have not an ounce of compassion?

Sir Henry turned on his heel and went upstairs as Chandra watched his retreating figure with apprehension.

Chapter 5

Two days later, Sir Henry and his wife took Chandra to London with them. She would have preferred to remain behind and escape their company, but she was given no choice and was bundled into the carriage with them. They gave no explanation for their sudden departure, but from their conversation as the carriage jolted along the rutted road, Chandra gradually discerned that the reason was a last-minute invitation to the Duke of Devonham's ball that night. The duke, who was the king's cousin, was famous for these balls. Invitations to them were cherished by those who received them and jealously coveted by those who did not. Lady Taylor, who until now had fallen into the latter category, was ecstatic.

Chandra could not help but wonder at the lateness of the bid. Surely the duke's invitations had gone out weeks ago. Why had theirs only now arrived, and why had she been included in it?

She looked out the window of the carriage. A light rain, little more than a heavy mist, had begun to fall. Even the prospect of seeing London, of which she had so long dreamed, failed to lift her spirits. Her intention in going to London had been to find Percy, and she had been deeply depressed since she had learned that he was in America. She had counted so on his rescuing her from Sir Henry.

As the coach rolled into London, its wheels rattling harshly on the cobblestones, Chandra pressed close to the window for her introductory view of the city. A stench rose from the slops tossed into the gutter and assailed her senses. The carriage vied with other vehicles and a large throng of poorly clad pedestrians for space on the narrow street down which they traveled. The houses were cramped together, and large signs projected out from their walls, casting shadows over the crowded street.

Chandra stared out in disappointment. Accustomed as she was to the freedom of the country, the openness and greenery, she was appalled by the squalor here. This was not the golden London of her dreams.

Worst of all, worse even than the odors, was the noise. Never had she heard such a din: the clatter of shod hooves, the clang of cart and carriage wheels on the paving stones, the bells of the scavengers, and the cries from the many peddlers, each trying to outshout the other in extolling his wares.

She gasped as the coach, swerving close to the buildings to make room for a landau coming from the opposite direction, nearly crushed a pedestrian against the wall.

His curses, including a colorful number that Chandra had never heard before, were still ringing in her ears when she saw ahead of her a tall, dark-haired man wrapped in a black wool cloak emerging from one of the buildings bearing a huge tavern sign overhead.

Chandra's heart leaped. The American! She pressed her face against the glass, but then she saw that the man's face bore no resemblance to that of the bold Yankee. Inexplicable disappointment seized her which was quickly followed by a wave of inwardly directed anger. Why could she not put the memory of that mannerless, arrogant American fool from her mind? She despised him and all of his countrymen. Yet his memory had plagued her for the past two days; and his kisses. She could not stifle the yearning deep within her when she thought of his caresses. He had been on his way to London the day that they met. Was he still here?

"You are being a fool," she told herself sharply. "You will never see him again. Nor should you wish to."

Still his face plagued her as the carriage jolted along, its occupants beset by the noise and stench all about them.

Gradually, however, the streets down which they traveled grew broader, the din quieter, and the odors less pungent. Now the sagging half-timbered buildings with shops on the ground floor gave way to impressive rows of Georgian town houses with united facades designed to dupe the observer into thinking that they were one great palace instead of a series of individual homes.

Sir Henry's carriage stopped in front of an impressive stone house with pedimented windows between engaged columns just off Berkeley Square. The plane trees lining the walk, disrobed by winter of their luxurious green plumage, displayed only the smallest buds on their white and mottled gray limbs. The house belonged to Lady Taylor's father, who was away at his country home in Derbyshire and had apparently placed his London establishment at his daughter's disposal.

A servant led Chandra up to the top floor, where she was assigned a small room, which to her delight looked out on the attractive square with its fine buildings and bustling life.

A maid came to take her blue silk gown for pressing. A little later, two other maids brought her a tub and hot water for a bath. She took a leisurely one, feeling both relaxed and revived from the jolting ride as she emerged from the tub and donned her pink wrapper of sheerest lawn.

Without warning the door flew open and Sir Henry entered, the evil look on his florid face frightening Chandra more than the fact of his barging in unannounced and uninvited. But she was determined that he not see her fear.

"How dare you invade my bedroom," she demanded, hiding her anxiety behind an angry bravado. "I am not dressed."

"So I see," he murmured, his voice strangely thick. He was dressed in fawn breeches and a white linen shirt, and was not even wearing a waistcoat.

As she stood beside the tub, clutching her garment about her, Chandra was acutely aware of how sheer the lawn of her wrapper was.

Sir Henry's casual stride picked up speed, and suddenly he was beside her. She tried to move away but he grabbed her arms and pulled her to him. She looked into his bulging eyes. They were filled with gloating triumph and lust, and she knew that she was in desperate danger. Chandra tried to twist from him, but she could not escape his grasp. He was standing against the end of the tub, and with all the strength that she could muster, she gave him a powerful shove.

He held on to her firmly as he fell backward into the tub, and they both came up soaked and sputtering.

Sir Henry momentarily lost his grip on her slick, wet body, and she flung herself from the tub, falling hard to the floor. She scrambled up as quickly as she could, impeded by the wet wrapper clinging to her, and she backed away. Too late she realized that in her frantic haste she had made a fatal tactical error. She had moved away from the window, her one avenue of escape.

As Chandra looked wildly around the room for some weapon, she caught sight of her own reflection in the gilt-framed mirror that hung over the small dressing table. She saw to her horror that her soaked lawn wrapper was virtually transparent, and it clung to her like a second skin. The garment was more provocative than had she been naked.

She looked at Sir Henry and saw his gaze roaming her body, fully revealed by the clinging lawn wrapper. His protruding eyes looked as though they would pop out of their sockets, and his bulging manhood pressed at his dripping breeches. She blanched with shame beneath his insulting perusal.

A short, cruel laugh rumbled in his throat, and he growled, "You proud bitch. You think you are too good for any man, but I will teach you differently, you wretched ingrate."

He started toward her, fumbling with the buttons of his breeches.

"No," Chandra screamed, backing away. She grabbed a chair, the nearest thing at hand that might offer any protection, and shoved it between her and her cousin.

He sent the chair crashing to the floor, and his hands shot out, catching the soaked cloth of her wrapper and pulling it open as he yanked her to him. He pinned her arms behind her, and she felt the hot pant of his camphored breath on her face. His mouth forced itself over hers and she felt the rough stubble of his face chafe her tender skin. She tried to keep her mouth clenched against his, but his tongue pushed through and probed her mouth roughly as he held her hard against him.

Sir Henry released his mouth and dropped his head. She caught a glimpse of the hungry look in his eyes as he directed his attentions to another part of her anatomy. His lips fastened noisily on the pink crown of one breast as water ran down from his wet hair and face and dripped onto her. His free hand assaulted her other breast, squeezing it so hard that she cried out in pain.

She struggled to free herself from his grip and so nearly succeeded that he hastily dropped a hand to her wrists to ensure that she did not break away. He forced her body against him, and the linen of his shirt scratched her naked bosom. She could feel the throbbing intensity of his lust hard against her as he pushed her back toward the bed.

Chandra's wits had saved her before, and now she resorted to them again. "What will the husband you give me to say when he finds you have foisted off damaged goods on him?"

This time her argument seemed to please rather than frighten Sir Henry. His eyes shone with a cruel satisfaction that terrified her.

"Your precious virginity will not matter at all to the man I have chosen for you, Chandra," he ground out, shoving her down upon the quilted coverlet.

"What do you mean?" she gasped as she fell. She thought of Lord Call's idiot son. Could he actually be arranging such a farce of a marriage?

But her cousin did not answer her. Forcing her arms

down along her sides, he hoisted himself awkwardly onto the bed and straddled her waist so that his knees held her arms imprisoned at her sides. He sat so hard upon her abdomen that a small cry of pain escaped her lips, but he paid no mind to her discomfort. Having securely pinned her to the bed with his body, his hands sought to liberate himself from his breeches.

Chandra squirmed wildly in a vain effort to free herself from the prison between his knees, but she was helpless beneath his weight. The look on his face plainly implied that he knew he had achieved his goal.

In his eagerness, his fingers could not manage the wet cloth. Finally, with an angry curse, he tore away the buttons, and they tumbled onto Chandra's heaving breasts. He rose to his knees so that he could extricate himself from his breeches.

As he did so, Chandra managed to loosen one arm. A heavy brass candlestick lay on the bedside table and she grabbed for it. Her hand closed around it, and she swung it upward as hard as she could against Sir Henry's skull. Her position made it impossible for her to put much force behind her swing, but the blow was enough to stun him momentarily.

He groaned and reached for his wounded head. Chandra gave a mighty lurch and pushed him off her. He slipped to the floor with an enormous crash.

She jumped up and ran for the door. She was a few feet away from it when it was flung open and Lady Taylor rushed in. "What is all the noise . . . ?" she demanded in a high-pitched voice.

She broke off, her eyes darting from Chandra's wet wrapper hanging open to her husband, lying on the floor clutching his head, and then back to Chandra.

"He attacked me," Chandra explained in a matter-of-fact tone.

Lady Taylor's fury exploded, but to Chandra's shock, it was not directed at her husband.

"You filthy slut," Amelia Taylor screamed at Chandra. "You dirty little whore, trying to trick my husband into bed with you."

Chandra was so stunned by this unwarranted abuse that she could only stare in shock. The thin, infuriated woman before her poured vituperation upon her in a crazed, uncontrollable manner.

When Lady Taylor finally paused for breath, Chandra tried again to explain. "Don't you understand, he . . ." She turned to gesture at Sir Henry and discovered that he had taken advantage of his wife's fury to slip unnoticed from the room.

"I swear, Lady Taylor," Chandra said firmly. "Your husband attacked me."

Lady Taylor glared at her. "You lie."

She turned and stalked from the room.

Chapter 6

The ride to the Duke of Devonham's palace, although it took but ten minutes, seemed to Chandra the longest she had ever had to endure. After her narrow escape from Sir Henry, she had not seen either him or his wife until they left for the duke's ball. They did not speak to Chandra even after they were settled on the brown velvet cushions of the carriage. Instead, they rode in silence that crackled with tension. Sir Henry, who sat with his wife on the seat opposite Chandra, watched her with a triumphant sneer that chilled her blood while his wife glared at her, eyes burning with hatred.

Chandra averted her eyes. She was so frightened and desperate over her hopeless situation that she no longer had the strength to return their gazes with defiance. Sir Henry obviously meant to marry her to Lord Call's idiot son after sampling her himself. With Percy so far away in America, she could see no means of rescue. But somehow, she thought anxiously, she had to come up with a scheme.

When their coach reached Devonham's palace, a massive imitation of one of Palladio's Vicenzan palazzos, two other carriages bearing early arrivals were stopped ahead of them. Chandra stared through the coach window at the palace as the Taylors waited their turn. Its great rectangular windows between the pilasters were blazing with light, and the soft strains of music drifted out through them. It was a rare night, unseasonably warm and soft, with brilliant stars and a quarter moon shining in the cloudless sky.

As Chandra was helped from the carriage by one of the duke's servants, she turned suddenly, sure that she had spied a familiar face. Could she be mistaken? No, it was indeed her former coachman, George O'Rourke, on the carriage ahead of Sir Henry's. George, looking stiff and uncomfortable in green livery trimmed with epaulets, saw her, too, and his prune-like wrinkled face broke into a smile.

With a tiny gasp of pleasure, Chandra started toward him. But, to her surprise, alarm flashed in his eyes and he warned her off with a slight shake of his head. She realized then that she had very nearly committed a terrible faux pas by going over to speak to him. The ton did not go about talking to other people's servants in front of dukes' palaces. Reluctantly, Chandra turned back and followed Sir Henry and his wife up the broad marble stairs to the palace.

George's new employer, a dissolute-looking man of about thirty, was ahead of them, and he staggered slightly as he tried to negotiate the steps. Lady Taylor, observing the uncertainty of his posture, said disdainfully to her husband, "I see Viscount Elliott has been celebrating before the ball. He is foxed already." Sir Henry merely grinned and nodded.

They stepped into a great hall that seemed to Chandra all arches supported by fluted columns, decorated with frescoes of mythological figures. Even the elaborate, carved marble overmantel of the fireplace contained an oval fresco of Zeus hurling a thunderbolt. Although the work was intricately and skillfully done, the overall effect was not pleasing—actually, Chandra thought, it was in rather poor taste.

The ballroom to which they were guided was quite unlike anything Chandra had ever seen before. It was dominated, indeed overwhelmed, by a gigantic chandelier, perhaps ten feet across, that hung in the exact center.

An orchestra in the musicians' gallery at the far end of the room was playing a waltz, and the floor was clotted with swirling couples. The women in silks and satins wore costly jewels that glittered in the light from the great chandelier, and the men were equally resplendent in velvet and satin coats and breeches.

As Chandra entered the room, several men turned to regard her with interest, and she felt extremely undressed in the blue silk ball gown. Its square neckline was so wide and low that it offered nothing more than the narrowest band of nearly transparent material as a covering across her breasts. Her hair was piled high upon her head in a confection of swirls and curls that crowned the delicate beauty of her face.

Lady Taylor was waylaid by an old dowager whose satin gown with wide panniers and elaborately constructed wig were both long out of fashion, and Chandra would have stopped to be introduced had not Sir Henry guided her on, muttering, "You shall not waste your time talking to that old bag."

It was the first time he had spoken to her since he had slunk out of her room that afternoon. He maneuvered her through the ballroom, glancing about him for appropriate partners. He did not stop for so much as an exchange of nods until he saw a plump but elegantly dressed young man in a coat of purple cut velvet over a cream brocade waistcoat. He wore a large diamond in the folds of his neckcloth and another equally as large in a ring on his middle finger.

Sir Henry nodded toward him. "Fitzhugh Flynn there has no title, but his father has more money than either of them can count," he said to Chandra.

After introducing Chandra to Flynn, Sir Henry was evidently anxious to move on. "My cousin is new to London society and knows no one here," he said. "Would you be so kind as to attend to her while I look for my wife."

Chandra blushed at the transparency of her cousin's ploy to leave her alone with Flynn, but could think of no way to avoid being left in this embarrassing situation. She watched Sir Henry walk off in silence.

Flynn made no attempt to talk to Chandra, but continued to examine the room, his lips twisted in supercilious boredom as the beautifully groomed women and their escorts in no less colorful plumage whirled by.

Chandra looked about her. The room was the most ornate she had ever seen. It made her feel as though she were at a sumptuous feast, each dish of which was, by itself, delicious, but when taken together were incompatible and overrich.

Chandra's attention was caught by a pretty young woman of perhaps three and twenty in a yellow Empire gown. She wore her curly brown hair in the Greek style with a bandeau in it, and her brown eyes roamed the room anxiously in search of someone. She looked so unhappy and nervous that Chandra could not help but feel sorry for this stranger. Somehow, she felt there might be a chord of sympathy struck between them were they to confide in one another.

Finally, embarrassed by the long silence between them, Chandra tried to engage Flynn in conversation. "It is a beautiful room, isn't it?" she remarked hastily and then wondered why she had told such a lie. Actually she could think of nothing else to say.

Flynn looked at her as though she were either quite mad or quite stupid, or perhaps both, and snorted, "It is grotesque. I cannot imagine a man investing so much in a room with such dreadful results. Devonham has no taste at all." He flicked at an imaginary bit of lint on his jacket sleeve. "I am a connoisseur of elegance," he sniffed.

A small voice behind Chandra interrupted them.

Chandra turned to see the young woman she had noticed earlier.

"Lady Margaret," Flynn said, bowing slightly to her. With a sardonic gleam in his eyes, he added slyly, "I took tea today with Lord William Pembroke."

Lady Margaret started and her voice quavered anxiously. "I have not seen him here tonight," she commented.

"He hated to miss the duke's ball," Flynn replied blandly.

"Miss . . . he won't be here? But he promised . . .

we were . . ." The girl's voice broke, and Chandra thought she was about to burst into tears. It was clear Lady Margaret was much in love with the absent Lord William.

"Unfortunately, his father commanded his company on his last night in England." There was a hint of malice in Flynn's voice. "And Lord William would not dare deny the Earl of Blandshire."

Lady Margaret was striving mightily to get hold of her emotions, and Chandra decided to break the awkward silence. "Where is Lord William going?" she asked.

"To America," Flynn replied.

"Why . . . why must he leave so soon?" Lady Margaret asked, still perilously close to tears.

"The *Golden Drake* is the only ship sailing for many weeks to that part of America where Lord William wishes to go. Besides, on such a dreadful voyage, one should sail aboard only the best that can be found."

"Where is he bound for?" Chandra asked.

"Washington," Flynn said with a sniff. "I tried to dissuade him, as it is a city fit only for hogs, but he protested that it was a necessity. Business, he says, although it's a strange place for an English lord to be conducting business these days."

Lady Margaret, who had conquered her threatening tears, seemed to regard Flynn's remark as a slur upon her beloved. "But you find nowhere satisfactory, Fitz, not even in England. I cannot imagine what possessed you to visit the United States when you knew how inferior they would be."

"On the contrary, some of the great plantations in Virginia are most civilized, even elegant."

Chandra started at the mention of the place. Her mysterious American was from Virginia. Of course, he would not live on one of those great plantations. Neither his inexpensive cloak nor his parrot-mouthed horse would indicate that he might be a rich land owner.

"What is the finest place you saw in America?" Lady Margaret asked.

"Willowmere," Flynn replied without hesitation. "It rivals anything to be found in England. Of course, it was built by a former Englishman, the Marquess of Pelham's brother."

"The son the old Marquess disowned?" Lady Margaret asked. "The one who was a leading agitator in the rebellion against the king?"

Flynn nodded. "His loyalties may have been questionable, but I assure you that his taste was not. Willowmere puts the Marquess's Pelham Hill to shame."

A young man came up to Lady Margaret to claim her for a dance, and Flynn gave Chandra a bored sigh as he led her away. "Lady Margaret is a fool, wasting her love on Lord William."

"Why? Does he not love her?" Chandra asked.

Flynn gave a harsh laugh. "It's not love, but money, that interests Lord William. Her dowry is substantial, but when Lord William bestows his title on a lady, it will be for considerably more pounds than Lady Margaret can bring him."

Chandra was assailed by the uncomfortable feeling that she was being scrutinized. Looking across the room, she saw to her shock that the Duke of Warfolk had entered the ball and was watching her intently. He was supported by a footman on each side. His green satin coat gaped untidily over his great stomach, and his white silk breeches strained to the point of ripping over his huge thighs. Chandra was frightened, and felt a bit ill at the sight of him with his eyes fixed upon her. Could it be that he had discovered whose daughter she was?

She heard one of two men who were standing near her remark, "The Duke of Warfolk becomes more gross all the time."

"And more sadistic, too, according to the girls at Madame de la Chartres's," his companion said.

"The madam's!" the first man exclaimed in surprise. "I would not have thought him able any longer. But then the madam does have the most beautiful and skilled whores in all England. I suppose that if any women could please him still, it would be them."

"I understand that the duke is nearly beyond even their great talents," the second man said. "He requires unspeakable things of them in order to become aroused."

The overheard conversation filled Chandra with disgust and fed the queasiness in her stomach. The ballroom seemed unbearably stuffy and noisy, and Flynn's disdainful manner oppressive. A dull throb began to pulse in her temple, and she desperately needed to escape to coolness and quiet.

Excusing herself to Flynn, she went out into the hall, which was empty except for Viscount Elliott, who was passed out in a drunken stupor on one of the chairs.

She wandered through several rooms, but all of them were occupied, some by small groups of men, others by couples linked together in varying degrees of intimacy. Finally, she found a small anteroom that was empty, and she took refuge in it. A lacquered Chinese screen in one corner concealed a chair and small table. Chandra slipped behind the protective barrier so that she might evade Sir Henry, should he notice her absence from the ballroom and come looking for her.

In her haste to conceal herself, she had not noticed a door ajar near the screen, and now she heard voices drifting through it. This room was undoubtedly a small waiting chamber for a larger room beyond the door.

As she was able to make out the sounds of voices coming from the next room, she realized that one of them was Sir Henry's. He was saying with great deference, "You have been most generous, Your Grace."

"Only make certain you uphold your part of the bargain," wheezed another voice very near the slightly open door. It was the Duke of Warfolk; that sound was unmistakable to her ears. Although he had not spoken directly to her, she had heard him ordering his footmen about.

"Not since her mother have I laid eyes on a woman who so fired my desires," Warfolk continued, "and I shall have her. I shall not be thwarted this time. If she escapes me"—the undisguised threat in the voice was so ominous that the skin on the back of Chandra's neck prickled—"I shall destroy you, Sir Henry, I promise you. I shall not be twice humiliated by your family."

"You shall have her, Your Grace," Sir Henry hastily assured him. "I shall deliver her to you myself tomorrow."

"Make certain she knows nothing of our plans until she is safely inside my palace or she will try to flee as her mother did."

"Why not take her there tonight?" Lady Taylor interrupted querulously.

"My security precautions are not quite finished. Once they are, her freedom will be at an end." The duke chuckled evilly. "And she shall rue the day her mother conceived her."

As Chandra realized the meaning of what she was hearing, she had to clasp her hands over her mouth to keep from screaming.

"I have warned Your Grace that Chandra is very difficult to handle," Sir Henry said nervously. "I am certain she will fight you."

"When I am done with her, she will grovel in terror at my feet, willing to do anything I bid."

Chandra heard a great deal of shuffling in the next room, then the door beyond the screen was opened wide, and the duke, aided by his two footmen, passed through the anteroom. Chandra sank behind the screen, terrified that they might discover her hiding place.

After the duke was gone, she heard Sir Henry's voice again. "You see how clever I have been, Amelia," he proclaimed triumphantly. "I shall reap a handsome profit from this. And you should be pleased, too."

"I don't understand why Warfolk wants her, the seed of the couple who so humiliated him."

"What better revenge than to ruin their daughter?" Sir Henry chortled gleefully. "He will make her pay royally for the transgressions of her parents. How I shall enjoy seeing the proud little bitch as Warfolk's slut. She thought herself too good for a sensible marriage to a man I would choose for her. Now she can put that thought out of her head. When the duke is done with her, no man will marry her."

Sir Henry and his wife passed through the door beyond the screen. Chandra stood motionless behind the screen as though she had been turned to stone. *The duke's slut.* She had been sold like a common whore to a sadistic old man who intended to abuse her in unspeakable ways. Even marriage to Lord Call's idiot would been less horrible than this fate.

Chandra was rocked in turn by revulsion, rage and terror. A new wave of nausea overwhelmed her. She hastened to a French door and, despite the coolness of the night and the scantiness of her gown, she hurried outside where she unburdened herself of her dinner in a flower bed.

Feeling no better, she came back inside, shaking with terror. Her mind was numbed by the thought of the hideous duke. He could not be dignified with the title of "man"; he was but a burned-out mass of corpulent flesh with a twisted mind. He saw her only as a way to gain his revenge at last upon her dead parents.

She could not—she would not—submit to him. She had sworn her vow to her father on his deathbed and she would not dishonor his name. What greater shame could there be than to become Warfolk's whore? Somehow she would, she must, escape.

But how to accomplish that impossible feat? She was without friends except for Percy, her only remaining hope, too far away to be of any assistance. Her mind worked frantically. Somehow she must reach Percy, even though it meant going to that awful land full of convicts and savages, the land that had been responsible for her father's ruin. The prospect dismayed her, but nothing was so terrible, nothing at all, as the thought of her fate in Warfolk's hands. And Percy would help her—he was the only one. She had to get to him.

Fitzhugh Flynn had mentioned a ship, the *Golden*

Drake, that was sailing tomorrow. She must be aboard it, she determined feverishly. The little money her father had left her would be enough to pay for her passage to Washington. Once she reached Percy, he would take care of her. Her only difficulty would be leaving Sir Henry's house undetected so that she could get to the ship.

She looked out into the hall and saw George O'Rourke bent over the body of his employer, the drunken viscount, who was still unconscious in the chair.

"George," she cried in a voice of such desperation that he straightened up in alarm.

"What be the matter?" he demanded.

Her fingers encircled his arm. "Sir Henry is forcing me to become the Duke of Warfolk's mistress."

George's wrinkled face grimaced in disgust. "That pig," he spat out. "Your father, he'll be aturning in his grave. And yer mother, too."

"You must help me escape," Chandra pleaded. "I . . . know what has to be done, if only you will assist me." The plan had come to her in a flash, and she outlined it for him. "You must come to the house of Lady Taylor's father in Berkeley Square with a carriage at dawn tomorrow to take me to the docks."

"Now, then, what would a lady like yourself be doing there?" George asked, scandalized.

Quickly, Chandra explained her need to flee to Percy. Seeing the doubt on his face, she added, "Percy Lunt is the only relative I have that will help me. You know that, George. You suggested it yourself when you spoke the name of Lord Lunt to me the day you left Northlands. There is no one else. There is no other way."

Still, George looked dubious. "But you cannot sail alone. 'Tis not likely the cap'n would even take you aboard, an unmarried lady traveling alone."

She stared at him, momentarily stunned, but then a solution formed in her mind. "I will pretend Percy is my husband, and that I am going to join him. Oh, please, George. You must help me," she begged. "Otherwise I will kill myself rather than submit to the man my mother spurned. You know me well enough—I would not hesitate."

Seeing her despair, George acquiesced. "Sure and I'll not be deserting you when you need me." He lay a comforting hand on her arm. "Be waitin' for me rig at dawn by your cousin's gate."

Chapter 7

Chandra's fur-trimmed cloak of forest green velvet scarcely warded off the sharp chill as she huddled in the foggy darkness beside the gate of the house in Berkeley Square, waiting for George—and the dawn. At her feet lay a portmanteau into which she had managed to jam an enormous amount. As the minutes passed without a sound of a carriage, her panic grew. What if George did not come?

The thought filled her with terror. She would walk, if necessary, to the docks, but would she find the way? Of whom could she inquire directions at this hour? Moreover, a woman dressed as she was, walking alone down the streets of London as dawn broke, was certain to attract unwanted attention. No matter. Somehow she must reach the *Golden Drake* before it sailed for America.

She pushed her hands deeper into the fur muff that matched the trim on her cloak in a vain attempt to warm them. She would find her way there. If she were lucky, the *Golden Drake* would weigh anchor before Sir Henry and his wife, who were both late risers, discovered her missing.

Sir Henry's rage would be great when he found her gone, but it would be nothing compared to the duke's fury. Much as she hated her cousin, she still could not help but pity him a little for having to face Warfolk and explain how yet another Taylor woman had eluded his loathsome grasp.

The first pale light of dawn penetrated the fog, heightening her apprehension. She stared eagerly into the gloom for some sign of a carriage, but the fog obscured the world about her.

A more unsettling thought assailed her. What if the sailing were delayed and she were found before she escaped England? She shuddered at the thought of punishment. A brutal whipping would be a preliminary to far worse once she was ensconced at Warfolk's.

Finally she breathed again as she heard a carriage approaching through the fog. As it pulled up, she did not wait for George to scramble down from his seat and help her. They did not exchange a word. She threw open the door herself and, tossing her portmanteau before her, she jumped inside. George quickly prodded the horses forward.

Chandra's ears strained for the sound of an alarm being given that would tell her her flight had been discovered, but she heard nothing except the clatter of the horses' hooves and the carriage wheels on the cobblestones. She sat back in the velvet-lined seat but could not yet feel safe. All her senses were on fire, attuned to every sound and movement about her.

After they had traveled some distance and were well out of Berkeley Square, George stopped and climbed down to talk to her.

"I found where the *Golden Drake* be docked," he told her through the window. "It be best, methinks, if me talks to the cap'n and secures your passage. I will tell him you be Master Percival's wife, prevented by illness from sailing earlier with him, and now you be joining him."

Chandra nodded her agreement. "Now when we get there," George warned her gravely, "you be staying in the carriage with the curtains drawn 'til me comes to fetch you to the ship. The docks, they be no place for a woman."

The carriage resumed its journey. The darkness inside the coach gave way to a thin gray light. To Chandra, the ride seemed to be taking forever. The carriage moved so slowly. Why didn't George make it go faster? But, of course, he wanted to draw no more attention to his vehicle than he absolutely had to. A new fear struck her. What would happen to George if he were caught aiding her? What would the duke do to him?

The carriage jerked to a stop. Chandra opened the curtains a crack to peer out. She saw George get down from his perch and hurry toward a row of decrepit buildings. Beyond them, the tall masts of ships with their sails trimmed loomed up like a ghostly forest of limbless trees through the fog. She could hear the creaking of their masts in the wind.

She let the curtains drop and leaned back against the seat. She had been far too distressed to sleep after the ball, and now she closed her eyes wearily. But they flew open again at the sound of raucous laughter near the carriage.

A man's voice rang out: " 'Ey lass, come 'ere."

Her heart pounding, Chandra peeked between the curtains and saw a sailor, a huge, brutal man, heading toward a woman who had just emerged from a ramshackle inn. She had the figure of a young girl and the face of a much used woman.

They began talking in low voices that grew louder as they argued. Finally the sailor, in a quick motion, caught her up in his arms and started down the street with her, despite her loud protestations.

Two other men, attracted by her cries, called out to the sailor, but he retained a firm grip on the struggling woman. "This 'ere 'ore don't like the price Oi've offered 'er," he explained, "though she ain't worth half."

The two men laughed and turned away. One called back over his shoulder, "Give the strumpet a good cuff. 'Twill teach her not to be so greedy."

The sailor, following the fellow's advice, dropped the woman to her feet and with his free hand administered a rough blow to her face, so sharp that Chandra could hear the crack in the carriage. The woman's head flopped, and she moaned pitifully as the sailor picked her up again, this time without meeting any resistance, and carried her into a doorway down the street.

The scene made Chandra more uneasy still. George

had been gone for a long time, and she began to fidget and curse herself, wondering if some evil had befallen him. At last she heard his footsteps, and looking out, she saw him approaching, defeat written in the slouch of his shoulders and the hesitation of his step.

"The ship be full," he told her sadly. "The cap'n refused to take another passenger aboard. Me tried to bribe him, but 'twasn't no use."

Chandra cried in panic, "He must take me." She began to tremble with fright. "What am I to do now? I must find another ship."

"The cap'n says his be the only ship leaving for that area this month." Seeing the anguish in her eyes, George added hastily, "Sure now, there'll be a ship asailing today, and I'll find her for you." But the stern set of his face belied his cheerful words. "Me dare not leave ye alone in the carriage too long. I'll find an inn where ye can hide."

Recalling the scene between the woman and the sailor, Chandra offered no objections. George resumed his perch, and Chandra closed the curtains as the carriage rumbled off. When it stopped, she peered out. They were halted before a shabby building. On a well-worn sign overhead, the letters spelling out *The Seagull Inn* had nearly peeled away, and the narrow street stank of excrement and rotting garbage. George hurried inside and Chandra pulled the curtains together again.

When he returned several moments later, he opened the door. "There be no fit place for a lady on the waterfront," he apologized as he helped her down. "This be the best of a bad lot."

As Chandra's feet touched the cobblestones, she noticed two dirty, unshaven men in tattered shirts and pantaloons watching from the shadows across the street. One was a giant of a man with an ugly scar that ran from the corner of his mouth past the edge of his left eye. His companion was smaller but looked equally unsavory. His small cruel eyes examined her velvet cloak greedily. She was greatly relieved when she and George were safely inside the inn.

The proprietor, angry at having been aroused at such an early hour, had already disappeared back to bed, so George, carrying Chandra's portmanteau, led her up to the room that he had secured for her.

"Lock yourself in and don't be opening the door to no one but meself," he warned her, eyeing the flimsy bolt upon the door dubiously.

After he left, Chandra slipped out of her velvet cloak. The room was mean and dusty, and she felt no solace in the knowledge that this was the last place Sir Henry would think to look for her. Trying to put some order into her chaotic state of mind, she set to folding her cloak neatly, and then she laid it across the one splintery chair in the room. She settled wearily on the bed, feeling a sudden rush of despair. George would not find another ship on which she could escape. Her cousin and the duke would turn London upside down looking for her, and they would find her. She would be forced into concubinage with the duke. Seeing in her the image of her mother, he would derive sadistic pleasure from abusing her.

His menacing words, "She shall rue the day her mother conceived her," echoed and re-echoed in Chandra's mind. Tears coursed down her cheeks and, lost in her misery, she did not notice the sound outside her door.

It was not until a sudden crack broke the bolt from its hinge and the door flew open that she realized her peril.

The two men she had seen in the shadows below dashed through the wrecked door. She had time for only one piercing scream before the big, scar-faced man clasped his hand roughly over her mouth.

His thick arms wrapped around her like bands of iron, and the stench of his filthy body mixed with the gin upon his breath nauseated her. Unable to escape his steely grasp, she shifted her strategy to a different kind of attack. She bit at the hand that covered her mouth just as she brought her foot down hard upon his instep.

He grunted with pain and loosened his grip on her

just enough so that she managed to twist sharply and break out of his arms.

She fled toward the door. Spitting out a violent string of curses, the man grabbed for her, but managed to catch only the shoulder of her dress in his hamlike hand. The muslin ripped, leaving her shoulder and the greater part of one breast exposed, but did not tear away entirely, and Chandra was trapped like a puppy on a leash.

He yanked her back to him and regained his grip on her arms. She tried to scream again, but the sound was quickly stifled when he stuffed a filthy rag into her mouth. She gagged and choked and vainly tried to snatch at it, but he was too quick for her. He captured her wrists and twisted her arms roughly behind her back.

"Ain't 'er a lively one," the smaller man said appreciatively as he watched his companion struggling with Chandra. " 'Er'll bring a pretty piece, 'er 'ill, from that cap'n bound for the West Indies. Likes the feisty ones, 'e does. Brings a better price, they does, at the brothels. Oi'd like a piece of 'er meself, Oi would, before we sell 'er."

Chandra, so crudely apprised of the fate awaiting her, redoubled her efforts to free herself, fear giving power to her already considerable strength. As she struggled, her hair tumbled down and cascaded about her in wild profusion.

With all the effort she could muster, she delivered a kick to her captor's shin that brought an explosion of pain from him.

"Gorblimey, giv' me a 'and," the big man panted. "Git 'er outa 'ere and us'll both 'ave our way with 'er. Now git 'er legs."

The smaller man pinned Chandra's feet to the floor, while the larger man bound her hands behind her back with a torn rag. When he finished, he pinched Chandra hard on the behind and the smaller man went to get her cloak, which he draped over her shoulders, concealing the torn dress and her bound hands. He tried to shove her toward the door but she refused to move.

"Git on 'er other side," the big man commanded.

With one on either side, they forced her toward the door, half dragging her along between them.

Chandra's heart pounded in terror as she realized she was doomed. No one on the waterfront would pay the slightest attention to a struggling woman caught between two men at dawn. They would assume she was just another whore being carried off by drunken sailors.

She was overwhelmed by the blackest despair she had ever known. She had managed to escape concubinage to a sadistic, loathsome duke, only to be condemned to a West Indies brothel.

Chapter 8

Miles Carrington awoke from a restless sleep, disturbed by dreams of a beautiful girl in men's pants and shirt; her hair, soft and lustrous as sable, flying in the wind; and her eyes as blue and deep as the ocean. It had been three days since he had met that mysterious creature upon the road to London, and still he could not put her from his mind. Never had he been so haunted by a woman.

The pale dawn light illuminated the grimy, soot-blackened ceiling above him. For a moment, he did not remember where he was. Then it came back to him: a dingy waterfront inn where he had reluctantly spent the night. With a sigh, he turned from contemplating the ceiling to Ninon, who lay beside him, her copper hair streaming across the pillow, her sleeping face contented from their lovemaking. She was an exciting creature, but hers was not the face of his dreams and it did not quiet his restlessness.

Ninon had insisted upon accompanying him to this miserable place despite his fears for her safety. Naturally, Miles would have much preferred to have spent his last night in England in her comfortable feather bed. But Ninon's house was on the far outskirts of London, and he had feared that if he stayed there he might miss the *Golden Drake*'s early-morning sailing. That fear was enough to make him put up with any discomfort, even this revolting hovel of an inn, the best the waterfront had to offer.

He smiled at Ninon's sleeping face. Aside from his worries about her safety, he had been glad enough for her company, for he had a long and celibate voyage ahead of him.

Slowly he eased his naked body from the bed, careful not to disturb his companion, and walked to the window to gaze at the London dawn, which he heartily hoped he would never see again. How totally alien he felt in this, his father's land, and how glad he was to be sailing from it this morning. His only regret was that he would never know the identity of that strange and beautiful girl.

As he watched the daylight grow stronger, a carriage, its curtains tightly drawn, stopped below, and its coachman disappeared into the inn. How strange, Miles thought, for such a fine carriage to be stopping at a waterfront inn at this hour. Miles's eyes narrowed as he noticed two ragged and unshaven men across the street also eyeing the carriage.

The inn door opened, the coachman emerged, exchanged a few words with the occupant of the carriage, then opened the door and helped her down. As the slim figure stepped out, Miles muttered an oath of astonishment.

It was the girl whose face had haunted him. But what was she doing at a place such as this, draped in a velvet cloak, looking every inch the grand lady? He frowned as he realized that he was not her only interested observer. The two ruffians across the street began whispering excitedly as she disappeared into the inn. Miles heard steps upon the stairs and the murmur of voices that stopped across the hall from his room. A few minutes later he saw the coachman emerge from the inn and drive away alone.

He turned from the window, musing about the scene he had just witnessed, and slipped back into bed. The woman beside him moved sleepily and opened her eyes.

"Where have you been?" she asked, her voice husky with sleep. Her hands began to caress his body.

"Looking at my last London dawn," he told her, too preoccupied and puzzled by what he had just seen from the window to pay her appropriate attention. But Ninon persisted, her hands wantonly urging his desire until finally he responded. When he lifted himself over her, she surged up to meet him, and they joined, moving together in unison.

Then he heard the scream from across the hall. The girl—it had to be her voice he heard. He and Ninon had been the only guests in the inn last night. He remembered those two miserable brigands he had seen in the street, watching the girl greedily.

Cursing, Miles bounded up, leaving his companion both astonished and unsatisfied.

"Be quiet," he warned her sternly as he grabbed the pair of dueling pistols that he had placed beside the bed as a precaution.

At the sight of the guns in his hands, she whimpered, *"Mon Dieu,* what is wrong?"

He darted to the door without a word and opened it quietly.

The two men were forcing Chandra toward the stairs. She was struggling but to no avail; her abductors were far too strong for her.

Miles's mind made lightning-fast calculations. If he called out to them to let her go, they might attempt to use her as a shield and still escape with her. If he disabled the big one who was pushing her toward the stairs, the companion might flee to save himself. Still, his goal was to free the woman; he would have to risk the man getting away.

Miles raised the gun and aimed at the big man's shoulder. He was a crack shot, but if the woman should twist at the wrong moment . . . Yet it was a chance he must take if he were to save her at all.

He fired. The shot hit the man just above the left armpit, its force half spinning him around as he yelled in pain.

His accomplice froze in shock. Chandra's instinct for survival overcame her astonishment, and she seized upon her captors' momentary confusion to jerk away from them and run, her arms still bound behind her back, toward the protection of the man standing in the hallway with two pistols, one of them still smoking, in his hands.

With the speed of a rattlesnake striking, the smaller man jerked a dagger from his waistband and hurled it at Miles's head.

He jumped aside and the blade whizzed by his ear, not more than an inch away, and thudded into the wall behind him. As Miles dodged the dagger, the man drew a dirk from his boot and lunged.

Miles fired the second pistol at him, and the man screamed in agony. Clutching at his shattered elbow, he turned and fled down the stairs.

While Miles's attention had been focused on the smaller man, he had failed to notice that the other had inched his way unobtrusively along the corridor and now, despite his wound, he leaped forward, pulling the dagger from the wall. He plunged toward Miles, who countered by hurling one of his now exhausted dueling pistols.

The weapon caught the man in the midsection, and he grunted, momentarily stunned. Miles leaped at him, delivering a hard right to the man's jaw. The brigand reeled backward and the knife fell from his hand.

Regaining his breath, he turned and fled down the stairs after his companion.

Miles, breathing hard with exertion, shifted his gaze to Chandra, who stood staring at him, her hair tumbling in wild profusion over her green velvet cloak. Her face was deathly white, making her eyes seem even bluer. He reached over and extracted the filthy gag from her mouth. He expected her to faint or dissolve into tears, but she only stood there quietly, staring at him. How stunningly beautiful she was, he thought.

"So we meet again," he said with a smile. "You are a trifle disheveled, milady."

"And you, Yankee sir," she replied easily, "are as naked as the day you were born."

He glanced down, and for the first time realized that he had abandoned his bed in such haste he had forgotten his clothes.

"My apologies, milady," he said with a slight bow, hoping fervently that his mocking tone concealed his acute embarrassment, "but the urgency of your scream indicated I should waste no time in rescuing you."

"For that, sir, I thank you," she replied, her voice cool, without a trace of emotion. "Would you be so kind as to free my hands? I find this position most awkward."

Miles stared at her in amazement. How relaxed she was. Most women would have been in uncontrollable hysteria by now. But she stood there calmly as though she were quite used to being abducted and conversing with naked men in hallways of waterfront inns. In fact, he had the disconcerting feeling that he was more embarrassed by his state of undress than she was.

"I have a knife in my room," Miles said, thankful for an excuse to beat a hasty retreat to it and his clothes. "If you will come with me, I will free you."

He hurried into his room where he was stopped short by the sight of Ninon sitting up in the bed, without even a sheet to cover her. Her tangled red hair spilled down her white shoulders and breasts. She held out her arms to him, obviously expecting him to carry on with their lovemaking.

Damn, Miles thought, his embarrassment soaring to new heights. He had totally forgotten about Ninon. Well, it was too late now. He would have to conceal his discomfort behind a pretense of casual nonconcern.

"Come, Ninon," he said briskly, his voice giving no hint of his upset. "It is time to be getting dressed."

She started to protest, but he cut her off firmly, saying, "There isn't time."

She glared at him and flounced naked from the bed, snatching at her clothes, just as Chandra entered the room. The two women stopped and glared at each other. Miles, on the other hand, turned his gaze to the ceiling.

Chapter 9

What Miles had supposed was Chandra's calmness was actually shock. There had been no time to react; it all had happened so quickly: her seizure by the ruffians, her futile struggle, and then the shot.

It was a moment before she realized that her rescuer was the American stranger she had met on the road several days ago. Even now that it was over, she still could not quite comprehend the sequence of events.

She followed Miles into his room in a daze. It was only after she was inside and saw the red-haired woman that her numbness began to lift. She was seized by an alien emotion, a mixture of dismay and inexplicable dislike toward this woman. Was she the American's wife?

At the sight of Chandra, the woman spewed out an angry torrent of French at such speed that Chandra, who read the language well enough, could make out only an occasional word. Miles silenced her with a firm admonition, spoken so low that Chandra could not hear.

The woman turned away from him with a pout, and he seemed relieved that introductions were not really in order. As he grabbed his knife and lifted the cloak from Chandra's shoulders, his eyes fell on the beautiful, perfectly formed breast, bared by the torn dress.

She blushed beneath his gaze, and said sharply, "If you were a gentleman, you would not stare."

"But, milady, I am a lover of beauty," he said lightly as he cut the rags that bound her wrists. He gently replaced the cloak about her shoulders. "If you will excuse me now, I will dress."

He gave her a tiny bow and slipped behind a screen in the corner.

Chandra started toward the door.

"Where are you going?" His harsh tone stopped her.

"A lady does not remain in a strange man's room while he dresses."

"You had better," he said flatly. "You are far safer in here. Haven't you just had a taste of waterfront manners?"

With uncharacteristic meekness, Chandra settled on a bench near the door, clutching her cloak tightly about her. His was a persuasive argument, in light of what had just transpired. Although Miles dressed behind the screen, the woman he had called Ninon displayed no such modesty. Instead she donned her clothes in the middle of the room, as though she took pleasure in displaying her voluptuous body.

"For one who insists she is a lady," Miles went on, the amusement in his voice rankling her, "you turn up in the oddest situations: riding a horse alone at dawn in men's clothes; and now, taking up residence in a waterfront inn.

"I cannot imagine your coachman being so foolish as to leave you alone at this inn." Miles's voice drifted to her over the screen. Although his words annoyed her, she could not deny that she found his deep, musical accent rather pleasing. "Surely he knows, even if you do not, that the waterfront is not safe for a woman."

"My coachman had no choice. As soon as he returns, I shall gladly remove myself from this inn and your presence."

"I hope his return is imminent, or it will be I who will have to remove myself from your presence," Miles replied as he came back into the room adjusting his stock. "I am sailing this morning for America, and I must leave for my ship very soon now."

"The *Golden Drake?*" Chandra asked.

Miles looked surprised. "Yes, that's her name, and I

must be aboard her. She's the last for weeks bound for Washington."

"I thought you lived in Virginia."

"I do, but I must stop in the capital before I return home."

Miles came around to stand beside her. The cloth of his garments was plain: nankeen breeches, cotton shirt, and a black worsted jacket, but the fit was excellent. Chandra could not help admiring his powerful body with its broad, muscular shoulders that tapered to a slim waist. And suddenly their last meeting flashed through her mind. She remembered with a strange warmth what it was like to be held in those strong arms.

She heard a vehicle rumble to a stop beneath the window. Praying that George had returned, she jumped up and went to look. But, to her disappointment, it was another carriage accompanied by two armed guards.

Miles, too, looked out, then turned to Ninon, who had donned a revealing and—to Chandra's surprise—very expensive gown. Why would this woman, consorting with a poor man in a waterfront inn, be so attired?

"Come, Ninon," Miles said. "It is time for us to part. Your carriage is here. I have taken the liberty of hiring two guards to protect you on your ride home."

He put her cloak about her and led her to the door. "Wait here," he instructed Chandra. "I shall return in a minute."

Chandra smiled, strangely pleased that the American was bidding the woman farewell. Obviously she was not his wife or she would be going home with him.

Chandra sank back on the hard bench by the door. The shock of all that had happened was wearing away and the full desperateness of her situation engulfed her once again.

How long could she possibly hide from her cousin and the duke? The dangers facing a woman alone and on the run in London had been brought sharply home to her by her narrow escape from the two scoundrels. Had it not been for the Virginian she would be the possession of a mercenary ship captain en route to the West Indies. She could not count upon such luck to save her again.

Her small white hands clenched into fists of determination. She must get aboard the *Golden Drake!* Then a wild scheme, born of desperation, formed in her mind. She must somehow persuade the Yankee to delay his departure so that she could sail in his place.

She shed her cloak and hastened to a broken piece of looking glass over a basin and chipped ewer, its glaze a grayish cobweb of fine cracks. The image that met her eyes was most unsettling. Her hair was disheveled, her face smudged, and the shoulder of her gown gone. She looked disgraceful, she thought, and quickly went to work to repair herself.

It would take all her powers to persuade the American to relinquish to her his quarters aboard the *Golden Drake.* He would undoubtedly not be an easy man to sway, and she wanted to look her most appealing when she tried. She managed to make her hair and face more presentable, but she could do little with the torn dress. She was about to hurry across the hall and change into another when she heard Miles's step in the hall. Quickly she snatched up her cloak and wrapped it about her again.

Turning to face him as he entered the room, she flashed a brilliant smile. "Pray, sir, what is your name so that I may know my benefactor's identity?" she inquired demurely.

Miles searched her face suspiciously for the reason for this sudden friendliness. "Miles Carrington. And yours, milady?"

"Chandra . . ." She almost said Taylor, but caught herself in time and substituted "Lunt."

"Chandra. It is an unusual name for an unusual woman. What are you doing at an inn in such a foul part of town?"

"Seeking a boat to America to join my husband who is a diplomat of His Majesty in the colonies."

Miles flushed angrily. "Your education has been most faulty. We have been independent for a quarter of a century."

Chandra bit back a retort. She dared not alienate him now. Although it galled her, she responded sweetly, "You must forgive me. I fear we British still tend to refer to your country as colonies out of habit."

Miles's eyebrow raised at her meek reply and he said drily, "You seem to have grown more charitable toward me and my country since last we met, Mrs. Lunt."

She realized that this was her moment and, swallowing hard to down her pride, she said in the most beseeching voice she could muster, "I pray, sir, that you will help me reach my husband. I have no one else I can turn to."

Her plea sounded stilted even to her own ears.

A sardonic smile played about Miles's lips. "How could I help you, milady?"

"I must sail on the *Golden Drake,* but I have been unable to secure passage aboard it." She gazed up at him, her sea blue eyes pleading through the thick dark lashes. "I pray, sir, that you will be so kind and generous as to give me your cabin and wait for a later ship to take you home."

He stared at her in astonishment. Then he gave a hearty laugh. "You jest! Why should I, rather than you, wait for a later ship?"

"I *must* sail today," she cried. "I cannot convey to you the urgency of my plight. I shall pay you well," she added, eyeing the plainness of his clothes and trying to calculate how much of her slender purse she would have to surrender for him to consider himself well paid.

Miles examined her coolly, obviously unswayed by either her plea or her offer of money. "Who is this husband you are so anxious to join?"

"His name is Percival Lunt."

Miles started in surprise. "I did not know that he had a wife, and one of such beauty at that."

It was Chandra's turn to be astonished—and dismayed. She had not thought there was the remotest chance this plainly dressed American should be acquainted with her cousin. She responded haughtily, "I should not have thought you would travel in the same circles."

Miles's eyes narrowed. "I met him briefly," he said in a cold voice. "We both gamble, although I am better at it than he is." This was not said in a boastful tone but as a matter of fact.

Chandra could scarcely conceal her upset at the news that Percy might still be pursuing his ruinous gambling in America.

"Your husband has kept your existence a secret," Miles said with a bemused grin. "You will be quite a surprise to many in Washington."

Chandra could not help smiling, too. Beyond a doubt, the most surprised of all would be Percival Lunt.

She asked, "You will help me?"

"Much as I should like to accommodate you, I cannot," he said, turning away and going to his sea chest from which he drew a fine rectangular case of walnut decorated with marquetry in an intricate arabesque design. "I have urgent business at home. I cannot delay my voyage."

"You cannot abandon me here amid kidnappers and thieves."

He set the flat case down sharply on the table beside his dueling pistols. "Madame, you abandoned yourself. I merely happened to be here in time to rescue you."

He picked up the pistols, a fine pair of flintlocks whose stocks were inlaid with silver wire.

"Sir, I am truly grateful to you," Chandra pleaded, "but I shall die if I cannot sail today."

"You appear quite healthy to me." Miles looked up from his weapon, a sardonic gleam in his eyes. "You had better make your story good. Go on—I'm interested."

Chandra's terror of the duke gave strength to her voice and sparked her imagination: "My family objected to my marrying Percy," she began slowly, "so we eloped just before he sailed for America. But they found us before we could escape England and dragged me away. Now they are attempting to annul my marriage."

Chandra, who had been raised to prize the truth and to despise deceit, was astonished at how easily these lies born of terrified desperation spilled from her lips. She even felt a hint of tears springing to her eyes.

"Perhaps your family knows what is best for you," Miles said unsympathetically as he opened the walnut box, which Chandra saw was fitted as a pistol case.

She studied his eyes and the set line of his jaw, and knew that, so far, he was unmoved by her tale. She continued more forcefully, "They will compel me to marry a man I cannot bear, a most horrid and repulsive man." Her pride would not let her tell him that she had not even been offered the respectability of marriage.

"Who is this lucky fellow?"

Chandra dared not use the duke's name. The American might know of him and would be loath to cross so powerful a man. "He is a neighbor of ours, a rich merchant," she lied. "But he is old and enormously fat." She shuddered as she thought of the repulsive Warfolk. "He has rotted teeth, a fearsome breath and many chins. His stomach is so enormous it strains even the largest garment, and his bulging thighs threaten to split his breeches. I have more than aesthetic objections," she hastened on. "He is as cruel as he is disgusting. His first wife killed herself shortly after their marriage because she could no longer bear his ill treatment."

Miles's deep skepticism had been apparent in his face until she described the duke. Her portrait of the man was drawn with far too much passion and fear for anyone to doubt the veracity of her story and the depth of her revulsion for the man. Now, to her relief, Miles looked more interested.

"I still don't understand why your dear husband hasn't come to rescue you instead of staying in America," Miles said.

Chandra gulped. "He . . . he has been forbidden to leave his post there."

"If he loved you, I would not think that would stop him for a moment."

Miles's questions about Percy made her nervous. "Don't you understand," she cried, "even if I were not married to my husband, I would rather kill myself than wed that hideous man. You cannot imagine what a monster he is." She gazed at him pleadingly through her long dark lashes. "Please." The one word was as much as she could muster. She began to cry, not the tears of a manipulative woman seeking her own way, but frightened, heartbroken sobs.

Miles studied her for a time, then a thoughtful look played in his hazel eyes and a strange smile formed on his lips. He placed the pistols in their case and shut the lid with a snap. He rose and tilted Chandra's face up to his. Tears flowed down her cheeks.

He said softly, "Chandra, I must sail today, I have told you as much, but I will help you escape to your husband if you are as desperate as you say you are."

Hope flared in her eyes. "How?"

Miles chose his words with care. "I am a tall man and a poor sailor, so I have booked the largest cabin aboard the *Golden Drake*. It will easily accommodate both of us."

"What," she stammered in horror, "are you asking of me?"

"Not to sell your body if that's what you fear," he replied indifferently. "I am merely offering to share my quarters for the voyage."

Her eyes widened with doubt. "You mean you will not . . ." she broke off, her face flaming with embarrassment, unable to continue.

"I do not take advantage of unwilling ladies, I assure you," he said in a matter-of-fact tone that held no trace of vanity. "There are too many who are willing, even eager, for my attentions."

Chandra was dumbfounded by this self-assured

American's answer and by his proposal. She wondered whether she could trust him. If only he were not an American. Her father had contemptuously dismissed them all as rogues. She remembered, too, Miles's assurance as he had stood naked in the hall, insolently unembarrassed by either his state of undress or the red-haired slut who shared his bed. And his behavior that day Chandra had met him when he had seized and kissed her, then mocked her indignation. But most unsettling of all was the memory of his kisses' effect upon her. Did she dare place herself in this man's hands?

"What is your answer, Chandra? Quickly, for I must be on my way to the ship. I am already late."

Despite his urgent tone, she sat silently. Her eyes, fixed on him with doubt and fear, mirrored the fight that was raging within her over his offer. Two hours ago, she would never have considered for an instant so preposterous and scandalous an idea. But the alternatives to his scheme—brigands who would sell her to a brothel or the sadistic duke, that great mountain of jelly-like flesh trying to possess her body—were even more horrifying. Anything, she thought, anything at all would be preferable to that degradation.

In a scarcely audible voice, she asked, "Will you give me your oath you will not force your attentions on me during the voyage?"

Miles smiled reassuringly. Again he seemed to speak with infinite care. "I swear that I will do nothing to you that you do not desire."

Chandra looked at Miles's handsome face and remembered his compassion as he comforted her that day near Blackstone Abbey. He was not cruel or repulsive and perhaps, she tried to convince herself, he was even a man of honor, despite signs to the contrary. She had no choice but to hope so: she had no other alternative.

"I will go with you." Her words came slowly, reluctantly, as if each one were a great stone whose weight she could scarcely move.

She thought she caught a disconcerting flash of triumph in Miles's eyes, but it was gone immediately.

"You have just become Mrs. Miles Carrington—at least in name," he told her. "We wouldn't want the captain thinking I was sharing my cabin with a woman other than my wife. Correct?"

Chandra nodded dubiously.

Part Two

Chapter 10

Chandra stepped into Miles Carrington's cabin aboard the *Golden Drake,* and gave a gasp of dismay as she noted the two bunks and narrow table with two chairs of the oak-paneled compartment. Overhead, paraffin lamps hung from gimbals. A commode, a small cupboard, and an oak armoire against the bulkhead, all of polished oak, completed the furnishings. Although the cabin was large by ships' standards, its size sorely disappointed Chandra. She was totally unnerved by the thought of spending the next several weeks with a man in such close confines.

"It is so small!" she exclaimed.

Miles was incredulous at her reaction. "I wish you could have seen the cabin I was forced to accept on my voyage over. It was scarcely half this size, reeked of potash and cod oil, and I had to share it with a dull clergyman who snored."

Chandra sat down nervously on one of the bunks. At the Seagull Inn her only thought had been that she must get aboard the *Golden Drake* at all costs, but now that she had achieved her goal her doubts about the wisdom of what she had done rose like the wind before a storm.

She watched Miles with trepidation as he saw to the stowing of his sea chest. Her uncertainty about him had been fueled anew when they had boarded the ship. Miles had played the role of husband to the hilt as he introduced her to the captain, his arm protectively around her and his hands at times a bit too possessive.

How far would he attempt to carry this charade? If he were not a man of his word, no help would be forthcoming for her from the others aboard the ship. They would surely not interfere with a husband claiming his recalcitrant wife. It would be even worse for her to confess that they were not married, since she had boarded the vessel with him voluntarily.

She was determined to retain her virtue. Who would wed her if she did not do so? How unfair it was, she thought. Men might do as they pleased. No one expected them to approach their wedding night unsullied. And if they took their pleasure, whether by guile or force, it was generally the unfortunate girl who paid the price of shame and ruin.

Miles carefully appraised the cabin as she watched with apprehension. There would be absolutely no privacy in this tiny space. Then he turned to her and asked pleasantly, "Shall we go on deck and watch England fade from view?"

She shook her head. The Taylors would be awake now and would have discovered her missing. Already a search might have been mounted, and she dared not risk being sighted on deck and caught just as escape was within her grasp.

"I am too tired, but," she added with sudden enthusiasm, " I hope you will go without me."

Miles grinned. "I'm sure you do."

After he left, Chandra lay back on the bunk. It had been more than twenty-four hours since she had slept, and she ached with weariness.

She was suddenly assailed by the enormity and recklessness of what she was doing. She could hardly bring herself to contemplate that she was leaving the beloved land of her birth for that savage, alien nation across the sea that her father had so despised. The thought was as unsettling as it was terrifying.

She trembled to think what her father would say were he alive. That land was hateful to him. He had explained time and again that it was populated by progeny of convicts and whores, by crude, ignorant, and uncultured louts without honor or principles. Were they otherwise, they should never have rebelled against the king, and his God-given right to rule.

But what other choice did she have than to go to America? The land that had ruined her father would have to be her refuge. Ironically enough, her flight there was the only way she could keep the vow she had made at his deathbed that she would not dishonor his name. And once there, things would right themselves again. She had not the slightest doubt that Percy would take her in and care for her. She would run his home and be his hostess. As a diplomat, he surely would have a fine residence and would entertain frequently. Perhaps she might even still manage a marriage of which her father might have approved to one of Percy's fellow British diplomats stationed in America.

At last, having somewhat reassured herself, her weary eyes closed in sleep.

Miles sat in a chair beside the table reading by the flickering light of a paraffin lamp. The *Golden Drake* had put to sea many hours earlier and day had faded into night, but still Chandra slept. Finally a movement on her bunk caught his eye, and he looked up from his book to discover her studying him in the dim light.

"I see you do not suffer from insomnia in awkward situations," he teased, shutting the book and laying it on the table. "I am afraid that you slept through supper. I have already dined with the other passengers, but if you are hungry, I will arrange for a meal to be brought here."

"Please. I have eaten nothing since yesterday."

Miles swung to his feet, his head nearly touching the top of the cabin. He ducked down as he passed through the doorway. His shoulders were so broad that they nearly filled the narrow opening.

He returned with a steward bearing a tray heavily laden with dishes: leek soup, fish, generous slices from a shoulder of lamb, and for dessert, an apple and cinnamon biscuit.

Chandra sat down before the repast and eyed it eagerly. "How long will it take our ship to reach Washington?" she asked.

Miles was pouring himself a generous shot of brandy from the supply he had brought aboard with him for the long voyage home. He looked up in surprise. "Washington? But we land at Baltimore."

"Baltimore! Where is that? You said you were going to Washington."

He took a sip of brandy. "I am. Baltimore is not far—perhaps forty miles. It will take less than a day to reach it, although the road's not all it ought to be."

She picked up her soup spoon. "I supose highwaymen and Indians lie in ambush along it."

Miles laughed. "We are not as uncivilized as you think. I promise you I shall see you safely deposited with your husband."

She pushed away her soup bowl. "Perhaps your country does not seem uncivilized to you, but I am used to culture and beauty," she said priggishly.

Miles gave her a sardonic glance. "Oh, yes, London is very beautiful and civilized with its footpads lurking around every corner to lighten your purse. I was especially charmed by the serene quiet of London and the sweet perfume of the slops in the streets."

He expected her to respond angrily, but instead she laughed. "It is difficult, I grant you, to decide which is worse, the smell or the noise."

He was surprised by her sudden affability, and he looked up from his mug. How beautiful she was when she smiled. He remembered the sweetness of her lips that day they had first met. Odd that she should have such a violent hatred of Americans. But there were many unusual things about her.

Abruptly he asked, "Who were the Americans that you knew before me?"

She looked up from her food in surprise. "But I have known none. You are the first."

"Then why do you hate us so?"

Chandra's incredibly blue eyes flashed angrily. "You

ruined my father, killed my brother and destroyed my mother's health."

Miles was startled by the vehemence of her words. "How?"

"It was that vicious pirate of yours, Captain Devil."

"Captain Devil?" Miles echoed in astonishment.

As Miles listened to Chandra's story of her father's ruin, he slowly came to understand the basis of her outlandish ideas. Evidently they all came directly from her father. How attached she had been to him.

She seemed to worship the man, who could do no wrong in her eyes. Her childish illusions about him were still intact.

When she finished her story, Miles said gently, "Your father was a fool to attempt such a scheme when he knew how successful our privateers were. And they were privateers, not pirates, licensed to seize British shipping just as yours were licensed to seize ours." Miles poured himself more brandy. "It seems to me that your father wished to shift the blame for his own folly to Captain Devil in particular and Americans in general."

"You defile my father," Chandra cried hotly, "in defending that evil monster, Captain Devil. Why, he was more animal than man! He had a great hulking body and a cruel, scarred face. A more hideous creature I have never laid eyes on. My father had a picture of him. He was a huge man with massive arms and legs that hung down like an ape's."

Miles could hardly keep from laughing aloud at her portrait. "I suspect that picture was naught but a British artist's conception of an enemy and bore no resemblance to the gentleman himself."

"But it did," she retorted heatedly. "It even had a caption beneath it, which read, 'The Yankee pirate Captain Devil, the archrebel. An admirable likeness.'" Sudden suspicion showed in her eyes. "Would you know this Captain Devil?"

Miles took a long sip of brandy and studied her face thoughtfully. When at last he spoke, he chose his words with great care. "We had many successful privateers during the revolution, and I have never been introduced to any man named Captain Devil. Perhaps I might recognize his real name. Do you know it?"

"No." She lapsed into silence, then burst out, "I wish he were still plying his trade now. Our Lord Nelson would make short work of him."

Miles smiled, drained the last of the brandy from his mug, put it down, and rose, hiding a yawn behind his hand. "I have not had the benefit of the long nap that you had, and I am ready to retire."

Chandra glanced quickly about the cabin, and her face flamed.

Miles noted her sudden blush and guessed the reason. "Come now, you were not at all embarrassed when you saw me without my clothes earlier today," he teased her.

She gasped and her color deepened.

Seeing her genuine distress, Miles said hastily, "I was only funning you." He grabbed a blanket from his bunk and fastened it to the beams to create a makeshift dressing room.

As he finished fastening the blanket and turned toward his sea chest, he was startled to hear Chandra's question. "Have you known Ninon long?" she inquired.

"Fifteen years."

A surprised little murmur escaped Chandra's lips. "Where did you meet her?"

"In France."

"In France? What could you possibly have been doing there?"

Cursing his loose tongue, Miles raised the lid of his sea chest and stared down at his neatly folded clothes. The less Chandra knew about him and his background, the safer it would be for Tom. Her husband, Percival Lunt, was a diplomat of the king, after all, and while Lunt was a fop, he was not a fool. If he were to learn from Chandra about his stint as Tom's secretary in France, he might start wondering about Miles's current voyage. The secrecy of this mission must be protected at all costs to ensure that Tom would not be embroiled in controversy. His Herculean task of trying to heal the nation's political wounds was difficult enough.

"What did you do in France?" she persevered as she picked up an apple from her dinner tray and bit into it.

"I tutored young aristocrats in the English language and in American thought," he answered, thinking this was not truly a lie for he had done that, too, in his spare time. "Foreign travel is most broadening." He paused and added with the specific intention of misleading her, "especially for scholars and teachers."

"Teachers? You are . . ."

"Excuse me," he said brusquely, cutting her off before she could force him to commit himself on the subject of his occupation, "I am retiring to my dressing room."

With a robe in hand, he slipped behind the blanket, leaving Chandra to munch thoughtfully on her apple. So he was a teacher. She was a trifle chagrined to learn that he was not a man of more exalted station, but she might have guessed his profession. His speech and demeanor were those of a well-educated man.

She heard someone moving down the passageway outside the cabin. Most likely it was one of their fellow passengers. None of them had been on deck when she had boarded that morning, although she had looked about for the Earl of Blandshire's son. He was the sort of eligible scion of good family that her father had so desired for her. What little chance she had now of fulfilling his dearest dream. Unreasonably, she was still filled with guilt as though she had somehow deliberately failed him and his dream for her.

She wondered if Miles were of good family. But were any Yankees? Papa had insisted they were all sons of thieves and murderers. If, in fact, Miles had such an ignominious background, then perhaps all her earlier doubts about him were not unfounded.

She rose from the table and went to her bunk where she sat uneasily on the edge. Would he force her to share his bed? She remembered her own disconcerting response to his kisses and quickly turned her back on him as he emerged from behind the blanket.

But Miles made no attempt to touch her. Instead, he got into his own bunk and turned his back on her. Instead of being overjoyed, she felt, to her surprise, a tinge of disappointment. She had simply assumed he would at least hint at his desire for her. Perhaps he was yearning for Ninon. Chandra had to admit grudgingly that the Frenchwoman had a fiery beauty with a sensuous boldness. And when a man had known a woman for fifteen years, well . . . Chandra blushed to think of it. She closed her eyes and let sleep claim her.

In the early hours of the morning, the wind rose rapidly, and the shouts of the sailors scurrying up the rigging to shorten the sails awoke Miles.

He heard Chandra turn in her bunk. He was much perplexed by the girl. His offer to share his cabin with her had been prompted far less by altruism than by visions of many leisurely hours of lovemaking with this exquisite creature on the long voyage home.

Actually, he had not really expected her to agree to his scandalous proposal that she accompany him across the sea. When she had, it had only confirmed his suspicions that she was not half so virtuous as she pretended. No woman, and a married one at that, who flouted convention as she did and who remained unflinchingly cool in the face of abduction by two scoundrels could be very innocent. Her charade, he decided, would only make the game more interesting. For, to Miles, seduction was a game, one that he played with the skill and assurance that come of much experience and success. Chandra might prove a more challenging opponent than most. So she could play the innocent as long as she liked, but before they were at sea a week, he had been certain, she would be happily sharing his bunk as well as his cabin.

Her conversation tonight, however, had much shaken his conviction that she was an adventuress with a good deal of worldly experience. If anything, she seemed less sophisticated than one would expect at her age. Her story of Captain Devil's picture had revealed a naiveté totally incongruous with the rest of her.

Once again, Miles was baffled by the strange contradictions in her personality. Well, he would have to do some exhaustive research in his subject before coming to any conclusions. This would be a task, he concluded, that might prove as enjoyable as it was enlightening.

Chapter 11

Chandra awoke late the next morning to discover that she was alone in the cabin. She hastened to dress before Miles returned, and she completed her toilette at the commode, where a handsome set of heavy silver brushes, engraved "M.C." in flowing script, lay beside the ewer and basin. The costly brushes intrigued her, as they contrasted sharply with Miles's inexpensive clothing. She wondered, as she began to brush out her tangled waves, how he had acquired them.

She coiled her thick sable hair neatly around her head, and when Miles returned to the cabin, she was putting on her fur-trimmed cloak.

"Where are you going?" he demanded as he ducked through the doorway wearing a greatcoat of black worsted and a pair of well-polished but somewhat worn Hessian boots.

"For a walk on deck."

"That would be unwise," he said, lifting the cloak from her shoulders before she could fasten it.

"Why?" His high-handed display of authority irritated her greatly.

"I met our fellow passengers yesterday while you were asleep." He folded her cloak neatly and handed it to her. "Unfortunately, we are richly blessed with traveling companions from the London ton."

"Are you disappointed that we are in such good company?" she asked tartly.

"For your sake, yes. You may know some of them. Even if you do not, your husband surely does. He may find it awkward explaining to them why his bride crossed the Atlantic posing as another man's wife."

Chandra drew her breath in sharply. In her desperation to escape the duke she had not even considered the other passengers. She would be ruined if one of them should recognize her, for there was only one plausible explanation for her peculiar traveling circumstances.

"I have let it be known," Miles said, "that you are of delicate constitution."

"Delicate constitution? What nonsense! I . . ."

"And that you are much troubled by seasickness," he continued firmly. "So I have ordered our meals brought here to the cabin."

As though in confirmation of Miles's statement, a steward appeared with a tray of food and two steaming pots, one of coffee for Miles and the other of chocolate for Chandra. He set them down and promptly left the cabin.

"You are missing little by having to forgo the company of our fellow passengers," Miles said soothingly. "There is Thomas Strum, a scrawny, peculiar second son of some obscure baron; Sir Egerton Chatwin, a dreary, middle-aged bore with his much too young and pretty wife, and His Lordship William Pembroke."

"Lord William is the son of the Earl of Blandshire," Chandra interrupted, expecting him to be impressed.

"So His Lordship has informed me on at least three occasions," Miles said drily.

"But he has every right to be proud of his connections," Chandra said as she sat down at the table to begin her breakfast. "It is a great recommendation to be a Pembroke."

"A man earns my respect only by his character and his courage. I have known too many weak sons of proud families." Miles joined Chandra at the table and poured himself a cup of steaming coffee. "Of course, if you like arrogant prigs, you will find Pembroke the most charming of men."

Miles's disrespect for the product of one of England's better families shocked Chandra. "Exactly the sort of comment I would expect from a coarse, common American."

Miles flushed. "I noticed you had no scruples about sharing a cabin with such a coarse, common fellow when it suited your purpose."

"Nor a choice, either. Had you been a gentleman, you would have given up your cabin to me rather than forcing me to share it."

He slammed down his coffee cup so hard that some of the contents spilled onto the table. "Your gratitude overwhelms me, madam. I need not have accommodated you at all, you know, and I suspect that if I had been wise, I would not have. Furthermore, you are most naive to suppose that, even had I abandoned my cabin to you, the captain would have permitted you aboard, alone without a chaperone or even an abigail, and fleeing your family in the bargain."

Miles was right, Chandra admitted to herself. And she was being petty. How could a poor American, with no family to be proud of, appreciate the importance of a connection like the Pembrokes? "I am sorry, truly I am. I am most grateful for your help," she said penitently.

The sincere contrition in her eyes seemed to cool Miles's anger. After a time, he asked, "Do you play chess, perchance?"

She nodded. Her father, who had loved the game, had made sure that she became a good player. In the previous year she had even been able to defeat him a fair number of times.

Miles got up and extracted from his sea chest a tiny chessboard with even tinier pieces of delicately carved ivory.

As he set up the tiny figures on the board, Chandra's eyes gleamed. This upstart American was about to be bested. But to her chagrin she quickly discovered that he was the better player, although she gave him quite a battle.

Miles laid out the pieces for another game. "Your father gave you a strange education for a girl," he remarked. "What else did he teach you besides the way to ride like a man and to play chess?"

She told him of her studies in Latin, philosophy, literature, even the rudiments of science. She did not confess that papa had also taught her to be an expert marksman. She doubted Miles would even believe this.

Miles toyed with a bishop as he pondered his next move. "Those subjects are hardly the normal curriculum for a young lady. Were you good at them?"

She nodded but did not elaborate. How could she explain to a stranger how determined she had been to excel at everything her father had taught her? His pleasure at her achievements had been her reward. Loving him as she had, it would have broken her heart to disappoint him.

They played in silence for a few moments, then Miles asked abruptly, "Tell me about your father."

Chandra hesitated. She did not wish to compound her life story with more lies, so she selected certain facts for him. She told him how papa had been a young member of Parliament with a brilliant political future when he had met her mother, and of the elopement and of the duke's terrible thirst for revenge. She did not, however, name Warfolk.

"Surely your father knew that he might have to spend years in exile."

Chandra shook her head slowly. "No, he realized there would be a momentary scandal, but he thought it would blow over soon enough."

Miles fingered one of the ivory knights thoughtfully. "Given this duke's vengeful, sadistic nature, I am surprised he did not find some way to snatch your mother back from Italy."

Chandra stared at him in surprise. "Perhaps he could not find her."

Miles's words generated a new fear in Chandra. What if the duke should learn that she had fled to America? Could he, powerful as he was, find a way to snatch her back across the Atlantic? She tried to banish the thought from her mind but she could not, and Miles won the game easily.

"You would have beat me this time were you not so preoccupied," he observed. "Perhaps you would prefer not to play again."

"No, I would like another try," she said, resolutely setting her mind to winning. How ridiculous to concentrate on such an irrational fear when she might be proving to an arrogant American just how skilled she was at the game.

The day passed so quickly that Chandra could scarcely believe it when supper was brought to their cabin. It had been by far the happiest day she had spent since her father's accident. Her distrust of Miles was considerably alleviated. His manners toward her were as impeccable as those of the finest English gentleman, and his conduct was unmarred by even the slightest hint of impropriety.

Being an innocent novice at romance, she did not suspect that his behavior was calculated to do exactly what it was doing—soothe her doubts and provoke her interest.

In the days that followed, Miles and Chandra spent many hours matching wits over the chessboard. At first Miles allowed her to win a game or two, as part of his strategy, but this patronizing attitude so rankled her pride that, in the face of her anger, he desisted. As a result, although she managed to give him stiff competition, she won few games.

On their third day at sea, Chandra had almost mastered the difficult art of dressing behind the blanket: she would twist and strain until finally she was able to close the vexing buttons on the back of her gown. Then she emerged and began subduing her long waves of hair neatly atop her head.

Suddenly, Miles's low, rich voice was so close to her ear that his warm breath tickled it. "Allow me. You have missed a button."

His fingers were at her back, and their provocative caress upon her bare skin made her draw in her breath sharply. The days at sea, she realized with dismay, had done nothing to improve her immunity to his touch, which sent excitement coursing through her.

He seemed to be taking an inordinately long time.

"What are you doing?" she inquired stiffly.

"I fear my clumsy fingers are having difficulty with this little button," he said so innocently that she was suspicious.

When at last he finished, she stepped away from him hastily, much flustered, and her thank-you was delivered in such an ungracious tone that Miles correctly assumed she was making a supreme effort to stifle her much stirred sensibilities.

A knock at her cabin door announced the arrival of breakfast. After they had sat down to it, Miles said, "You were very close to your father, weren't you?"

Chandra looked at him quickly. He had demonstrated an enormous interest during their time at sea in her father and in Percy, asking dozens of questions about them. Naturally, she was eager to discuss the former—but not the latter.

"Yes, we were close," she said. "Papa knew so much, and he spent hours and hours making sure that at least some of his knowledge would be passed on to me."

"What else did he have to do?" Miles asked.

His question startled her. "Not a great deal," she admitted. There had been little to occupy papa at Northlands except the horses he bred, and George had done much of the work with them. "But understand," she went on, anxious to correct any misimpressions, "that papa was a wonderful man. He never treated me like I was a silly girl. He respected my ideas."

"No doubt," Miles said quietly, "since they so often coincided with his own."

"What a mean thing to say. Papa respected my thoughts; he took me seriously."

Miles was silent and she ceased her defense, feeling suddenly that she was protesting too much.

* * *

As the days passed, Chandra found Miles's conversation even more challenging than his chess. Rather than the crude, ignorant dolt she had imagined all Americans to be, she found to her surprise that this one possessed wide-ranging knowledge. Sometimes Chandra argued with him sharply, something she would never have dreamed of doing in similar discussions with her father, but other times she found she agreed with Miles and was much entertained by his dry, ironic observations. Papa had always been so solemn, but Miles was more often amused than reverent.

Miles, too, enjoyed their discussions. He disliked simpering females without spirit, and Chandra did not soften her views to please him. He could not recall a time when Sally Humphreys, his neighbor's eager daughter, had *not* agreed with him. She was determined to snare him as a husband and her strategy seemed to be flattery and simpleminded acquiescence. Miles thought wryly that if he were to tell Sally that her health would be vastly improved if she would swallow arsenic, she would immediately agree with him.

Chandra was courageous as well. Not many girls would have dared to cross the Atlantic with a stranger. No, it could not be denied that Chandra was an unusual and exotic flower. And on top of that, he liked her. Not only lusted for her, as he assuredly did, but liked her, even when they argued. Their stiffest battles revolved around the respective merits of their nations and their governments. She could not imagine a nation without a king, nor could she see the point of a president who could be replaced every four years at the pleasure of the people.

"But why should a man who may be utterly incompetent rule a nation simply because of the accident of his birth?" Miles challenged her with this one day as he and Chandra were finishing a chess game that, as usual, he had won.

"But are your people capable of choosing the best man?"

"They just have," Miles nodded as he placed the tiny

ivory chess pieces carefully in their case. "We have a new president who was inaugurated while I have been on this trip."

"What is his name?"

"Thomas Jefferson."

The name was familiar to Chandra, but it took her a moment to place it. "Not the one who wrote that infamous Declaration of Independence?" she gasped incredulously, remembering how her father had rallied against its author as a mad revolutionary and a godless anarchist.

"Infamous!" Miles sputtered. "It is one of the noblest documents ever penned by man. Have you read it?"

"No," she admitted, much embarrassed.

"Well, you might try doing so before you condemn it."

She sat contritely before him and vowed that she would do so when she reached America. Miles gave out with a hearty laugh. "I do enjoy our talks, but for now, let us rest a bit. Perhaps some music might be in order."

Miles reached beneath his bunk and pulled out the guitar that he had brought with him to while away his long, lonely voyage, which had turned out not to be lonely at all. Even though the companionship he had found so far with Chandra was not precisely what he had originally intended, it was certainly pleasurable.

Frequently in the evening he would play his guitar, and Chandra would join her light soprano to his melodious baritone. Sometimes, he would merely accompany her on the guitar, listening to her sweet, clear voice. Other nights they would read to each other from the small library—a collection of Shakespeare, a volume of Ben Jonson, a book of Greek dramas and poetry—that Miles had brought with him.

Chandra loved to listen to him read. His voice was so rich and full of expression. He had an actor's dramatic flair for imbuing the words with nuances and emotion, and his soft Virginia accent instilled his phrases with music.

One night as they were sitting side by side at the nar-

row table, he read to her from Jonson's poetry. His
voice had dropped lower and lower, and she had unconsciously moved her head very close to his to hear
better.

> *The thirst that from the soul doth rise*
> *Doth ask a drink of divine;*
> *But might I of Jove's nectar sup,*
> *I would not change for thine.*

His eyes were soft and warm and his lips were very
near to her own. "Let me but taste your drink divine."
His voice was seductive, and his lips met hers.

She felt as though her limbs had turned to water. She
could not resist his kiss. His arms stole around her, and
the kiss grew more intense. She thrilled to be in his
arms: this man had a mesmerizing effect upon her. She
was faintly conscious of his strong fingers holding her
and his chest against her bosom. Once again, she felt
within her those deep stirrings of pleasure and longing
that she so little understood.

This is madness, she thought, knowing that if she
did not end the embrace very quickly, she soon would
not have the strength. She would never break her vow
to her dying father. She cursed herself for her weakness,
and with a wrench of will she pulled away from Miles,
her eyes mirroring the conflict within her.

"Please, don't," she gasped. "I cannot break my vows.
I beg you, don't try to make me do so."

"You are determined to be faithful to your marriage?"
His question carried a hint of wonder and respect.

He had no way of understanding her real meaning.
Well, she was not about to tell him that hers were not
vows made to a husband.

To her relief, he did not protest. So, she thought, she
had found the proper weapon to keep him at his distance.

The next day, after the steward carried away their
breakfast tray, Miles asked her if her parents had been
happy at Northlands.

"Mama was. She would have been happy anywhere that papa was, she loved him so. But it was difficult for him." Chandra paused, considering that proud, complex man that she had adored. "The people there were not his kind. The local squire was jovial, but only half educated with rustic manners and crude speech. Papa found the parson who held the living in the village ignorant and boring. So my father became something of a recluse, devoting himself to his horses and books."

"And to his daughter," Miles said softly, thinking to himself that she was the only one around who could have possibly measured up to his snobbish standards. And of course for Chandra there had been no other man around against whom she could measure her father.

"Yes, I guess so," Chandra agreed, "especially after mama died. He was so lonely, and we became inseparable then."

Miles gave her a thoughtful look. Her dear father had tried to make her the replacement for the son who had died. And then when his wife was gone, he had turned her into the companion he had lost. "So that is why he educated you as he did, so that he would have company in his interests," he said aloud.

Her eyes flashed. "I suppose you are one of those men who think education is wasted on a mere woman."

"Education is never wasted, but I understand that in England it is the size of a girl's dowry, not her education, that is important to a prospective bridegroom."

"Isn't it the same everywhere?" Chandra asked bitterly. "Would you marry a woman who had no dowry?"

"Of course, if I loved her. Then it would not matter if she had only the clothes on her back."

Chandra looked at him in wonder. The man was amazing, truly.

As the days passed, Chandra, who had never been taught guile, found herself laughing and confiding in Miles under his skillful questioning as she would have in an old and dear friend. Only on the subject of Percy was she evasive, and Miles could not help taking note of that. But her frankness startled him. She seemed as clean of artifice as her face was bare of those poisonous white powders that Englishwomen so liberally employed.

One night as they were eating supper in their cabin, Chandra asked, "Why have you never married?"

Miles shrugged. "Why should I take on the shackle of marriage when I can have its pleasures without its burdens?"

"That means you must have a mistress," she said. "Am I correct?"

"That is not a question a lady asks a gentleman."

"You did not answer it, so that means you do."

"Yes, I do, but that is not why I don't marry. I have always preferred adventure to routine." He grinned at her. "And my impression of you the first time I saw you was that I had found a kindred spirit."

She blushed and clutched her napkin hard. "I fear that you drew the wrong impression of me that day."

By now, he knew he had, but he could not refrain from teasing her. "You hardly ran away from me."

"I know I should have, but I was certain a stranger who quoted so knowingly from the classics would surely be a gentleman. So, you see, I, too, was quite misled."

"But when I took you in my arms to soothe you, you did not object."

She sighed and poked at the food on her plate so that she could look away from him, from his searching hazel eyes. "I suppose I should have swooned the moment you touched me. But I have never swooned in my life, and I fear I don't know how."

His mouth twitched as he struggled to keep from laughing aloud at her honesty, which he found quite as bewitching as her beauty.

"But you went quite too far when you kissed me," she reproached him. "I had never been kissed like that before."

His eyebrows rose. "Not even by your dear husband?"

She blushed violently and stammered in confusion. "I mean, by a stranger, of course."

Miles was sure he had just touched a sore spot. He had always found the story of her marriage odd, and whenever he tried to discuss Percy with her she changed the subject.

"The only reason you married Percy was to escape that repulsive merchant your guardian had picked for you, wasn't it? Percy was the only one you knew that you could turn to, wasn't he?"

"No, no, of course not." Chandra was flustered. "I love Percy."

Miles doubted, from her tone, that the marriage had ever even been consummated. After all, they apparently had been dragged apart shortly after the ceremony, and Percy had had to set sail for America. What a weakling he was, Miles thought contemptuously. She was a woman of far too much spirit to be wasted on that young fool.

Occasionally, late at night or in the early morning when the other passengers were safely in their cabins, Miles would take Chandra walking on the deck for a breath of air.

On one such night, as they emerged on deck, the moon was bright and full and the sky was a vast field of starry lights. The great square sails of the *Golden Drake* billowed above them in the wind, the topgallants seeming to reach to the sky itself.

They stopped at the taffrail and stared down into the dark and impenetrable sea before moving away into the protection offered by the quarterdeck. Here, sheltered from the wind, it was almost warm.

Nothing disturbed the night's silence except the wind in the sails and an occasional noise from the livestock that had been brought aboard as food for the long voyage.

The big moon gave a romantic feel to the night, and Miles found himself irresistibly drawn to Chandra, her face so lovely in the pale light. He took her in his arms and brought her close. He gathered her into the cover of his body, and slowly he kissed her. She did not resist him, and he pressed his advantage, exploring the tender recesses of her mouth, caressing the fine, full curves of her hips. He felt the quickening within her as she returned his embrace.

Encouraged, his hands slipped to the fastening that held her green velvet cloak and he touched her throat lovingly, delicately, as he undid the clasp and let the garment drop from her shoulders. His lips burned a trail of kisses down her throat. His hands slipped behind her and held her body tightly to his. Her breath was coming more quickly now.

Then suddenly, she thrust him away from her, and he saw torment in her eyes.

"You said you would not press me—I believed you," she said in a voice so full of reproach that he felt like a cad. "I have told you I will not break my vows. Why must you persist?"

"I am not forcing you," he protested. "I told you I would do nothing that you did not desire. But I think there is much you desire."

"Please," she cried in a choked voice. "I cannot."

Much as Miles wanted her, he could not act counter to her wishes. In truth, he was much impressed by her determination to remain faithful to her husband, particularly when he was certain that she had made a loveless bargain. He admired her integrity and her faithfulness. Were he ever to take a wife, he would demand just such fidelity of her.

He stared down into Chandra's troubled face. She was naive, contrary to his first impressions, and Miles had no taste for taking advantage of young innocents. His private code of honor did not permit it, which was why Sally Humphreys still retained her virtue despite her enormous willingness to relinquish it to him. Nor had he ever, despite his reputation as a rake, enticed an unwilling wife to betray her husband. The faithless wives who had come to his bed had done so eagerly and had been no strangers to forbidden fields. He would make no further efforts to seduce Chandra, he decided. The game was simply not played for such high stakes.

Chapter 12

Miles quickly discovered his good intentions were more painful than his bad. Having seen that Miles was a gentleman of his word. Chandra grew careless in their communal living—to his acute distress. Ignorant of the ways of men and the small things that set their blood afire, she had no inkling of how much she tempted him. As he watched her unfastening the long coils of sable hair and shaking them in a cascade down her back, as he caught her adjusting a collar or a hem, he felt a rush of excitement he could not subdue.

But even more tantalizing to him were her movements behind the blanket that formed their makeshift dressing room. The soft, rustling sounds of garments being discarded, and the sight of delicate ankles stepping out of petticoats beneath the curtain, fired Miles's desires, and in his imagination he undressed her soft body. Had Chandra stood naked before him, he could not have been more aroused.

He felt besieged—her beauty, her tempting curves, and her lavender scent all seemed to permeate the cabin. Her constant nearness in these small confines drove him wild with desire. He had never been a celibate man, and this long voyage and Chandra's innocent provocation were testing him in a way that he had no will to be. Nor was he altogether certain that he could manage to resist what was becoming to his mind a superhuman challenge.

And so, as the days passed without relief, he grew irritable. One night as the wind and the swell of the sea rose ominously, he sat reading, watching Chandra out of the corner of his eye, sitting upon her bunk brushing out her hair. How he longed to go to her and take her in his arms. Angrily, he gritted his teeth and tried to fix his attention on his book, but the sea was so rough it was unlikely he could have read it even had he been able to put his mind to it.

Chandra put down her brush and started toward the makeshift dressing room to get ready for bed. But she stopped beside his chair, and looking down she asked, "Where do you teach?"

It was a question he had successfully evaded answering in the past by skillfully turning the conversation to other channels. But he gathered from her tone that tonight she needed to know for some reason and was determined not to be fobbed off again.

"I don't," he replied curtly.

"But you said . . ."

"I did not. You presumed. I merely said I had done some tutoring when I was in France."

"But what do you do, then?"

Miles gave a careless toss of his head. "Whatever I like."

"I mean, what is your occupation?"

Her persistence further stretched his temper, which was already strained by her challenge to his self-restraint. He thought of the great stock she placed upon a man's position, and this further whipped up his mood. With a certain bleak humor, he replied, "I am a farmer."

Her shock was engraved in her face and her voice. "A farmer! I mistook you for a gentleman."

While her response did not entirely surprise Miles, it added fuel to his building anger. "In America, madam, a man can be both a farmer and a gentleman. The two are not mutually exclusive."

Chandra's snobbery, evidently inherited from her adored father, was the only thing Miles did not like about her. Philip Taylor had taught his daughter to judge a man by his family, title, and fortune, rather than on the essentials of character, courage, and achievement.

"You must have a large and profitable farm," Chandra said stiffly.

He shrugged indifferently. "Enough to supply my few needs."

"Are you poor?"

He shrugged again and quoted: " 'It is not the man who has too little but who craves more that is poor.' "

She could not keep the disappointment from her voice. "What brought a poor farmer like yourself to England?"

"It was not a trip of my choosing." The conversation was turning down a path he had no wish to travel, for Tom's sake. "I was on important business for a friend. I cannot discuss it."

"He must be quite wealthy to send you abroad in such style," Chandra observed, nodding at the cabin.

"He has some resources at his disposal," Miles said drily. He rose from his chair, went to the cupboard, and poured himself a glass of Madeira. If only the girl would go to bed and be done with it!

"Your father—was he a farmer, too?"

The hint of contempt in Chandra's tone raised a dangerous glint in Miles's eyes. "Of course," he replied, turning toward her.

"And his father? Or do you even know who your grandfather was?"

Miles took a long sip of wine and stared at her stonily. "Oh, I know very well—the old reprobate." Sardonic amusement played about his lips. "Were I to tell you, you would be shocked speechless. But I shan't drag my family skeletons out of the closet."

He sat down again, stared moodily at his wine, then gestured at their makeshift dressing room. "If you're not going to use it, I will."

Chandra, puzzled by his mood, hastily went behind the blanket to undress, and as she did so, they heard from the deck an urgent summons to the crew. "All hands lay aloft."

The wind and the seas were picking up fury.

Miles sat fuming. He was angry at Chandra's snobbishness, angry at her for tantalizing him, angry at himself for not pressing his attempted conquest, angry that he would soon have to turn her over to her fop of a husband, angry, in fact, at the whole damned world.

He drained his wineglass and stood up. Just then a sudden crosswave slammed into the ship and Chandra, who had just unlaced the bodice of her thin lawn shift, was hurtled from behind the curtain's protection. Miles reached out and caught her before she fell. She had had no time to pull her bodice together, and the pink tips of her breasts lay bare for his eyes to feast upon. Miles looked down at the pale, perfectly formed fruit, and his desire rose hard and urgent. This, coupled with his anger, consumed his honorable intentions toward her.

"What the hell," he thought bitterly. "Since she is so certain that I am no gentleman, I might as well confirm her belief."

His hands began to fondle her soft white breasts as his lips settled warm, moist kisses on her throat. The shift fell to each side of her bosom, and he eased it off her shoulders. The imprint of his fingers was burned into her yielding flesh.

Caught by surprise—and by a surge of passion stronger than anything she had ever before experienced—Chandra was powerless to rebuff him. She found herself eagerly meeting his questing lips as they closed over hers. His tongue probed her mouth as his caressing hands excited her bosom, her back, and buttocks. When at last they drew apart, his lips lowered again to her throat and then to the pink crowns of her breasts which seemed to harden and rise up to meet his lips. A strange, divinely pleasurable sensation swept over her as he teased the pink peaks with his tongue, and she moaned.

Miles, feeling her body responding so eagerly to him, could not resist mocking in a voice husky with passion. "You see, my lovely, stubborn one, you want me as much as I want you. Even if I am only a poor American farmer."

His words enraged her and brought her back to her senses. She was not some red-haired harlot or eager farmer's daughter to amuse him during a boring voyage. She was a gentleman's daughter and a lady. Her fury spurred her to belated action. As he tried to nudge her gently onto his bunk, she gave him a shove and fled to the far corner of the cabin, where she glared at him as she fumbled with her shift, trying to cover her naked breasts and to subdue the desire that Miles had aroused within her.

He took a step toward her. "Don't you come near me, you crude, arrogant jackanapes," she cried.

Miles stopped, furious at himself for having allowed his foolish words to send him to defeat just as he was about to conquer her.

"I warn you that my husband is an excellent marksman, and he will not let my honor go unavenged." Actually Percy was a terrible shot and hated guns, but she was searching desperately for something to hold Miles off.

"So your husband concealed his skill with his pistols as well as his beautiful wife, did he?" Miles stood beside his bunk watching her, his lip curled sarcastically. "Possibly you noticed at the Seagull Inn that my marksmanship was most accurate. Should it come to a duel between Percy Lunt and myself, I have no doubt who the winner would be."

Chandra could make no convincing argument on this score. Instead she snapped, "My husband is a well-born gentleman, far superior to you in every way."

Anger glowed in Miles's eyes. "You, my foolish beauty, will one day learn the hard truth that titles are no indication of character or integrity. You love the shadow of a man, and not his substance. You love the wind that ruffles the tree's branches and not the tree itself. Give me an honest farmer any day to a sly, conniving aristocrat."

With that, Miles stalked from the cabin, a black scowl upon his face.

Chapter 13

The days that followed were miserable for both Chandra and Miles. Her trust in him had been destroyed, and now she was wary. The easy, frank camaraderie that they had enjoyed had been dealt a deep blow that might, it seemed, prove fatal.

Her snobbish rejection rankled Miles. His anger at her, however, did not lessen his desire for her, and he could find comfort only in the thought that their voyage was well past its halfway point and his frustration would soon be ended. For solace in the interim, he stayed out of the cabin and turned to Sir Egerton Chatwin's wife, who had been boldly angling for him since they had met the first day of the voyage. Although Miles was only mildly interested in her, he enjoyed her willingness after Chandra's reluctance.

The day after their harsh exchange of words, Chandra welcomed his absence. But without him there, she quickly found the confines of the small cabin unbearable. Much as she hated to admit it, she missed Miles dreadfully. Time, which had passed so quickly in his company, now dragged endlessly.

When Miles did return to the cabin, a cloying scent of musk clung to him. Chandra inquired, "Did you perchance fall into a perfume vat?"

Miles laughed sardonically as he hung his coat on the peg beside the door. "So Lady Chatwin has left her calling card upon me."

"Lady Chatwin!"

"Unlike you, the lady is far from averse to a little

pleasure with a man who is not her husband, even if he is a poor American farmer."

Chandra felt a prick of jealousy. "You conceited fool. You malign Lady Chatwin. You are not so irresistible as you think." But even as Chandra said it she knew she was wrong. Devilishly handsome as Miles was, and charming and attentive besides, he no doubt had more than enough willing wenches to warm his bed.

Miles gave Chandra a lascivious grin as he went to the cupboard to pour himself brandy. "You don't know what you are missing until you try it."

She glared at him and tried to cheer herself with the thought that Lady Chatwin undoubtedly was stupid and dull, but this speculation made her feel no better. She felt as though she could not stand the tiny cabin another instant, and she announced that she was going for a walk on deck, her first in daylight hours since she had boarded the *Golden Drake*.

"You will be making it difficult for your adored husband," Miles warned, replacing the brandy decanter in the cupboard.

"I don't care." Chandra grabbed her cloak from the peg where it hung beside Miles's coat.

He took the cloak from her and placed it over her shoulders. "Do as you please, then. And be it upon your head."

He grabbed his greatcoat and accompanied her to the deck. She breathed deeply of the air, heavy with the tang of salt, and stared up at the great clouds of square white sails billowing from the vessel's tall masts. But the scene beyond the boat was less inspiring. The sky and the sea were the same depressing gray, blending together into one misty, dreary whole, so that she was not certain where one ended and the other began. A brisk wind tugged at Chandra's hair and cloak. It was colder on deck than she had expected, and she wished that she had brought her fur muff. Still, she uttered not a word of complaint. She would not fuel Miles's fiery tongue by acting the lady.

They had walked scarcely fifty feet along the deck

when they were approached by a petite young woman with an angelic face who was entirely wrapped in fur. She fastened her discontented brown eyes eagerly upon Miles, who bowed and introduced Lady Elizabeth Chatwin to Chandra.

Lady Chatwin was at least four inches shorter than Chandra and not over four and twenty years. Chandra, to her chagrin, had to admit that the young woman was beautiful, although the whiteness of her skin might be attributed to mercury water rather than nature, and the color on her cheeks and lips to carmine rather than good health.

Lady Chatwin's eyes narrowed as she gave Chandra the critical appraisal a rival reserves for her competition. So Miles had not overestimated his effect upon the lady after all.

Lady Chatwin's voice dripped with sweetness. "I understand, Mrs. Carrington, that you have been weathering the trip very poorly." She smiled with false innocence. "Fortunately, I have had no such trouble. My husband says nothing is more boring than a sickly woman."

Chandra was diverted by a man's voice behind her asking, "What have we here, a new passenger picked up in mid-Atlantic?"

Miles gave the newcomer a cold look. "My wife has finally found her sea legs, Lord William," he replied brusquely.

Chandra examined the Earl of Blandshire's son with some disappointment. He was handsome, but his heavily lidded eyes were hard and calculating. Even when he smiled, the eyes remained cold. He had a narrow nose, slightly hooked at the end. Creases furrowed the corners of his thin mouth, giving him a sullen, one might even say a cruel, expression. His greatcoat was of the finest wool collared in velvet, and of impeccable fit, but he did not cut as fine a figure in it as Miles did in his plain worsted.

He was a lord and the scion of a noble family, of course, but Chandra was forced to admit reluctantly that Lord William seemed hard and passionless, and without any of Miles's warmth. Nonetheless, she told herself, such a man of high breeding and birth would never act toward her as that crude farmer had done.

Pembroke studied Chandra appreciatively. "Are you American, too?"

"No, my lord, I am English." She gave him a dazzling smile.

His interest increased visibly. "How do you like your new home in a strange land?" he asked.

"I am afraid I still await my first glimpse of America."

"So you are newly wed. How terrifying it must be for you to leave behind all you love."

"On the contrary," Miles interjected, "I could scarcely restrain her, she was so eager to board this ship for her new home."

Miles's eyes glinted with mockery, and Chandra wanted to hit him for teasing her when he knew she dared say nothing in her own behalf. He put his arm possessively through hers. "If you will excuse us . . . ," he said as he guided Chandra away.

"Why did you rush me off?" she protested when they were well beyond the others on deck. "I enjoyed talking to Lord William."

"I cannot abide him," Miles said irritably. "Besides, we cannot risk much inquiry about how we met and where our courtship was conducted. The more lies we must tell now, the more difficult for you later. You seem to forget, my dear," he said as he steered her into their cabin, "I have only your best interests at heart."

Chapter 14

Chandra saw little of Miles in the days that followed. To escape the loneliness of their cabin, she frequently went on deck by herself. Whenever she appeared, Lord William or the baron's son, Thomas Strum, vied to reach her side first. She was naturally flattered by Lord William's interest in her. How pleased her father would have been to see her with the Earl of Blandshire's son. Whenever they were together, he hovered about her and showered her with extravagant compliments.

"How could my idiotic countrymen have permitted such a rare and valuable jewel as you to be carried off by an American?" he asked her one day. "If only I had met you earlier . . ."

The next day, as they stood at the railing gazing out at the seemingly endless expanse of sea, he burst out, "Your beauty eclipses the sun itself." She blushed and nodded her thanks. He continued. "Your husband is a very lucky man. Where in America is he from?"

"Virginia," she responded.

"How amusing a coincidence. I plan to offer for a plantation there called Willowmere. I have already written the owner of my intention. Perhaps your husband has told you of it. It was built by an Englishman, Lord Scott Leigh, the brother of the old Marquess of Pelham, and is one of the most beautiful mansions in America." He gave her a suggestive smile that she did not find particularly inviting. "Will you visit me there? Its beauty should be a fitting setting for your own."

But at that moment Chandra's interest in Lord William and in Willowmere was shattered by the sight of Miles and Lady Chatwin walking together on the deck, her arm in his.

Lord William's company, even his lavish compliments, soon began to pall on Chandra. His conversation was not nearly so lively or amusing as Miles's was. But as tedious as she found him, he was still far preferable to her other admirer, Thomas Strum. Although she had bristled when Miles had called Strum peculiar, Chandra realized now that the description was only too accurate. The obscure baron's younger son was a dull man with a pinched face and the unhealthy pallor of one who continually shuns the sun. He fancied himself an elegant dandy, but his attire was more often ludicrous than impressive. The first time Chandra had seen him on deck, he was wearing a many-caped scarlet riding coat with enormous gold buttons, fine leather riding boots, and buckskins.

She had asked Miles with barely suppressed laughter, "What do you suppose he means to ride in the middle of the ocean?"

"Sea horses, perhaps," Miles had quipped with a grin.

In that rare moment, she and Miles had recaptured a shadow of their former ease together, and she felt a sharp stab of regret for what had been lost between them. Since he was spending most of his time now with Lady Chatwin, she did not even have an opportunity to discuss Strum further with him.

But Chandra was very displeased by Lady Chatwin's attentions to Miles. She was as quickly at his side when he appeared on deck as Lord William and Strum were at Chandra's. It was disgraceful, Chandra thought angrily, how Lady Elizabeth fawned over Miles.

Chandra's greatest pleasure in Pembroke's company came from the anger that flashed in Miles's eyes when he saw her with him. It seemed to Chandra that this was the only time now that he even noticed her. Whenever Strum came near her and Miles happened to be there to take note, she thought she saw a hint of amusement in his infuriating, mocking eyes. It was as if he were saying, "You see? Everything I told you about those pompous dolts was absolutely true."

And "dolt" was the term she would have used for Strum. When he met Chandra, the first thing out of his mouth was a question about the names of her family's estates. He quickly informed her he was not acquainted with Blackstone Abbey, although he had heard a dreadful report of it somewhere. When she mentioned Northlands, he said, "Don't believe I've heard of it. Can't be too much. A pity you have not seen my home. Quite the best there is, you know."

His main topic of conversation was his father's splendid estate. He could not understand how Chandra had failed to hear of it. He took great pains to convince her of its grandness by describing every piece of furniture, every objet d'art, every flower and topiary in the garden, until Chandra thought she would die of boredom.

It came as an enormous shock to her that the standards her father had so carefully imbued in her did not hold up. A poor American farmer of dreadful lineage was more comely in appearance, education, manners, and intelligence than a pearl of British aristocracy. Or so she had come to feel. How disgusted papa would be with her, she thought guiltily.

One afternoon, Strum, inappropriately resplendent in a moss-green coat of cut velvet and black velvet breeches, with two large emerald rings on his fingers and a third in the folds of his neckcloth, bested Pembroke in the sprint to her side. Chandra suffered politely through a ten-minute dissertation on the difficulty his father's gardener had once encountered in coaxing a recalcitrant boxwood into a splendid unicorn topiary.

Unable to stand another moment, she excused herself and fled to the quiet of her cabin. As she opened the door, she was greeted by a sudden commotion on Miles's bunk, and she heard him say nonchalantly, "I believe, love, that we have company."

He rose from the bunk, casually fastening his breeches

and disclosing to Chandra's shocked sensibility considerably more of Lady Chatwin than Chandra cared to see.

Her shock gave way to fury. "You trollop," she spat out at the woman, who rose hastily, fumbling with her dress. Seeing murder in Chandra's eyes, Lady Chatwin quit the cabin with graceless speed.

Chandra glared at Miles. "How dare you bring her here?" She spat at him in outrage.

He returned her expression, his hazel eyes flashing dangerously. "I remind you, madam, this is my cabin. It is I, not you, who paid the fee, and I shall invite whomever I please and for whatever purpose." He gave her an insulting look. "If you are going to play the jealous wife, I shall expect you to act the wife in all other respects, too."

"I am not jealous," she cried and turned to escape the cabin. But she found her arm caught in a hand of steel.

"Where are you going?" Miles demanded.

"Back on deck. The air here is much polluted."

But he held her arm more firmly. "In that case I shall walk with you."

"I prefer to walk alone."

"If you must interfere with my relationship with Lady Chatwin, I see no reason why I should not return the favor for yours with Pembroke."

"Lord William and I are not lovers," she snapped.

"Nor, unfortunately, are Lady Chatwin and I, thanks to your untimely interruption."

As Miles guided her along the companionway, she asked stiffly, "Pray, what do I owe you for the cabin? I will not be beholden to you."

"I don't want your money, only your love," he mocked, then said with a graveness that surprised her, "Keep your money. You will need it. And keep it a secret from your husband, too."

She looked up at him with startled eyes. "Why?"

"If you do not, it will soon vanish at the gaming tables," he said as they reached the deck and came face to face with Pembroke, the velvet collar of his greatcoat turned up against the sharp wind.

"Mr. Carrington," Lord William said, "I've been told you are a Virginian." Chandra was relieved that once again she would be spared a discussion about Percy. But it troubled her to think that the rumors about his gambling might be true. "Are you familiar with the plantation Willowmere?" Lord William asked. "It is said to be spectacular."

"I've heard rumor to that effect," Miles replied indifferently. The wind was increasing, and it tugged at his thick brown hair, pushing it back from his face, which was set in a hard, irritated expression.

"Have you never been invited to Willowmere?" Lord William's tone dripped with condescension.

"No." Miles toyed angrily with a belaying pin, and Chandra was certain he was holding back some choice comments.

"A pity. I hoped you were acquainted with its owner, the Marquess of Pelham's nephew."

"We in America have no use for titles. We fought too hard for our independence from such foolishness."

Lord William's mouth twitched angrily. "Perhaps if your countrymen paid more attention to such foolishness, yours would be a more civilized country."

Miles gave him a cold, piercing look. "Then tell me: Why would an English lord travel to a country he considers so uncivilized?"

Pembroke looked uneasily away at the tars scrambling aloft to shorten the sails in the rising wind. "Because I understand many owners of great plantations like Willowmere are in severe financial straits, and their holdings can be bought at bargain prices. It seems extravagant tastes were not matched by extravagant incomes. I, on the other hand, have the means to increase my estate, and I intend to do so."

"It is the outrageous prices we must pay you English for your goods that drives the planters to bankruptcy."

Pembroke smirked. "Come now, we cannot be blamed for everything."

Miles was silent for a moment. "No," he acknowledged generously, "the foolishness of some planters in relying solely on tobacco, which has exhausted the soil, must share the blame."

"What price would Willowmere bring?" Pembroke asked abruptly.

"You will not find Willowmere for sale at any price." Miles's fingers drummed impatiently on the railing and his eyes drifted up to glance at the sailors struggling with the wind-filled canvas. "Its owner is in no distress. He is the richest planter in Virginia."

"Are you one of those great plantation owners floundering in debt, Mr. Carrington?"

"No, I am a farmer." Miles withdrew his attention from the sailors aloft and stared Pembroke squarely in the eye.

The corners of Lord William's mouth curled in contempt. "What do you raise?"

Miles fixed the Englishman with a cold look. "Pigs."

"Pigs!"

"Pigs," Miles reiterated with enormous enthusiasm.

Pembroke gave Miles and Chandra a slight, hasty bow and hurried away as rapidly as if he had just learned Miles suffered from a highly contagious social disease.

Chandra was mortified. "Is that true? You raise pigs?"

Miles seemed to enjoy her embarrassment. "But, my dear wife, I told you of my occupation."

"I am not your wife!"

"Not too loudly." His grin infuriated her. "If you are chagrined to be thought the wife of a pig farmer, think how much worse to have it thought you are merely his mistress."

Chandra's face flamed. She turned and marched back to their cabin.

Chapter 15

Within half an hour, the word was out. The other passengers pretended not to see them or suddenly walked in a different direction at their approach. Chandra could almost hear them hissing, "the pig farmer and his wife." As the days passed, she stayed more and more in the cabin, reading and embroidering. But humiliated as she was, she had three small consolations: the voyage was almost over, she was spared so much as a nod from Thomas Strum, and Lady Chatwin had ceased her attention to Miles. Naturally, Lord William's interest in Chandra vanished.

While Chandra hid in the cabin, Miles, who seemed amused by his status as an outcast, spent more time than ever on deck.

One afternoon, tiring of her needlework, Chandra looked about for Miles's collection of Shakespeare but could not find it. She assumed he must have put it away in his sea chest. When another hour passed and he had not returned, she grew impatient. Finally she went to his chest and opened it to search for the book.

Miles's plain cloak was folded neatly on top. She lifted a few of the carefully folded layers. Although his garments were plain, he was as meticulous with them as he was with his appearance. She lifted another layer and to her surprise found a most expensive coat of amber brocade and beneath it a pair of white breeches of the finest silk.

The cabin door opened behind Chandra, and she

heard Miles say, "We are almost to Chesapeake Bay. It won't . . ." He broke off and slammed the door behind him. His voice turned furious. "What the hell are you doing! You call yourself a lady, but I find you going through my clothes like a common whore searching for valuables."

"I was only looking for your Shakespeare," she stammered. "I did not mean any harm."

"Liar." Miles's tone was low and menacing. "You were going through my papers. Are you happy with your discovery?"

"I swear I found nothing except some fine clothes."

She shrank back as he strode angrily to the chest and began examining its contents. The clothes were folded back at the point where Chandra had come upon the brocade coat. Seeing that nothing below it had been disturbed, he returned the upper garments to their original position.

"How can a poor pig farmer afford such an elegant coat and breeches?" Chandra demanded, daring to speak only when she saw the flush disappear from his face.

He rose from the chest and slammed the lid. "Gambling is nothing to be ashamed of, unless one loses like your dear husband does."

She snatched up her embroidery again and flounced down on her bunk. "I should think, then, that he would be precisely the sort of man that you would seek out as a partner."

"I play to match wits with my opponent, not to relieve him of his purse." He retrieved his greatcoat from the chair where he had tossed it.

"How noble of you."

He ignored her comment and, as he hung his coat on the peg by the door, asked thoughtfully, "Just how well do you know your husband?"

"What a silly question. I am certain that once I am with him, he will forget his gambling," she said, determined to talk sense into her cousin. Yet she wondered what kind of reception she would receive from Percy when she arrived in Washington.

The *Golden Drake* sailed into Chesapeake Bay, signaling that the end of the voyage was near.

Miles was up before dawn on their last morning aboard, eager to watch as the *Golden Drake* moved past the shore of his beloved Virginia on its way to Baltimore.

Chandra, awaking at the first pale appearance of light, was surprised to see him already dressed and about to leave the cabin.

"We should dock by midmorning," he told her as he departed.

She got up, stretching lazily in her nightshift, and looked out the porthole at the welcome sight of land and an occasional house against the horizon. She felt a twinge of anticipation as she scanned the horizon. Whatever her father's prejudice against this strange land, it was her new home and she intended to make the most of it.

She heard the door open and turned to find herself staring at the pale face of Thomas Strum.

"How dare you come in here?" she demanded, furious at his invasion. "Get out."

"Don't worry." Strum seemed oblivious to her anger. "I just saw your husband go on deck. We shan't be disturbed."

His eyes feasted hungrily upon her body, clad as it was in the revealing nightshift.

Chandra was more angry than frightened by his audacity. "You are bold and impertinent beyond belief," she snapped. "Now leave."

She might as well have been addressing a statue for all the heed he paid her.

"We'll have our moment together before we part." His words were slurred. "Shan't disappoint you."

He staggered slightly as he came toward her, and she realized as he grabbed at her that his unsteadiness was not due to the motion of the sea. He reeked of stale alcohol.

Wrapping her in a clumsy embrace, he licked his white lips. "I could not acknowledge you in public, of course. My position as the son of Lord Strum would not permit me to be seen with a farmer's wife. But I've wanted you . . . oh, I have . . ."

"You are quite mad," Chandra cried as she struggled to free herself from his arms. "And soused besides."

"Been celebrating the end of our voyage, but I ain't more than a trifle foxed," he protested, planting slobbering kisses upon her as she tried to squirm away.

She managed to free her right hand, and she slapped him hard across the face.

The blow seemed to confuse him and he loosened his grasp on her. "You should be honored that I, the son of Lord Strum, have deigned to make you the object of my attention," he whined in a hurt tone.

Chandra choked in rage at his conceit. "It is an honor I want none of," she cried as she jerked free.

As she turned to flee, he reached out and caught a handful of her nightshift, ripping it from her.

The sight of her naked seemed to drive him beyond the point of sanity, and he seized her greedily, his eyes rolling back in his head. He was grunting—a strange awful sound of anticipation emanated from deep within him. She gave a piercing scream as he forced her down on the bunk, and they struggled furiously. She twisted and pummeled him with her fists, but for a man who seemed all bone and no muscle, he was surprisingly strong. He fumbled with the buttons of his breeches and forced her legs apart. He stabbed at her, unable in his drunken frenzy to find his target.

The cabin door flew open with a crash, and Miles stormed in, looking for all the world like an avenging devil. With murderous rage in his eyes, he picked up the skinny Strum as though he were a rag doll, set him upon his feet, and slammed a rocklike fist into his face. Chandra heard a crack as the blow found its mark.

Strum gave a strangled yelp of pain, then sank limply into Miles's arms, blood pouring from his nose.

Throwing open the cabin door, Miles tossed the unfortunate Strum into the passageway as though he were a particularly odious piece of garbage and slammed the door shut.

Miles strode quickly to Chandra, who was huddled on her bunk. He picked up her wrapper and tried to put it around her, but when he touched her, she shrank from him and her eyes filled with fear. She began trembling so violently that he knew he would not be able to get her into the garment. He grabbed a blanket from his bunk and wrapped her in it, then gathered her in his arms.

She tried to pull away from him.

"I won't hurt you, Chandra." His voice was compassionate and reassuring. "Not all men are fools and brutes like that one."

She clung to him desperately and began to cry with great wrenching sobs. As his gentle hands stroked her hair, he murmured soothingly in her ear.

She did feel safe in his arms. Safe and comforted. She clung to him, wanting him never to release her. After her crying subsided, Miles laid her gently back on the bunk and smoothed back her damp hair. He rose and went over to pour her a generous shot of brandy.

He handed her the glass. "Drink it. It will help."

She sipped the fiery liquor, her eyes watching Miles over the rim of the glass. Suddenly she reached up and touched his arm. "Will you accept a word of thanks?" she asked softly. "And call a truce?"

He smiled, took her hand, and squeezed it.

A surge of affection for him swept over her. It pained her to think that by nightfall she would be with Percy, and Miles would be on the way to his farm in Virginia. It was not likely that she would ever see him again.

A great sadness and sense of loss welled up in her.

Part Three

Chapter 16

It was nearly 3 P.M. when the hackney coach Miles had
hired at the dock in Baltimore lurched into Washington.
He had promised the hackman a handsome bonus if
they reached the capital by late afternoon, and the man
had been determined to earn his reward. He hustled the
horses along at a speed that, given the condition of the
rutted road, made it seem unlikely to Chandra that they
would even reach Washington in one piece.

Some of the old rapport that had existed between
Miles and Chandra during their first weeks at sea had
been reestablished during the ride from Baltimore. The
tender moment they had shared before they docked
brought up the former feelings, and they softened toward
each other, talking and laughing easily together.

Chandra had expected Baltimore to be a rough, crude
seaport, little more than a collection of shacks along the
waterfront, so she was impressed by the bustling city
and its attractive main avenue, Market Street. The
houses along it, while not elaborate, were spanking new,
and there was a general air of prosperity about the street
and the city.

As the coach rounded a sudden curve on the road
that climbed out of Baltimore, Chandra looked down
at the city spread beneath them. "Baltimore must be
quite large."

"About 20,000 people, I believe," Miles replied.
"Many of your countrymen, and those of other lands,
have found the living here quite pleasant."

They passed farms interspersed with forests of oak

and birch along the road. Chandra was full of questions
and observations about this new country. Although the
land did not seem as deep a green as in England, it had
a beauty all its own, and Chandra's excited discovery of
this brought a smile to Miles's lips.

Washington, however, was a grave disappointment:
little more than a raw village in a humid swamp. True,
some substantial new homes were going up here and
there, but for the most part the town was a motley collection of small, mean cottages scattered among the
trees. The bare branches added to the general air of
desolation. Only the peach trees were in bloom, their
pink blossoms giving a little color to the otherwise dismal scene.

Chandra stared through the coach's window as they
drove through the streets. "Is this truly your nation's
capital?" she asked incredulously.

Miles smiled. "Now you see why Senator Morris of
New York says, 'This is the best city in the world to
live in—in the future.'"

"But why was it built in a swamp?" she demanded.

"Partly because of political horse trading, partly because it was George Washington's choice," Miles said
succinctly. "I suppose the old general had a fondness
for the place."

Chandra turned from her scrutiny of the new capital
and faced Miles. "We must find Percy first," she said
with more resolution in her voice than in her heart. Now
that the moment of parting was drawing near, she was
becoming more and more reluctant to say goodbye to
Miles. She sensed once again that vibrant connection between them and could call up at will the feel of his
touch on her.

"I believe I heard that your husband was living at
Mrs. Hanna's boardinghouse," Miles said. "We'll try
there."

"A boardinghouse!" The image conjured up smells of
overcooked cabbage, dingy rooms, and rank poverty.
"Surely Percy has a fine house of his own!"

"As you can see," Miles said, nodding at the sparsely

settled land beyond the window, "there are very few homes, fine or otherwise, yet in Washington. Given the shortage, boardinghouses are a favorite accommodation of men living alone here. Even Tom . . ."

"You mean the wealthy friend who sent you to England?" Chandra interrupted.

"Yes, that's the one." Miles pointed at a gash of mud through the trees that served as a street. "He stayed up there on New Jersey Avenue at Conrad and McMunn's while he was waiting for . . ." Miles broke off hastily and fell silent.

"Waiting for what?" Chandra asked, hoping to find out more about the mysterious Tom.

"Oh, never mind. At any rate, he has the beginnings of a nice house here now. It will be quite grand when it's finished." Miles rapped to get the coachman's attention and, after issuing him instructions, settled back on the seat. "Mrs. Hanna's place is not more than a couple of minutes from here," he told Chandra.

She closed her eyes, ruefully regretting her dreams about presiding over Percy's mansion. When she opened them again, her attention was caught by a boxlike sandstone building of classical design, complete with flat balustraded roof, on a nearby hill. It was the most impressive building she had yet seen in this pathetic little village. Oddly enough it had been built slightly to one side rather than centered on the top of the hill.

"What is that building?" she asked, pointing toward it.

Miles followed the direction of her hand. "You mean over on Jenkins' Hill? That's our Capitol, or at least what there is of it so far. That's the north wing, which is to house our Senate. The foundation has recently been laid for the south wing, where the House of Representatives will sit. I understand the two wings are to be joined by a domed structure in the center." Chandra listened with interest. Did all Americans have this much detailed knowledge of their capital's buildings? Or was even architecture a passion of this Virginia farmer?

Mrs. Hanna's turned out to be a neat two-story house

of red brick and white shutters. A little black maid in a white cap and apron opened the door and led them to a small sitting room where they waited while she summoned her mistress. A high-backed pine settle and two hoop armchairs were arranged around a fireplace, where a collection of pewter plates, chambersticks, and tankards were displayed on the mantel.

When Mrs. Hanna, a woman of middle years, ample figure, and pleasant countenance, appeared, she gave Chandra and Miles a sharp glance. "I do not take couples, only single men," she said quickly.

"It is not a room we seek," Miles explained, "but one of your boarders, Percival Lunt."

Disapproval was stamped on Mrs. Hanna's face. "Lunt has not lived here for weeks. He sneaked out in the middle of the night, owing me a month's back rent. Not that I was sorry to see him go. With his drinking and gambling until all hours, he wasn't the type I cared to have in my house."

Chandra suppressed a gasp of shock. "Do you know where he is living now?" Miles persisted.

"No, but I can tell you it isn't in any of the respectable places here on New Jersey Avenue."

As Miles and Chandra started toward the door, Mrs. Hanna called after them, "If you find the young scoundrel, remind him what he owes me."

Chandra climbed into the coach and sank back upon its seat, humiliated and dismayed. Miles got in after her and sat opposite. "Aren't you going to say I told you so?" she asked bitterly.

His eyes were grave, filled with obvious concern for her. "I assure you, Chandra, that this is one time I wish I might be dead wrong."

The coach turned off New Jersey Avenue onto a wide muddy swath cut through thickets of alder. They visited three boardinghouses without success. Finally, at the fourth, they were told to "try the widow Murphy's down the road a piece."

Chandra was horrified when they pulled up before the weathered wooden building. It was dilapidated and unpainted; apparently it had been converted from a barn to living quarters.

"Surely, he is not here," she protested in disbelief.

"No, of course not, but perhaps we can get further directions," Miles said comfortingly.

The widow Murphy herself answered the door. A slovenly woman of considerable girth and years, she peered suspiciously at Chandra and Miles. When he asked her about Percy, she replied contemptuously, "You'll probably find him abed as usual. Don't usually get up before the sun's down nor to bed before it's up again." She nodded toward a ramshackle stairway that looked as though it would collapse beneath a child's weight. "Sure, and I suppose you be another one of his gambling creditors," she sneered, exposing her broken, tobacco-stained teeth. " 'Tis all that ever comes alooking for him. There be a long line ahead of you."

"If that's the case, you will be a welcome change for him," Miles told Chandra drily. "Let's go up." He turned toward the stairs.

"No!" She laid a restraining hand on his arm, humiliated at the thought of Miles witnessing her meeting with Percy in this hovel. She was also terrified at how Miles might react should he learn that she had deceived him about being Percy's wife.

"Come. Why this sudden hesitancy to see this husband you adore and have risked so much to reach?"

"Please," she begged, "you need not come with me."

"I promised I would deliver you safely to your husband, and I shall not leave you until I have done so." He took her arm and started toward the stairs.

Reluctantly she accompanied him up the bare splintery steps. The upper hall was dank and smelled of mildew. Compared with this, the dreary waterfront inn in London had been a palace.

When they reached Percy's door, Miles pounded heavily upon it.

A weary voice that sounded both old and young called out, "Go away, whoever you are. I don't want to see you."

"Percy," Chandra called. "It is I. It is Chandra."

A strange, strangling noise came from within and in a moment Percy, wrapped in a frayed robe, flung open the door. Chandra scarcely recognized the thin, dissipated man before her. Percy's delicate handsomeness had faded. His face had aged way beyond his five and twenty years, his sandy hair was thin and straggly, his eyes were puffy and bloodshot. A rough stubble, wheatlike in color and texture, stood out on his cheeks and chin.

At the sight of Chandra, his mouth worked in silent astonishment. At last he managed to ask, "What in God's name are you doing here?" His voice held no affection, only anger and shock.

Miles bowed slightly to Percy, who was a good half foot shorter. "I have brought your wife safely to you," he said to explain his presence.

"My wife! What are you talking about? I have no wife."

Miles turned, disbelief in his eyes, to Chandra. "Then what are you?"

She flushed crimson and lowered her eyes, unable to meet his furious gaze. Her reply stuck in her throat.

Percy answered for her. "She is my cousin."

"I had to lie to you, Miles," Chandra said hastily. "You would not have helped me if I had told you the truth."

Miles's hazel eyes flashed, their yellow flecks dancing like summer lightning. "So all that prattle about fidelity to your marriage vows was a pack of lies. And I thought you were a woman of integrity and honesty."

She flinched at the bitter disillusionment in his voice. "But that was not a lie. I said that I was being faithful to my vows. You only assumed that they were those sworn in marriage."

"Will someone explain to me what is going on?" Percy demanded.

A door down the hall opened, and a man's grizzled head peered out curiously. Percy hastily stepped back into his room and beckoned Chandra and Miles to enter.

The place was small and furnished only with a narrow bed, a washstand and a chair. It had a musty smell, as if it were rarely aired or cleaned. Clothes had been tossed carelessly on the bed and chair and spilled onto the floor, which had no carpet to cover its rough surface.

Miles turned on Chandra in fury. "What *is* the truth? Why in hell were you so anxious to reach your cousin in America? What could possibly have induced you to gamble your reputation as well as your virtue?"

"My story was not all a lie." Chandra trembled at Miles's rage. "The part about escaping a loathsome man was true. I had no one to turn to but Percy."

"But why me?" Percy's dismayed voice piped up. "We have not seen each other for years."

Her hopes and her heart sank at his coldness. "But that day at Northlands when we parted . . . You promised that you would help me if ever I needed it."

"I was a child then, making a child's promises, Chandra. You were a fool to carry your dreams with you so long."

"Am I to believe, then, that there was a rich, fat old merchant?" Miles interjected.

Before Chandra could answer, Percy said sourly, "If he were so rich, you should have married him. He could have provided for you far better than I."

Tears welled up in her eyes. "Percy, I would never have seen a penny of his fortune, and little good it would have done me regardless. He was cruel and sadistic, and he would have made my life a living hell if, indeed, I survived it at all. He said he would make me rue the day my mother conceived me. He did not mean to marry me, only make me his mistress." Her cheeks burned with shame. "He wanted me only for revenge on my parents."

"I don't understand," Percy said. "Who is this man?"

"The Duke of Warfolk."

"The Duke of Warfolk!" Miles and Percy repeated in horrified unison.

Percy turned white. "You fool, don't you realize he is one of the most powerful men in England?" Percy sat down on the edge of his disheveled bed as though his legs could no longer support him. "Don't I have enough trouble already? If he learns you came to me, he will destroy me."

"You little devil," Miles snapped, whirling Chandra around to face him, "when you put a man in deadly danger, you might at least have the conscience to warn him. What a short and unhappy life I should have had had I been discovered aiding you. If somehow I managed to escape with my life, I would even now be rotting in Newgate."

"You see," Chandra retorted, "it is just as I said. You would not have helped me if you had known the truth."

Miles gave her a withering look. "To the contrary, if I had known the identity of the man you were fleeing, I would have insisted upon helping you escape him. But I also would have been far more careful about how I got you aboard the *Golden Drake*. God, when I think . . . ! I should have disguised you so that your own mother would not have recognized you." He paused, as if contemplating the enormity of his mistake. "There were hundreds of people around the docks that day, and perhaps you didn't notice, but your beauty and that velvet cloak you were wearing drew considerable attention." A deep frown creased his face and he asked abruptly, "Have you ever been limned?"

"Yes, of course, several times," Chandra replied, confused by this seeming non sequitur. "Only a month before papa died, he had an artist come to Northlands."

"Damn!" Miles interrupted. "I'll wager that copies of your likeness are being shown all over London accompanied by reward notices. Someone may well remember your boarding the *Golden Drake* that day. So don't be certain that you have escaped Warfolk yet."

The color drained from Chandra's face. "What am I to do?" she muttered, suddenly so terrified that she could not manage a whole breath of air into her lungs.

"If your whereabouts are learned, your guardian can require you be returned to him," Miles said thoughtfully. "So I would strongly advise you to procure documents proclaiming you are Percy's ward. That will create enough confusion and delay to perhaps enable you to elude Warfolk again."

Miles turned on his heel and strode to the door. As he opened it, he turned over his shoulder and spat out at Chandra, "Let me congratulate you. No woman has ever before so successfully made a fool of me."

He slammed the door so hard behind him that the windows rattled. New tears sprang to Chandra's eyes. Her heart ached at the realization that not only would she never see him again, but that he would remember her with anger and bitterness for having lied to him, for having repaid his kindness with deception.

Percy broke into her reverie "Whatever am I to do with you? I suppose you have no money," he wailed.

She remembered Miles's warning, and now she appreciated its wisdom. "No. I spent it all on my passage."

"How do you expect to live here?" he asked sourly.

"I thought you would help me."

"That was presumptuous of you. I tell you, I am drowning in debt!" His face convulsed, and beads of sweat broke out on his forehead. "My creditors have threatened me. I fear they may do me bodily harm if I do not repay them very soon."

Chandra was so shocked she could barely raise her voice above a husky whisper: "Surely they would not dare. You are a diplomat. If you tell the British minister that you have been threatened, he will . . ."

Percy cut her off with an angry snort. "The British minister. That's a joke. There is no minister here. Nor is there likely to be one assigned since that Republican rebel Jefferson is president. Everyone knows he has always loved the French and hated the English." Percy wiped his perspiring brow with a soiled handkerchief. "Edward Thornton, the legation secretary, has been in charge since Liston left last year, and I suspect he'll continue. Thornton makes no secret of his dislike for me. Trusts me with nothing and would love to get rid of me."

Chandra studied the face before her. It was a puffy caricature of the pretty child that Percy had once been. She shook her head sorrowfully. "How could you have gambled yourself into such straits, Percy?"

He shrugged his shoulders. "What else is there to do here? There's no social life—even less now that Jefferson's egalitarian ideas are in vogue. He never goes out at night, and 'tis said he's in bed by ten. He even canceled the formal weekly leaves at the President's Palace that have been long-standing tradition. The women are livid. It was their only opportunity to dress up and be seen in this godforsaken mud hole."

He strode over to the washstand and picked up a comb. Squinting into the fragment of mirror above the stand, he began trying to set his sandy hair right, arranging it to cover his bald spot. "This Jefferson's a true democrat," he scoffed, pronouncing the final word with a sarcastic sneer. "He sees whoever wants to see him. And the common way he dresses is shocking. He looks like a farmer. In fact, it's said he prefers the company of farmers to that of diplomats. He rides about alone on horseback, talking to everyone he meets on the road. Many of them have no idea they're speaking to their president. It's little short of scandalous."

Percy put down his comb and turned away from the mirror. "I tell you, this is a rough and uncivilized country, and one survives here only by his wits. Gambling comes naturally to me, so why shouldn't I do it? But my creditors are not men to be fooled with." He gave her a poisonous look. "And now I am burdened with you as well."

"Not for long," Chandra retorted with a proud toss of her head. "Only until I can find a position as a teacher or governess."

"Perhaps you could marry this man, Carrington."

"Percy, he is nothing but a poor farmer."

"How particular you are," he sneered. "Anyway, when I met him at the countess's a few months ago, he told me he was a gambler. And if that night was any indication, he's a bloody good one, too. I wanted to take him on, but he told me I wasn't in his league. How did you meet him?"

Chandra took a deep breath and started at the beginning. There was no need to conceal her story from Percy. When she finished, he whistled softly. "So you traveled the entire voyage as man and wife."

"Posing as man and wife," she corrected him.

"Come now." He leered at her. "You cannot tell me that you two shared a tiny cabin for weeks and were not intimate. I am not such a fool."

She swallowed hard. If Percy would not believe her, she wondered who would. "But it is true," she told him firmly.

"Then Carrington is a fool," Percy scoffed, with a strange little gleam in his eyes that unnerved her.

"Percy, what are you thinking?" she demanded sharply.

"Nothing," he murmured. He strode over to the one small window which was streaked with rain-spattered grime, and stared out moodily. "God, how I hate this dreary swamp," he cried. "My dear, kind uncle could have secured me a post in a civilized European capital, but instead he let them send me to this wretched bog."

Poor, foolish Percy, Chandra thought, watching his pouting face in the slanting late afternoon light. When they were children, he had evaded reality by spinning exciting fantasies about his future in the glittering social whirl of London. Now he evaded it by gambling away his future. What would become of him?

What would become of her?

Chapter 17

Miles slammed the front door of Mrs. Murphy's boardinghouse and bounded down the steps toward the hired vehicle. He snapped out his destination on Pennsylvania Avenue to the coachman and jumped in.

As the coach joggled forward, Miles, seething, leaned back against the leather cushions. He had trusted Chandra, thinking her frank, honest, innocent—totally different from the conniving, silly, dull creatures that he abhorred—and she had blatantly lied to him. He had befriended her, and she had repaid him by playing him for a fool. How easily she had duped him!

Miles's pride was stung. She had rejected him as a **lover not out of** fidelity to her husband, but no doubt because **she thought that** he was beneath her. All that damn fool nonsense her father had stuffed into her head about titles and lineage. Miles had never before been found deficient by a member of the opposite sex, and this rankled him. And on top of everything, the little snob had had no scruples about using him as her means of escaping Warfolk.

Warfolk. Miles shuddered, remembering that night at Madame de la Chartres's on his visit to London two years ago. Seeking relief after the celibacy of his long voyage, he had gone to London's most elegant brothel. But when he arrived, a pall hung over the establishment. The girls were nervous and obviously frightened despite their best efforts to hide it.

When Miles asked the girl he had chosen, a delicate blonde named Annis, what was wrong, she wouldn't tell him at first. But, as he persisted, she gave in. "The Duke of Warfolk is expected tonight. All the girls are terrified that they will be among those he chooses."

Miles's eyebrows had raised slightly at her use of the plural. "The duke cannot content himself with just one companion?"

"There is nothing simple about the duke's tastes," Annis had replied bitterly. "He is as cruel and sadistic and depraved a man as ever passed through these doors. After the girl has been the object of his attentions, it is often some time before she can work again. Madame had a room done for his visits, specifically paneled and lined with heavy draperies to deaden all sound."

But these precautions had not been sufficient to swallow entirely the shrieks of agony that caused Miles's flesh to crawl. He would have tried to go to the girls' rescue had not Annis clung to him.

"Don't be a fool," she had begged. "There is nothing you can do, and the duke might have you killed. He would not hesitate, for human life means very little to him."

And that, Miles thought in horror as the coach ground through the mud of Pennsylvania Avenue, was the man Chandra had fled. No wonder she had been willing to gamble anything to escape England. Had she told him the truth that day at the Seagull Inn, he would have been as determined as she that she get away. But instead, the foolish, headstrong girl had thought it necessary to trick him.

The coach rolled to a stop in front of an unfinished mansion on a knoll above the muddy road. Miles instructed the coachman to deliver his sea chest to Conrad and McMunn's boardinghouse, paid him off, and started toward the big house, which was built in the Palladian style of the same sandstone as the Capitol wing. Here, however, the stone had been whitewashed.

Miles walked very slowly, dreading the rapidly approaching moment. Tom would be enormously disappointed that the mission he had conceived had failed. His plan had made such eminent good sense at the time.

Tom had been thoroughly advertised in Britain as a Francophile who harbored an implacable hatred for the English, who, in turn, regarded him with strong suspicion and mistrust. Some among them might even seize upon this as an excuse to once again harass the United States.

So, naturally, as soon as he was elected, Tom had sent a personal envoy to Pitt. If he could reassure him of his sincere feelings of friendship for England, he might win assurances from Pitt that his friendship would be reciprocated. After all, Pitt had sympathized with the Americans during the revolution, calling England's war with its rebellious colonies "most accursed, wicked, barbarous, cruel, unnatural, unjust and diabolical."

Pitt could have given that assurance had he still been chief minister, Miles swore softly to himself. Who could have foreseen his sudden fall from power? He had been chief minister for seventeen years and was still a relatively young man—only forty-one. It seemed inconceivable, yet it had happened. He had been turned out and replaced by that nonentity Addington.

Miles reached the steps of the mansion. Not even the entrance was finished. The wooden steps were obviously temporary, and he had to cross a wooden platform to reach the front door. He was admitted to a great hall by a servant.

Miles had scarcely given his name when Tom hurried into the hall, his strong, square face wreathed in a broad smile and his ruddy complexion heightened by his obvious pleasure in seeing Miles. The unruly red hair had faded to gray, but he still had a few freckles. Tom's blue coat showed signs of much wear and was far from the latest style. Beneath it he wore a scarlet vest, which was a bit snug. His breeches were of corduroy and his stockings of white cotton. His slippers, Miles noted with amusement, were down at the heel.

He greeted Miles with all the warmth of a father welcoming a son home.

"Where is your baggage?" Tom asked.

"I had it sent to Conrad's."

"Nonsense. You'll stay here. I'll have a servant bring it back."

Miles opened his mouth to protest, but Tom stopped him with a grin and an upraised hand. "You can't argue that I don't have the room. Of course, the upstairs isn't finished yet, but still my secretary and I rattle around here like two mice in a church."

Tom guided Miles across the large hall to a room on the other side of the mansion. "Come, I am having dinner. You must join me."

Miles tried politely—and reluctantly, for Tom's taste in food and wines was justly famous—to decline, but Tom brushed off the refusal. "I have acquired an excellent French chef," he boasted. "I think you will approve. We must celebrate your return."

"I am afraid there is no reason to celebrate," Miles protested sadly as he followed Tom into the dining room. "My mission was a failure. Pitt was no longer in power when I arrived."

"Yes, I know," Tom said calmly. "Word reached us ten days after you had sailed."

He went back to his seat at the head of the long mahogany dining table and gestured for Miles to take the chair at his right.

"Did you go ahead and meet with Pitt, anyhow?" Tom asked.

"Yes, but purely out of politeness, I fear. He has no power."

"But he will again," Tom said consolingly. "I understand his successor is not much of a leader and probably will not last long. Pitt will be back, and he will remember my efforts. Your mission may yet pay a dividend."

Miles smiled. How like Tom to place his failed mission in the most optimistic light and strive to ease his disappointment.

A servant hurried in to lay a cover for Miles, and the steward arrived with champagne, which he opened and poured into heavy cut-crystal glasses.

Tom lifted his glass toward his guest. "Welcome

home. And now I want to hear more about your trip.
Did you try to contact Addington?"

"No," Miles said, watching Tom's face carefully for
his reaction, as he was still far from certain that he had
acted correctly. "I thought of doing so, but it seemed to
me the letter I carried was meant for Pitt's eyes alone."

Tom's relief was reflected in his face. "You were absolutely right, Miles. You did everything just as I had
hoped you would. You have always seemed to have a
talent for managing under unforeseen circumstances."
He gave Miles a warm smile.

"I do have one thing to report," Miles said, sipping
his champagne slowly. "Pitt warned me. He said he has
heard of a well-financed plot afoot among some of the
English aristocracy to sow dissent among us with our
government. The hope there is that we will become so
unhappy, we will reject it and opt for reunion with Britain."

Tom set his glass down hard on the table. "God, that
galls me! We are so vulnerable to a tactic like that right
now. Such mischief could not come at a worse time.
Damn!"

A servant presented Miles with an array of tempting
dishes, and he requested a little of everything. With a
grin, he said to Tom, "I would not want to judge your
chief on an insufficient sampling of his work." The grin
faded. "I gather from what you just said that the bitter
wounds have not healed in my absence?"

"No. I have been trying mightily but they are deep
and grave. They could be fatal if they are further in-
fected by outside meddling. What tactics will these plot-
ters employ?"

Miles shook his head. "Again, I must disappoint you.
Pitt did not know. He only knows that the rumors would
not be so strong if there were no truth to them."

"Who is behind the scheming?"

"He had a strong suspicion, but he would not divulge
a name to me without concrete evidence. He would only
say that he believed it to be a lord of great power who
is very close to Prinny. And, of course, with the king's

latest bout of madness, Prinny could become regent."

The two men ate in silence for a time, Tom preoccupied with the information Miles had just given him and Miles savoring the excellent repast. It was the best meal that he had had in months, and he told Tom so.

"I'm happy you arrived to share it with me. How long shall I have the pleasure of your company here in Washington?"

"Only tonight. I am anxious to get home as quickly as possible, and there is nothing to keep me here," he said, bitterness tinging his voice as he thought of Chandra.

"Very well then," Tom sighed. "Thanks for your help, Miles. You are a man one can count on. And I need you now, more than ever."

Chapter 18

Chandra was given the vacant room next to Percy's, which was even tinier and mustier than his. As she looked dubiously at the gray linen on the narrow, lumpy bed, Percy shrugged. "It's all I can afford," he said sullenly. "It's not Northlands or the Duke of Warfolk's palace, but, of course, you chose to abandon that."

It wasn't even clean, she thought, but the room was the smallest of her concerns. She knew that Miles was right about the duke's long arm and his great power, and the thought that she might be forced back across the Atlantic to him set her trembling. When she anxiously told Percy she wanted to secure documents showing him to be her guardian immediately, to her surprise he readily agreed.

"I have a lawyer friend who might be able to arrange it," he said. "I will go at once to see him."

Chandra looked at him sharply, her suspicions aroused by Percy's sudden affability, and she watched his departure with vague misgivings.

It was nearly dark when she finally saw him returning. As he approached the boardinghouse, two evil-looking men dressed in ragged homespun accosted him and fell into step beside him. Instead of coming to the door, the trio left the path and set off for a clump of trees behind the boardinghouse. Each man had linked an arm through one of Percy's and they appeared to be forcing him along.

Chandra flew downstairs and was about to start after them, but Mrs. Murphy restrained her.

"Don't be a fool, mixin' in somethin' that ain't none of your concern," she barked. "Them's a couple of his gambling friends, them is. Ain't the first time them's been here."

"They do not look like proper creditors," Chandra said.

"Your cousin ain't been particular about the people he borrows from."

Chandra watched as the trio disappeared into the trees. A few minutes later, she heard a shriek. It was Percy's voice. Not heeding Mrs. Murphy's admonition, she ran out the door and toward the trees, Percy's screams guiding her.

The foliage was thick and the bushes caught at her clothes as she ran, but she ignored them, having no thought of the danger in which she might be placing herself. Her only thought was to reach Percy. Although he had not been kind to her since her arrival, she could not help thinking of him as her dear childhood friend. She was almost upon them when she saw him.

The two had stripped him of his jacket, waistcoat, and shirt, which lay in a heap on the ground, and had tied him to a tree. The smaller of the two men was holding a cat-o'-nine-tails.

She ran to him and grabbed his arm as he raised it to apply another stroke.

"Stop it," she cried, hanging on to his arm.

The man stared at her in astonishment through his one good eye. He wore a patch over his left. "What 'ave we 'ere?"

"Stop it," she ordered again. "Leave him alone."

"Her's as gutsy as her's pretty," commented his companion, a bull of a man with thick, knotted muscles and an array of scars on his face that gave mute testimony to the violent life he led. He leered at her, then laughed and said, "Sure, and he's all yours. 'Twas only a wee warning of what's coming to him if he don't pay Murchison within seventy-two hours." He spit a wad of chewing tobacco on the ground at Percy's feet and nodded at it. "There'll be less of him left than that, I can tell you."

The man pulled a knife from his waistband and cut the rope that bound Percy to the tree. He crumpled into a heap, moaning piteously like a hurt animal. The taller man gave him a kick with his heavy boot, and the pair disappeared through the trees. It was some time before Chandra was able to get Percy to his feet. Half supporting him, she dragged him back to the boardinghouse.

In his room, she washed his back. The men had only been toying with him, she realized. Although his back bore several angry red welts, it was not shredded as it would have been had they whipped him in earnest. Still he sobbed as though he had been beaten within an inch of his life.

"What am I to do?" he whimpered.

"What do you owe this Murchison?" Chandra asked, wondering how much of her tiny hoard she would have to surrender to save her cousin.

"More than a thousand pounds."

She drew in her breath sharply. "Percy, whatever possessed you? What shall we do?"

"I don't know. There is no one left to borrow from. If only I could put together a small stake; I am due for a run of good luck." His eyes were bright, the eyes of a dreamer who has lost touch with reality.

When Chandra finished her ministrations, Percy lay upon his stomach on his bed whimpering, until Mrs. Murphy gave him a draught of laudanum to put him to sleep. Just before he drifted off, he murmured to Chandra, "I almost forgot. I got the papers you wanted. They were in that envelope I had with me. You must sign one."

She hastened to the washstand, where she had deposited his garments and the envelope, which she ripped open. They were very official-looking documents decorated with handsome seals. The one that required her signature stated her oath that Percy was her guardian. Eagerly she snatched up a pen to sign it, but as she affixed her name a wave of anxiety swept over her. She hated placing herself in Percy's control. He had grown into a weak man, one without any sense of right and wrong. Yet no prospect was half so terrifying as that of being forced back to England and Warfolk's concubinage. Percy's guardianship was her only alternative.

She considered her current situation. She could not depend upon Percy for support, and her small inheritance would not go far. She had to find herself a position at once.

She asked Mrs. Murphy where she might begin to look for employment, but the old woman just looked her up and down. Exposing her broken, stained teeth, she leered, "Only one kind of work me know of for a woman of your looks, and plenty of business you'd have, too. Many a man's here without his wife and anxious to have his needs taken care of."

Chandra blushed a vivid shade of red and turned from the woman in disgust.

It was with a heavy heart that she went to bed that night, and she grew sadder still when she thought of Miles, of his anger at her. If only she could have a few minutes with him to explain that in her desperation to escape the duke it had not occurred to her that things could go badly for him.

Large tears trickled down her cheeks. How she would miss his strength and protection! Well, there was nothing she could do. She was alone now, and she would have to learn to manage.

Chapter 19

Miles Carrington was up early the next morning. He left his saddlebags at Tom's and set out for Thompson's stables, where his horse was quartered, prepared for the long ride home. When he reached the stables, he was surprised to find Percy Lunt there waiting for him.

"What do you want?" he growled at Lunt.

"I want you to meet your responsibility to my cousin."

"What are you talking about? I've done far more for that lying wench than anyone could have been expected to, fool that I was."

"She told me everything. How you forced yourself upon her repeatedly aboard the *Golden Drake*." Percy's bravado did not entirely mask his nervousness. "And how she is now carrying your child."

Miles stared at him in fury and disbelief. Percy rushed on: "You must assume your rightful expense for the child."

"And what would that be?" Miles asked in a deceptively cool voice.

"A lump sum payment of $10,000 and Chandra will relinquish any and all future claims upon you for the child's support."

Miles was so enraged that he was utterly incapable of rational thought. That deceitful, lying girl! She, whom he had thought so innocent, so totally lacking in guile. Why, she was nothing more than a light-fingered extortionist! As though they had romped their way over the ocean! Worse yet, no one, least of all a judge, should it come to that, was likely to believe his word against hers that they had crossed the Atlantic in chaste friendship. In fact, it was hard for him to believe it himself. Never had he been so betrayed by a woman.

Miles turned on his heel, and Percy grabbed anxiously at his sleeve. "Where are you going?"

"To see that blackmailing trollop of a cousin of yours."

Percy clung desperately to him. "No, no, you can't do that," he cried in alarm. "She won't see you. She never wants to lay eyes on you again. You are to give me the money and be off."

"You go to hell," Miles snapped. "I'm surprised she doesn't want a name for her brat, only a fortune."

"Oh," Percy protested. "She would never marry you. She told me so. She said you were nothing but a poor farmer."

At this, Miles's rage exploded like a disintegrating star. He struck Percy hard, flattening him.

Quickly summoning his horse, Miles rode at a gallop to Mrs. Murphy's boardinghouse.

When Chandra awoke that morning, she found that Percy was already gone.

"Them two yesterday must hav' put the fear of the devil in him," Mrs. Murphy said. "Never seen him up so early in all the days him's been here."

He must have gone in search of a loan, Chandra thought, wondering whom he could have found still gullible enough to apply to. As she poked at the gray mush that Mrs. Murphy served as breakfast, Chandra wondered how far out of Washington Miles was by now.

As she pushed her scarcely touched dish away, Mrs. Murphy came in. "A gentleman to see you," she announced. "The one who brought you here yesterday."

Chandra jumped up in surprise and happiness. Her heart leaping with joy, she rushed to the front hall. But she stopped abruptly when she saw Miles's face. Wearing buckskins and a brown caped riding coat, he was stalking up and down like a caged beast, his whole body exuding rage.

Seeing her, he whirled and reached out for her. He seized her roughly and shook her. "You little vixen. You will not blackmail me," he growled.

She was stunned by his attack. "Blackmail you?"

The muscles in his face twitched with rage. "I thought you were different from the usual run of females, but now I find the innocent lady who proclaims herself of impeccable bloodlines and high morality is at heart a conniving whore."

Tears welled up in Chandra's eyes. His fingers bit painfully into her arms, but she was more deeply hurt by his incomprehensible words. "I don't know what you're talking about."

"Oh no," he sneered. "No, you just send around that mincing cousin of yours to demand a small fortune for having allegedly robbed you of your virtue and gotten you with child."

"What?" Chandra's eyes widened in astonishment. "Percy has been to see you?"

"As if you did not know! Percy's nursing a bruised jaw as his payment, and that's but a small token of what I should like to do to you."

Chandra's knees grew weak as she realized what Percy, in his desperation, was capable of doing.

Miles increased his pressure on her arms, and he shook her again. "And you know it is all a lie, you blue-eyed witch. Whoever your brat's father may be, we both know it cannot be me. You were exceedingly stupid not to at least have given me reason to think your brat might be mine." His eyes raked her with scathing contempt. "Too bad the thought of me in your bed was so repugnant when the thought of my money in your pocket was so attractive."

Chandra was sickened. Miles actually thought her capable of these things.

His voice turned cruel. "I will not pay you blackmail, but I will hire you."

"Hire me?" she asked in bewilderment. "For what?"

He gave her a long contemptuous look. "You know

what for," he said insultingly. "How much you earn shall depend upon how well your services satisfy me."

Her disgust at his offensive proposition was written on her face. "I would die in the gutter first," she muttered between clenched teeth, trying in vain to free herself from his iron grasp.

"And your bastard with you?"

"There is no child," she insisted, her voice choked with emotion. "But if there were, I would not use it as a weapon to force a man to support me."

Miles stared at her suspiciously.

"Percy lied to you," she explained. "I swear that I knew nothing of what he was about, nor will I be a party to it. I have no designs on you or your purse."

Miles released her arms, but he still looked skeptical. "If what you say is true, why is your cousin trying to blackmail me?"

"He is desperate. He has incurred enormous gambling debts, and last night one of his creditors sent two men to beat him into sensibility. They did not hurt him badly but only reminded him that if he did not pay his debts at once to this man called Murchison, his life would hang in balance."

"Percy is more stupid than I thought to get involved with Murchison," Miles said thoughtfully. "He is notorious."

The front door opened to admit Percy, his cheek puffy and swollen. Seeing Miles, he gave out a shout and turned to flee.

"Percy, come back here," Chandra ordered.

Reluctantly he obeyed, his stiff body moving slowly toward them.

"Percy," Chandra demanded, "how could you have told Mr. Carrington those lies?"

Percy's face was sullen. "I told him no lies," he said with feigned innocence, "only what you had told me. He is the father of your child and with his skill at the gaming tables, he should be able to raise a handsome settlement."

Chandra threw up her hands. Percy was so audacious

that he continued to persist in this tale even in the face of her denial.

With a contemptuous glare at Chandra, Miles said, "You are the most troublesome piece of baggage I have ever encountered. My ill fortune, but thank God it's at an end." With that, he turned on his heel and stalked through the front door.

Chandra lashed out at Percy, and gave him a hard shove. "You are despicable. If you attempt to pursue this evil blackmailing scheme of yours, I shall denounce you as the liar you are."

"Don't you understand what will happen to me?" Percy's eyes were wild with fear.

"There must be other ways to raise the money."

"Chandra, it is my life," he pleaded.

"Some things are more precious than life."

"That's easy for you to say."

"If it were my life, I would act differently."

Percy started up the stairs to his room two at a time, but midway he changed his mind. He stalked down them again, and headed for the front door.

"Where are you going?" Chandra asked.

"It's none of your affair. Since you have destroyed my plan to save myself, I must come up with another."

Percy slammed the door hard behind him, leaving Chandra to worry about the next reckless scheme he would concoct.

Beset by widely vacillating emotions, Miles rode at a gallop from Mrs. Murphy's down the wide, muddy gash that was Pennsylvania Avenue, to pick up his saddlebags at Tom's. How he wanted to teach Chandra a lesson! Despite the help he had given her, she could see him as nothing but a conduit to her new life.

Despite his anger, he could not help being worried about her. What would Percy try next in his desperate attempt to save himself? It would surely involve Chandra—she was the only asset that unscrupulous weakling had.

When Miles reached the president's house, he was

met in the hall by Tom's secretary, Captain Lewis. Tom wanted to see him at once.

Curious about the summons, Miles went to the big library in the southwest corner that Tom used as his office. There, to Miles's even greater surprise, he found Tom with Jim Spenser, the nephew of Miles's neighbor, Fred Humphreys.

"What are you doing here, Jim?" Miles asked the gangling youth, who stood head to head with him. When Miles had first seen the lad seven years ago, he had been runtish, ill-fed, ill-clothed, and much neglected by his uncle, who had become his guardian upon the death of his parents. Miles had taken the boy under his wing, and become almost a second father to him. Humphreys was too eager for Miles's favor to object and only wished that Miles would exhibit half so much interest in his daughter, Sally, as he did in his nephew.

The boy hesitated, and Tom answered for him. "He came to warn you. It seems Jim's uncle has set a trap to force you to marry his daughter."

Miles turned to Jim. "What nonsense is this? No one traps me into marriage, least of all Fred Humphreys and his silly daughter, whose brain is tinier than her waist."

"Do not underestimate them," Tom cautioned. "Their plan sounds clever."

"Not clever enough, no matter what it is." Miles settled down in the chair next to Tom's. "Tell me about it, Jim."

The youth pulled nervously at the buttons of his coarse shirt. "Well, sir, as soon as you left for England, my uncle announced that you and Sally had become engaged the night before your departure and would be married when you returned. He hinted you tried to seduce her, but that she held out for marriage, and you finally yielded."

"My lord! I had not seen Sally for a fortnight before I left, nor have I ever tried to seduce her. Indeed, I never wished to!"

"You know that and so do they." Jim squirmed uncomfortably in his chair. "The story was doubted by many at first. But after Sally had her wedding gown and trousseau sewn, and the invitations were sent out, everybody had to believe it."

Miles's face was clouded with rage, and his hazel eyes darkened. "We shall see how much Sally enjoys her wedding without a bridegroom. What the hell inspired your uncle to this stupidity?"

Jim stared down at the floor, poking at it with the scuffed toe of his boot. "I should not be telling you this, but I care nothing about my uncle." The youth looked up and his eyes mirrored his affection for Miles. "The man is desperate. He would have lost his land last month had he not invoked your name as his son-in-law to be and drawn upon your credit."

"Both he and his creditors will be sadly disappointed." Miles jumped angrily to his feet and strode to the window, where he stared out over the trees to the Potomac River. "But why did Sally agree to her father's mad scheme? She has plenty of suitors vying for her hand. There was no need to trap an unwilling husband."

"She has always wanted you, Miles," the boy replied.

"And she seems to have gotten you," Tom concluded. "It's one thing to bed willing widows or faithless wives, but you cannot make false promises of marriage to the daughter of a respected family and then break them after the wedding invitations have been sent out."

"But I did nothing of the sort," Miles protested, turning back from the window.

"Of course not, but all you have is your word against hers."

"I don't believe my honesty has ever been questioned."

"No, but your morals have," Tom said bluntly. "I do not see how you can escape marrying Sally unless you can prove she and her father are liars."

Miles knew that Tom was right. If he simply walked out on the marriage, he would be unjustly branded a cad, a pariah in decent society.

It was certainly his day for deceitful women and their scheming relatives, Miles thought bitterly. One too proud to marry him and the other too eager. Well, they could both be damned, and their conniving families with them.

One thing was certain: he was no more going to bow to Humphreys' plot than he had to Percy's blackmail. Nor was he, if he could help it, going to spend the rest of his days as a social outcast for refusing to marry Sally. He stood deep in thought for several minutes, oblivious to his two companions. He would find a way to foil the Humphreyses and show them up for what they were.

Finally, he heard Tom saying, "When you get that evil gleam in your eye, Miles, I know it is time to start worrying about what you're up to."

Miles only smiled enigmatically. He turned to Jim and asked, "How did you manage to come here to warn me?"

"My uncle sent me to Washington. The date he and Sally set for the wedding is growing very near, and he was getting nervous that you might not return in time. Since you'd said you would stop in Washington before coming home, he sent me to see if I could find out about you."

"Remain here a little longer, Jim." Miles's mouth curled up in a pleased smile at the plan that had begun to take shape in his mind. "In a day or two, I may be able to send you back to your uncle with news of me that I wish him and his daughter to hear."

Chapter 20

Chandra was far too disturbed to do anything but pace the bare, splintery floor of her room.

What would Percy try next? She must get away from him. But how? Her cheeks burned as she remembered Mrs. Murphy's assessment of her employment prospects. Miles had been her only friend, and now he had turned against her. In a certain way, she could not blame him when she considered the provocation of Percy's outrageous charges. Tears of hurt mixed with anger sparkled in her eyes. She wanted desperately to find Miles and convince him of her innocence.

It was afternoon before Percy returned, and his mood had lifted. He walked with a carefree gait, his thin shoulders thrown back, and he whistled as he came up the steps.

Chandra observed the change with foreboding. "What have you been up to?" she asked nervously.

He ignored her question. "I know you are angry at me, and I can't blame you." He was, she recalled, an expert at placating those he had offended. Even as a child he knew how to get his way. "I am truly sorry for what I did this morning. I was so desperate I lost my head. Can I ever hope you will forgive me?"

Chandra's suspicions escalated. "What have you done now? Tell me, Percy."

"I tell you, I have done nothing," he replied with an air of hurt innocence, "although I have managed to persuade a banker to make me a loan to pay my debts to Murchison."

166

She regarded him skeptically, but he tossed off a winning smile and said casually, "I am going to make up for the terrible thing I did to you this morning by buying you a new gown from Mrs. Hoben. She's the most fashionable dressmaker in Washington, Chandra. She even makes Dolley Madison's gowns. You will love whatever she concocts for you."

"Who is Dolley Madison?"

"The wife of the Secretary of State. She acts as President Jefferson's hostess."

"But, Percy, we cannot afford to spend a farthing on anything other than your debts."

"I'm flush now. Come, don't argue."

Mrs. Hoben's small shop off Pennsylvania Avenue was in a frenzy of activity. It was apparent from the bustling confusion and from the dressmaker's rapid-fire instructions to her minions that the shop had just received a large order that was to be delivered posthaste.

Despite this, Mrs. Hoben herself, to Chandra's surprise, carefully took her measurements and spent more than an hour asking her opinion of fabrics and sketches. Chandra felt guilty for taking so much of the woman's time when she was so busy. Mrs. Hoben obviously expected that Chandra would become a frequent and free-spending customer, and it was with some embarrassment that Chandra finally ordered one simple gown.

The next day Percy announced gleefully to Chandra that they were going that night to the Countess de Beroit's.

"Who is she?" Chandra asked, delighted at the prospect of escaping Mrs. Murphy's miserable establishment for a few hours.

"She is the most famous . . ." Percy hesitated as though at a loss for the right word to describe her, "ah . . . hostess in all of Washington."

"And why has she honored us with an invitation?" Chandra was still suspicious of her cousin's devious notions, so naturally she questioned him closely about everything.

Percy gave her a peculiar look. "I did not ask her,"

he said hastily, "and while I think of it, wear that blue ball gown you brought with you from London."

Chandra nodded. It was only as she was dressing that she thought to wonder how Percy knew about the gown, which she had packed away out of sight.

As the hack coach Percy had hired pulled up in front of the countess's residence that night, Chandra could not hide her admiration. This was the most substantial house she had yet seen in Washington: a large two-story brick structure with large windows through which the music of a pianoforte drifted softly. A flagstone path rimmed with boxwood protected her blue satin slippers as she walked to the door. Chandra had forgotten how revealing the décolletage of her blue gown was, and she was feeling a little nervous. In the United States, particularly, such a display of exposed bosom might be frowned upon.

She and Percy were greeted at the door by a tall, muscular black man, whose forbidding countenance was incongruous with his servant's livery.

He bid them wait in the entry hall while he summoned the countess, and went through a set of double doors to the left, revealing a large drawing room with a surfeit of gilt and brocade. It was every bit as ornate and ostentatious as the Duke of Devonham's ballroom, but in considerably worse taste. Chandra wondered with amusement what the sharp-tongued Fitzhugh Flynn would have had to say.

There was a sizable group, perhaps twenty-five in all, already gathered in the room, and oddly enough, most of them were women—all of them young, beautiful, and expensively gowned. In fact, Chandra could count only three men in the room. She might have imagined that she had stumbled into a young women's school, except she knew of no establishment where the students wore such daring gowns. They made Chandra's seem almost modest by comparison.

Everyone in the room was attentively listening to a man seated on a low sofa in the center of the room. He was so well surrounded by the group that Chandra could see little of him except for a snatch of his peacock velvet coat. Then he rose to his feet, and Chandra's heart leaped. It was Miles Carrington.

What in the world was he doing here? But then Chandra recalled his comment about passing for a wealthy man in Washington homes. Certainly he looked the part tonight. His white silk breeches were tailored to perfection over the broad shoulders, slim hips and muscled thighs. The white of the lace frill at his neck accentuated his sun-bronzed, handsome features, and he wore the velvet coat as though it were a second skin. There was nothing about him that gave the slightest hint he was a farmer, or anything other than an elegant gentleman, completely at home among the best of society.

A lump rose in her throat as she remembered how furious he had been with her when they last met. But was it any use to try to soothe his anger toward her? She noted with a pang of jealousy that he seemed to be well acquainted with the ladies who hung about him, eager for his attention.

The countess detached herself from the group surrounding Miles and came to greet Chandra and Percy in the hall. She was slim and attractive, and her black hair was piled high on her head in an elaborate arrangement which sparkled with diamond-studded combs. A diamond necklace lay in the curve of her bosom above the lavender satin of her dress. Although she had a youthful bounce to her step, she was not as young as she had appeared at a distance. Heavy makeup and powder concealed most of the telltale lines of her years.

The countess examined Chandra critically and her dark, almost black eyes sparkled. When she had finished her appraisal, she turned to Percy. *"Eh bien,* the cousin is as beautiful as you describe her, *chéri.* I regret a little I do not do business with you."

Chandra was mystified by the woman's words, but before she could ask a question, the countess led them down the hall to a small room at the back of the house.

At the center was a table on which lay two decks of cards. A bucket of chilling champagne and several glasses rested on the white marble top of a mahogany side table.

The countess blew a kiss and left them there. Chandra turned angrily to her cousin. "Percy, what is the meaning of these cards?"

The corners of Percy's mouth twitched in a thin, nervous smile. "The countess is a superb hostess. She caters to her guests' every wish."

"We are leaving, and I want no argument from you. I will not permit you to gamble."

She turned toward the door and found herself face to face with Miles. Glaring at her icily, he gave her a tiny, brusque bow, and her heart sank as she realized she was not forgiven. He walked past her and pulled out one of the chairs at the table. "Shall we begin?"

Percy nodded and settled in the seat across from Miles.

"Percy!" Chandra cried in alarm. "Surely you are not going to play with him. You yourself have said he is too expert for you." She turned to Miles. "And you, what have you to gain by this? I warn you that he has no money and already is deeply in debt."

Miles smiled, a strange hard smile. "So I understand, but I am softer hearted than you think. I cannot turn your cousin down. He says his very life hangs in the balance."

"Not any longer. He found a banker to loan him the money to pay Murchison."

Miles laughed. "So that is what he told you. I am afraid he was not entirely truthful." Miles began shuffling one of the decks with easy, graceful hands. "I am not a banker, as you well know, and I did not loan him the money. I only agreed to make it possible for him to win $10,000. We will gamble up to that amount. If he wins, he keeps it and pays off Murchison."

"And if he loses?"

"Chandra, be quiet," Percy interjected impatiently.

"I shall not lose. I shall be very lucky tonight. I can feel it."

But she persisted: "And what if Percy loses? You know he cannot pay you." Her voice took on a sharp edge of sarcasm. "Or are you too soft-hearted to care?"

"No indeed." Miles set the deck down on the table. "That is why I have required Percy to pledge collateral in case he loses. He is not totally without assets."

"I should like to know what they are," she said sourly.

"Would you now?" Again the hard smile played over Miles's lips. "While they are not, strictly speaking, his, he can assign his control over them to me."

Chandra was livid. She turned to Percy and objected angrily, "So now you are signing away your inheritance even before our uncle has died."

"You are becoming tiresome, Chandra," Percy said. "Shall we begin, Mr. Carrington?"

"Is ten dollars a point agreeable?" Miles asked casually.

Percy nodded sullenly and began dealing the cards two at a time, his hands trembling slightly.

Chandra sat on a chair near the wall. What holding of Lord Lunt's had Percy mortgaged away? And what would their uncle say when he found out?

Percy did well during the first few hands, and Chandra began to relax a bit. But then a new doubt struck her. Where would a farmer get $10,000? Miles could not possibly have that kind of money. He was so certain that he was skillful enough to defeat her cousin that he had decided to bluff and lighten Percy of part of his inheritance. She almost rose from her seat to protest, but then sighed and bit her tongue. Percy would have to learn the hard way.

Miles ignored Chandra as he played, giving her not so much as a side glance, and despite her anger at him for setting up this impossible wager, she was still piqued by his cold indifference.

The play began going badly for Percy, and the numbers on Miles's side of the scorecard soared. It was as though Miles had been toying with Percy in the beginning, lulling him—and Chandra—into a false sense of security. Now he had settled down to play in earnest. Percy was in trouble, and the more he lost, the more desperately he played. As Miles took yet another game, Chandra looked at the score and saw to her horror that Percy was down nearly $8,000.

She grew anxious as she watched the cards being dealt for a new game. Again, the hand was a disaster for Percy. He scored only a paltry seven points to Miles's sixty-four. If the next hand were equally bad, Miles's points would be doubled.

Percy seemed to realize his predicament. His hands shook so violently that he could scarcely manage to deal the cards. When he picked up his hand, a look of enormous relief crossed his face, and Chandra felt a faint glimmer of hope.

His luck held and he took the point.

"*Quatrième,*" Miles said.

"Not good, a quinte," Percy replied.

Chandra breathed more easily. The quinte gave Percy fifteen more precious points, and she felt certain that he would take this hand. But her elation was short-lived when Miles called out, "*Quatorze.*" She gave her cousin a nervous glance.

"*Quatorze* twice," said Miles.

Percy looked as though he had been stabbed through the heart.

Miles led with the ace of hearts and Percy put the nine on it. Miles tossed down the king of hearts next, drawing the queen from Percy.

Chandra was sure Percy must be out of hearts. Her fear was confirmed when Miles led the jack and then the ten, and Percy was forced to place two diamonds on them.

When the hand was over, Miles had taken all the tricks, scoring an additional forty points for the capot.

Chandra calculated hastily in her head. Percy had managed only twenty points this time to add to his seven from the last hand. His losses would be doubled.

She knew the worst even before Miles announced in

a lazy voice, "You lost this game by 123 points doubled. That puts you down to me by $10,140. I am afraid, sir, that our game is over, and I shall collect the collateral now."

"How can you collect it," Chandra demanded, "when it is in England and still belongs to my uncle?"

Miles regarded her with genuine puzzlement. "What are you talking about?"

A small knot of anxiety grew in her chest. "What have you won?"

"You," Miles said coldly.

"What?" she gasped. The world grew black in front of her eyes and, for a moment, she thought she might faint. As she swayed, Miles grabbed her and held her tightly. His hands were not gentle.

"No," she moaned. "No." It was all a nightmare. Percy could not have done this to her, could not have wagered her as though she were nothing more than a piece of merchandise! It was monstrous, unthinkable, inconceivable that she should have been gambled away to this American farmer.

But when she opened her eyes and saw the frightened hangdog expression on Percy's face, she realized he had done just that. Her spirit caught fire and she turned in rage upon him.

"I am not a slave. You have no control over me."

"But he does," Miles told her coolly, still holding her in his powerful grip. "You are his ward and he has the documents to prove it."

The papers she had signed . . . She had made Percy her guardian! In horror, she recalled her apprehension when she affixed her name to the document. Oh, why hadn't she listened to her fears?

Miles pushed her chin up roughly, forcing her to look into his hard, expressionless face. "You belong to me now."

His harshness confused and unnerved her. His hard face held no affection for her, and she remembered his insulting proposition. Her arms bore the bruises he had inflicted on her yesterday.

"So you will force me to become . . ." Her voice broke and she could not finish.

"A farmer's whore?" he supplied.

She winced as though he had slapped her. "Percy!" she cried in anger and shame. "How could you have sold me to this man? You are worse than Sir Henry."

Percy paled. "He, he said he would marry you. I made him promise."

The thought was too much for Chandra's overwrought nerves, and she began to laugh wildly, hysterically. "How good of you, Percy," she gasped finally, "to make a poor pig farmer promise to marry me."

Miles's grasp on her arms tightened, and a muscle near the corner of his left eye twitched angrily. "You should be more grateful for my generosity in giving you an honest name and a home."

"An honest name and a hut for a home and hogs for society," she spat at him.

Although only an hour ago Chandra would have given anything to dispel Miles's anger toward her, all the tenderness that she had felt for him had vanished. Now she felt a burning rage for his arrogance and humiliation of her. What was worse, he was about to force her to break her vow to her dying father.

She struggled fiercely to free herself from Miles's grasp, but he was far too strong for her. Her hair came out of its fastenings and tumbled down about her in a sable cascade. She realized at last that she could not get free of him and finally acknowledged defeat. Miles released her and shoved her toward a door.

"Go repair yourself," he told her roughly. "I have a bit of unfinished business with your cousin."

She did as she was bid, praying that the room to which he directed her would contain another exit. But to her despair it turned out to be a small drawing room. There was no other door except the one through which she had entered, although there was a narrow window. She quickly threw up the sash and, crushing her skirts to her, she climbed through. The blue silk of her skirt caught on something as she dropped to the soft dirt be-

low and she heard the material rip. Frantically, she tried
to free it, but when she could not, she tore the gown
away, leaving a sizable piece of silk attached to the
window ledge.

She ran through the soft dirt and emerged on a side
street. Turning blindly, she fled headlong down a dark,
muddy road, running she knew not where. Somehow
she had to find her way back to Mrs. Murphy's and the
small hoard of pounds she had secreted there. Then
she would escape. She had no idea in which direction she
was going, only that she must run, run, run!

After a while, her lungs began to ache and her weary
legs slowed, but she forced herself on. Suddenly her feet
were knocked out from under her as she tripped over
a tree root protruding above the ground. She sprawled
headlong onto the soft dirt, her ankle stabbing with pain.
For a moment she could do nothing but lie there panting for breath.

Then, without warning, she felt strong hands encircling her like bands of steel and lifting her to her feet.

"Did you have a nice little run?" Miles mocked her.

A tiny sob escaped her throat. How had he found her
so quickly? "How silent you are. I did not hear you
approach," she told him bitterly.

"I was taught to track by an Indian. They make no
sound. However, I hardly need an Indian's training to
follow the trail you left—torn skirt on the windowsill,
footprints in the soft earth. A child could have found
you."

"I am sorry I was not more of a challenge to your
talents. I shall try to do better next time."

His hold on her tightened. "There will be no next
time, not even if I have to chain you to our bed. You
are a bond servant indentured for debts and I may do
anything I choose with you. The law protects me in
that." He told her this as he lifted her in his arms and
started down the road.

"Where are you taking me?"

"We will spend the night at the countess's house."

"Together?" Her voice quavered.

"Most assuredly together."

The hint of amusement that tinged his words further angered her.

"I will not spend a night with a man I am not married to," she snapped.

"May I remind you, my sweet, that you have already spent a good many nights with me unmarried," Miles said drily. "Furthermore, as you appear to have a penchant for trying to escape, I fear I do not dare let you out of my sight until we are wed tomorrow."

Chapter 21

Miles carried Chandra through a rear door into the countess's house and up a back stairway.

"You seem to be quite at home here," she quipped sarcastically. "I take it you are on friendly terms with the countess if you can requisition a room in her home whenever you wish."

"I have visited a few times." He set her down in front of a door at the rear of the second floor.

As he opened the door, Chandra heard the unmistakable animal moans of passion from the room across the hall. She stared at its closed door in astonishment as Miles pushed her inside.

The room was all mirrors and gilt with pastels of naked men and women decorating the wall. Their activities did not merit a lady's scrutiny.

"This is dreadful," she said primly.

Miles shrugged indifferently. "As bawdy houses go, I've seen worse."

She looked at him in astonishment. "I will not spend a night in such a place."

"You should be thankful it is only for a night." Miles locked the door carefully and removed the key, placing it in his pocket. "If your cousin had had his way, you would have been a permanent resident of this establishment."

"What are you saying?"

"I found Percy here attempting to barter you to the countess in exchange for the money he needed."

She recalled the countess's strange statement to Percy

when they arrived. Now she understood its meaning. Tears glistened in her eyes. "Surely they both knew I should never . . ." She broke off, unable to fiinsh.

"You would not have been the first reluctant one the countess has had here," Miles said coolly, sitting down on the big bed. "She has a reputation for firmness with her girls." Miles kicked off his black leather pumps and settled back against the bed's plump pillows. "So you see, my sweet, you should be thankful that I have saved you, as they say, from a fate worse than death."

His sarcastic tone provoked her anew. "I hardly see any reason to be grateful for having been gambled away like an object."

Miles's hazel eyes narrowed angrily, but his voice remained calm. "Your cousin would have sold you outright. At least I gave him a chance to redeem his debts without sacrificing you."

"Did you now?" she demanded contemptuously. "Where would you have gotten $10,000 to pay Percy? What would you have done if Percy had defeated you?"

"He would never have managed it," Miles said with an arrogant certainty that further infuriated Chandra. "He is too poor a player." Miles gave her a long, appraising look. "Still, you are most astute. Your cousin never even gave a thought to the fact that a poor farmer like myself could not possibly have that kind of money."

"So you got me fraudulently, offering a stake you did not have, because you were certain you would win."

"And I did." Miles shrugged and examined Chandra critically. "Although, looking at your rather unkempt appearance at the moment, I am not certain that I have acquired any great prize."

She flared in anger, then caught sight of herself in one of the mirrors. Her face was smudged; the beautiful blue gown, stained with mud from her fall, with a jagged piece missing from its skirt, was hardly recognizable; her hair had tumbled down about her in a wild profusion of unruly curls. But regardless of the way she looked—did this merit his cold harshness toward her? She wondered how he meant to treat her now that she was his. He acted as though he thoroughly disliked her, and she had to admit that she had given him some reason to. But why on earth, then, was he going to marry her? It made no sense at all. She was suddenly filled with foreboding about his motives.

"I don't understand why you want me to be your wife," she said at last, deciding it would be better to discover his true feelings now.

"I don't."

The curt reply confirmed her worst fears. "But why then?"

"Unfortunately, I find that I am forced to marry. You are preferable to my one other alternative." He briefly told her of the Humphreyses' plot.

"You, my dear," he concluded, "are my trump card in their game of coercion. And it shall be our little secret, Chandra, that we were married here in Washington, rather than in England before we sailed."

She glared at him. "What of me? Merely because you wish to spite your neighbor, you are condeming me to a loveless marriage."

He gave her a cool look. " 'Many can brook the weather that love not the wind.' " Then he threw back his head and laughed triumphantly, "God, I wish I could see Fred's and Sally's faces when they learn of my marriage. No one will believe their story now. They will be exposed for the liars they are."

It was as though he had pierced her heart with a dagger. Her worst fear was confirmed: Miles cared not a whit for her. To him she was simply a means of out-witting his scheming neighbor. She hastily turned her back, hiding her face so that he could not see the pain and despair recorded there.

"At dawn tomorrow," Miles went on, "my young friend Jim Spenser will ride hard to spread the word at home that I have acquired a bride while in England, and that the reason for my sudden, mysterious voyage there was to claim her."

"But how would you have known me?"

"I met you on my first trip to England two years ago

and have had eyes for no other since." He twisted his face into a parody of a lovesick swain, then laughed. "God, what a marvelous joke."

"What if I will not go along with your story?" Chandra demanded as she went over to the basin and dampened a cloth in some water to sponge her face. She could see Miles in the mirror in front of her, and she watched his reflection carefully.

"Would you rather tell the world the truth: that I won you in a card game after your guardian tried to peddle you as a whore?"

The man was impossible! How did he know exactly what would anger her most? "Why don't you marry this Sally?" She vowed she would not lose her temper. "At least she wants you, which I don't."

"I refuse to be forced into marriage."

"But you are forcing me to marry you. Why is that different?"

He looked at her in surprise as though the thought had never occurred to him. "A woman marries whom she must, especially a woman in your position. A man, unless he is a fortune hunter or a weakling under his father's thumb, marries whom he desires. And regardless of my feelings for you, at least I find you interesting. Whatever else our lives together may be, my pet, I am certain they will not be dull." His eyes seemed to undress her with his penetrating gaze.

"I am not your pet!"

"But you are," he smirked. "A little wild and unruly yes, it's true, but I shall tame you."

She sputtered in fury and grabbed the first thing at hand, which happened to be a heavy soap container. She hurled it at Miles, but it fell short of its target.

"What a terrible aim you have," he mocked. "Remind me never to let you have a gun."

She looked around wildly for something else to throw, but Miles bounded up from the bed, and was beside her in two strides, his hands biting cruelly into her arms as he pinned them to her sides.

"You will be wise to desist from such unladylike displays of anger in future," he told her fiercely. "Now get out of that dress and into bed. I should like some sleep tonight." His impatient fingers began undoing the blue gown's fastenings.

She tried to pull away from him. "At least have the decency to turn your back while I undress."

"So you can bolt for the window," he jeered. "I don't advise that this time. It is a long drop to the ground."

"You are no gentleman."

Miles's eyes glittered. "But, my sweet, I am merely doing my best to live up to your boorish expectations of me. Now are you going to take that gown off or do I have to do it for you?"

Hastily she shed the torn blue gown, and stood, red with embarrassment, in her thin cotton shift. Miles's gaze roamed over her body, so lightly veiled by the flimsy undergarment, as though he were a buyer sizing up the merits of a mare.

Tears of anger and humiliation spilled down Chandra's cheeks. How could she ever have thought this vulgar lout was in the least attractive or have harbored the slightest tenderness for him? "I hate you," she lashed out at him. "You won't drag the marriage vows from my lips."

"Your choice, milady." Miles shrugged nonchalantly as he folded his peacock velvet coat and laid it neatly over a chair. "Do you prefer to be mine without marriage? I warn you that if you refuse to speak your vows quietly tomorrow, you will never have a second chance." He slipped off his white satin waistcoat. "Which role do you prefer, wife or whore?"

She stared into his hard hazel eyes and knew that he would do as he threatened. There was no affection there to temper his treatment of her. Despair seized her as she thought of life tied to this cold man.

"I await your answer," Miles said harshly as he removed his shirt, disclosing a powerful, tanned chest, well protected by a mat of dark curly hair.

Chandra bowed her head in defeat. "I will do as you wish," she whispered.

"That's better." Miles's gloating smile made her capitulation seem all the more bitter. "But there is one wifely duty I will never perform of my own free will," she added between clenched teeth. "Of course, I imagine a man like you has no compunction about rape."

For an instant, Miles's casual indifference was rent by a flash of fury in his eyes, but it was gone quickly. It was another moment, however, before he seemed to trust himself to speak, and when he did, his face and his voice were as icy as an English winter.

"You underestimate me. I have told you I coerce no woman into my bed. If you wish to share its pleasures, you will have to seek them. If you do not desire them" —he shrugged indifferently—"others are more than willing. Ours is, after all, a marriage of convenience." He grinned in that insouciant manner that so infuriated her and nodded toward the bed. "Get in."

"I just told you I shall not share your bed."

"The pleasures of my bed," he corrected, "and I shall offer you none. But share my bed you will. I won't take any chance on your escaping me."

With that, he grabbed her, tossed her upon the bed as though she were a sack of grain, and got in after her, pinning her next to the wall so that his hard body lay between her and the door.

"Although," he added in a low, suggestive tone just when she thought he was falling off to sleep, "the day will come when you will hunger for my attentions."

"Never," she sputtered, outraged by his calm confidence.

Miles made no attempt to touch her, and his even breathing indicated that he was nearly asleep. But Chandra lay awake seething with rage. The impudent jackass! She would never willingly submit to him, and she vowed she would make him regret the day he decided to take her for a wife.

She huddled as close to the wall and as far away from

Miles as she could. She did not lack the courage to try to creep from the bed, find the key to the door, and flee into the night, but the difficulties seemed insurmountable. Even if she somehow avoided awakening Miles, her gown lay in ruins, and she could hardly run through the streets of Washington in her thin, nearly transparent shift.

She might be able to filch a dress from one of the house's occupants, but the thought of what scene she might stumble upon in another room brought a blush to her cheeks. What if one of the male visitors should mistake her for a hired girl? She shuddered.

Her movement brought an instant reaction from Miles. He reached out and his hand descended firmly upon her belly. His touch sent another tremor through her, but this one was not of disgust.

His eyes opened. "You weren't thinking of going anywhere, were you, my precious?"

"No," she quavered, utterly disconcerted by the response his hand had stirred in her.

"That's good. I am a very light sleeper, and you would not get far."

He stroked her belly provocatively, suffusing it with a warmth and a throbbing excitement unlike anything she had ever experienced before and arousing deep within her such exquisite sensations of growing intensity that she could not catch her breath. Beneath the gentle assault of his hand, her body cried out for his caress even as her mind rejected it.

"Please," she gasped finally in a strangled voice, shoving his hand firmly away, "don't."

"What's the matter, my sweet?" he mocked her. "Are you discovering that you are not so impervious to my touch as you would like me—and yourself—to believe?"

He had hit upon the truth, and she cursed herself for her weakness. "I hate you," she stormed, turning to the wall.

He chuckled. "Do you now?" he queried softly. He ran his hand over the curve of her hip and her thigh.

Then, abruptly, he rolled over so that his back was to hers and promptly went back to sleep.

When she woke the next morning, Miles was already up and was pulling on a pair of white silk breeches.

"Come, Chandra," he announced in a delighted tone, "it's time to get up. You should be more eager to greet your wedding day."

She rolled over and gave him a poisonous look.

He began to don a ruffled shirt of fine white cambric. "Do you wish for Percy to give you away?"

"He already has," she snapped, sitting up in bed. She carefully kept the sheet high about her neck.

"You know what I mean. Percy is the only relative you have here."

"I fervently hope I shall never set eyes on him again. If it weren't for him . . ."

Miles cut her off. "Hurry up and get dressed," he said brusquely.

"In what?" she inquired, still clutching the sheet about her. "My gown is ruined. Perhaps you wish to parade me through the streets of Washington in my shift."

Miles pulled from an oak wardrobe an enchanting gown of white silk trimmed with ruffles of lace at the neck, wrists and bodice, and a new chemise of the softest batiste also trimmed with lace and delicately embroidered flowers.

He laid them on the bed, saying, "You will wear these."

Although Chandra's eyes lit up at the sight of the lovely garments, she would not give him the satisfaction of a happy smile. "Are they borrowed from one of the 'ladies' of this distinguished house?" she asked in a sarcastic manner.

"No, I bought them for our wedding."

Her pleasure with the new clothes vanished. "You were well prepared, then. I see you felt totally certain of Percy's lack of skill at cards and of my helplessness to escape you."

Miles angrily jerked an embroidered white satin waist-coat from the wardrobe. "Your gratitude for my largess overwhelms me. Now damn it, get dressed." Deliberately, he turned his back on her.

She rose hastily and put on the chemise and the gown. "These must have cost you a substantial portion of your gambling winnings," she mused as she fingered the fine silk.

"I have been uncommonly lucky at the tables in the past few days." He pulled on a red velvet jacket. "And you, my sweet, are more the beneficiary than the victim. Imagine—just imagine—where you might be now had you not met me."

He turned toward her, shaking out the white lace ruffles at his wrist that contrasted vividly with the red of his coat. His garments were superbly tailored to his lithe body, and their materials, like those in the clothes he had given her, were the finest that money could buy. Despite her hostility, she had to concede that he cut a handsome figure. Her life with him might be poor and hard, but at least she was being married in style.

"Allow me." He reached out and began fastening the back of her gown. Once again, she found she could not subdue the excitement that his touch aroused.

"Tom and another friend will act as our witnesses," he said as his fingers worked the buttons.

So, Chandra thought, she would at last meet the mysterious Tom about whom Miles had been so reticent.

"Do they approve of your winning a bride in a card game?" she asked tartly.

"They know nothing of that, only that you are obliged to make a marriage of necessity."

"The necessity is yours, not mine. What have you told them?"

"The truth," he said, finishing with the buttons and going over to the wardrobe where he withdrew a large box. "That you fled England to escape the vengeful Warfolk and dare not return; that you find yourself alone, friendless, and penniless in an alien land and are desperately in need of a protector."

"A protector! Is that what you call yourself?"

He ignored her comment and, opening the box, he produced an exquisite bridal veil of the sheerest white chiffon embroidered at the crown with seed pearls. "And that your need coincided with mine for a wife. Consequently, we are getting married. If you weren't so stubborn you'd admit that you need me." He finished with a small glint of amusement sparkling in his eyes.

"I may need a protector, but I don't need a marriage to a man who won me in a card game. I certainly don't need *you*."

"You stubborn little fool," Miles said quietly. "If out of spite you tell my friends of last night's card game, it is yourself whom you will embarrass and demean, not me. Nor will your loose tongue stop me from marrying you. I am determined to outwit Humphreys at all costs. You will have gained nothing except my anger, and you will have lost a great deal."

She turned away from him, still defiant. "I will do as I please."

Chapter 22

The little church where they were to be wed was, like almost everything else in the new capital, unfinished. As they stopped in front of the modest wooden structure, which still wanted paint and half of its steeple, Chandra looked around, half fearing that Percy might have decided to make an appearance. While it was true that she had no wish to see him again, she could still not stifle her anxiety over what would happen to him today after the deadline passed and he was unable to pay Murchison. She was not a vindictive person and, angry as she was at her cousin for what he had done to her, she did not want him hurt.

But when Miles helped her down from the curricle that he had hired, the street was empty except for a stranger on horseback who was riding toward them. "Here comes Tom now," Miles said, waving to his friend.

Chandra studied the man. Although he was plainly dressed in a simple black suit with white silk hose and linen, he was a distinguished figure. His handsome square face, open and honest, was that of a vigorous man, full of vitality and curiosity, who seemed much younger than the years indicated by his longish gray hair.

As he dismounted, Miles introduced them. "Chandra, meet Thomas Jefferson."

"The president?" Her incredulous question slipped out before she could stop herself, and she felt very foolish. What was she supposed to do? How was she

supposed to address an American president? Did one
bow as one did before the king? She supposed not.

"Sir, I mean Your Excellency, I mean Your Maj . . ."
She broke off, certain that *your majesty* could not be
right. "I don't know what I mean," she confessed frankly. "I've never met a head of state before, and I don't
know how to address you. Am I supposed to curtsy?"

"Certainly not," Jefferson replied, his eyes twinkling
with delight at her candor. He smiled at her with such
a kindly and pleasant smile that he immediately won her
affection. "We are a republic here, and we are all
equals."

Chandra nodded, still somewhat dazed by the fact
that Miles was on such close terms with the head of his
country. But then she remembered what Percy had said
about Jefferson preferring the company of farmers.

A coach was rapidly approaching them. "That must
be Dolley," Miles said. "She will be our other witness,"
he told Chandra.

Chandra was dumbfounded. Could this be the Dolley
Madison of whom she had heard at the dressmaker's?
The woman who acted as Jefferson's hostess?

The coach rattled to a stop, and a statuesque woman
with the liveliest dark eyes and the most irrepressible
smile that Chandra had ever seen descended like a
whirlwind. She was in her early thirties and her black
hair seemed even blacker in contrast to her lovely fair
skin. Dolley Madison was not a beauty in the classic
sense, but her vivacity obscured that fact. Her simple
yellow silk gown with its empire waist and slim skirt was
in the latest fashion.

"How lovely you are," Dolley said, without waiting to
greet the gentlemen, bestowing her dazzling smile on
Chandra. "Now I see why you have coaxed Miles out
of his confirmed bachelorhood."

She turned to Miles, her eyes sparkling mischievous-
ly. "And I understand that I am not at your wedding
at all, that actually it took place a month ago in England, and that what is about to happen is all a dream
which I shall, of course, forget the instant I awaken."

Miles grinned. "I knew I could trust you, Dolley."

"I think it's shameful, just shameful, what that dreadful Fred Humphreys tried to do to you," she said. "You are so clever to have outwitted him."

"The rector is waiting for us," Jefferson said. "We had better go in."

Chandra stiffened. She had dreaded the moment when she would be compelled to break her vow to her father and bind herself to this American, and now it was at hand. She saw that Dolley had caught the sudden panic that had shown in her face and was watching her with concerned eyes.

"Now you men go inside," Dolley said quickly, "while I adjust Chandra's veil. We'll be but a moment."

After the two men had vanished into the church, Dolley turned to Chandra, her warm brown eyes full of sympathy. "I know how apprehensive you must be, believe me. You are not marrying out of love but because of necessity. But sometimes when circumstances force us to do what the head instead of the heart dictates, we find that what was wise, because it was wise, also brings us great happiness."

Dolley reached up and arranged the layers of chiffon in Chandra's veil. "I, too, was full of secret misgivings when I married my beloved husband. I admired him more than any man I knew, I was awed by his brilliant mind, and I was certain that he would be a good father to my son and a staunch husband to me, but I cannot say I truly loved him." She took Chandra's hands in her own and held them comfortingly.

Chandra smiled at her as best she could, hiding her true feelings, and she nodded. This perceptive woman had sensed her unhappiness, but, of course, she knew only part of the story. What would Dolley say if she were aware that Chandra was not merely a reluctant bride, but a totally unwilling one? But it would serve no good purpose to tell her. As Miles had said, it would be Chandra who would be most shamed by the revelation.

Dolley went on, "I was still full of misgivings after

my wedding. Now, however, so precious is my husband to me that I cannot bear to be separated even for a day from him. Now, come, we must go in, or they will be out looking for us."

The rector was a serious young man, bespectacled and nervous. He began reading the service in a soft voice. Chandra stood at the altar flanked by Miles and two strangers, one the president of the United States and the other the wife of his secretary of state. She felt numb, as if perhaps all this were not happening to her but to some other, less fortunate woman.

When it came time for her to repeat her vows, she waited as long as she dared before responding. Only when she felt Miles tense beside her and saw, out of the corner of her eye, that his face had grown stormy did she end her silence. In a tiny voice she pledged herself to this strange, angry man until death did them part.

Afterward Jefferson insisted the newlyweds go back to his residence for a toast and refreshments. Dolley, however, regretfully excused herself. "I must get home to my husband. He has been very ill, and I am so concerned about him."

The deep brown eyes could not hide her feelings and told Chandra as clearly as had her earlier words how greatly she now loved the husband she had married reluctantly.

When the curricle stopped in front of the white-washed mansion on Pennsylvania Avenue, Chandra commented, "So this is the President's Palace."

Jefferson looked pained. "Please, the president's *house*. I dislike all the trappings of royalty." He smiled. "I hope it pleases you?"

As they crossed the wooden platform to the door, Jefferson ushered Chandra before him and asked if she would like a tour of the house. She quickly accepted his offer. As he led her through the large public dining room, an oval room intended as a vestibule which Jefferson had turned into a drawing room, the library that he used as an office, and the antechamber next door, he told her and Miles of his plans to add east and west wings that would house offices, a smokehouse and a laundry.

He led them back to the private dining room, where a feast had been laid out for them: roast beef, ham, oysters, crab, eggs, at least a dozen different kinds of fruits and vegetables, a wedding cake, and other sweetmeats.

After toasting the couple with champagne, Jefferson smiled. "I hope you will not think it presumptuous of me, Chandra, to discuss your most intimate secrets right before you, but Miles is an old friend and we always speak the truth with each other." He turned to Miles and said quietly, "You know I was much distressed last night when you told me of your marriage plans. I feared your precipitous action was dictated solely by your determination not to marry Sally. But now that I have met the beautiful and charming bride that you have won, I feel more sanguine."

Chandra was sorely tempted to confide in the president and tell him how, indeed, she had been "won." But she had held her tongue up to this point and she would now. She was stubborn but she was not—whatever Miles might think—spiteful. She would gain nothing by telling Jefferson except to trouble the gentle and kind man greatly and to very likely alienate Miles forever. She would not destroy the president's confidence in his friend, either.

Chandra was fascinated by Jefferson. He was so gracious and attentive, he talked so lovingly of his daughters and grandchildren, and his wide-ranging mind could converse easily—even brilliantly—on any subject that was raised. How her father would have relished spending time with this man! But then it came back to her with a sudden start that her father had raged against this, the most sane of men, as "that mad revolutionary."

"By the way," Jefferson was saying, "I did as you asked last night and talked to Edward Thornton about sending Percival Lunt back to England." The president turned to Chandra. "Miles told me of the grave danger your cousin was in because he could not pay his gaming debts. He thought it would be safest for Lunt if he were sent back to England."

"Did Thornton object?" Miles asked.

"On the contrary, he was delighted. Said he had been looking for an excuse to do that very thing. I am afraid, Chandra," Tom said apologetically, "that Thornton did not think highly of him. In any event, your cousin was put aboard a boat at Georgetown this morning bound for Norfolk, where he will be put aboard another ship sailing for England. So he is safe."

Chandra was greatly relieved. "Thank you. I am most grateful to you."

"I suppose you will miss him," Jefferson remarked.

"Never." The word, spoken with such intense vehemence, slipped out before Chandra realized it.

She saw the confusion on Jefferson's face and turned to Miles with a silent plea for help in her eyes.

"I am afraid Percy was thoroughly unscrupulous as well as a compulsive gambler," her husband explained. "He tried to blackmail me, and when that failed, he tried to sell Chandra to the Countess de Beroit."

Jefferson looked thoroughly shocked and troubled. He sat in silence for a moment. Then he said sadly, "I wish, Miles, that you had told me that last night. I would never have had him sent home."

"Why not?" Chandra asked in surprise.

The president looked grave. "If he is that unscrupulous, what is to stop him from selling his knowledge of Chandra's whereabouts to the Duke of Warfolk?"

Part Four

Chapter 23

The curricle sped along a Virginia road so narrow it was hardly more than a ribbon through the thick woods of oak and birch. At times the ruts that had been grooved in the road during the spring rains were so deep that Chandra half expected the vehicle to vanish into one of them. A thick canopy of green formed by arching branches that intertwined above the road shaded the curricle from the direct rays of the hot sun.

She cast a surreptitious glance at Miles, sitting stiffly on the seat beside her, a deep frown on his face. They had scarcely spoken a word since they had left the president's house, as Jefferson's fears about Percy had cast a pall over them. Was she never to escape the specter of the cruel Warfolk? A forlorn sigh escaped from Chandra's lips as she thought about it.

Her husband, hearing it, scrutinized her sharply, but when she said nothing, he turned his attention back to the pair of grays that he was skillfully guiding at a rapid clip. His frown seemed to grow deeper.

At last she spoke, thinking to clear the air between them. "Who are you so angry at?"

"Myself. I was so stupid I didn't even think of what Percy might try. I just couldn't conceive of even him being that base, but I know Tom is right."

"How is it," she asked, giving voice to a question that had nagged at her since they left Jefferson's house, "that you can so despise me and yet care about the duke taking me from you?"

Her words further fueled his anger, bringing a flush

of red to his face. "I have told you before, madam, that I do have some integrity, despite your opinions to the contrary. I would not see unjust harm come to any man or woman."

How little she knew about this stranger who was her husband: only that he was a farmer, despite his education and gentleman's bearing, who apparently did better at the gaming tables than with his pigs and who numbered among his friends the president of the United States. He was such a multifaceted individual. She was enormously curious about him. And about his life which, after all, she would soon be sharing.

"Where is your farm?" she asked.

"On the Rappahannock River. It's one of the four great tidal rivers in Virginia that drain into the Chesapeake Bay."

She tried the name on her tongue, liking its rolling sound. "Rappahannock. What does it mean?"

"It is an Indian word that perhaps best translates as 'ebb and flow stream.' "

"How large is your house?"

"Large enough for me. But you with your grand tastes may find it cramped." An odd, superior look glinted in the hazel eyes. He was evidently very eager for her to see her new home.

In the distance, a frisky chestnut mare frolicked on a green carpet of grass. Chandra wondered whether she would ever again be able to indulge her passion for riding. Could a farmer like Miles afford a horse? Timidly she asked him.

"Yes, I have one," he replied. "And you may ride the poor nag when it is not busy with the plowing."

Her anticipation dimmed considerably. She pictured the poor swaybacked, splayfooted beast that would become Zeus's successor in her life. The dismay written on her face seemed to amuse Miles.

Sometime later, they passed a cottage with a dirty, nearly naked boy of about two playing in front. "Its windows have no glass," she noted.

"Many of us cannot afford such luxuries. Glass is very expensive."

"But it is a virtual necessity," she countered. "Surely the rain pouring inside must ruin the wood of the floors."

"Wood?" Miles raised his eyebrow quizzically. "Why do you assume that they are wood? The rain does make the dirt a trifle muddy about the edges, but it dries in a day or two."

"Dirt floors!" She was aghast.

Miles grinned. "Come now, they are most practical. You need never scrub them."

She sank back in dejection upon the seat, thinking of the life that lay ahead of her. She would be a dreary farm drudge: cooking, washing, cleaning, feeding the pigs. She could not bear the thought of such a wretched existence. What irony to have been married to this man with two of the nation's most important people as her witnesses. To be fêted by the president of the country on the event of starting her new life in a dirt-floored hovel. Of course, if Miles would consent to abandon farming for gambling, things might change for them. He apparently was so much better at the latter, and enjoyed the game as well, that he might be persuaded to alter his profession.

"Percy said that when he first met you, you told him you were a gambler. Why?" she asked, testing the waters.

"The fool was making a nuisance of himself insisting that I play a few hands with him. I had no wish to do so because, as you saw last night, he was no match for me. I thought to get rid of him by telling him I was a professional gambler, and he was not in my league."

Miles abruptly raised his whip and pushed the pair of grays to a furious pace. While Chandra admired his skill in handling horses, she could not help but question the wisdom of such speed, given the sorry condition of the road.

"When shall we reach your farm?" she asked anxiously, dreading her first glimpse of the miserable sty she was to share with this farmer.

"I hope by late tomorrow."

They passed a substantial brick house whose entrance was guarded by the spreading boughs of two yew trees. They reminded Chandra of those that had grown at Northlands. How far away it seemed now in time as well as miles. Her father's death might have happened years ago instead of months.

All her life Chandra had striven to please her father and now she had failed him in the one thing he had wanted most from her. She knew that he would have found her betrayal of his dream for her future beyond forgiving. The thought filled her with misery that was made even more painful by Miles's lack of caring. If she had married for love, at least, it would be some compensation to do without money or title. But this man felt nothing for her. A firm resolve grew in her aching heart to resist his lovemaking—why, the very word was a mockery, considering their relationship. He would find his "indentured" wife had a will of her own that could not be so easily bent to his. No blood of his would flow in her children's veins to shame her father if she could prevent it.

The sunset was fading into darkness when they reached a substantial roadside inn, three stories high with a wide veranda and dormer windows on the top floor.

"We will spend the night here," Miles announced, reining the horses to a stop.

Chandra offered no objection, pleased at the thought of one final night in pleasant surroundings. As Miles helped her down, she noticed a large box stowed beneath the curricle's seat.

She nodded at the box. "What is that?"

"Seed," he replied carelessly.

The innkeeper, a fat, pleasant man of fifty named Tilham, welcomed Miles by name. His effusive greeting indicated that Miles had stayed in this establishment more than once in the past.

Upon his introduction to Chandra as the bride that Miles had acquired on his recent trip to England, the innkeeper plied her with compliments and Miles with congratulations for having found such a beautiful wife. He served them a hearty dinner of oyster soup, baked ham, and a strange orange tubular vegetable that Chandra had never seen before.

"They're called yams," Miles explained, as he consumed his dinner with gusto.

Chandra, nervous over what lay ahead of her in their hired room, scarcely touched her food. She was determined to keep her silent vow to resist her husband.

The Carringtons' room on the second floor was small but clean with cheerful braided rugs, white Georgia pine floor, a fireplace of English brick, and a large feather bed with snowy linen that Chandra eyed apprehensively. She did not believe Miles's boast that it would be she who would have to seek the pleasures of their marriage bed, but no matter, she was ready to tackle him with her wits and her will.

Miles shut the door, locked it and, without a word to her, shed his clothes. He folded them neatly over a chair and climbed into the bed naked.

"Hurry up," he growled. "Get into your nightclothes and put out the candle. I'm tired and I want to get an early start tomorrow."

His brusque tone was certainly not romantic. Swallowing hard, she shook her head. "I have no nightclothes with me."

"Sleep in your chemise if you want."

Biting her lip, she reached back to unfasten her wedding gown, but she soon discovered that no matter how she twisted and struggled, she could reach only a few of its many buttons.

"Damn it," Miles grumbled from the bed, "I told you to hurry."

"I can't get my gown unfastened," she confessed.

"Why didn't you say something sooner?" he demanded as he bounded up. Despite his forbidding tone, the touch of his fingers on her back as they skillfully undid the buttons filled her with a sense of well-being

When he was finished, he pushed the gown from her shoulders and it fell about her feet.

She stiffened, but he only laughed.

"Were you expecting something else from me?" he asked in mock innocence as he climbed back into bed.

Chandra longed to throw something at him. She stepped out of her gown and draped it neatly over a chair. She fingered the soft batiste of the shift that Miles had given her. It was finer than any she had ever had, and she hated to think of sleeping in it, especially since she was unlikely to ever have another so nice again. But it was either that or crawl naked into bed beside Miles, and neither her pride nor her modesty would permit her to do that.

She snuffed out the candle and got into bed gingerly, clinging to the edge as far away from Miles as she could get. His back was turned to her, and she waited nervously for him to make his move. She steeled herself to resist him. But he did not even acknowledge her presence.

Eventually his breathing grew even, indicating he had fallen asleep. She had girded herself for any ploy—his raging at her, his pleading with her or brutally seizing her. She had been prepared for anything but his ignoring her. Now she lay beside him, an unloved bride, and tears of humiliation glistened in her eyes.

When she awoke, the first gray light of dawn was creeping into the room. Miles had tossed the sheet aside, leaving his powerful bronzed chest bare, and she took this advantage to examine his sleeping form. In sleep his face was relaxed and his dark hair curled about it in unruly fashion. Whatever else Miles might be, he surely was a handsome figure of a man, she thought with a perverse twinge of pride.

His eyes opened, and seeing her watching him, he taunted with a mocking grin, "Did you enjoy your chaste wedding night, my beloved?"

All her shame and resentment at him surfaced at that moment. He was insolent, arrogant and insufferable.

"It was a most peculiar wedding night . . ." she began hotly, but he cut her off.

"Did you think you were so irresistible that no man could restrain himself at the sight of you?" His scorn left her hurt and speechless. "Perhaps you wish to plead for my loving attention."

Her already strained temper was stoked higher by his words and she flounced up from the bed, giving Miles a generous view of her shapely leg, thigh and bosom. Although his desire was kindled, he gave no indication of it.

Chandra could think of nothing now but hurting him as he had hurt her. She lashed at him with a string of almost incoherent complaints, ranging from his lowly station in life to the inadequacies he most certainly must have as a lover.

"You arrogant, swaggering fool! You could never make me desire you, you crude farmer," she cried.

As her attack grew wilder, Miles's bewilderment turned to determination. He was seized by a desire to prove to this haughty termagant the gross falsehood of her harangue against him. By God, he would teach her how he could make her body hunger for him! His eyes blazed with such intensity that Chandra suddenly realized she had gone too far. She broke off and stared fearfully at him.

He jumped from the bed. "I will demonstrate to you what nonsense you prattle, madam," he said between clenched teeth. She could feel his hot breath on her, they stood so close.

He grabbed her new chemise in his powerful hands and ripped it from her, leaving her standing as naked as he. His insolent hazel eyes roamed her body.

Her cheeks flaming, she tried to shield her nakedness with her arms, but he grabbed them and held them above her head, then tumbled her down on the bed. She felt the exciting warmth of his bare skin and of his strong, warm body pressing against hers. She began to struggle, but he was far too strong for her and easily held her pinned.

"I shall scream unless you let me go," she whimpered.

"And what shall you scream, my sweet?" He took both her hands in one of his large ones and moved the other down to rest on her thigh. "That your husband is claiming his conjugal privileges? The only response such a complaint is apt to bring is the advice that the husband deal sternly with such contrariness."

She knew he was right. No one would interfere. But still, she refused to give in. Her tongue had served her as a weapon before and now she employed it again. "So you will rape me with the excuse that you are my husband. I thought you did not force yourself upon unwilling women."

"I shall not take you against your will," he replied coldly. "I am merely going to demonstrate to you how much you want me."

"Want you? You are mad!" she spit out, still trying to struggle free.

"You fight me because you fear to find out the truth about yourself and your desire for me."

Stung by the realization that there was far more truth to his accusation than she cared to admit, she lay back stiff and passive beneath him, determined that he would find no response in her body.

His hands began to roam over her, and despite the anger in his eyes, they were extraordinarily gentle. He stroked her face and hair. He slowly moved his hand down to her breasts and toyed with them until the pink peaks rose up in hard excitement against his fingers. Her will began to crumble despite her determination. The tenderness with which he caressed her stirred a pleasure deep within her that shook her to the core of her being.

His lips began to tease her breasts as his hand moved lower, stroking her thighs, then her belly, brushing it lightly until she moaned with pleasure.

Now his hands and his lips seemed to be rioting over her body, taunting it, teasing it, tempting it and caressing the spots most likely to drive her to ecstasy. In a few moments, he succeeded.

She writhed and burned with pleasure beneath his touch, caught now on the waves of her own awakened passion. She was swept away by a force beyond herself that she could neither understand nor subdue. She would never comprehend how it happened, but suddenly her arms were encircling him, and she was clinging to him, returning his kisses as hotly as he gave them, caressing his body eagerly with her untutored hands.

The fire of her response and of his own desire consumed both his anger and his control. He wanted her now as he had never wanted a woman before. He lifted himself over her. As he entered, she stiffened and tried desperately to get away, her panic rising as she realized too late where her passion had taken her. "No," she moaned.

But he was no more able to stay his need than he could have halted an earthquake. His lips closed over her, silencing her cries of protest. He murmured softly, reassuringly to her, as she struggled beneath him. Then with a sharp thrust that split the virgin barrier, he possessed her. A strangled cry escaped Chandra's lips.

Now he strove with all the considerable skill he possessed to erase her pain with pleasure. He wanted her to delight in their lovemaking as much as he. He longed for her to experience the full depth of joy that could be hers.

At first Chandra felt only a sharp, stabbing sensation. But then Miles's skill fired her perverse yearning, and her body, almost against her will, began to respond to him. Her struggle gave way to a rhythm that matched his in mounting intensity. She seemed on the edge of a great precipice from which she would plunge into some sweet, unknown paradise. Finally, when she thought she could not bear another moment of the tension that was building within her, she was rocked by spasms that welled up from the very depths of her being. She stiffened, her breath coming in quick short pants. She moaned in ecstasy and receded into a serene contentment greater than any she had ever known.

For a long moment Miles remained one with Chandra, reluctant to break their union. When at last he parted from her, he rolled to one side, propped himself on an elbow, and stared down at her in wonder.

She lay as though suspended in a trance. Her eyes were closed, and her beautiful face seemed filled with the ecstasy that they had just found together. He had suspected that she could be passionate, but the heat of her response amazed him. If she could attain such heights now, he trembled to think of what joys awaited them as she grew more willing and more experienced.

Chandra opened her eyes and looked up at Miles, who was watching her closely. She read the strange expression on his face as a sign of triumph. He was gloating over her, the insolent rogue!

Her contentment evaporated in anger. This man who cared not at all for her had conquered her with scarcely an effort. He had promised her confidently that he would make her hunger for him, and how easily he had done so the very first time he had bothered to try. Not that he had deigned to try on his wedding night. Nor would he have today if she had not goaded him into it with her insults. How pleased he must be with himself.

She had not wanted to surrender to him, but he was like a sorcerer, coaxing her body beyond her control, casting a spell over her that made her do his will. She was filled with loathing for her own weakness. With no effort at all, he had seduced her into breaking her vow to resist him, just as easily as he had caused her to break her vow to her father. She knew deep within herself that despite her brief struggle she had ached for him, hungered for him.

Most galling of all to her was the knowledge that she had betrayed herself and her father for a man who harbored no affection for her, but regarded her merely as a pawn in his game of revenge. To him, she was but a pet to be played with and brought to heel.

Her anguish and her humiliation boiled up. She was livid at the thought that this man could so easily bring her body to his bidding and make it ignore everything she held dear.

"You forced me," she cried out wildly, knowing it wasn't really true but too consumed by her own self-loathing to care.

Miles laughed a low, indulgent laugh. "If that's the way you respond to rape, my sweet, I can hardly wait to experience your reaction when you are willing."

"You are intolerable," she cried in fury made all the more intense because she knew his amusement was justified. "You forced me to break my vows."

"You keep prattling about your vows," Miles said irritably. "Are these the same mysterious vows that you were so determined to keep aboard the *Golden Drake?*"

"Yes," she affirmed loudly.

"From the way you're carrying on about them, I am beginning to fear I have bedded a nun. Were they religious?"

"No, certainly not. They were made to my father on his deathbed."

At the mention of her father, Miles's eyes narrowed. "What was the nature of these vows?"

"That I would marry a man of good family, and that I . . ."

Miles's body stiffened and his dark brows knit together. "What in the hell is so fine about your family? At least I do not gamble my women away in card games or sell them as whores."

His harsh words failed to stop her tongue, and she cried, "Even now I may be abreeding with your brat."

"And what would be so terrible about that? I am not averse to an heir."

"An heir to a pig sty!" Only half coherent by now, she poured out the story of her father's expectations of the man whose blood would flow in his grandsons' veins. "And you," she cried bitterly, "are not a worthy sire. You are nothing but . . ."

Miles's bellow of rage drowned her words. "Not a worthy sire!" he roared in such fury that the room seemed to tremble. The terrible look in his eyes told Chandra that she had just dealt him the worst insult of his life. She had wounded him to the very core of his pride.

"You ungrateful little chit," he thundered. "I saved you from ruination and worse at the hands of Warfolk and sheltered you across the Atlantic. I rescued you from your weakling cousin who would have sold your body as if you were a horse. I have made you my wife, a position a good many women have done everything in their power to secure. I have just pleasured you as you have never before been pleasured. And you have the effrontery to tell me that I am an unfit sire for your children!" He was shaking with rage. "I swear I will make you pay for your foolish pride."

Jumping up, he seized her and yanked her to her feet. "You want me," he told her brutally. "If I had had any doubt of that previously, your response to me just now dispelled it. But your infernal pride and the nonsense your father instilled in you won't let you confess it. You prefer to deny your own nature than let your father's foolish fantasy for you die a natural death. Don't you realize that he was counting on your marriage to somehow erase his own disgrace and banishment?"

"Don't talk about papa like that," she whispered brokenly, the fire gone out of her.

Miles glared at her. "You blind fool. For once in your life face up to what your father really was: an embittered recluse who shunned society because it did not meet his snobbish standards. He had lost touch with reality! Otherwise he would have known that the daughter of a penniless outcast had little hope of marrying an exalted nobleman. If you think otherwise, you are most naive."

She began to speak, then stopped as she realized that she could not defend her father against Miles's indictment.

"Philip Taylor may have left you penniless in pounds, Chandra, but he bequeathed you a fortune of pride. Take care that it does not destroy you as it did him. I have no title, but I have given you an honorable name and security. You sneer at me for being a poor American farmer, but if you had an eye in your head you would realize that I offer you more than a good many men would. You should be delighted to have a strong, honest husband who will care for you and please you well in bed."

He turned away from her and strode to the wardrobe, flinging open its doors with such force that they nearly snapped from their hinges. Then he whirled to face her.

"I promise you, madam, that you will not have to worry about my attentions again. If you are ever to have the pleasure of my lovemaking again, if you are ever to bear my child, you shall beg for it on your knees."

Miles turned back to the wardrobe and snatched at his clothes. "Get up," he ordered Chandra. "I want to be home tonight, and we have a long way to go yet."

Chapter 24

His face as black and forbidding as a thundercloud, Miles urged the horses along the brutal pace as though by doing so he could somehow exorcise his rage. They careened past newly cultivated fields, greening with the tender shoots of spring, through pinewoods whose boughs screened out the warm sun, and by plantation houses, some of them great brick mansions with imposing facades shaded by oaks and elms. Chandra sat beside him, gripping her seat with both hands to prevent herself from falling as she was jogged up and down in the curricle. She felt such a mixture of emotions: on the one hand, confusion at her visceral physical response to Miles; on the other, sadness at her shattered dreams. Life was simply not as her father had painted it for her —the man sitting beside her who had taken her in wedlock and in the marriage bed was teaching her that. She eyed enviously the grand houses they passed and thought of the mean cottage that awaited her at the end of their journey.

But not all the plantations were so impressive. Some showed the beginnings of decay—trim in need of repainting, roofs that had to be repaired, hedges that should have been clipped. And, as further proof of the owners' failing fortunes, the fields that surrounded these deteriorating houses were often brown and scarred by erosion's ugly little gullies. Their crops were yellow sedge and an occasional scrub pine. Chandra recalled what Miles had said to Lord William Pembroke about exhausted soil.

Despite the reckless haste at which the curricle traveled, Chandra found the day passing as slowly as eternity. At least yesterday Miles had been merely indifferent toward her, but since her cruel challenge of his paternal fitness this morning, he had been in a silent, seething rage.

Chandra stole a glance at his strong, muscled body so straight and angry beside her. She could not blame him in the slightest for his mood. Painful as it was for her to accept, Chandra had to admit to herself that Miles had been right about her father.

Papa had extracted vows that were impossible for her to keep, binding her to his hopeless fantasy. For the first time in her life she saw her father not through an adoring child's eyes but as he really was: a snobbish, selfish man who always blamed his own failures on others, yet was unforgiving of the smallest defects in them. He had demanded a great deal of everyone but himself. She no longer felt guilty for having failed him.

And hadn't his cherished notions about titles and family bloodlines been as foolish as his fantasies for her marriage? Chandra had only to consider the Duke of Warfolk or Sir Henry or even that wretched Strum to be convinced. Again Miles was right. It was a man's character, not his title, that was important.

For the first time, Chandra seriously considered the virtues of the man to whom she was wed. He was handsome of face and form, fastidious in appearance and dress, strong in spirit and body. And he was intelligent and well educated. She remembered the pleasure that she had found in his company on the voyage from England, and the excitement that his mere touch was capable of raising in her. Perhaps her body, which had betrayed her to his caress, had been more honest than her mind, which had been blinded by her pride.

Her flesh burned with the memory of his lovemaking that morning. Her body was awake, alive as it had never been before. She had not imagined it could be so wonderful. She glanced down at Miles's strong slender hands, which had brought her to a state of unbearable excitement. The memory made her warm and weak and fed an aching desire deep within her for more of that bliss. She yearned for him physically; her breasts, her belly newly molded under the powerful touch of his hands. Had Miles suggested at that moment pulling the curricle off the road into the woods and making love to her on a bed of tree boughs, she would have been delighted.

An image of the fat, disgusting Duke of Warfolk came into her mind and she shuddered, half in revulsion, half in fear. The terror that Jefferson's warning about Percy had generated in her yesterday welled up again. The thought that she might yet be dragged back to the duke nauseated her.

She gave a sideways look at Miles and offered up a silent prayer of thanks. Life as Miles's wife would be hard, but she would not be brutalized or degraded.

She might not have a fine house or beautiful clothes, but at least she would not share the plight of so many wives who were the passive recipients of their husband's attentions, which left them at best cold and unsatisfied, and at worst filled with loathing.

However, Miles had no affection for her and pretended none. That was the sad truth. And, Chandra felt, to a great extent this was her fault. In her pride she had done her best to convince him—and herself—of her aversion to him. Had she been more honest, their relationship would surely be on a warmer plane now. In those early days aboard the *Golden Drake,* after all, they had built a companionship that could have formed the firm foundation of a marriage.

But her proud tongue had alienated him. She had no illusion about how deeply she had wounded Miles, and she wondered whether the scar would forever mar their life together.

She stole another surreptitious glance at her husband, wondering it it were possible to win his affection despite all that had passed between them. She must swallow her pride and try. She searched for anything to break the tense wall of silence between them and finally asked, "Shall I meet your family when we arrive at your farm?"

He kept his grim face fixed upon the road as he answered curtly, "My parents are dead. The only family I have is my sister, Ondine, and she lives far away in the Carolinas."

"Does she have children?" Chandra asked, desperately trying to keep the conversation from dying.

"Four."

"Who is her husband?"

Miles turned and looked at her, an odd expression that she could not decipher on his face. "His name is Devin Darcy."

"It's a nice name. Do you get along well?"

Her question seemed to amuse Miles. "My sister and I get along with him splendidly, but he undoubtedly would not meet your exalted standards."

She ignored his sarcasm and, summoning up her courage, she touched his arm. He gave her a sharp, bitter look that very nearly scattered her resolve.

Clutching the side of the curricle seat, she stammered, "I am sorry, Miles, for what I said to you this morning at the inn about . . . about . . . children."

She flinched at the hurt and the pain in his eyes. She would not have believed that her tongue had had the power to inflict such a grievous wound on him.

"But it was what you believed, wasn't it?" he shot back.

She lowered her eyes in confusion. She would not lie to him. "Yes," she began in answer to his question, meaning to explain to him the metamorphosis she had undergone that morning in her thinking about her father's ideas, but she got no further than that one fatal word.

Miles bristled and cut her off. "Spare me your thoughts, madam. I have had quite enough of them already today."

"Please, Miles," she persisted.

"I said I wanted quiet," he snapped, turning away. His hard body was set like a wall against her.

Her courage and her tongue both failed her, and she sank back, totally dejected at his refusal to accept her attempt at reconciliation. Her heart ached. Would the bitter fruit of her pride be Miles's permanent animosity? She had come to care so much for this man who now seemed to hate her.

She was determined to make things right, but it was foolish to press her case now. She would wait until to-night after they had reached his farm and were in bed. By then his fury would have had time to cool, and she would demonstrate to him by her actions as well as her words how much she had come to appreciate him. Yes, it was best to wait. His wound was still raw.

Suddenly Chandra was entranced by a spectacular sight ahead of them: a small village surrounded by dog-wood trees in full bloom, stretching their flowered limbs in great splashes of pink and white against a green background of taller trees. The village was neatly laid out, and its structures ranged from tiny cottages to substantial buildings. Reigning over them all on top of a broad knoll overlooking a river beyond was a magnificent double-fronted mansion with two-story-high colonnaded porticos that reminded Chandra of a Greek temple.

"How beautiful," she murmured. "What is that village called?"

"It is not a village, but a plantation."

"It is extraordinary!" she exclaimed. "But that looks like some great church or temple on top of the hill."

"The owner lives there," Miles said as he slowed the horses.

"You mean all of this belongs to him?" she asked in dazzled surprise. It was by far the grandest plantation she had yet seen.

He nodded, his lips curled in a sardonic smile. "Don't tell me there exists a house in America that could actually meet with your approval?"

"You are being cruel, Miles. Of course, it does. It is spectacular."

"Since you like it so much, I shall give you a closer

look." He turned the curricle off the main road and started it up the drive that led to the complex.

"What is it called?" Chandra asked.

"Willowmere."

She drew in her breath. So this was the Willowmere that had so charmed Fitzhugh Flynn, the Willowmere that Lord William wanted to buy.

The curricle rolled along a winding avenue lined with elms, past small cabins where black children played and flowers bloomed in a profusion of rich colors: the yellow of forsythia and daffodils, the white and blue of hyacinths, the lavender and pink of azaleas. The air was heavy with the perfume of the flowers, and Chandra breathed in the sweetness eagerly.

As they drew near to the mansion, they passed several more buildings, then a formal garden edged in boxwood that rivaled anything she had ever seen in England. If Chandra had been able to create her dream estate, she decided, it would have been Willowmere. She stared at the temple-like house and wondered what it would be like to be its mistress, living in such luxury, presiding over such beauty. She pushed the thought quickly from her mind. She would learn to be content with what Miles could give her and would cease longing for things she could never have.

The avenue of elms ended in a circular drive in front of the mansion, where Miles stopped the curricle.

Chandra, embarrassed by their trespassing, asked nervously, "Shouldn't we go on now? I have seen the house."

"Since you are so interested in Willowmere, you must see it inside as well as out. I am always eager to please my loving bride."

The last was spoken with such sarcasm that Chandra cringed inwardly. Was he trying to embarrass her by invading a place where, by his own admission, he had never been invited? Willowmere's owner, the Marquess of Pelham's nephew, would think them unconsciously rude for such an intrusion.

"We cannot burst in uninvited."

"What worries you, madam? Are you ashamed to be seen with your poor farmer husband?"

"Of course not!"

A surprised look crossed Miles's face at the quickness and force of her response, but he said nothing. He jumped down from the curricle and went round it to help her down.

"No," she cried, shrinking back as he held his arms out to her. "I prefer to remain here until we leave."

His hard, emotionless eyes stared up into hers and he said quietly, "Then you will have a very long wait indeed, for this is your new home."

Chapter 25

Chandra blinked at Miles in astonishment, unable to comprehend his words.

"You mean," she asked finally, "that you are a tenant here?"

"No." His handsome, tanned face was a mask, his voice brusque. "I own it."

As though to confirm his words, the front door opened and a tall woman with an air of authority about her hurried across the portico and down the steps to greet Miles. She was perhaps forty; her lined face was too narrow to have ever been pretty. Her once dark hair was now well sprinkled with gray and was coiled severely around her head. She gave Miles a fond look, not unlike that a mother might bestow on a son after a long absence.

"So you're home." Her voice was totally colorless despite her obvious happiness at seeing Miles. She gave Chandra a curious, sidelong glance. "Young Jim Spenser tells us you took a wife while you were in England."

"So I did, Sarah." Miles nodded at Chandra, who was sitting stiffly in the curricle, frozen by the revelations of the past few moments. "This is my wife, Chandra." To Chandra, he said, "Sarah is the general in command of my house, and you will find her invaluable."

She could manage nothing more than a nod in response. Sarah appraised her critically, and Chandra realized that she, who had made such a point of challenging Miles's background, was now the one whose breeding was being questioned. As her firmest beliefs had been demolished over the past several hours, she wondered uneasily if she measured up to Sarah's expectations.

"I thought young Spenser was joshing when he came riding home with the news that you'd married," the woman said. "His uncle thought he was fooling, too. What a whipping Humphreys gave that poor lad. And Sally's still abed from the shock. I'd told everyone you weren't planning on marrying her, no matter how many wedding invitations she sent out. No one believed me then, but I guess they will now."

A strange smile curled on Miles's lips. "So Sally took the news of my marriage hard, did she?"

Sarah nodded and gave him a quick, sharp look. "Not as hard though, I hear, as Mrs. Keating did."

Miles colored slightly and said nothing.

Sarah's look, coupled with Miles's reaction, told Chandra that Mrs. Keating was surely the mistress Miles had mentioned. She felt instantly jealous at the sound of the other woman's name.

Miles lifted Chandra down from the chaise and, holding her in his arms, he crossed the portico. The feeling of having his arms about her once more made her heart thud wildly. He carried her over the threshold into Willowmere's entry hall and she looked around at its gracefully curving staircase, its floor of marble inlaid in geometric patterns, and its yellow brocade banquettes. She was still in a daze, her thoughts rolling in confusion. This lovely place, which she had looked at so longingly minutes ago, was to be her home.

Miles set her down. "Welcome to Willowmere," he said.

He led her into a huge dining room furnished with French settees and armchairs upholstered in rose damask. Elegant commodes and tables decorated with marquetry and ormolu mounts were scattered about the room.

Chandra was dazzled by the room's splendor. Rose brocade draperies with matching swags and pelmets framed the tall windows, and the white wall panels were decorated with carved, gilded detail. A crystal and bronze chandelier sparkled overhead, and an Aubusson carpet lay beneath Chandra's feet on the polished hardwood of the floor.

Tears welled up in her eyes as her frustration and confusion grew. She felt like such a fool. But how was she to know? How could Miles not have told her the truth?

"Why did you lie to me?" she asked him, her voice quavering. "Why did you torment me with stories of hogs and dirt floors and swaybacked plow horses?"

Miles, who had been watching her closely, seemed to be goaded to renewed fury by her question.

"If you had not been so determined to believe the worst of me, it would have been perfectly obvious to you that I was more than what I said." He held out his well-formed hands with their long, tapering fingers and well-groomed nails. "Are these the work-callused hands of a poor farmer? Were my manners and my conversation those of an ignorant yokel? You would have known immediately that I was not a rustic bumpkin had you not been so prejudiced against me. There are none so blind as those who refuse to see. To you, I was merely one of those dreadful Americans that your father so despised."

Chandra, her cheeks flaming, whispered, "Still, you might have told me."

"Would you have believed me?" Miles asked scornfully. "I don't think so. Even yesterday it never occurred to you to question my station when you saw that I was such a close friend of the president."

He was right, of course. Her mind had simply refused to put the pieces of the puzzle together. But then another question occurred to her. "I thought Willowmere belonged to the Marquess of Pelham's nephew."

"I once told you that you would be shocked if you knew who my paternal grandfather was." Miles's voice dripped with venom. "He was the ninth Marquess of

Pelham, and even you, my haughty snob, must admit the House of Leigh is among England's finest."

Angrily Miles took her elbow and guided her toward the great marble staircase. "You see, madam, despite your diligent efforts to avoid it, you have made a far more impressive marriage than that foolish prig of a father could ever have managed for you in England."

The knowledge that he was right again only increased Chandra's misery. She turned her head away so that he could not see the pain in her face and murmured, "But your name?"

"Carrington is my mother's maiden name. She was the daughter of James Carrington, one of the largest landowners in the colonies."

"Why do you not bear your father's name?"

"If you are asking if I am a bastard, I am not," Miles snapped.

She spun round to face him, a stricken look upon her face. How could he think that was what she had meant?

"My father was disowned by his father," Miles continued, "and came to America, where he worked for a time for grandfather Carrington, who had lost both his sons to a putrid sore throat. My mother was his only child who survived to adulthood. When my parents were married, my father took the Carrington name as his own to preserve it. It was the finest present he could have given to my grandfather."

"You might at least have told me who your ancestors were."

"Why? Because they make me a fit sire for your children? I am the same man with the same character regardless of what I choose to call myself or who my father might have been."

They had reached the top of the stairs, and Miles led her into his bedroom, which was so large that its canopied bed, although huge, was dwarfed. Memories of their lovemaking that morning stirred in Chandra's imagination, and she looked longingly at the big bed with its hangings of pale blue silk that were bordered in the same deep blue velvet that covered the bed itself.

The motif reoccurred at the tall windows where deep pelmets and borders of pale blue drapes were also of matching velvet.

It was a bedchamber unlike any she had ever imagined. There were bombe chests on each side of the bed, a divan and chairs upholstered in white velvet, marquetry tables and chests of satinwood, a secretary of burl and walnut with glass-paneled doors, and a fireplace of white marble, veined with blue.

Miles did not stop here for even a moment. Instead, he abruptly guided her through his room to an adjoining one that seemed austere after the splendor of the last. This room had not been furnished with either the elegance or the care of the other rooms she had seen; it seemed like an afterthought. It had a stuffy, neglected air about it that indicated it was never used. Its bed was considerably narrower than the one in Miles's room, and its hangings were of yellow linen. A rocker, with a mahogany tripod table beside it, a mahogany dressing table with a yellow skirt, and a highboy completed its sparse furnishings.

"My mother never used this bedroom. She would not have dreamed of sleeping anywhere but at my father's side. Therefore, you shall be the first to occupy it unless"—his tone was icy—"you wish to plead to share mine. No doubt you find my bed more appealing and my parental fitness no longer in question now that you know I am the Marquess of Pelham's rich nephew."

Chandra felt as if Miles had physically struck her. The contempt in his voice seared her very soul. If she bowed to him now, she realized with a sinking heart, he would always regard her with scorn and contempt. He would be convinced she was nothing but a shallow, mercenary female delighted at the fine bargain she had unknowingly made. He would never believe the truth— that she had come to realize that day on the road how pathetic her father had been and how much she cared for Miles; that she had wanted to be his wife no matter what his station in life.

If only she had persisted in her apology and her admission of how wrong she had been about him. But she had not, and now it was too late. Much as she longed to share his bed, she dared not tell him, not because she cared for him too little, but because she cared for him too much.

With a breaking heart, she said meekly, "This room will suit me."

Miles gave her a brusque little bow and was gone.

Chapter 26

No longer able to suppress her anguish, Chandra threw herself down on the yellow linen bed cover and buried her head in the pillow to muffle the sound of her sobbing. A knock at the door a few minutes later roused her.

She wiped her eyes hastily. "Who is it?" she called.

"Sarah." The housekeeper entered without waiting to be asked. She was followed by a slender girl of perhaps seventeen with chocolate skin and eyes, who was staring shyly at the floor. The girl carried the seed box that had been stowed beneath the curricle's seat.

"Patty here will be your maid," Sarah said, her face set in guarded, unsmiling lines. "She will help you unpack and dress for dinner." With that, she turned and left the room, shutting the door smartly behind her.

Chandra was embarrassed by her lack of luggage. "I am afraid I have little for you to unpack."

"Ah'll do dis," the girl replied softly, opening the box she was carrying and pulling out a deep maroon velvet gown trimmed with lace at the neck and wrists.

Chandra came over and peered into the box. There were more layers of clothing beneath the velvet dress. "Where did you get this?" she asked Patty in surprise.

The girl stopped in confusion, holding up the maroon gown. "Massa Carrington sez it's yours."

Chandra reached in and pulled out a filmy black nightgown of silk and lace. She held up the lovely garment, wondering bitterly if her husband would ever see her in it. After the nightgown came two morning dresses and two embroidered batiste chemises that rivaled in quality the one Miles had ruined that morning.

She put on the maroon velvet and, feeling less in need of food than of a long, long cry, she went down to dinner.

Miles, who was in the hall talking to a short stocky man, scarcely glanced at Chandra as she appeared. The stranger had a square, serious face and an unruly thatch of straw-colored hair. Chandra guessed his age at about eight and thirty. Miles introduced him as James Dunlop, Willowmere's overseer, and told her he would be staying for dinner.

As Miles led her into the dining room, she whispered, "That was lovely seed you were carrying in that box. Thank you."

Miles shrugged. "Mrs. Hoben and her minions had time to complete only a very few of the things I ordered. The rest should be along in a few weeks."

Chandra remembered the busy flurry at the dressmaker's and the woman's keen interest in her. "You had Percy take me there, didn't you?" she asked incredulously.

"How else was she to get your measurements? She's an excellent dressmaker, but not *that* good," Miles said as he helped Chandra into her chair, which was upholstered with Gobelin tapestry. The one in which she was seated was one of a dozen drawn up around the long mahogany table, which had been set with Meissen china, Ravenscroft crystal, and a gleaming pair of heavy silver candelabra, each holding five tapers.

"What would you have done with all the clothes you ordered if Percy had won your game?" Chandra asked.

"But, as I told you before, I knew that he would not."

During dinner, Miles talked constantly to Dunlop of plantation problems and neighborhood news. Chandra felt quite left out. The dinner was as splendid as its setting: oysters on the half shell, followed by sherried consommé, then baked shad with a roe soufflé. But Chandra had no appetite, and she scarcely touched her portions. Instead she sipped frequently of her wine, which was always immediately replenished by an observant servant hovering in the background.

"How is Fred Humphreys taking my marriage?" Miles asked Dunlop casually.

The overseer choked on a bite of shad and shot a quick, embarrassed glance at Chandra.

"Don't worry," Miles assured him, "we both know about his plot."

"Don't underestimate Humphreys." Concern creased Dunlop's serious face. "He is a dangerous and a desperate man, and as enraged as a wounded boar to have been so humiliated. I fear his first meeting with Mrs. Carrington may be unpleasant."

"Not if I can help it," Miles said, signaling the servants to remove the dishes.

The wine had begun to go to Chandra's head, making her feel giddy and reckless. She found herself wishing that Dunlop would disappear into the night and leave her alone with Miles.

When they finally rose from the table, Miles took Chandra's arm. "I know you are exhausted after our long trip," he said hastily, "and you have my permission to retire." He turned back to Dunlop. "We shall have brandy in the library."

Startled by his abrupt dismissal, she walked silently with them into the hall. The front door was open and Jem, the butler, was talking to a lad of about thirteen who was holding a missive in his right hand.

The boy was saying, "Miz Keatin' tole me ah's to wait for a reply."

As Miles took the sealed, folded sheet from Jem, Chandra spied her husband's name written on it in a graceful feminine hand. Miles broke the seal and a broad smile appeared on his lips as he read the contents. "Tell Kitty yes," he told the waiting boy.

Chandra felt Dunlop stiffen beside her. Her cheeks burned with embarrassment and her mind with envy. What gall the woman had in sending a message to Miles on the very first night he was home with his new bride!

It was outrageous. Chandra was angry, but beneath the anger was fear and, yes, jealousy.

As the butler closed the door after the boy, Miles took Chandra's arm and led her to the staircase. "Goodnight, madam." He relinquished her arm and left her to make her own way up the stairs.

She ascended slowly, her head held high, her pride not permitting her to betray hurt to the two men below.

Did Miles intend to continue his affair with Kitty? Perhaps this was the same question that the woman had asked him in her note, which he had answered with such alacrity. Would he rush to Kitty at the first opportunity tomorrow?

No, Chandra swore to herself, she would prevent it. The wine had erased her inhibitions. She put on the lacy black nightgown, then let down her hair, which cascaded to her waist in rich brown waves.

She hastened into Miles's room, pulled back the velvet cover, and slipped between the cool sheets. Miles would find her there when he came upstairs. The wine had given her the courage she had lacked earlier, and she was determined that tonight Miles would hear her apology and her new understanding of him. She prayed that he would believe her. If only Dunlop would leave quickly, before the bolstering effects of the wine wore off and her courage faded.

A few minutes later she heard a horse departing. Running to the window, she saw the overseer ride away.

She lingered there for a moment. The moon was full and very bright, and a blanket of stars like a million tiny candles sparkled in the sky. The perfume of the hyacinths and jasmine drifted up to her window on the night air. Willowmere lay soft and enchanting in the pale light.

As Chandra stood musing by the window, a groom led another horse up to the house. Miles emerged, mounted and rode off, disappearing into the darkness beyond Willowmere. The sound of his horses's hooves beat like a hammer inside Chandra's disbelieving mind.

Miles was so eager for his mistress that he was hurrying to her on his very first night at home with his bride.

She was engulfed by anguish and rage. How triumphant Kitty must be to snatch back her lover from his new wife so quickly. Tears filled Chandra's eyes as she thought of Miles's icy indifference toward her. He had, after all, married her only to spite his neighbor. He would not have consummated their marriage had she not taunted him into it. How naive she had been! She could never win Miles Carrington's affections by trying to please him or by explaining her newfound self-awareness.

She had nearly made a fool of herself tonight. He wanted only his mistress, of course. He did not want her. Chandra swore to herself that she would never give Miles the satisfaction of knowing that she cared in the slightest whose bed he occupied. Nor would she ever plead for his attentions. She would never humble herself to him now.

But despite her resolution, she could not entirely subdue her longing for him. Even now, as he rode to an assignation with his mistress, Chandra's body still cried out for him. If only once again he would take her to that paradise she had so briefly visited that morning.

It was a long time before she fell into a troubled sleep, exhausted from the long journey and from her tormented emotions.

When she awoke, the sun was already bright in the sky. As she arose, she heard a horse gallop up, and she hastened to the window. It was Miles. He dismounted and tossed the reins carelessly to a waiting groom.

From the look on his face, she was certain he had not spent the night alone in a joyless bed.

Chapter 27

Chandra dressed slowly. She could scarcely bring herself to face the reality of her situation or the servants, whose principal topic of conversation this morning undoubtedly was their master's strange sleeping arrangements. Her fury of the night before had spent itself, leaving a bitter aftertaste of defeat and despair. She told herself that she hated Miles, but then an unsettling thought pricked her. If she truly hated him she would not be so miserable.

When Patty arrived, she was startled to find her mistress dressed and staring out a window at the formal garden with its geometric divisions outlined in boxwood parterres. "Breakfast is waiting for you," the little maid said.

Chandra's stomach churned at the thought of facing Miles. "Please bring me a tray here."

The maid nodded and withdrew. But it was Sarah rather than Patty who arrived a few minutes later. The housekeeper's eyes were hostile as she told Chandra bluntly that Mr. Carrington expected her at breakfast.

Chandra was furious. Did he have to have his servants deliver his orders for him? And why had he insisted she come down? Did he wish to crow about his night's pleasures?

Reluctantly, Chandra went downstairs. To her relief, Miles was not in the dining room, but she still had no appetite. A vast meal was spread on the marble-topped sideboard: bacon, ham, eggs, fish, griddle cakes, and beaten biscuits, as well as a silver pot of steaming coffee and another of tea. There was enough food to feed a regiment. She served herself a few tiny portions, but she could not manage more than a couple of mouthfuls.

She dawdled over her tea, as she had nothing else to do or any idea of what was expected of her when she finished.

Suddenly Miles burst into the room. Chandra yearned to vent her anger at him, yet, looking at the handsome face and the hard muscular body clothed in buckskins and a cambric shirt open at the neck, a lump rose in her throat. Her heart ached as she thought of him with Kitty.

"Come." He pulled impatiently at her chair. "I will give you a tour of Willowmere. It will have to be a quick one, for much has accumulated in my absence that I must attend to."

"I am honored that you could find the time for me."

Miles's left eyebrow raised slightly at her sarcasm, but he let her remark pass. He guided her to a long, open colonnaded passageway that led from the main house to a small building, which she discovered was the kitchen, complete with two fireplaces and a huge assortment of pots and pans. Two young black girls were paring and chopping vegetables at a long table. Miles nodded at them and led her on.

Chandra marveled at the scope of Willowmere. Next to the kitchen was a smokehouse with brick ovens for curing hams and bacon. In addition, there were a dairy, an icehouse, a spring house and a tailor shop. On the other side of the gardens were a blacksmith, a carpenter shop, a coach house, barns for storing tobacco and granaries for corn. At the far end of the complex were the neatly whitewashed cabins where the slaves lived.

Her first impression of Willowmere as a village had not been far off the mark. Among the slaves were blacksmiths to make and repair plows and harrows; sawyers and carpenters to construct and repair the buildings; spinners and weavers to turn the plantation's cotton and flax into cloth; a tanner and a currier to prepare leather, in addition to the less skilled hands who worked the fields.

Then there were the animals. There were stables housing an impressive array of horses, cattle enclosures, a hen coop, a dovecote, and a pigpen.

Miles stopped at the last and nodded at the dozen or so pigs with a grin.

"So you see I am a hog farmer—among other things."

Miles took her arm and led her toward the garden. "By the way, I have received a letter from your friend, Lord Pembroke, addressed to 'Mr. Leigh,' telling me of his close friendship with my uncle, the present Marquess of Pelham, and soliciting an invitation to Willowmere."

"Will you invite him?"

"I shall not even answer his letter."

Miles turned his attention to his vegetable garden, pointing out the rows of carrots, beets, parsnips, turnips, pumpkins, peas, lettuce, lentils, broccoli, kale, eggplant, endive, watermelon and cantaloupe.

As he talked, Chandra forgot his rude comment about the letter. How proud he was of Willowmere! Like a child displaying his most cherished possession. Never had she seen him so enthused before.

They left the garden and walked through an orchard that included apple, peach, cherry and nut trees in its ample acreage. Miles turned to her with a mocking half-smile. "Did you find your bed comfortable last night, my dear?"

"Very," she responded coolly. She forced a false, sweet smile to her lips and said with careful indifference, "I hope Kitty welcomed you back to hers with sufficient warmth to make up for your long absence."

The grin vanished from Miles's face. "I am delighted to learn," he retorted, irony tinging his voice, "that I have not married a jealous wife."

"I assure you that it matters not in the least to me whose bed you occupy so long as it is not mine."

"I am grateful for your kind permission to take my pleasures where I please." Miles's voice was oddly choked, as though he had swallowed something the wrong way.

"And I shall do the same."

"Like hell you will!" His temper exploded with such suddenness and violence that Chandra started. "If you do not desire me that is your affair, but I shall not be cuckolded."

"But you feel free to do the same to me."

"It is different for a man."

His reply fired her own temper. All her life she had been told women could not do things—ride astride, hunt, shoot—because such activities belonged only to men. Only her father had taught her how wrongheaded that attitude was. And in this, at least, he had been right.

"Why is it different?" she demanded. "If you can do it, I can too, and I will."

Her defiant words seemed to push him beyond control. His face contorted with rage and Chandra, thoroughly frightened now, instinctively stepped back from him. His hands shot up and he seized her hair, holding her head so tightly she thought he intended to crush it in his huge hands. He forced her to look into his eyes, which seemed to flame like the fires of hell itself.

"I will have no bastard inherit Willowmere. Should that prospect appear likely, so help me God, I will kill both you and your lover."

Chapter 28

The rest of the day seemed to Chandra to drag on forever. Dinner, a sumptuous spread served at three in the afternoon, broke up the tedious hours.

When Chandra expressed some surprise at the enormous culinary display, Miles curtly told her that in Virginia the main meal was taken at this time and a light supper would be served at eight.

"And don't tell me it is not done this way in England," he said sourly. "I don't give a damn."

The remainder of the meal was a dismal, silent affair. The tension in the room was so heavy that Chandra's head ached violently by the time it was over.

During the next three weeks, she saw Miles only at their agonizing meals. She could scarcely choke down a few bites of the food and she began to lose weight. Each night after supper, her husband rode away and did not return until morning.

Chandra was without function or position at Willowmere. She was not needed and not wanted by Miles, and Sarah ran the house. Kitty obviously sated the needs Chandra might have satisfied in the marriage bed. Despite her protestation that she cared not where Miles took his pleasure, Chandra quickly came to realize that she cared very much, indeed. There was no more bitter sound to her ears than that of Miles's horse riding away each night. Chandra was wildly jealous of Kitty Keating.

She spent most of her time in her room, poking disinterestedly at her needlepoint or trying to read a book from Miles's vast library.

One afternoon when the humidity hung like a stifling curtain beneath the hot sun, Chandra made up her mind not to come down to dinner. She simply could not tolerate the hostility in his face as he sat across from her at the table.

When Chandra did not appear in the dining room, Miles came up to get her. "What do you find so attractive about this room that you refuse to leave it?"

"Do you think I enjoy it here? I stay here because I have nothing else to do."

"Nothing except thinking up ways to disrupt my household, demanding your meals on a tray in your room as though you were a chair-bound invalid."

"I did not ask for a tray."

"What do you plan to do, go hungry?"

She nodded. "I could not eat if I came to the table."

His face set in a grim forbidding mask. "So now the quality of my table does not suit your tastes, my haughty bride. What is it you find so inferior about it?"

She looked at him wearily, wondering why their conversations always seemed to provoke such misunderstandings. "The food is delicious."

"Then what the hell is the matter?"

When she did not answer, he swept her up in his arms and headed toward the door. "You shall come to the table when meals are served if I have to carry you down each time and tie you to the chair."

He held her roughly, expecting her to fight him. Instead she buried her face in his shoulder and pleaded in a tiny, misery-filled voice, "Please, Miles, I beg of you. Don't make me go down."

Her quick tears dampened his shirt, and he sat down on the bed with her. He turned her face to his.

"Why are you crying?"

"Can't you understand that I cannot eat when there is so much tension between us at the table?" She brushed at her tears. "We sit there in that terrible silence, like two strangers. My stomach churns and the sight of food makes me ill."

"I have not noticed you making any attempt to alleviate the situation."

"A conversation can only take place between two people."

With an oath of exasperation, Miles said, "You gave me no indication that you wished to converse with me."

He pulled his handkerchief from his pocket and wiped away her tears. It reminded her of that day she had first met him by the fallen oak near Blackstone Abbey. Then he had finished his ministrations by kissing her, and she found herself hoping that he would do the same now. But instead he merely set her upon her feet and, offering her his arm, he said gently, "Will you join me for dinner now, my sweet? I promise that I shall try to be better company, and I hope that you will do the same."

She nodded and took his arm. This time, she swore to herself, there would be no misunderstandings.

When they were seated at the table, Miles looked across at her with a teasing gleam in his eyes. "I have been amazed, my dear, that I have not been besieged by requests from you to redecorate. I thought women loved nothing better than turning houses upside down and putting their own stamp upon them."

"Why should I want to change perfection?" she asked.

Miles smiled, obviously pleased by her compliment. "There is no improvement, then, that you would like?"

She studied him for a moment, then with an impish grin playing at the corners of her mouth she said innocently, "Well, perhaps three small things."

"What are they?" Miles asked suspiciously.

"Perhaps a bit of glass for the windows, wood for the floors, and a ride on the swaybacked plow horse of yours if you could spare him," she teased.

He laughed, that wondrous low, rich laugh. "How long it has been since I have heard you laugh, and how nice it is," she told him.

"And how pleased I am that you are giving me reason for mirth for a change," he said seriously. Then his tone lightened. "I had a letter from Tom today. He has invited us back to visit him in Washington when I have the time."

Chandra's face lit up at the prospect of seeing Jefferson again. "Can we go?" she asked.

"So you like the thought of revisiting the president's house?" Miles commented.

"It is not the house, but its occupant. He is a charming and fascinating man."

"Even if he did author that infamous Declaration of Independence?" Miles asked drily.

Chandra blushed. "I have since read it. I found a copy in your library, and I can find no fault with it or with its author."

Miles gave her a long, searching look. "That pleases me," he said quietly.

Although the meal still had several strained and awkward moments, all in all it was by far the most pleasant that Chandra had yet had at Willowmere.

Supper that night continued on the same improved note. When they had finished, Chandra, unwilling to lose Miles's attention, challenged him to a game of chess. Obviously surprised, he agreed, and they settled over a board in the library. She strove to play at the top of her ability, not because she wished to defeat him, but because she wanted the game to be difficult enough to hold his interest. In the end, using every bit of her concentration, she won, and she hoped it was due to her skill.

She could not help but wonder whether he had let her do so, but when she asked him outright, he only laughed and said wryly, "You play a better game than you think, my pet." His voice grew thoughtful. "A much better game."

He took her arm and escorted her upstairs, the first time since he had arrived at Willowmere that he had done so. Her heart beat with excitement, but he led her directly to her room. He did not tarry but went into his own, shutting the door behind him.

Chandra swallowed hard in disappointment. At least, he had gone to his room instead of to Kitty. That was some progress. As she undressed, she wondered what it would take to win him back entirely. Perhaps tomorrow she . . . But her heart sank when she heard the sound of a horse outside her window. Jumping up, she got there just in time to see Miles's great bay carry him away in the moonlight.

Her heart heavy with disappointment, she turned back to her bed. At least, she thought, I made him keep that woman waiting tonight. And tomorrow night I may succeed in my goal.

The next morning, when Chandra came down the stairs to breakfast, Sarah's querulous voice drifted up to her from the dining room.

"She is not a fit wife for you, Miles. You need a woman like your mama or sister. Even Sally Humphreys, and lord knows I think little enough of her, would have made you a better wife. At least she . . ."

"Sarah," Miles cut her off sharply. Then his voice dropped, and Chandra, although she strained to hear, could not make out what he said. How dare that meddling servant talk so about her mistress! Miles should fire her for her impertinence, Chandra thought bitterly.

As she reached the bottom of the stairs, she heard Miles say, "I will wager you fifty dollars against that old thimble of your mother's that within a year you will agree with what I have said about Mrs. Carrington."

"That woman has turned you into a greater fool than I thought," Sarah scoffed. "You used to be a smart gambler."

Sarah came into the hall, wearing the black bombazine gown of severe cut and long-outmoded style that seemed to be her uniform. When she saw Chandra standing near the foot of the stairs, she gave her a long, cold look. Then she turned and walked toward the back of the house. It was obvious that Sarah was pleased, rather than discomforted, that her new mistress had overheard her speaking to Miles in such derogatory terms. Once again, it was clear to Chandra that Sarah was more mistress here than she was.

As Chandra entered the dining room, Miles was helping himself to a large serving of eggs, bacon, ham and beaten biscuits. She took a plate and began to put more delicate portions of food on it from the platters on the sideboard. "I hear you are becoming a most reckless gambler," she remarked casually.

Miles frowned. "So you overheard my bet with Sarah?"

She shook her head. "Only the sum wagered. You give most generous odds. I want to know what I must do to save you from losing fifty dollars."

Miles's frown gave way to a grin. "I dare not tell you. You might make certain I lose."

"What little trust you have in your wife," she said, as she sat down across from him. "Tell me, why does Sarah dislike me so?"

"You have failed to win her respect. If you win that, her affection will follow. I fear, at the moment, she finds it difficult to appreciate your charms."

"No more than you do," she retorted tartly.

His eyebrows raised. "I am not unappreciative of your charms, my sweet. 'Tis your tongue that strains my temper."

"Sometimes with good reason, I must admit."

His fork stopped halfway to his mouth and he lowered it to his plate as he stared at her in surprise.

Jem appeared in the doorway to announce a visitor, Ben Dickson.

"How strange," Miles said in surprise. "Show him in, Jem.

"Dickson lives near Norfolk, a considerable distance from here," he told Chandra after Jem left the room. "I cannot imagine what would bring him this far to see me." Miles smiled. "It's hard to say which Ben likes to do more, eat or talk, but he's a good-hearted soul, even if he is something of a worrier."

Just then, Dickson came through the door of the dining room. His girth readily attested to Miles's statement about his love for food. He was a roly-poly little man with a bald head and a cherubic face that today looked decidedly worried.

"What brings you here, Ben?" Miles asked, as Chandra poured coffee for him. To their surprise, he had declined the offer of breakfast.

The worried frown settled deeper. "You might say I'm delivering a message, a very strange message. It happened more than a fortnight ago, and it's been bothering me ever since." Dickson stirred a generous amount of cream into his coffee. "At first, I was going to write you about it but now, with the pirates and all, I thought I had better ride over and tell you."

The cherubic face was apologetic as he turned to Chandra. "Do you have a cousin named Percival Lunt?" he asked.

Chandra stiffened. "Yes," she replied apprehensively. What could Percy have done now?

Dickson looked relieved. "Then perhaps 'tis nothing after all. But what with the pirates and all, one can't blame a body for being nervous when a stranger asks all the questions that he did."

"Who are these pirates you talk about?" Miles asked.

Dickson's face wore an expression of amazement. "You haven't heard of them? Why, they're the talk of the coast. They're English apparently, and they've been the scourge of the Carolinas for the past two months. They started out with one ship, the *Black Wind*. Now a second's joined it, and one of the pirates was overheard to say a third ship was on its way."

Dickson cast a hungry glance at the heaping plate of biscuits on the table. "Perhaps I'll just have one biscuit to go with my coffee."

As Miles passed the plate, Dickson went on, "As I was saying, those two ships have played havoc with our merchant vessels. At least a dozen have been seized, practically in sight of the coast. All right if I take two?"

Dickson was smearing the biscuits with a thick frosting of butter. "It's not just ships they're after, either.

They've hit a number of coastal plantations as well. And they are brutal beyond belief, torturing the men and forcing them to watch while, one by one, they rape the women. Then they put the buildings to the torch. They seem as bent on terrorizing their victims as on robbing them." Dickson piled marmalade on both his biscuits. "I tell you there is a terrible hue and cry along the coast about how Jefferson and the government are doing nothing to protect the people from these brigands."

"Let's hope they stay in the Carolinas," Miles said grimly.

"But they haven't. Last week, they hit a plantation on the James River, burned it and tortured the people. And they say the pirates knew the layout of that plantation exactly and where all the valuables were hidden, as if they had inside information. So you can see why I got uneasy about Lunt after all the questions he asked."

"Where did you meet him?" Miles gave Chandra a nervous glance.

"On a boat going down the Potomac from Washington. I'd been there on business, you see. Lunt asked me if I'd ever heard of you, Miles. Said he'd heard you'd married a cousin of his that he was particularly fond of. He seemed to be under the impression that you were some kind of hog farmer. I tell you I set him straight quick enough on that ridiculous notion," Dickson said indignantly. He cast an envious glance at Chandra's plate. "My, those eggs do look good. Perhaps I'll just have a taste."

Miles nodded at the servant hovering behind them, and he brought Dixon the silver-covered platter from the sideboard.

Dickson helped himself to a generous portion. "You would have thought that Lunt would have been pleased when I told him you were probably the richest planter in Virginia and the owner of the famous Willowmere. But instead of being happy that his cousin had married so well, he cursed you, Miles, called you . . ." Dickson stopped, shot an embarrassed look at Chandra, and said lamely, "He, ah, questioned your parentage. Then he wanted to know exactly where Willowmere was located and just how one got here. Said he wanted to visit his dear cousin before he had to leave for England in a few days."

Chandra sat staring into her plate. She felt as though something inside her had snapped.

"Perhaps I'll have just a bit of ham to go with my eggs. It smells so good," Dickson said, looking longingly at the sideboard.

Miles signaled to the servant, who brought over the platter. Dickson took large slices, then continued, "That was when I first got on the boat. Lunt had a flask on him, and I tell you he made some heavy indentures while we were en route."

He took a sip of his coffee. "The odd part was after we docked in Norfolk, and I found Lunt getting on a ship sailing that very day for England. That's when I got suspicious. I tell you I marched right up to him and asked him why he'd lied about going to Willowmere. That's when he gave me the message."

"What message?" Miles demanded.

"He laughed drunkenly in my face and said—his voice was very slurred—'The next time you see that . . . Miles Carrington, tell him that the duke will be most pleased to hear about his prize.' "

The color drained from Chandra's face, and she bit her lip to keep from crying out. Jefferson's fears were confirmed. The duke's cruel face loomed in her mind, and she was suddenly sick to her stomach. She jumped up from the table, choking and swallowing hard. "Please excuse me. I am not well." She fled from the room.

Miles jumped up after her. "You must excuse me, too, Ben. Just a moment."

Dickson nodded placidly, guessing the cause of Mrs. Carrington's sickness. "I hope it's a boy," he called after Miles, who had run up the stairs after Chandra.

He found her sitting ashen-faced on her bed, having already disposed of her breakfast.

He took her icy hands into his. "Chandra, I promise

you I will never let you be dragged back to Warfolk. Trust me."

She looked at him sadly. She wanted to believe him, but what could he or anyone do against the power of that hideous man? His long, terrible arm had reached to India to destroy Lord Lunt's son!

Miles drew her to him and held her comfortingly, silently, for a long time, stroking her hair.

Finally, he said, "I should have simply paid off Percy's debt to Murchison. I thought of doing that, but I knew if I did, it would be only a week or two before he was in as much trouble as before, and I would have to bail him out again. There would have been no end to his demands on me, you see. I felt the simplest solution was to have him returned to England. I was wrong."

Chandra felt her husband's muscles tighten as he held her. "It never occurred to me that Percy, unscrupulous as he is, could be so vile and low as to go to the duke."

After a while, he released her. "I left our guest most abruptly. I had better go back down to him," he said regretfully.

Dickson evidently understood that the couple wished to be alone, for he made his apologies and left at once. After he had seen his guest to the door, Miles went back up the stairs to Chandra's room. "Come, my sweet, walk down to the stables with me," he said briskly. "I have something to show you."

Numbly, she allowed him to lead her from the house. They walked for several minutes in silence until they reached the stables. The something Miles wanted to show her was a beautiful Arabian gelding that brought a cry of appreciation to her lips.

"I have no use for this poor, old, broken-down plow horse," Miles said with a grin, "so I thought I'd let you have him."

"Oh, Miles," she cried, her troubles momentarily forgotten in her excitement. "He's beautiful. Thank you. What is his name?"

"Gray Dancer. Would you like to try him now?"

She looked at her husband with a curious expression

on her face. She had no riding habit, nothing to wear except the man's pants and shirt that she had stuffed into the corner of her portmanteau when she had fled England. When she told Miles her plight, he smiled. "So wear them," he said carelessly.

"I won't embarrass you?"

"I shall be delighted to see you in that costume again. After all, it's what first attracted me to you."

She blushed as she remembered their first meeting— and their first kiss.

When she had changed, Miles mounted his own horse and they started out to cover the length and breadth of Willowmere. They rode for more than an hour without ever leaving the plantation's boundaries. Chandra marveled at its size and noted with pride how neatly cultivated and productive its fields were in contrast to some of those that they had passed on the journey from Washington. At Willowmere, no broom sedge spread its yellow warning of exhausted soil across the fields.

When she commented on this, Miles told her how many of his neighbors had initially laughed at his theories of crop rotation and fertilization. Now, however, those techniques were paying rich dividends, and his debt-ridden neighbors looked on with envy.

"That's what happened to Fred Humphreys," Miles explained. "His fields no longer support him in the manner to which he was accustomed, and he did not scale down his way of life to match his diminished purse."

"What will happen to him?"

Miles shrugged indifferently. "His mortgages are being foreclosed and he will lose Dana Grove. I suppose he could always try to start afresh on the frontier, but frankly I think he is far too soft in both body and spirit to succeed."

Miles pointed to the west. "Humphreys' plantation lies over there. The land bordering Willowmere on the north belongs to Howard Haughton. You'll like his wife, Martha, I think. She's an intelligent, sensible woman, and was a good friend of my sister, Ondine."

They spent another half hour touring the land before

starting back to the stable. Chandra felt a kind of lightness as she rode along next to her husband. She felt protected, safe with him. When they returned, Chandra asked eagerly, her eyes aglow, "Can we ride again?"

"Of course. And if you wish to ride when I am busy, Tam will have a groom accompany you."

"I don't need a groom," she protested as she dismounted.

"It isn't wise for you to ride alone, my sweet," Miles said gravely.

Chandra realized he was thinking of the duke, and she shivered as if a cold wind had suddenly begun to blow.

Part Five

Chandra's spirits were lifted by the compliment, and she turned to find a woman of perhaps forty in a pink lutestring gown. The newcomer had a warm, generous smile that seemed to embrace not merely her lips but her entire face, and Chandra found herself immediately

Chapter 29

Percival Lunt drained the little wine remaining into his glass and called for another bottle of claret. He took a gulp and wiped his mouth with the back of his hand. Even the wine in this second-rate London gambling hole was inferior. He was still burning with indignation that he had been denied entrance to two of the more reputable gaming houses in St. James for lack of a card.

"But I am Percival Lunt, heir of Lord Lunt," he had insisted as the hard-faced man tending the door of the second establishment began to turn him away.

"I don't care if you be Prinny himself," the man had replied. "Without a card, you don't come in here."

Percy was livid. This had never happened to him before. He wondered uneasily—although it had been only three hours earlier that Lord Lunt had disowned him—if word of his uncle's action had already gotten around. That wasn't possible, of course.

He had finally gained entry at this seedy establishment where the dealer at the faro table had suspiciously quick wrists. He lost the little cash he had within a matter of minutes, whereupon he sat back, drinking sullenly and watching the room's fifteen or so occupants crowded around the faro table.

The gamblers gathered round the table were all men except for an aging dowager and a pretty, black-haired woman in a red empire gown that was daring both in its low décolletage and in the translucency of its fabric, which clearly revealed the woman's handsome form. Her gown, Percy noted, was attracting greater, if more oblique attention, than the cards, as the other gamblers kept stealing sidelong glances at her.

Percy did not share their interest. The only woman who had ever fascinated him was Lady Luck and, Percy thought sourly, today she had treated him most cruelly.

He drained his glass greedily, as if the claret could wash away the bitter memory of Lord Lunt's denunciation. Instead of a proper welcome after Percy's long absence in America, the puritanical old skinflint had greeted him with a furious tirade about how America had been Percy's last chance to straighten himself out and stop gambling.

"You have thrown that chance away just as you have thrown away half my fortune at the gaming tables!" Lord Lunt had thundered. "I am taking the only possible action: I am disinheriting you. Now get out."

"You can't turn me out," Percy had whined. "I have no money."

"That is solely your concern," his lordship had snapped, turning on his heel and stalking out.

Percy picked up the empty claret bottle and looked around the room for the waiter. Where the hell was he? Damn, it was all that bastard Miles Carrington's fault, he thought. It had been Carrington who had sent Percy back to England—to disinheritance.

Talk about skinflints, that Carrington headed the pack. When that fat little fool on the boat, Dickerson or whatever his name was, had said Carrington was the richest planter in Virginia, he had exploded in rage. Why, he could have paid the debt owed to Murchison and not missed a halfpenny of it. How pleased Carrington must have been with himself. He'd gotten Chandra, and it hadn't cost him a cent.

Well, he wouldn't feel so smug when he heard the duke might take his prize away.

"Percival Lunt," a voice came from the doorway. Looking around, Percy nearly groaned aloud his dismay at the sight of Archibald Platt bearing down on him. Just his luck, Percy thought, to run into the biggest gossip in London his first day back.

"I thought it was you," Platt said as he reached Percy's side. Platt, who fancied himself a dandy of the first stare, wore a wine velvet coat and an enormous, intricately folded neckcloth that must have taken his valet an hour to arrange. "When did you get back from America, Percy?"

"This afternoon."

Platt raised an inquisitive eyebrow. "And at the tables already?"

"Just having a drink at the moment," Percy replied airily as the waiter returned with the new bottle of claret and removed the empty one.

"But in a place like this?"

"I was wondering myself what you were doing here," Percy parried.

"Came to see Lord Riverton's latest lightskirt." Platt nodded at the woman in the translucent gown. "Heard she gambled here. Quite a looker, isn't she?"

Percy drank down the claret and poured himself another glass.

"I suppose your uncle was overjoyed to have you home," Platt said with a distinct sniff as he fluffed up the lace at his wrists.

"Delighted," Percy replied. He was not about to tell this gossiping fool the truth. Platt would have that choice bit of news all over London within ten minutes.

"Say, isn't Lord Lunt's sister the one who jilted the Duke of Warfolk?"

"That was more than twenty years ago," Percy said brusquely, taking another long gulp from his glass. What did this ass know about it?

"But there's a postscript to the story, don't you know?" Platt lowered his voice to a more intimate level. "Seems her daughter's guardian promised the girl to Warfolk for his mistress, but the girl flew. Can't blame her. The stories about how Warfolk treats women would curl your hair. They say the duke's rage was so great when he learned of her flight that the walls of his palace actually shook. He's offering a huge reward for her return. So's the guardian, who is presently residing in

Newgate prison, where the duke had him thrown on some trumped-up charge. People say it serves him right for selling his ward off to Warfolk like that."

Platt broke off as Percy nearly knocked over the bottle's rapidly diminishing contents in his haste to pour another glass. "I say there, Percy, dipping pretty deep, aren't you?" Platt said, looking at the man's bloodshot eyes.

Percy glared at him. Damned old gossip sounded as sanctimonious as Lord Lunt. "What business is it of yours?"

"None, I'm sure," the insulted Platt replied. "I won't keep you, then," he said and quickly took his leave.

Percy slumped in his chair and stared morosely at his glass. So Warfolk had had Henry Taylor tossed into Newgate. What would he do to Percy if he found out Chandra had gone running to him? On the other hand, Percy thought, brightening, what would the duke do *for* him if he told His Grace how to find her. A rich reward, Platt had said. And Warfolk was a powerful man. It wouldn't hurt at all to have him indebted to Percy. The duke could do a great deal for him. He'd go to Warfolk this very minute, Percy decided, staggering up from his chair.

By the time he reached the duke's mansion, not far from Carleton House, his dreams had taken form. He might collect not only the rich reward but a fat sincere thank-you as well from the grateful duke.

Percy was left to cool his heels for some minutes in a small anteroom and he planned carefully just how he would impart his information. He wouldn't give it all away at once, but would drop hints. When he was assured that he would be well paid for his pains, then he would tell the whole story. At last, just when he was starting to nod off, a servant came and he was led up the stairs to the ducal presence.

His first glimpse of Warfolk was staggering. He was the fattest, grossest creature that Percy had ever laid eyes on. He must have weighed fifty stone, and those cruel eyes! No wonder, Percy thought, Chandra had been so desperate to escape him.

The duke's many chins trembled as he intoned, "You know where Chandra Taylor is." It was not a question, but a statement.

"Yes, Your Grace."

"Where?" Warfolk delivered the word like a bullet.

"I, I think we should discuss the reward you're offering," Percy said nervously, beginning to wish he had never come.

"I'll do the thinking, you impertinent puppy, and if you don't speak up quickly, you'll get your just desserts instead of a reward."

Percy was sweating now. This conversation was not going at all as he had imagined it. "She's fled to the United States. She's married to a rich Virginia planter named Miles Carrington."

"Where do they live?"

"On a plantation called Willowmere on the banks of the Rappahannock River."

An evil smile spread across the duke's face. "Yes, I know of Willowmere. How convenient. I have an agent in America already, who can see to her return."

"An agent?" Percy blurted out.

"Curiosity is a dangerous vice," the duke snarled.

"Yes, Your Grace." There was a moment's silence. "My reward, Your Grace?" Percy ventured at last.

"You'll get it when she's returned to me," the duke said as he rang for a servant to escort Percy out.

"But I can't wait until then," Percy cried in a panic.

"You'll wait. Now get out of here." The duke turned to the servant who had answered the bell, "Show him down the back stairs. I don't want swine like him going out my front door."

Thoroughly frightened, Percy followed the servant down the back stairs and nearly collided with a rough-looking man on his way up.

The back stairs, Percy thought. Another insult.

* * *

Captain George Mondello didn't care in the slightest how he entered the mansion of the duke. He was impressed just to be in the house of such a swell. Apparently the back stairs were used frequently for visitors, Mondello thought, as he nearly bumped into a pale, thin young man being led down them. Mondello's long years as a sea captain and as a pirate had taught him to sum up a man quickly. He pegged this one with the badly bloodshot eyes immediately for a whining weakling. Wouldn't last two days in a sailor's berth, he wouldn't.

As Mondello reached the duke's door, he tugged at his simple black coat. He'd heard some unsettling things about his new patron, whom he was about to meet for the first time, but he certainly couldn't fault his generosity. Not only had he financed construction of the *Black Grace,* which promised to be the fastest, sweetest pirate ship that ever sailed, but he was taking only one quarter instead of the customary half of the profits from the booty. Not that Mondello planned to tell his men of the duke's generosity. He'd pocket it himself. Still, he couldn't help but wonder why a man as rich and powerful as Warfolk was dabbling in piracy at all. And Mondello didn't much like the idea of raiding plantations. He'd have to talk to the old boy about that.

Mondello strode through the door and faced the duke. He had seen some bad-looking men in his business, but nothing quite like this.

"Mondello, the *Black Grace* sails tomorrow," the duke said, wasting no time on preliminaries. "I hope everything is in order."

"Yes, Your Grace," Mondello murmured.

"And in return for my generosity toward you," Warfolk went on, ignoring the interruption, "I require absolute obedience to the orders that I and my agent in America give you. As you know, you will be on one of three ships. The other two are already there plying their trade. Keep in mind that the most important thing is the plantations. I've told you what must be done."

"But, Your Grace," Mondello protested, "why bother

with raiding plantations? There is far richer plunder in the merchant ships."

"You fool." The look in the duke's eyes cowed even as hardened a brigand as Mondello. "I am not in the slightest interested in plunder. That's why my terms to you are so generous. I am interested in creating terror, in stirring up dissension among the rich plantation owners against their government. That's why I want them tortured and their women raped by each and every member of your crew. Their plantations must be burned to the ground. Do you understand?"

Mondello nodded.

"My agent in America," the duke went on, "knows more fully what is expected. His instructions will be passed along to you through Captain Flint of the *Black Wind*."

"Who is this agent?"

"That is my secret."

"I don't much like taking orders from a man whose identity I don't even know," Mondello protested.

"I don't care what you like," the duke snapped. "He's far too valuable to have his neck stretched at the end of a rope should one of you be captured and decide to divulge his identity in exchange for your life. This way you will have no valuable information to give away. Even Captain Flint doesn't know his real name. Of course," he said, turning toward the window in obvious disgust, "if you don't like the terms, I'll find another captain."

Mondello saw his rich prize slipping away. "No, Your Grace, they're acceptable."

"Good. Now I have a message for you to deliver to Captain Flint for my agent. There is a woman in America that is to be brought back to me. Her name is Chandra Carrington, and she is married to the owner of a plantation called Willomere. My agent is already familiar with its location. As one of the richest plantations in America, it is a prime target."

The duke handed Mondello a miniature picture of Chandra from the small table beside his chair. "This is the woman. Have Captain Flint tell my agent that no matter what else you accomplish, that woman is to be brought to me."

Mondello stared down at the portrait in his hand. What a beautiful creature she was. "What if . . . ?" he began.

"You will bring her." The look the duke gave Mondello was cruel, nearly inhuman. "If you fail, none of you will ever dare set foot in England again."

Chapter 30

Meals at Willowmere were now lively affairs between Chandra and Miles. Their discussions ranged over a wide variety of subjects and were punctuated with much laughter. In fact, they were reminiscent of those that they had enjoyed during their first weeks aboard the *Golden Drake*. Chandra now found herself eager for mealtime and the opportunity it afforded to be with Miles.

But still, her heart was gravely troubled. First, of course, was her terror that Warfolk could somehow force her back across the sea to him, if Percy had indeed alerted him of her whereabouts.

The second thing on her mind was Miles. Although he was personable and considerate, he made no attempt to exert his marital rights. Instead, to Chandra's anguish, he rode away from Willomere each night and did not return until morning.

She was very confused. It was clear to her now that Miles was true to his word. If ever he were to be her husband in more than name, she would have to beg for his attentions. But she was not at all certain even if she did this what the outcome would be. Not when he continued to spend his nights with Kitty.

So Chandra hesitated, held back by her pride and her uncertainty. Despite her pique at Miles's nocturnal forays, however, she gave no outward sign that they displeased her—or even that she was aware of them. She knew that acting like a jealous shrew would likely destroy the fragile relationship that she was nurturing with her husband. And at least, Chandra told herself, although they were not yet lovers, they were becoming friends.

On the day before the Stratfords' ball, more than a month after her arrival at Willomere, two trunks arrived from Mrs. Hoben's and were placed in Chandra's dressing room. She was astonished at the richness of their contents. Each was piled high with elegant gowns and other expensive garments and accessories.

As Miles watched, Chandra slowly pulled gown after gown out, her face aglow with pleasure like a child's on Christmas morning. She was dazzled by the array of silks, satins, brocades and muslins that Miles had purchased for her. Although the items themselves were wonderful, she was really more reassured by her husband's largess. Surely he would not have bought all these lovely things if he did not care at all for her, and the hope in her heart grew stronger.

"You have been far too generous," she told him as she lovingly fingered the skirt of a pink brocade gown. "Where shall I wear them all?"

"Here, of course." The softness in his eyes moved her as much as his generosity. "My reward will be seeing you in them."

"Did you choose them all yourself?"

He nodded, grinning broadly. "I created quite a sensation at Mrs. Hoben's."

She could well imagine he had and wished she might have seen the spectacle of him surrounded by swatches and sketches. "Your taste, sir, is superb."

"From you, my dear, that is a grand compliment. Which will you wear to the Stratfords' ball tomorrow?"

Chandra picked up a frothy confection of lilac silk and lace, embroidered with pearls. It was a gown a queen would have envied. "This—if it meets with your approval."

"My choice exactly." He rose and started for the door. "I must be off. I was supposed to have met Howard Haughton and John Dunlop half an hour ago.

We are going down river to look over some stock for sale."

He turned away but she came around and intercepted him. Looking earnestly into his hazel eyes, she said, "Thank you for everything, Miles. You have been so good to me." Impulsively, she reached up, pulled his head down, and kissed him. The touch of their lips seemed to electrify them both, and suddenly she was clinging to him, kissing him passionately.

He drew back, it seemed to her reluctantly, and tilted her chin up. Staring down into her sea blue eyes, he asked gently, "What is it you want, my sweet? I want to know."

Emboldened by his tenderness, her arms still encircling him as though to emphasize her words, she cried, "I want you, Miles. I want you so much." The words spilled out almost before she realized what she was saying, and she bit her lip. She had laid her heart bare before him.

But in an instant her doubt was dissolved by the warmth of his lips on hers. He returned her kiss with an intensity that left her breathless. His skillful hands caressed her face and teased her breasts. His touch filled her with pleasure, and she gave a tiny moan of delight as his eager lips moved down to her neck and then even lower.

Suddenly Sarah's voice cut the air like a sharp knife: "Mr. Haughton and Mr. Dunlop are waiting downstairs for you, Miles."

Instead of retreating after delivering her message, Sarah remained in the doorway, surveying the Carringtons with a cold eye.

Chandra's cheeks flamed with embarrassment while Miles cursed Sarah under his breath.

"Later, my love," he promised in Chandra's ear. "I shall be home as early as I can tonight."

The day seemed to drag on forever. As evening approached, Chandra found herself glancing eagerly out the window every other minute to see if Miles was yet in sight. Even the threat of the duke, never far from her mind these past few days, receded before her impatience for her husband's return.

Finally she saw him in the distance on his big bay, accompanied by Dunlop. Her body trembled at the thought of what would surely pass between them that night. Remembrances of their first time passed through her mind—it was as if she could actually feel his hands on her again just by thinking of him.

When Miles and his companion were only a few hundred yards from the house, a black boy emerged from a clump of trees where he had obviously been waiting and stopped them. Chandra recognized the boy. He was the young slave that Kitty Keating had sent on their first night at Willomere.

The boy and Miles talked, then Dunlop resumed riding toward the mansion while Miles turned his horse in the direction of the woods that lay to the southwest, the same path he took each night to meet Kitty.

Chandra watched him in horrified disbelief, her happiness crumbling into pain and anger. She ran to her wardrobe and hastily changed into her shirt and riding pants, then raced downstairs.

As she rushed out the front door, she nearly collided with Dunlop. The surprised overseer stared at her. He could see the fury in her eyes. "Mr. Carrington bid me tell you he would be somewhat later than he thought, but will be home as soon as he can," he stuttered nervously, but she rushed past without bothering to reply.

So Miles was so eager to taste his wife's charms that at the merest nod from his mistress he stopped for a romp with her!

Chandra caught up with the slave who was leading Dunlop's horse away, snatched the reins from the astonished man's hands, and flung herself on the mount, digging in with her heels to spur him on. The surprised animal responded by breaking into a gallop, and horse and rider quickly reached the woods into which Miles had vanished.

Chandra reined in the horse and moved more slowly along a path that led through the trees. Suddenly she reached a clearing where a small, neat brick cottage nestled amid towering pines. She was puzzled. The house must be on Willowmere land, but Miles had never shown it to her during their rides, nor had he ever mentioned it.

She stared transfixed for a second, then wheeled around in despair, her heart feeling as though it would surely break. She could not bear to gaze upon the scene in the cottage, and she turned her back, her mind besieged with pain and outrage. Her first impulse was to rush into the house and tear the adulterous couple apart. But doing so would only result in her own humiliation. Miles had always preferred his mistress to his wife, so Chandra would accomplish nothing by confronting him now, but to have him confirm that fact in front of her rival.

With a sob, Chandra turned and fled to her horse. She mounted and pushed it blindly onto the path toward Willowmere, tears streaming down her cheeks as she remembered Miles's promise to her that morning. *Later,* he had said, but later meant only when he had nothing more enticing, such as Kitty, to occupy him. This was, indeed, a marriage of convenience, she thought bitterly—his convenience. She hated him for toying with her.

"He has no affection for me," she raged. "Why can I not remember that I am merely a prize won in a card game!"

When she reached Willowmere, she ran blindly past Sarah and up the stairs to her room, where she slammed the door shut and threw herself upon her bed, wishing with all her heart that she would die.

Chapter 31

Miles galloped back to Willomere, chafing at the delay that had kept him from Chandra. The scene with Kitty had been most distasteful, although he believed he had at last convinced her that their affair was over.

He had not seen his mistress since the night of his return to Willowmere with Chandra, and that time had been sheer disaster. He would not have gone to her then except for his rage at Chandra's challenging his parental worthiness and then rejecting his bed. By the time Kitty's invitation to meet him had arrived, he had been half out of his mind with anger and frustration and had seized upon it.

But that homecoming night had only worsened his plight. Although Kitty had eased the ache in his loins, she had done nothing to relieve the pain in his heart. He had discovered then that after having tasted Chandra, his appetite was spoiled for any other woman. Even as he had lain beside Kitty, Chandra had haunted him, and he had realized to his dismay that it was she—and only she—that he wanted. Without trying, she had won him totally and forever.

He had told Kitty then that their affair was over, but she had refused to believe it. Her incredulity had soon turned to fury as she had stomped around the cottage and screamed at him.

"I will not give you up," she had stormed.

"You have no choice."

She had cursed him, then pleaded with him, then cursed him again.

In the month since then, he had ignored all her notes, but today she had threatened that if he did not meet her at the house in thē woods, she would invade Willowmere and confront him in front of his wife. Damn Kitty! Her timing was exquisite. Any other day he would still have refused, but he did not dare risk such a scene when Chandra was on the brink of capitulation. Reluctantly he had obeyed the summons.

He had found her waiting in the bedroom of the cottage wearing only a thin silk wrapper. When he walked in the door, she had let the wrapper fall to the floor, and stood naked before him, her body inviting his. But instead of exciting him, he found her wanton ploy disgusting. He had never liked women to throw themselves at him. He preferred to do the wooing.

He had seized her and told her bluntly that she was making a fool of herself. Then he had turned and left the cottage. The Carrington family had always referred to this place as the Honeymoon House because his parents had lived there after their marriage until his father could build Willowmere. What irony, he thought, that he himself had ended up spending the initial nights of his own marriage there alone, driven from his big comfortable bed at Willowmere by the torment of having Chandra so near him in the next room. He could not have trusted himself had she been too close. He was determined to vanquish her infernal pride and have her admit to herself—and to him—how much she wanted him. Until she did that, he would be her husband in name only. The solitude of the Honeymoon House was his only recourse to assure himself that he would not be overpowered by his desperate desire to make love to his wife.

As he reined his horse to a stop before Willowmere, he thought with satisfaction that his determination had succeeded. Chandra had confessed her desire for him, and there would be no further need for pretense. He dismounted quickly, eager to claim his bride at last.

To his disappointment, Chandra was not downstairs to greet him. Perhaps, he thought with a smile, she was awaiting him in his bed. He hurried up the stairs but his bedroom was empty. He crossed into Chandra's room and was disconcerted to see her sitting near a window, staring blindly out at the twilight sky.

"Chandra," he said softly.

Slowly she turned toward him, and he saw as he approached her that her face was swollen and her eyes were red from weeping.

He tried to take her in his arms, but she flinched at his touch and pushed him away violently.

"Don't come near me," she cried. "I hate you."

He found the agony in her eyes even more disconcerting than her words. She looked as though she had been whipped and her spirit destroyed.

"Chandra, my darling, what the devil is wrong?"

"Leave me alone." Her tone was lifeless.

Seriously concerned, Miles retreated and sought Sarah.

"What happened to Mrs. Carrington while I was gone?"

The housekeeper denied any knowledge of what might be the matter, so Miles, quite baffled by the turn of events, went back up to Chandra's room. The door was locked.

"Open the door," he ordered. "This is my house and I will not be locked out. Open it or I will break it down."

Silence.

Furious, he slammed his shoulder against the wood, shattering it. The door flew open with a crash and he strode angrily over to Chandra. She was huddled on the bed like a frightened child.

Sitting down beside her, he pulled her to him and held her against her will. "My sweet, what has distressed you so?"

She pulled away from him. "As if you did not know."

"No, damn it, I don't know," he said irritably, "and I do not understand your moods, but I most certainly intend to fulfill your desire of this morning. You had no objections then to my touch, and I must assume that you are merely playing a little game which, I warn you, I intend to win." He began to undo the top button of her high-necked muslin gown.

She jerked away. "Don't touch me!"

She jumped from the bed, trying to flee, but he was too quick for her. He caught her as she reached the shattered door and wrapped his arms around her. She fought him furiously as he nudged her back toward the bed. Holding her in the circle of one arm, he lowered her onto the yellow coverlet. In the fray, her skirts had become tangled about her waist, leaving her long white thighs exposed to his appreciative eyes.

He held her down on the bed. "It is useless to fight me like this," he said softly as she continued to squirm in a vain effort to free herself. "I am strong and I don't intend to let you go."

At his words, she ceased her struggling and lay rigid on the bed, glaring up at him, her resistance now passive but just as firm.

Miles was determined to awaken her passion. He would not take her by force, but he would make her want him. He had, once, and he knew just how to arouse her. His lips sought the sweetness of her mouth, but he found it was barred to him by clenched lips and teeth. He began to lavish kisses upon her face and hair.

"My darling, what's wrong?" he murmured in her ear, drinking in deeply the tantalizing jasmine-and-rose scent of her hair. "How lovely you are. I'm your husband, my sweet. Don't deny yourself what we both want. This morning I saw desire for me in your eyes and I knew that at last you had allowed yourself to accept the truth. You are a passionate woman, Chandra. Let me give you pleasure."

He raised his head to look down into her blue eyes and found that they were still glaring up at him. Still he persisted. His hand caressed her bare thigh leisurely, then abandoned it to start on the buttons of her bodice.

When he had undone them, his hand slipped beneath the muslin and toyed with her breast. Still she remained unyielding. At last, beneath the gentle insistence of his fingers, her nipple hardened. An involuntary response, Miles thought, but a beginning at least.

Her blue eyes were closed now. He returned his attention to that portion of her bared by her raised skirt, and at last he felt a yielding within her. Her smooth belly trembled beneath his touch.

He sought to reassure her. "Trust me, my love."

At his words, her eyes flew open, ablaze with anger, and her body again hardened against him.

He redoubled his efforts. But this time, there was no answering softness in her.

What in God's name could be wrong, he wondered. He wanted her, but not like this: cold, hating, ungiving. Never in his life had he felt so frustrated as he did now in the face of his wife's abrupt change of heart. He had looked forward to tonight only to be denied once again.

A disquieting thought struck him. Had she been merely teasing him, this morning, tantalizing him purely for the satisfaction of seeing him hurt?

At that moment Chandra, as though in confirmation of his suspicion, asked coldly, "Am I to be spared another rape?"

Her words doused his passion as effectively as a pitcher of ice water, and he stood up abruptly. "Do not wish for the impossible, madam. My only intention is to leave you alone."

He turned and stalked from the room.

Moments later the sound of his horses' hooves echoed in the still night as he rode away from Willomere.

Chapter 32

Chandra remained in bed until noon the next day, her mind in a turmoil. Miles had returned to Willomere an hour after sunrise but, to Chandra's relief, he had not demanded her appearance at the breakfast table. She was not ready to face him, still shaken from last night. Despite her determination, he had stoked the fires of her passion until she could barely stand it. In another second, her desire for him would have driven her to wrap her arms around him and let him take her. She hated herself for her weakness, burning so eagerly for a man who cared more for his mistress than he did for her.

Yet she was troubled by the puzzled, hurt look in his eyes. Could it possibly be that he did not appreciate how deeply he had wounded her by going to Kitty? Perhaps it would have been better if, instead of retreating into sullen silence, she had screamed out her pain and anger. But her pride would not let her. She could not bear to see the smirk of satisfaction that she feared would settle on his face.

Now he had sworn to leave her alone. Her heart ached. Could there be a worse punishment than living here in his house, ignored and unloved, while he contented himself with another woman?

Would Kitty be preening herself at the Stratfords' ball tonight? Chandra's lips tightened. No matter, she would outshine Miles's mistress at the ball. Filled with purpose, Chandra summoned Patty to help her dress. She would use every wile she had ever read or heard about to assist her in her cause.

She did not emerge from her room until it was time for her and Miles to depart for the Stratfords'. As she left the house, she saw Miles waiting for her at the foot of the stairs. Her hair was piled high in an intricate crown of sable curls, giving her a regal air. The lilac of the gown enhanced the delicate translucence of her complexion and heightened the color of her eyes with their luxurious veil of dark lashes. She thought she saw a gleam of appreciation in Miles's eyes.

As they met, Chandra avoided his eyes and her hand trembled as he took it. He did not speak, but merely gave her a curt bow and led her to the portico beyond which his coach, its walnut panels and silver mountings polished to a high sheen, awaited them. As they approached the carriage, young Jim Spenser galloped up on a spotted mare and halted beside the coach. "Sir," he yelled, and then lowered his voice. "I must warn you of the evil stories my uncle has spread about you and your wife."

The gangling youth dismounted and stood nervously before Miles, shifting from one foot to the other. Jim had grown so quickly that his height had outstripped his body's ability to catch up, and he was all skinny arms and legs.

"What stories?" Miles demanded.

Jim poked nervously at the ground with his toe. "That you did not marry in England, but merely made up the story to get out of your promise to wed Sally."

"If I concocted the story, how does your uncle account for the fact that I am married?"

Poor Jim turned crimson and stared at his feet, avoiding Chandra's anxious gaze. "He says your wife isn't your wife. She's a . . . a . . . a whore you hired to put on an act."

Chandra gave a strangled cry, and Jim squirmed nervously beneath her gaze.

In exquisite detail, Miles cursed Fred Humphreys's parentage and the circumstances of his birth. "I will kill him for that vicious lie about my wife. How did Fred conceive such a ludicrous idea?"

"I fear it is Martin Davis's fault. He said he thought he saw you leaving a . . . a house in Washington with Mrs. Carrington."

Miles slammed his fist hard against one of the portico's doric columns. "If Fred seriously thinks he can spread such evil talk without my calling him out, he is either stupid or far braver than I thought."

"Neither," Jim protested. "He and Sally have convinced young Sam Bernard, who's never been known for being too bright, that he should redeem her honor by challenging you. And hothead that Sam is, he's just aching to do that. He's been sweet on Sally for months. Fred's counting on it."

"Sam is a strong man with not a bit of savvy," Miles dismissed him contemptuously.

"Aye, but he's also a crack shot and a little crazy. It's been said he fired a second too soon in that duel he won." Jim turned his horse about to leave. "Please, sir, be careful," he called over his shoulder to Miles. "Sam will be at the ball."

The four matched grays hitched to Miles's coach pawed impatiently at the ground as Miles handed Chandra into the coach.

She settled on the velvet cushions with all the eagerness of one being driven to the guillotine, and clasped her hands in her lap to keep them from trembling as Miles got in after her. Their wretched scene last night in itself was enough to unnerve her, but now she was also about to be forced to face a ballroom full of hostile people who thought her an imposter and a whore.

She cast a sidelong glance at her husband as he settled down beside her. His dress coat of lilac velvet complimented the hue of her own gown. The coat's collar, border and tails were heavily embroidered with silver flowers and he wore it over a lilac silk waistcoat with silver embroidery in the same floral pattern as the coat's. Snowy white lace fell from the jabot at his neck and from his wrists. How elegant and handsome he looked, Chandra thought, despite the forbidding sternness of his face. She could almost feel affection for this man—were it not for his abominable behavior.

They rode in silence, Chandra painfully aware of his hard muscled thigh resting casually—and she was certain deliberately—against hers on the seat. His mere touch made her heart and her stomach pulse. She found herself longing to take his hand in hers, to gather strength from him for the ordeal ahead of them. Most of all, she wanted to beg him to be careful. But Miles was grimly silent, and Chandra, remembering last night's scene, could not bring herself to speak. She was much relieved when Rosewood, the Stratfords' mansion, came into view in the distance, its lights glittering like beacons from the hilltop on which it was perched.

Miles looked through the window at the long line of carriages moving slowly up the driveway. "It looks to be the best turnout the Stratfords have ever had," he commented.

"I wonder why."

"You." Miles's lips twisted in a sardonic smile. "My neighbors are most curious to see you."

"No doubt, since they think I am a whore."

His face grew hard. "Don't worry, my love. Humphreys will apologize for his insults before the night is over, and no one will ever again question your honor."

But his words, instead of comforting her, reminded her of the threat of Sam Bernard. She pressed her small hand over Miles's large one, and pleaded, "Please, Miles, be careful, I beg of you. This Bernard sounds dangerous."

Miles's hazel eyes searched her face intensely. Then he said softly, "But just think, Chandra. If I were killed, you would not only be free of me, but an exceedingly rich widow as well."

She drew back in horror. "You cannot seriously believe that I would wish you dead."

He shrugged carelessly. "Only last night you told me you hated me." His unreadable eyes seemed to bore into her soul. "Do you hate me, Chandra?"

She looked away, unable to meet his gaze, and her voice faltered. "No."

She expected him to gloat over her reply, but he merely studied her in silence for a moment, then reached into his pocket and pulled out a long, narrow case. He opened it, and she saw on its satin lining a necklace set with hundreds of small diamonds in circular links and with one magnificent, many-carated stone in the shape of a teardrop in the center. It was an extraordinary necklace. He casually placed it about her neck, saying, "It was my mother's. I almost forgot to give it to you."

She was so surprised and awed by the magnificent necklace that she could only stammer her gratitude in disjointed fashion.

"I think, my sweet, such a present is worthy of more effusive thanks."

Blushing, she leaned over and kissed him on the cheek.

"That would hardly be payment for a paste necklace," he complained, seizing her in his arms and planting a searing kiss on her lips. It stirred within her those deep longings that he seemed able to kindle so easily. He did not release her until their coach pulled into the line of carriages waiting to give up their occupants at the front door of the Stratfords' red brick mansion.

Chandra was much shaken by his kiss, but she took a deep breath to help herself recover. And then she recalled their problem. She whispered in sudden panic, "I cannot go in there, knowing what all those people think I am."

Miles's hand closed over hers reassuringly. "They will know at once what a lie that is. Despite your poor opinion of Americans, Virginians are quite able to recognize the difference between a lady and a whore. They will appreciate you, believe me."

"Too bad my husband doesn't."

Miles's eyebrow raised. "If you wish me to appreciate you more, you must give me more opportunity to do so."

"And you must tear yourself away from your more engrossing pursuits."

' Surprise crossed his face. "What in the devil do you mean by . . ."

But his sentence was cut short by their arrival at the door. A Stratford slave opened the carriage door.

The Stratfords, a handsome couple in their middle years, were the epitome of gracious hospitality as they greeted Chandra and Miles, and Chandra's apprehension was eased by the genuine warmth of their welcome.

Still she found her knees trembling nervously as she entered the big ballroom. The women's perfume mingled with the fragrance from the urns and vases and bowls of flowers—lilacs, peonies, daffodils and bouquets of half a dozen other varieties in profusion; and she felt a bit dizzy as she gazed about.

The Carringtons were not the first to arrive, and their appearance was like a magnet drawing the attention of everyone in the crowded room. Chandra was painfully aware of the cold stares she drew from the women and the smirks from some of the men. Her cheeks flamed with embarrassment, and she was thankful for Miles's protective arm about her waist, holding her reassuringly, as he acted every inch the proud, loving husband. She looked over the sea of strange faces, searching for a crown of thick copper hair, but to her relief she saw no one resembling Kitty Keating.

Chandra was soon caught up in a flurry of introductions that followed one upon the other so quickly that the faces became an indistinguishable blur. At first, she was greeted politely, but coolly. Then, as Miles had predicted, her new neighbors quickly realized that at least part of Humphreys's tale was a lie.

"You have outdone yourself in choosing a bride, Miles," she heard a woman behind her say in a soft, approving voice.

Chandra's spirits were lifted by the compliment, and she turned to find a woman of perhaps forty in a pink lutestring gown. The newcomer had a warm, generous smile that seemed to embrace not merely her lips but her entire face, and Chandra found herself immediately liking and trusting her.

Miles greeted her affectionately. "This is Martha Haughton, one of our neighbors," he told Chandra, "and a dear friend of both my sister Ondine and myself since childhood."

Martha clasped Chandra's hands in her own. "I hope you will visit me."

"I should like to," Chandra replied, delighted at the prospect of having this warm, cheerful woman as a friend.

"Have you heard from your sister lately?" Martha asked Miles.

"No. As you can well attest, Ondine has never been a frequent letter writer."

A worried frown settled on Martha's placid face. "I hope she and her family have not been troubled by the pirates. I am concerned about them, since their plantation is very near the sea."

Amusement played in Miles's eyes. "What a surprise the pirates will be in for if they tangle with Ondine. I have little doubt who would win the encounter."

" 'Tis not a laughing matter," Martha reprimanded him gently as they were joined by her husband, a portly man in a plum velvet coat. He had a high sloping forehead, round eyes and a smile that was as friendly as his wife's. "Even Howard has bought additional weapons."

"Including a pair of French two-shot pistols that might interest you, Miles," Haughton said.

"Indeed," Miles agreed. "Perhaps you could bring them over some day soon."

"Gladly." Howard looked about quickly to make certain he would not be overheard. "Have you heard about Fred Humphreys and what he has been claiming?"

Miles's smile turned to a scowl. "If Humphreys is wise, he will not come tonight."

"But Fred is an idiot." Martha gave a scornful little toss of her head. "And he's certain to come with the Beaumonts. They have a rich Englishman visiting them who is looking for a plantation to buy. Humphreys hopes to sell him Dana Grove to save himself from the humiliation of foreclosure."

"He shall not live long enough to be foreclosed upon if he does not apologize for the lies he has spread about my wife," Miles snapped.

"Fred's a desperate man—and perhaps a little mad in the bargain," Martha said thoughtfully. "I, too, hope he won't come tonight, but I would wager he will."

And come he did, a short, heavy man with a red bulbous nose that belied his fondness for whiskey and with hands as plump and soft as his body. He was accompanied by his daughter, a petite girl of delicate blonde beauty with snake-like green eyes and a pouting mouth. Her carriage and the tilt of her chin were defiant, and she was laced into a green satin gown that matched her eyes and accentuated the tiniest waist Chandra had ever seen. With them was a smallish young man with a lopsided, buck-toothed grin and a strange intensity in his eyes that frightened Chandra, who guessed this must be Sam Bernard.

Quiet descended like a curtain upon the previously boisterous room. A path cleared as if by magic between the group in the doorway and the spot twenty feet away where the Carringtons stood with the Haughtons.

Time seemed frozen for one long moment. Then the tense silence was broken by a startled exclamation from one of the men who had followed Humphreys into the room: "Mrs. Carrington!" The two words echoed through every corner of the quiet chamber, drawing attention to the speaker.

"Lord William!" Chandra gasped in surprise.

Recovering, the English lord bowed and said with a supercilious smile, "I would not have expected to see you here."

Humphreys's eyes fairly bulged and his voice was unsteady. "You mean you know this woman, Lord William?"

The Englishman nodded. "She and her husband— Mr. Carrington there—were my fellow passengers on the voyage from England."

At this, Sally let out an unearthly wail that turned the scrutiny of the gathering full upon her. At this unwanted attention, she turned and fled from the room as though all the hounds of hell were in full pursuit of her. After a moment, Sam Bernard hurriedly followed her.

Humphreys, his face ashen, turned, too, and would have followed his daughter, but Miles's shout stopped him.

"Fred Humphreys," he said in a voice as sharp as steel, "you have spread vicious lies about my marriage. I care little what you say about me, but when you attack my innocent wife and question our union, you have gone too far—much too far." Miles stripped off his white kid glove. "I demand satisfaction for the lies you have told about her. What will your weapons be?"

Humphreys's shoulders slumped and he hung his head, seeming to shrink several inches in the process. "Sam, Sam," he croaked. But Sam was gone and he was forced to face Miles's rage alone.

"You cannot be serious," Humphreys blubbered. "I am a sick old man. You are young and strong. It is outrageous that you should challenge me."

"Not nearly so outrageous as the malicious lies you have spread. As Lord William there—and all the other passengers aboard the *Golden Drake*—will verify, Mrs. Carrington and I sailed as man and wife from England." Miles swept Humphreys with a look of contempt. "No, it is not she who is an imposter, but your daughter. Sally tried to pass herself off as my betrothed when she knew I had never mentioned marriage to her. Nor did I ever attempt to seduce her." Miles's voice was as ominous as his scowling face. "You, Fred Humphreys, will admit your lies or you will accept my challenge."

Humphreys had turned the shade of gray clay. He was a cowardly man trapped in the consequences of his own scheming. The guests' eyes were all fixed upon him, awaiting his response, and there was not a sound in the room.

"I admit it," he whimpered. His words were scarcely audible, even to those standing nearest to him, but there was no doubt from the look on his face that he had admitted the charges against him. He turned slowly and shuffled from the room, a broken man.

"I should have done him a greater favor had I killed him," Miles said with distaste, watching him go. "He will be ostracized even if somehow he manages to keep Dana Grove."

With Humphreys's departure, the room suddenly exploded in a nervous clamor as though the guests sought to drown out the unpleasantness of the past moments in loud chattter. The small orchestra, two violins and a French horn, began playing spiritedly, adding to the hubbub.

As the music resumed, Chandra quickly found she had no shortage of eager dancing partners. She was gratified that she was so well accepted by her new neighbors, but she was shaken by the scene between her husband and Fred Humphreys. Everything she had imagined about the uncivilized nature of the new world was perfectly true. She hoped the unpleasantness was at an end. Miles had handled it well, but still, despite his defense of her, he scarcely gave her a glance and seemed not to notice her popularity. Only when Lord William asked her to join him in a quadrille did she find Miles suddenly watching her, his eyes narrowed and his brow furrowed in a displeased frown.

Chandra quickly discovered his lordship's attitude toward her had undergone a metamorphosis upon learning she was the mistress of Willomere. When after a time Pembroke ran short of glowing adjectives to apply to Chandra's beauty and her gown, she found the opportunity to ask him how long he had been in the neighborhood.

"I arrived two days ago."

"But it's been more than a month since the *Golden Drake* docked. Have you been traveling here since then?"

He hesitated, then replied. "I was looking over some large plantations for sale on the James River."

"But there were none that captured your fancy?"

His eyes were feasting hungrily on her diamond necklace and the tempting curve of her bosom as he answered absently, "Oh, I found several that suited my purpose."

"Did you buy one?"

The question seemed to take him by surprise, but he answered smoothly, "My heart was set on Willowmere."

"If that's so, I am surprised you tarried so long in coming here."

"I delayed, hoping to receive an invitation, but now that I know who its owner is, I understand why he chose not to extend his hospitality to me." Despite his lordship's determined effort to be charming, he could not keep the anger from his voice.

Chandra longed to cut short the dance, but she caught sight of Miles watching them with a dangerous glint in his eye. *Could it be that he is jealous of Lord William?* she wondered. The thought made her eagerly consent to a second dance with the Englishman, although her heart was not amenable to it.

As they whirled into it, the scowl on Miles's face darkened. Seeing her husband's reaction, Chandra flirted with Pembroke, hoping that Miles might taste a bit of the pain she had felt last night when she had seen him about to make love to Kitty.

His lordship took his advantage and boldly sought Chandra's permission to visit her at Willowmere. She was far from pleased at the prospect but agreed to it because she knew it would irritate her husband.

When the music ended, Miles quickly reclaimed Chandra, his arm encircling her waist none too gently. As he guided her away, he said, "I have ordered our coach. It is waiting."

As they climbed inside, Chandra managed to seat herself across from her husband so that their bodies could not touch and they would face each other. The small carriage lamp outside diluted but did not vanquish the darkness.

As the coach started up, Chandra protested, "Why did we have to leave so soon? I was enjoying myself."

She saw the hard set of her husband's face in the deep shadows cast by the lamp.

"I have just put to rest one rumor about our marriage, madam. I do not care to have Lord William's attentions to you—and your obvious appreciation of them—start another."

She gave him a smile as sweet as it was false. "I am honored by his lordship's attention to me."

"Are you now?" Miles said. He leaned forward and raised his hands to her neck, tracing the diamond necklace down her throat. When his fingers reached the end of the big tear-shaped stone, they slowly moved lower down the curve of her bosom and slipped beneath the lilac silk of her bodice to tease her breasts, stoking in her that aching desire for him that his touch unfailingly aroused.

She could not stop the rapid thumping of her heart nor her body's response, and the mocking smile on his face told her he had correctly measured her longing for him.

"You may be honored by Lord William's attentions, my sweet, but you are excited by mine," he told her, his voice lazy and insinuating.

Furious, she tried to push his hands away. "I prefer an English gentleman's courtly lovemaking to an American's pawing," she snapped.

His smile faded and he withdrew his hands. "I may not choose to taste your fruit, madam, but I promise you no one else will harvest it either."

His words brought tears to her eyes, but she managed to spit out at him, "You bastard."

The remainder of the journey to Willowmere passed in a seething silence that crackled with tension.

Chapter 33

Lord William called on Chandra at Willowmere before noon on the day following the Stratfords' ball, and she, still smarting from Miles's words, welcomed the Englishman solely to defy and annoy her husband. The second day after the ball, Pembroke called again upon her. On the third morning, when Sarah announced his arrival, Chandra could have groaned with exasperation. Her distaste for his lordship was growing apace with his persistence, and she longed to have the housekeeper tell him she was out. But the disgust on Sarah's face when she named the visitor was enough to make Chandra exclaim with false brightness, "How nice. I shall be down directly."

Chandra knew that Sarah wasted no time in informing Miles of the Englishman's visits and that they irritated her husband mightily. In fact, Chandra thought bitterly, they seemed to be the only thing concerning her that attracted his attention at all now. After their quarrel on the way back from the ball, their relationship had slid back to that tense, stony silence that had prevailed during those first terrible weeks at Willowmere. Chandra despaired that her marriage would forever be a bitter charade, one that she found unbearable even if her husband did not.

Lord William's visits had an unforeseen consequence upon Chandra. He was proving to her beyond a doubt just how silly her father's foolish notions had been. The more she was exposed to his lordship, the more she came to appreciate Miles.

She slowly and reluctantly made her way down the stairs toward the drawing room where Lord William awaited her, and it was with a distinct sigh of relief that she bid his lordship goodbye an hour later. During the dull visit, he had plied her with flattery as hyperbolic as it was insincere. Instead of endearing him to her as he intended, it served only to increase her distaste for him and the ache in her heart for Miles.

That afternoon, Howard Haughton arrived at Willowmere with an oblong mahogany box that held a pair of over-and-under flintlock pistols Miles had wanted to see. The two men, accompanied by Chandra, walked down behind the smokehouse where a target had been set up for practice. She was delighted to have some company other than Sir William, and she found Howard's company even more enjoyable than she had at the ball.

"Surely you don't think the pirates would venture this far north?" Miles said as he loaded one of the flintlocks with its two stubby barrels.

"They are bolder than you think," Howard replied as he loaded the other pistol. "I have just had word they have disabled two navy vessels that Jefferson sent after them. They say the captain of the *Black Wind* is wilier than Captain Devil was."

Chandra started at the mention of her father's nemesis, but he raced on before she could ask Haughton about him. He threatened, holding up his flintlock, "If they come sneaking up to Haughton Hall, I plan to have twice as many shots at them. Speaking of sneaks, Miles, when I rode over here today I saw Sam Bernard about a quarter mile from here on Willowmere land. Has he given you any trouble?"

Miles looked up in surprise. "No, nor have I seen him hereabouts."

Haughton, having finished loading his gun, raised it and fired at the target. The shot hit several inches from the center.

Chandra watched enviously. She would love to have a chance at it. It had been so long since she had handled a gun, though, that she wondered if her marksmanship was still as sharp as it once had been.

Miles raised his gun and fired. The ball penetrated the target with deadly accuracy.

"You always were the best shot in the county, Miles," Haughton said without rancor.

Miles raised the flintlock to fire again, but Chandra raised her hand and placed it over his.

"Please," she asked, "could I try it?"

Miles's surprise was evident as he handed her the gun. To the amazement of the two men, her ball followed Miles's squarely through the center of the target.

"That was quite a shot," Haughton exclaimed. "I wager you can't do that a second time."

He handed her his gun, with a look of amusement on his face. She cocked the weapon and fired again, her second shot duplicating her first. Silence greeted her feat. Miles's face was inscrutable, while Haughton looked amazed.

Miles took Chandra's arm. "Now that my wife has demonstrated that she is a better shot than either of us, shall we return to the house?" he said drily.

They spent another hour talking with Howard at the house and Sarah brought them coffee. After their visitor had left, Miles turned and asked Chandra, "Did your father teach you how to shoot?"

She nodded.

"He did give you a most unusual education." Miles shook his head.

"Do you mind?" she asked hesitantly.

"Not at all, my dear," he laughed. "I just wouldn't want it getting around that you are a better marksman than anyone in the county."

The next day, Chandra was sitting listlessly at her dressing table and Patty was coaxing her hair into a neat coil when Lord William was announced. Chandra was not eager for his company, but she noted it was a scant thirty-five minutes until dinner would be served. If she received him now, he would be here when Miles came in. It would be the first time the two men met face to face at Willowmere, and Chandra was curious to see Miles's reaction. So she welcomed his lordship with more warmth than usual and flirted with him in the drawing room until her husband arrived.

Only a slight tightening of Miles's lips and a cold glint in his hazel eyes betrayed his anger at finding Lord William with his wife in his house. After a few minutes of strained conversation in which Lord William announced his approval of Willowmere, Miles said brusquely, "I am afraid you must excuse us, Pembroke. Our dinner is awaiting us."

Chandra was horrified at Miles's rude dismissal of their guest.

Pembroke rose stiffly to his feet, anger stamped on his face. "A thousand pardons for detaining you. It seems Virginia hospitality is not all it is reputed to be."

"I am sorry you find it a disappointment," Miles replied smoothly. Chandra quickly walked to the door and saw Lord William out, where he bid her a rather curt farewell.

After Lord William had gone and the Carringtons were seated at the table, Chandra chastised Miles roundly for his rudeness. He was silent as Jem finished serving them their first course of sorrel soup and waited to speak until after the servant had left the dining room. "It was his lordship who was rude," Miles said. "He came uninvited in the hope of forcing a dinner invitation from me."

"Could it be you are jealous of him?"

"Of Lord William Pembroke?" Miles's lip curled in disgust. "No, madam. But I refuse to have that prig at my table. So take care that you do not extend him an invitation to dine with us that I will have to repudiate."

" 'Tis not your company in which he is interested," she snapped.

"Nor yours, either. He did not deign to speak to you when he thought you the wife of a farmer, but now that he finds I own Willowmere, he is all honeyed smiles and flattery." Miles raked her with searing eyes. "And you are a greater fool than ever I would have thought, madam, if you believe otherwise."

The contempt implicit in his words was evident. It was bad enough that he had no love for her, that he preferred his mistress, but that he should consider her a fool to think any other man could be interested in her was more than she could bear. "You insult me most cruelly!" She was consumed by an anger beyond her control and, rising from her seat with her wineglass in her hand, she hurled its contents in his face.

The sight of the claret running down his face and staining his snowy white shirt brought Chandra to her senses. She stared at him in horror. His face was burning with a fury that terrified her. With a wrenching sob, she turned and fled to her room.

A few minutes later, Chandra heard Miles slamming about his bedroom. She cowered on her bed, expecting him to come in and rage at her. But after a few minutes, she heard his door bang and his angry steps retreat down the stairs as he called irritably for Sarah. The woman's voice answered him from below stairs, and several minutes later Chandra heard him ride off.

She sank back on her bed in utter despair. The afternoon was oppressively hot, which added to her misery. Black clouds rolled across the sky but brought no rain to relieve the humid air. Listlessly she went to a window in the hope of catching even a hint of a breeze. To her surprise, she saw Sarah riding out of the woods, back on the path from the house Chandra had come to think of as Kitty's.

A few minutes later Sarah came to Chandra's room. "Since Mr. Carrington won't be here for supper, I thought you might like a tray here in your room." The woman's tone was uncharacteristically friendly, but her eyes were calculating.

Chandra felt certain the housekeeper had some ulterior motive but she was at a loss to figure what it might be. "Why isn't he going to be here?" she asked.

Sarah gave her an enigmatic smile. "He's invited a guest for supper and thought they would find it more congenial at the house in the woods. I have been down getting it ready."

Sarah's words pierced Chandra like a knife. She had no need to ask who the guest was. Chandra's heart felt as though it would explode. This time, she realized, she had driven her husband straight into the arms of his mistress.

Chapter 34

Chandra turned Gray Dancer toward the woods, as though she were drawn by some evil magnet toward the house there. As she reached the path that led through the closely spaced trees, a movement perhaps a hundred yards away caught her attention. A man leading a horse hastily drew back into the concealing shelter of the trees, but not before she recognized his thin, lopsided face. It was Sam Bernard.

What, she wondered nervously, was he doing creeping about Willowmere? Howard Haughton had seen him doing the same thing yesterday. She remembered his desire to avenge Sally Humphreys's honor and wondered if he were seeking an opportunity to ambush Miles. Her fear for her husband prompted her to call out, "Sam, Sam Bernard, what are you doing there?"

There was no answer. She called again, and this time she saw him spur his horse from beneath the protective trees and gallop away from her toward the road that led from Willowmere.

Much troubled by this, she pushed Gray Dancer on to the red brick house nestling below the giant pines. The front door was open and she heard no sound. So, walking softly and slowly, she went inside. Shaded as it was by the towering trees, the house was considerably cooler than Willowmere. She walked through the drawing room and into the dining room, where the table had been laid with covers for two. Filled decanters of red wine and brandy rested on the sideboard.

Slowly she crossed the hall into the bedroom where

she had seen Kitty and Miles. The covers on the bed had been turned back. On a marble-topped commode rested a pair of silver brushes with the initials "M.C." engraved in flowing script upon them. They were the brushes that Miles had used aboard the *Golden Drake*. She touched them once, thinking of that trip that now seemed so far in her past, and then withdrew her hand quickly.

She moved on to a massive walnut wardrobe that occupied one corner of the room and opened it, disclosing dozens of gowns in the richest of fabrics—velvets, satins, silks, brocades. Obviously these were gowns that Miles kept here for Kitty. The garments were not of the latest fashion, but of a more opulent style, now passé, that Kitty apparently favored. Miles had given his wife some beautiful clothes, but he had also been most generous to his mistress, Chandra thought bitterly.

She turned and found herself once again staring at the bed. She thought of Miles making love to Kitty there and was suddenly wildly jealous. Was he more passionate with her? Did he reach greater fulfillment? Did he wish to please her more?

Chandra whirled around to flee from the house, but at that moment the long-threatened storm finally broke, sending rain down in sheets and trapping her there. She would simply have to wait until it subsided.

She retreated to the drawing room and settled in a chintz-covered wing chair. The house's furnishings were sturdier and more rustic than those at Willowmere, but the place, in general, looked comfortable and inviting.

She listened to the rain pounding down on the roof. When she was a little girl and it had rained like this, she had loved to sit on papa's lap before the fire and have him read her stories. She thought sorrowfully of her father and all that she had learned since his death about him, herself, and the world.

There are none so blind as those who will not see, Miles had said to her, and she had been very blind. Indeed, especially when it came to him.

She might have won Miles the morning after their

wedding if only she had swallowed her pride and admitted her own desire. Instead, she had deeply wounded him with her wild insults. This man, who had saved her life and opened her eyes to reality—she dreaded to think what her fate might have been had she never met Miles.

The rain had stopped as suddenly as it had begun. Chandra, eager to escape, left the house and remounted Gray Dancer. She walked the horse slowly down the path between the trees. The temperature had dropped sharply during the storm and now a stiff breeze tugged at her hair. Once beyond the woods, Chandra turned toward the banks of the Rappahannock, still holding Gray Dancer to a slow walk as she tried to sort through her turbulent thoughts.

When she had first seen Willowmere, she had marveled at what it must be to be the mistress of such a beautiful place. Now she knew that without the love of the man with whom she shared it, she would only find misery here. She was tormented by the thought that she had now been responsible for severing the only contact she had with Miles—their meals together.

Was there any way she could win her husband back now?

She reached the edge of a marsh where she knew Miles went to hunt wild fowl, and urged Gray Dancer to a gallop, hoping that a good run might help quiet her thoughts. A flock of angry gray mallards, startled by this invasion of their terrain, rose up in a startled swarm. Two bitterns aroused from their slumbers let out booming cries of protest.

Suddenly, without warning, the saddle seemed to slip, and Chandra found herself flying through the air.

"Oh God, what is happening?" she thought, panic-stricken in the instant before she hit the ground. The air was pushed from her lungs as if she had been hit in the chest by a sledgehammer, and the world went black.

Sometime later, she knew not how long, she regained consciousness and tried to clear the fog from her mind. Why was she lying here among the tall marsh grass? The wet spongy ground beneath her had soaked her shirt and pants. She tried to move but her body did not seem able to respond. Her limbs ached terribly and her head throbbed with unbelievable pain. She felt as though she had been run over by a team of oxen.

As her mind cleared, she realized she had been thrown from her horse, although she could remember nothing after leaving the house in the woods. Gray Dancer was nowhere in sight. Disjointed questions flickered through her dazed mind. How would she get back to Willowmere? Would Miles even bother to look for her? He had no more need for her now that she had saved him from marriage to Sally. Perhaps he would think Chandra had run away and would be delighted to be so easily rid of her. If only her head did not ache so. Even if a search was begun for her, would anyone find her, so well hidden as she was here in the marsh?

She slipped into unconsciousness again, and when she came to, she heard the baying of hounds in the distance. Someone must be exercising the dogs. The baying of the hounds grew closer and she heard the sound of pounding hooves behind them. Suddenly the dogs were upon her, sniffing and pawing at her, and sending up a clamorous roar.

The hoofbeats stopped a few feet from her, and an instant later Miles was kneeling beside her, a wild look upon his face. She had never seen him this way before. When he spoke, however, his voice was very gentle. "Did you hit your head when you fell?" he asked, smoothing the hair back from her forehead.

She tried to think, but finally had to admit: "I don't know . . . it's all . . . very vague. I don't think so."

His fingers probed her skull beneath her hair, then moved down her body, searching for swelling or broken bones.

Another horse stopped nearby and she heard Dunlop's voice ask, "Is she all right, Miles?"

"She doesn't appear to have hit her head, and nothing seems to be broken," he replied. "I think she may have only had the breath knocked from her, so it's probably safe to move her." He looked down into her eyes and brushed the weeds gently away from her face. "Tell me what happened."

She closed her eyes, trying to remember. "I don't know. I was riding along when suddenly I went flying through the air."

"Miles, come here," Dunlop's voice from some distance away called out urgently.

Miles left her and Chandra heard the two of them consulting in tones so low she could not make out what they were saying. Then the voices moved toward her and she heard Miles say, "Fortunately, she fell where the ground is soft and spongy. If it had happened anywhere else, she might have been killed. You ride back to Willowmere, bring a wagon to move her, and have Sarah send one of the slaves to bring a physician as fast as he can."

Chandra heard a horse ride off, and Miles returned to her, his face angrier even than it had been when she had hurled the wine at him. She shrank from him, wondering if he was thinking of that incident. Perhaps he was planning now that they were alone to confront her with it. "What is it?" she quavered in a small voice.

"Nothing." Without much success, he tried to force a smile to his lips.

"I am sorry . . ." she began, but then she was racked by uncontrollable shivering, whether from her wet clothes and the soggy ground beneath or from shock and fright or perhaps some of all those things, she did not know.

Miles scooped her into his arms and hugged her against him, trying to infuse some of the warmth from his body into hers. She lay languidly against him, strangely happy in the protection of his arms. How comfortable she was. If only she could remain there for the rest of her life. Gradually her shaking subsided and she looked up at his face. There were deep lines that she had never noticed before etched around the corners of his mouth and his eyes.

"I am sorry I have caused you so much trouble," she

said softly. "I have never in my life fallen like that before."

He smiled at her and teased, "You see, my sweet, you are not the infallible horsewoman you thought you were. Where did you go riding?"

"Along the river," she said evasively, not wanting to tell him of her destination.

"Where did you stop?"

The question caught her unaware. How had he known she had stopped? Had he seen her in the cottage? She dared not lie to him, and she stammered, "At the house in the woods."

She expected him to rage at her for invading the private sanctum he reserved for Kitty, but his voice was disinterested, as though he were merely trying to make conversation. "How long were you there?"

"I'm not sure. The rain came after I arrived, and I waited until it stopped. I suppose about an hour all told."

Suddenly his voice was harsh. "I forbade you to go riding by yourself. Why did you disobey me?"

She was startled by the sudden change of his mood. "I hadn't planned to ride far," she whispered.

"I would call this quite far."

To her relief she heard the approach of a wagon and horses. Miles and Dunlop lifted her carefully into the wagon. A bed of straw had been spread on the floor with an eiderdown quilt over it. Miles covered her with another blanket and settled down beside her as the wagon began to move. Despite the cushioning, the bouncing of the wagon as it traveled across the fields hurt her bruised body. Miles, seeing her grimace, pressed her hand tightly in his and stroked her forehead soothingly.

When they reached Willowmere, Miles carefully carried her upstairs and lay her on her bed, then sat beside her until the physician arrived. He was a thin, nervous man who looked rather hastily put together. His neckcloth was badly tied and his black broadcloth jacket appeared to have been donned on the run. He had obviously ridden at top speed, knowing it would not be wise to keep an agitated Miles Carrington waiting, and he was somewhat breathless as he was ushered into Chandra's bedroom.

After examining her, he confirmed Miles's diagnosis. No bones had been broken and she did not appear to have suffered a head injury.

"You may be sore for a day or so," he told her, "but don't fret. You are young and should be as good as new very quickly."

After the physician left, Miles resumed his seat beside her bed. When she again tried to discuss her accident with him, he shrugged it aside lightly, remarking, "We all fall once or twice. You are silly to dwell on it."

When Sarah arrived with a tray for Chandra's supper, she was startled to see it contained not only broth, tea and custard for herself but a more substantial repast for Miles.

Chandra remembered the two covers that had been laid at the house in the woods and realized that she had inadvertently managed to keep Miles from dining with his mistress tonight after all.

"I am afraid I am keeping you from an important appointment," she said slyly.

"It was nothing that important," he replied cheerfully, raising his wineglass to his lips. As he did so, Chandra was harshly reminded of the terrible conclusion to their last meal together. She put her spoon down abruptly.

"What's wrong?" Miles asked in alarm. "Are you feeling worse?"

She reached out and touched his hand. "Miles, I so regret what I did today at dinner. I swear I didn't realize I was holding the wineglass until I threw it."

His hand swallowed hers up, and he said gently, "I had forgotten about that. I am afraid that I gave you provocation." He grinned. "Just promise me that you won't do it again or I shall have to lay in a more extensive supply of neckcloths."

They finished eating in an easy silence, and every once in a while, Chandra glanced up to see Miles staring at her with a concerned and tender expression on his face. When the tray had been cleared away, she lay back on the pillows and took Miles's hand in hers, holding it tightly, determined to keep him as long as possible from his night with Kitty. But almost immediately, overcome by weariness, she fell into a restless sleep marred by nightmares.

In one she lay chained on the cold stone floor of a damp dungeon. The Duke of Warfolk, a whip in his hand, stood leering down at her. "You will never escape me again," he told her emphatically, "and before I am done with you, you shall beg to die."

In another she was pursued down a long, ever-narrowing tunnel by a man armed with a sword whose face was hidden by a mask. When the tunnel grew so narrow that she could run no further, she was forced to turn and face her masked pursuer, who raised his sword to sever her head from her neck.

She let out a piercing scream and awoke to find herself thrashing wildly. Suddenly comforting arms were holding her. "It's all right, my darling," Miles murmured soothingly, stroking her long, damp hair. "It was only a nightmare."

She clung to him, shaking. "I'm so frightened, Miles." She told him of her nightmare about the masked man. "It all seemed so real."

"But you can see, it was only a bad dream," he comforted her. His face was gentle in the flickering light of the chamberstick that had been left burning beside her bed. She rested her head against his strong furry chest and, glancing down, she realized with a start that he was naked. Her mind whirled in confusion. He had been sleeping in his own bedroom. He had not ridden out to Kitty, but had remained here at Willowmere to be near her. A wave of happiness swept over her, and she embraced him fiercely. "Please don't leave me," she begged. "I'm afraid."

He looked skeptically at her narrow bed. "I fear this little pallet is not wide enough to hold us both. Do you want me to put you in my bed?"

She nodded, still clinging to him. He gathered her up in his arms and carried her into his room where he laid her down on the big canopied bed. The sheets were warm from his body. He lay beside her and drew her tenderly into the protection of his arms where, soothed by the nearness of his body, she quickly fell asleep again.

Miles lay awake a long time, drinking in her scent that was far sweeter to him than that of any flower. How he loved her. He had not been able to admit how great and fierce that love was even to himself until this evening when he had seen Gray Dancer return to Willowmere, missing both its saddle and its rider.

For a moment, he had felt as though he himself had died. Yelling like a madman for his horse and his hounds, he had set out in frantic search for Chandra. He could not bear the thought that perhaps he had lost her before he had ever won her.

When he found her lying there, so white amidst the tall marsh grass, he feared the worst. But then her eyes flickered open and looked up at him. Never in his life had he felt such relief and thanksgiving.

He knew then that he had to find a way to bury the differences that kept them apart. His love for her was boundless, and he would prove it to her somehow.

His anxiety over her safety had brought his true feelings to the surface. All their fights and misunderstandings seemed so trivial now. All that mattered was that she was alive and well. As it happened, Chandra's nightmare had been closer to reality than she knew. Her fall from Gray Dancer had not been an accident. The cinch of her saddle had been cut so that it would snap altogether once she urged her horse to a gallop. Fortunately she had walked her horse until she reached the marsh. Had she let him run among the trees, she very likely would have been killed.

Not wanting to alarm her, Miles had spared her the truth about her fall. He had brushed it aside as an accident and now faced the difficult task of keeping her safe from her unknown enemy without her realizing. Who would want to kill her and why?

He thought immediately of Warfolk, but quickly dismissed the possibility. Even if the duke had learned of Chandra's whereabouts from Percy and had dispatched men to reclaim her, they could not yet have reached America. And secondly, whoever had cut Chandra's cinch had meant to kill her. Miles sincerely doubted that Warfolk would want her dead in a distant land. No, he would want her brought back to England where he could inflict his tortures upon her personally and revel in her pain.

But who could wish her harm here? The cinch almost certainly had been cut during her stop at Honeymoon House, but who would have even known she was there? He sighed anxiously and drew her closer to him as though by this small gesture he could somehow protect her from the danger that threatened her.

Chapter 35

Chandra awoke the next morning to find herself pressed against Miles's back. In her sleep, her gown had become entangled about her waist, and she thrilled at the touch of his bare skin, warm and tantalizing, against hers.

She remembered waking last night and the drama she had suffered through, but then she recalled the strength of Miles's arms, how safe and comforted she had felt when he held her. It had seemed to her that no danger, nothing—not even the dreaded duke—could touch her when she was within the magic circle of his embrace, and she had fallen at once into a peaceful sleep.

Miles stirred, awakened, and rolled over to face her. His dark hair was tousled and his hazel eyes were soft and affectionate, making him look younger, almost boyish, and strengthening Chandra's slender hope that perhaps if she could keep him from Kitty one night, she might well do so again. He smiled at her.

"How are you feeling this morning?" he asked with deep concern.

She stretched and twisted, then reported, "Only a trifle sore."

"Any more nightmares?"

"None. It must have been the change of bed. Yours is most comfortable." Now that she was in it she resolved to do everything she could to remain there—with him at her side.

"I am pleased that you appreciate it," he said drily. "I only wished that you appreciated what went with it as well."

Lowering her eyes to the dark curly hair on his chest and blushing slightly at her boldness, she whispered, "I am sure I might if only you would teach me."

His hand tilted her chin up so that he could look into her eyes. His own were guarded and his voice was cool. "If you wish such lessons, you must ask for them. I will not be wrongly accused of rape again."

Her blush deepened, and she dropped her gaze from his. "Did you not hear me? I just made such a request," she whispered almost inaudibly. She snuggled closer to him.

"Take care, my sweet," he warned her, "or your lessons will begin immediately."

"Why should they not? I've always been an eager student."

Miles looked dubious. "So soon after your fall? I don't think . . ."

"Silly," she interrupted and silenced any further objections on his part by covering his lips with her own.

Their kiss was long and deep and searing. His fingers stole up to the bows that fastened her nightgown at the shoulders and untied them, freeing her breasts from their thin veil. His lips moved down the curve of her neck, planting a trail of fiery kisses before seeking new fruit.

He was a patient, tender teacher. He leisurely explored her body as if she were some new continent whose contours he wished to imprint forever on his mind. With infinite care, he caressed all of her—her hair, her face, her breasts, the flat warmth of her belly, her long, smooth thighs. She marveled at the tumultuous sensations that he aroused in her.

Only once he stopped, and then just to inquire, "Do I hurt you? Your fall worries me."

His concern was as reassuring to her as his tenderness. In answer she kissed him and hugged him to her. He inhaled sharply and she felt the press of his desire.

Still he did not take her. He continued his attentions to every curve and recess of her body. His mouth bathed her with kisses, sometimes light and nibbling, other times fierce and demanding, until she moaned and writhed beneath his touch and his tongue.

When he had made love to her before, she had been at war within herself over him, but now there was no doubt to cloud her mind or her senses. She reveled in the pleasure he was giving her. Her blood was pounding, her breath came fast, and the deep throbbing need for him was rising to a frenzy within her.

He caressed her most intimately until she groaned, but in pleasure so intense she felt she might not be able to tolerate much more of it.

At last he moved over her and took her. For a moment he was quiet, as if to reassure himself that he was not hurting her, then he began to guide her up, up, toward a blazing sun that turned their bodies to liquid fire and at last consumed them in its convulsive power.

They lay together, their limbs intertwined, their breathing synchronized, one with the other. Chandra was exhausted, but wildly happy. If only this peaceful interlude could continue forever. But the silence was broken by a knock on the door. Sarah called out that Tobias Toberman, Miles's shipping agent, was awaiting him.

"Damn," Miles complained, "I forgot he was coming this morning."

He gave Chandra, still lying contentedly on the bed, a long farewell kiss. "Stay in bed today, my sweet. I want you to rest after your accident."

"I'm perfectly fine," she complained.

"And besides," he said, teasing, "I want you well rested for my attentions tonight."

After Miles had closed the door behind him, Chandra lay on his big bed staring up at the blue silk canopy, thinking her happiness would be complete if Miles told her during his pleasuring of her that he loved her—and if the threat of Warfolk could somehow be dispelled. She shuddered as she remembered her nightmare about the duke and tried to push it from her mind.

Miles remained closeted in his office with Toberman until well into the afternoon, and the day dragged by.

Chandra was so bored by one o'clock that she decided to walk down to the stables and check on Gray Dancer.

As she approached the stables, she realized with dismay that her head had begun to ache and her throat was getting sore. She must have taken a chill from lying on the wet marsh grass yesterday.

Tam was in a far stall with a mare who was about to foal, so he did not see Chandra. As she passed the tack room, she glanced in and noticed her saddle with its cinch dangling. She went in and bent to study the cinch more closely. The leather had been cut cleanly almost all the way through with a knife.

In a daze, Chandra walked from the tack room, then collapsed on a pile of straw by an unused stall, her legs no longer able to support her. No wonder she had fallen. Someone had meant her to. Someone had tried to kill her.

Her mind spun in confusion. But who? Who would have any reason? And why had Miles dismissed her fall so lightly? Surely he must have seen that the cinch had been cut. Why, then, had he been so unconcerned, unless . . . ? She shivered in terror, remembering her nightmare of the man in the mask trying to kill her. Did the face behind the mask belong to Miles?

Had her suspicion yesterday been correct? She had now served her purpose in providing him with an escape from marriage to Sally, and a divorce would be messy, giving rise to many questions. He had never made any secret of the fact that he had not wanted to marry Chandra. Had he thought murder made to look like an accident would be the only way out?

Or had he thought that there was anything between her and Lord William? She remembered Miles's uncontrollable fury that day she had threatened to take a lover. He had sworn to kill her if she did. Perhaps her flirtation with the Englishman, designed only to make her husband jealous, had led him to think she was unfaithful.

But could this man, this tender and concerned lover, could he really be trying to kill her? It was inconceivable. Or had he, after his scheme to kill her had failed, decided to play the loving husband to allay any suspicions she might have?

Her head was aching horribly now, and her throat was raw. She felt hot and feverish, and her mind was as confused as it had been when she had first regained consciousness after her fall.

She no longer knew what to believe or whom to trust. Every man she had trusted had betrayed her, she thought wildly. Her father with the snobbish nonsense he had instilled in her; Sir Henry—of course she had never trusted him, but still he had been her guardian and legally responsible for her well-being—Percy, the cousin she had so loved as a little girl. Why should Miles be any different?

And who else here had any reason to wish her dead?

She fled from the stable and back to the house. When she got to her room, she threw herself upon the yellow linen cover of her bed, her heart leaden. Her head was throbbing intensely now, and she felt very hot, indeed.

If what she feared about Miles were true, she must not let him know of her suspicions if she were to have any chance at all of surviving. But she would have to be wary and watch for any signs—anything at all that might give him away.

She heard a great commotion outside and dragged herself off the bed. She got to the window in time to see Miles dash from the house toward the stables. A few minutes later, he rode off on his big bay.

At three, to Chandra's surprise, Patty appeared at her room with a dinner tray that Miles had ordered for her.

"What was all the shouting about a while ago?" Chandra asked her maid.

"One of de field hands done took after another with a pitchfork, and de Massa done rode out dere," she replied in a matter-of-fact way.

It was well into evening when Miles reached home, as the field where his slaves' fight had occurred was in the far corner of the plantation. Apparently they had quarreled over a woman, and it had taken all of Miles's skill at haranguing, cajoling, and reasoning to make peace between them.

Miles was seething with impatience by the time he reined his big bay to a halt at Willowmere's door. He had so looked forward to a leisurely dinner with Chandra this afternoon and an even more leisurely night of even more pleasant pursuits.

But he had been anticipating more than a night of passion. Chandra must answer the questions that perplexed him. What had motivated her sudden capitulation to him, admitting at last her long denied desire for him? Why now, when their relationship seemed at its very worst? And what had caused her to pull back from him that night before the ball?

That she reciprocated his passion, there was no doubt. But did she reciprocate his love? Oddly Miles, who had always been so self-assured in his love affairs, now found himself feeling as shy and uncertain as a boy in pursuit of his first infatuation. She had grievously wounded him once with her insults, and he was reluctant to confess his love for her until he had some indication of hers.

No, their marriage could not flourish until she could discuss frankly with him not only her true feelings but the differences and misunderstandings that had been built up, block by block, like a brick wall between them.

He hurried to his bedroom, but to his surprise, the big canopied bed was empty.

Puzzled, he crossed to Chandra's room, and his heart sank at the sight of her, clad in a silk wrapper, sitting on her bed, staring out the window, exactly as she had been that night he had returned so eagerly after his meeting with Kitty.

"Chandra." His voice was as soft as a caress.

She turned to him, and this time it was not anger but fear that he saw in her sea blue eyes.

Miles was nonplussed. "Chandra, for the love of God, what is the matter now?"

She stared down at the floor and refused to meet his eyes.

He saw the happy night that he had so anticipated slipping away, and his temper rose apace with his perplexity and his frustration.

"Chandra, I don't understand this. When I left you this morning, we . . . Why are you suddenly afraid of me?"

She stiffened. "I am not." But her voice lacked conviction.

Miles sat down beside her and took her in his arms. She did not attempt to repel him, but her body was unresponsive to his embrace. He sought her lips but again, although she did not evade him, she merely endured his mouth upon hers. Where was the fire that had burned so brightly between them this morning?

He pulled back and looked into her dull eyes. Too dull, he thought. And how warm her body was. He put his hand to her forehead. She flinched at his touch.

"You have a fever," he exclaimed, much concerned. He scooped her up in his arms and again felt her shrinking from him. As he pulled back the covers of her bed, he pleaded, "Chandra, please tell me what has happened to frighten you."

"Nothing," she insisted sullenly as he lay her down between the sheets.

He summoned Sarah, who examined Chandra's throat and went to get one of the remedies that she was so skilled at brewing.

After Chandra had drunk the concoction, she lay back down, turned her head away from her husband's anxious gaze, and closed her eyes.

He stood there for a long time studying her feverish face. Was he always to be rebuffed just as he thought he had conquered her? The woman was maddening— and he was sure her illness was not the sole cause.

Finally he retreated to his bedroom where he poured himself a large snifter of brandy from the decanter he kept there.

*   *   *

Miles was up early the next morning. When he checked on Chandra, he found her in a deep sleep. He touched her forehead and, to his relief, it seemed much cooler.

Still baffled over her reaction to him last night, he went down to the stable to check on the condition of the new foal that had arrived the night before.

He was examining the pretty black-and-white filly when a messenger rode up, the heavy lather upon his horse attesting to the speed of his ride and the urgency of the message that he brought. It was from President Jefferson.

Miles broke the seal and began reading the letter written in Tom's own hand. He was to come at once to Washington to meet with Jefferson and several other leaders on a matter of gravest and most urgent importance—what it was he would know when he arrived. Tom would not have written such a pre-emptive summons had not the situation been most serious, but naturally the call could not have come at a worse moment. He dared not leave Chandra alone at Willowmere while her unknown enemy stalked her, nor could he take her with him on an arduous, breakneck journey to Washington in her condition.

He pondered his dilemma, and decided finally that the only possible solution was to approach the Haughtons and see if she could stay with them while he was gone. He trusted the couple implicitly, and he knew Chandra liked Martha. Quickly, he ordered his horse and told Tam to send a slave to fetch John Dunlop. Upon his return from Haughton Hall, Miles would meet with him and discuss the matter.

At Haughton Hall, Miles found Martha and Howard just finishing breakfast. Their blue dining room had always seemed a comfortable and cheery place to him, but now he seemed unaware of his surroundings. He declined their offer to help himself from the platters on the sideboard, but agreed to join them in a cup of coffee.

As Martha poured it for him, he explained everything: the urgent summons to Washington, the threat from Warfolk that hung over Chandra, the attempt on her life, and his reluctance to leave her alone and unprotected at Willowmere.

"Who would want to kill her and why?" Howard exclaimed when Miles finished. "I have never heard of such a shocking thing!"

"But, of course, she will stay here," Martha said. "We'll get the carriage and go at once to bring her back. And you needn't be concerned, Miles. I shan't let her out of my sight." Martha's kind face was filled with sympathy. "Poor Chandra must be terrified."

Miles looked at her across the rim of his cup and said, "She doesn't know."

"Doesn't know!" Martha was aghast.

"I don't want her to find out. It will only frighten her."

"But, Miles, it is far more cruel and dangerous to keep it secret," Martha protested. "How else is she to be on her guard? You must tell her, Miles."

He had to agree with the wisdom of Martha's argument. As he rode back to Willowmere, he considered how best to impart the awful information. He dreaded doing so. It was bad enough that Chandra had the threat of the duke's long arm, and now to have to add this new danger . . .

He was a quarter mile from his home when Dunlop rode up and joined him. Miles told his overseer of his summons to Washington.

"I shall leave within the hour, and you will be in charge. I know we have a great deal we need to discuss, but I am afraid we must postpone it once again. First our supper night before last being canceled because of my wife's . . . accident, and now this."

"We both know, sir, that your wife's fall was not unintentional." Dunlop's voice was grave. "You remember it was me discovered the cut cinch, and I know a knife cut when I see it." As they rode up the elm-lined path that led to Willowmere, Miles was silent and Dunlop kept his peace. But finally, as they neared the stables, he blurted out, "Do you have any idea who might have tried to kill Mrs. Carrington?"

"No. I wish to God I did." Miles turned to his overseer. "Do you?"

Dunlop colored slightly beneath his broad-brimmed straw hat and and dropped his gaze nervously to his saddle.

"Dunlop, damn it, tell me!"

The overseer stammered, "Mrs. Keating."

"Kitty!" Miles exclaimed in disbelief. But as he thought about it, he realized it was not so preposterous. Kitty had a terrible temper, and she was bitter about her ouster from Miles's life. Still he could not imagine Kitty a murderess.

"What evidence do you have to support your suspicions?"

"None." The overseer obviously wished he had never begun this uncomfortable conversation. "It is only . . ." He broke off, unwilling to continue.

"Only what?" Miles prodded him.

The overseer's ruddy complexion grew redder. "I could not help but wonder what happened between the three of you that night Mrs. Carrington followed you to the Honeymoon House. The time when you met Mrs. Keating there."

Miles swung around in his saddle and stared at his overseer as if he had taken leave of his senses. "Followed me there? What are you saying?"

"I saw her ride after you."

Although the day was hot, Miles was suddenly chilled as he thought of what Chandra must have seen. He remembered Kitty naked before him in the bedroom, trying to tantalize him into making love to her. If Chandra had glimpsed that, there was no interpretation save one that she could possibly have made.

Of course Chandra had changed toward him that night! She must have thought him more eager to meet his mistress than to claim his wife. Miles groaned aloud. But why hadn't she railed at him, cursed him, even hit him so that he could have answered her suspicions?

Why had she remained silent, covering her rage with cold spite?

But could he have answered her if she had spoken? Had he himself witnessed such a scene, would he have believed the truth? Most certainly not.

When Miles and the overseer reached the stable, Miles dismounted and, for the first time in Tam's memory, he turned and walked away without so much as a word, his face down. He looked like a man who has seen his love destroyed before his eyes.

He stalked up to his bedroom where he removed a japanned box containing a tiny pistol, so small it looked like a toy, and its accouterments from their resting place in the corner of a chest. The gun had been his mother's and he had put it away as a keepsake when she died. He jammed the gun into the pocket of his green broadcloth coat, picked up the japanned box, and marched into Chandra's bedroom. He found her in a thin wrapper of yellow that displayed the perfection of her body. She was standing by a window, staring listlessly outside. She turned sullen eyes toward him.

"How are you feeling?" he asked.

"Much better. I still ache a little, but Sarah's potion did wonders for my throat."

He smiled with relief and reached into his pocket for the tiny gun.

As he drew it out, Chandra, to his amazement, flinched and drew back at the sight of it. Fear was inscribed across her face.

"Chandra, my God, what is the matter?"

She did not answer but only stared at him with wide, frightened eyes.

Nonplussed by her strange behavior, he took the tiny barrel in his hand and pushed the butt, inlaid with mother-of-pearl, toward her. "This was my mother's," he said gruffly. "Do you know how to use it?"

She looked at him with an odd expression on her face. Then she took the weapon, examined it, and nodded. "Yes," she replied tonelessly. "My father had a similar one. Why are you giving it to me?"

"I must go to Washington immediately." He told her of Jefferson's summons and of his arrangement to have her stay with the Haughtons while he was gone. "I want you to promise me, Chandra, that you will carry this gun with you at all times, and sleep with it beside your bed. And you must promise me that while I am away you will not go anywhere without Martha or Howard."

"Why? Because of Warfolk?"

"Partly." He reached out and caught her hand. She tried to snatch it away from him, but he held on to it, pressing it gently.

He tried to soften the blow as much as he could. "I did not tell you this before because I did not want to frighten you, but someone is trying to kill you."

To his astonishment, her face changed and her eyes sparkled with relief.

"Madam," he protested, "I am at a loss to understand your happy reaction to news that someone has the intention of murdering you."

"I know about that, but I thought it was . . ." She broke off.

But the meaning of her half-completed statement was not lost on him.

"My God, you thought that—what kind of beast do you think I am?"

The pain and the reproach were so heavy that Chandra reached up and touched his cheek as though to soothe away his hurt.

"What else was I to believe? I saw the cinch—it had been cut. Yet you joked about my fall, blaming it on my poor riding."

"Is that why you were suddenly so afraid of me?"

She nodded.

He groaned. "Here I sought only to spare you fear and instead succeeded in increasing it." He studied her face with troubled eyes, and then burst out, "But why on earth would you think I wanted to kill you?"

The look of pain that filled her eyes wrenched his heart. She said haltingly, "I suppose because it was the easiest way to get rid of me. I had served my purpose by saving you from marriage to Sally, and you made it obvious you preferred your mistress to me."

"So Dunlop was right. You did follow me."

An angry flush spread over her face, confirming his fear.

"Chandra, I swear to you that the situation was not what you thought. I swear to you I did not make love to Kitty that night."

"What about all the other nights?"

"What other nights?"

"Every one since we have been here save the past two."

Miles seized her hands in his. This woman he loved so dearly, whom he had struggled to avoid for fear of touching her, had thought he had been unfaithful to her all those long wretched nights he had spent. "Chandra, I have not been spending my nights with Kitty."

Chandra tried to pull her hands away but he refused to relinquish them. "Where have you been then?" she demanded, her voice choked with anguish.

"Alone at the Honeymoon House."

"If Kitty was not with you, why are her clothes in the wardrobe?"

"Those were my mother's."

"But you were going to dine with Kitty there the night before last."

"No, of course not. I had an appointment with Dunlop." He dropped her hands. "I had asked him to supper to discuss business and after the wine bath I got at lunch that day, I preferred to do it away from Willowmere."

"But why," she asked in wonder, "would you go to that house every night if Kitty were not there?"

It was a question that Miles could not answer without betraying the depth of his love and his need for her, and the torment she had caused him.

He hesitated, then said slowly, "After the insults you hurled at me the morning after our marriage, I swore that I would never again touch you except were you to beg me. If ever I made love to you again, it would be at your bequest. But it was an oath I feared I might find impossible to keep with only a single door between us. I was determined to put myself beyond temptation, beyond the torture of having you so near where I would be tormented by the lingering perfume of your scent and the sound of you moving about in the room beyond mine." His tone turned bitter. "You see, my sweet, you were the winner in our game of love after all."

He swung around, half expecting to see triumph in her eyes at his admission, but he found only innocent wonderment in their depths.

Suddenly she was before him, her arms encircling him, her hands caressing him, her lips eagerly seeking his. He embraced her then, holding her as though he could never let her go.

Their kiss was interrupted by Sarah's toneless voice announcing the arrival of the Haughtons, who had come for Chandra.

Miles held her tightly to him, unable to bring himself to let her go. His overwhelming desire for her warred with his duty. Finally, with the greatest reluctance, he released his wife, but she clung to him resolutely.

"Please, Miles, stay," she pleaded.

"If only I could, but I cannot ignore Tom's urgent summons."

She nodded sorrowfully and released him. "Promise me then that you will hurry back."

"I promise," he said, praying silently that she would be waiting for him when he returned. Nothing, not her unknown stalker, not the unseen hand of Warfolk, must come near her while he was away.

Chapter 36

The Haughtons were most congenial hosts and were much concerned about Chandra's safety. They watched over her carefully but unobtrusively, so that she felt both secure and welcome at Haughton Hall. She found herself caught up immediately in its bustling activities. The Haughtons' five lively children, ranging from Philip, who was fourteen, to Susan, who was four, seemed to regard Chandra as another member of the family.

Chandra quickly learned that a planter's wife, despite her slaves, did not lead a life of leisure. Indeed, Martha never seemed idle. She was constantly overseeing the cooking, the smoking, the cleaning, or was visiting an ailing child in the slave quarters. In the evening her hands were always occupied with knitting or sewing.

Martha was especially busy now. The Haughtons' annual barbecue, an event to which all the planters and their families for miles around were invited, was only a few days away, and the seemingly endless preparations consumed much of Martha's time. Chandra offered assistance wherever she could, but she found that often things were so well taken care of she was more a hindrance than a help.

Chandra felt she would be perfectly happy when Miles returned. When he did, their marriage would know a true beginning.

And then she realized she could never be completely happy until she had solved the question of who had tried to kill her. It seemed to her there were only two suspects, Sarah and Sam Bernard. Even though Sam had a dubious reputation and had been near the woods that day Chandra's cinch had been cut, she was inclined to dismiss him. He was so dumb and cowardly. Sarah was, in Chandra's mind, the prime suspect. She had made no secret of her feeling that Chandra was an inferior wife for Miles. Only Sarah knew that Chandra had gone to the house that day, and Chandra was certain that she had deliberately provoked her into going. Chandra wondered if Miles also suspected Sarah. Why else would he have suggested that she stay at the Haughtons' during his absence?

Chandra sighed as she thought of Miles. She was so impatient for his return, she could scarcely contain herself. Her body ached for his beside her in bed and for his strong, kind presence.

The day after Chandra's arrival at Haughton Hall, she was in the cutting room with Martha. She was helping to arrange two vases of roses for the fireplace in the dining room when Lord William Pembroke's arrival was announced.

Chandra looked at Martha in dismay. She could think of nothing less appealing than entertaining the Englishman. Indeed, she had only used him before to make Miles jealous.

"Please," she begged, "could he be told I am indisposed and not able to receive visitors?"

Martha was obviously surprised but she nodded, saying, "If that is what you wish."

"It is." Chandra was emphatic. "And please tell him it is likely to be several days before I shall be well enough again to receive visitors so he will not call again tomorrow."

Martha's calm eyes studied Chandra's face. "I thought you were exceedingly fond of Pembroke."

Chandra was horrified. "Wherever did you get such a nonsensical idea? I cannot bear him."

Martha held a rose above the vase as she decided where to place it. "I am afraid rumors have been flying. You apparently make him most welcome at Willowmere and even prefer his company to that of your husband."

"Oh, no!" Chandra cried in dismay.

"Isn't it true that he has been a frequent visitor of yours since the Stratfords' ball?"

" 'Tis true," Chandra admitted hastily, "but I did it only to make Miles jealous." This sudden burst of candor startled her nearly as much as it did Martha.

"Such a game as that, Chandra, is very dangerous." Martha's normally placid face was rebuking. "And 'tis one that often hurts the player more than anyone else."

Chandra hung her head. "But it seemed to be the only way I could win my husband's attention," she protested.

"What?" Martha was incredulous. "That is quite the silliest thing I ever heard. Don't you realize what laid to rest the rumors about your marriage so quickly at the Stratfords' ball? It was obvious to everyone there that Miles was wildly in love with you, obvious that his marriage was not a sham. He is more in love than I, for one, would have ever thought it possible for him to be."

If Chandra had had any doubts about the veracity of Miles's statements before his departure for Washington, Martha's words laid them to rest. Oh, her foolish pride that had prevented her from admitting to Miles how she really felt! Had she done so in the beginning, how happy they might have been together these past weeks, instead of being miserably separated by misunderstandings.

Miles had expected to be gone no more than three days, and as the third day drew to a close, Chandra found herself hurrying to the window at any sound of a horse in the distance.

But she was disappointed. Miles did not return that day or the next either, and Chandra began to fear that he had met with an accident. As the hours passed without his return, her expectation gave way to sickening fear. Could fate be so cruel as to snatch him from her just as they at last had quelled the misunderstandings that had kept them apart?

Martha tried in vain to calm her, assuring her that

he must have been detained for some valid reason, but Chandra was not to be soothed.

The morning of the barbecue came and went with no sign of Miles. Chandra, her heart aching, went about helping Martha, seeing to the setting of the tables on the broad lawn that lay between Haughton Hall and the Rappahannock.

Tantalizing odors arose from the great barbecue pits where beef, lamb and pork were roasting under Howard's direction.

"Chandra," Martha said, her arms full of fragrant fresh mint that had just been cut for the juleps the men favored on hot days, "I must warn you that Kitty Keating will undoubtedly be here today. It is our custom to invite all the planters and their families, and if I know Kitty, she will be here even though her husband cannot attend. Poor old John had a stroke last November, and the end is not far off for him." Martha paused, seeing a coach approaching in the distance. "If I am not mistaken, that is our first guest arriving," she announced. "Come, Chandra, we must hurry upstairs and dress."

The knowledge that Kitty might be at the barbecue caused Chandra to discard the gown of pink and white checked dimity that she had planned to wear in favor of a fine white cambric with tiny puffed sleeves and a low-cut bodice embroidered in blue that set off her porcelain skin and sable hair most becomingly.

By the time she had completed her toilette and emerged from the house, two score people already dotted the broad lawn. The sun was at its noon zenith, and the promise of a fine party was written on the guests' faces.

The day had grown hot and humid, and gray clouds threatened on the horizon as Chandra descended the stairs to join the guests. Many of them were already quenching their thirst with the cooling drinks that had been set out: lemonade, mint juleps, wine, cider, and several others. Chandra gratefully accepted a glass of cherry shrub.

As she took her first sip, she saw a gig pulled by a

brown hackney arrive at a brisk trot. One of the Haughton slaves jumped to take the reins and help the gig's sole occupant down. It was a woman in a wide-brimmed straw hat, its crown tied with a wide green bow. As she alighted, her clinging gown of green jaconet muslin revealing her full figure, Chandra recognized the newcomer as Kitty Keating. Beneath the brim of the hat, which protected her pale skin from the scourge of the burning sun, copper ringlets curled about her face. The softness of the curls contrasted with the hard set about her eyes and her wide, sensuous lips.

Kitty was very determined about something, Chandra thought, watching as the woman eagerly searched the faces of the crowd. Finally, disappointed, she joined the other guests.

Lord William Pembroke arrived about one-thirty, and Chandra found herself greatly challenged to avoid his company. Finally, in desperation, she retreated into the house and hid there for several minutes before going out onto the back portico. Since it faced away from the river, it was out of sight of most of the guests on the lawn. She settled herself in the swing suspended there and congratulated herself on having given his lordship the slip.

But her triumph was short-lived. Within a couple of minutes Pembroke was beside her, audaciously seating himself in the swing without so much as asking permission.

Chandra would have risen but he grabbed her hands firmly in his own. "Why, after giving me every reason to believe my company was most pleasurable to you, have you suddenly begun to avoid me?" he asked bluntly.

When she tried to free her hands he only held them more tightly. She was unnerved by the hard, calculating look in his eyes. It was hardly the tender entreaty of a hurt swain.

As lightly as she could manage, she said, "My lord, I fear you read too much into the natural friendship I feel for one of my countrymen when we are both far from home."

The gray eyes narrowed angrily and he looked away, his mouth tightening as though he were struggling to control his temper. Suddenly, without warning, he dropped his hands, seized her in his arms, and kissed her hard upon the lips.

For a moment she was paralyzed by shock. Then, as she began to struggle to escape him, he hastily released her. Instantly he was on his feet and, as if divining her reaction, he jumped back from the swing, beyond the reach of her hand. She had never felt so impelled to slap a man's face.

Her hand dropped back, unable to reach its target. "How dare you," she sputtered. "Don't you ever . . ."

The outraged tirade into which she was launching was cut off by the apologies flowing in a rushing torrent from Lord William's lips.

"I beg you to forgive me . . . I swear I did not mean to do that . . . I fear you have so bewitched me that I quite lost my head . . . Take pity on my poor distraught heart and forgive me my moment of madness."

The words tumbled smoothly, fluently from his lips, and Chandra thought she sensed a gleam of triumph, as disconcerting as it was inexplicable, in those cold gray eyes.

His profuse apologies did little to cool Chandra's ire, and when they had run their course, she snapped, "Get away from me and leave me alone, you arrogant prig!"

He departed, affecting nonchalance despite his rather hasty gait.

As he left her, Chandra saw to her horror that a young couple whom she did not know had been watching the scene intently from some distance away. Several other persons were near them on the lawn, and Chandra wondered how many of them had witnessed Lord William's kiss.

Certainly this would strengthen the rumors already circulating about her and Pembroke. But, worst of all, what if Miles should hear of this? She could not expect him to believe her version. If only she had acted on impulse and actually slapped the man, but from a distance it must have appeared that she had acquiesced to his advances.

Chandra was reminded yet again that the behavior of titled gentlemen was often execrable. She glared after Lord William with murder in her eyes and saw to her surprise that instead of joining the other guests on the lawn, he was retreating in the opposite direction, around the other side of Haughton Hall. What could interest him there? But she was too distraught to reflect upon this further and retreated into the house to compose herself.

If only Miles had returned, none of this would have happened. Tears crept down her cheeks at the thought that he might have met with an accident on the road from Washington. And now she had the added fear that if and when he did return, he might be told by someone who did not know better that she had committed an indiscretion with Lord William. That might be enough to destroy the fragile relationship between her and her husband forever.

She struggled to subdue her emotions so that she could face the crowd of guests on the lawn with some semblance of calm. Somehow she would have to think of a way to squelch the stories that no doubt were already beginning to circulate about her and Pembroke.

Chapter 37

Miles was delayed two additional days in Washington by a series of meetings. Jefferson had summoned his closest advisers to discuss the British pirates, who were continuing to take a heavy toll of American merchant shipping and coastal plantations. Secretary of State Madison, slight of stature, his face still drawn from his recent illness, attended. So did Albert Gallatin, the Swiss-born secretary of the treasury; Henry Dearborn, the secretary of war; as well as a covey of ship owners and planters, including Miles's brother-in-law Devin Darcy, from the southern seaboard states.

Listening to the talk around the long mahogany table in the president's house, Miles was quickly apprised of the situation. The *Black Wind* and its companion ship had struck terror into the hearts of shippers and coastal residents from Georgia to the Chesapeake Bay with their lightning raids. Their boldness and their cruel brutality toward the residents of the plantations that they plundered had wreaked havoc. Some of the panicky planters were muttering darkly against the government for failing to protect them from these barbarians.

The attacks could not have come at a worse time, on the heels of the bitterly fought presidential election that had already weakened the tenuous union that bound the young country together. Many Americans were questioning whether separation from England had been the wisest course. The shippers and planters gathered around the table grumbled that if they had still been under the protection of the Union Jack, they would not have to fear being set upon by English pirates.

"It's suspected that the brigands are being aided by some of our own people," said Eustace Farnefold, a portly planter and politician from the James River, which had been one of the pirates' targets. "The scoundrels seem to know exactly which vessels are carrying the richest cargo and which plantations offer the greatest treasure as well as where it is hidden within the houses.

"Surprise has been their greatest weapon," he continued as the other men nodded their agreement. "They sweep in on dark, cloudy nights, tie up the men, torture them, and force them to watch as their womenfolk are raped. Page Owsley's wife has gone mad as a result of their treatment of her."

"I don't understand why these pirates are also raiding plantations," Devin Darcy said in his deep, commanding voice that exacted attention and respect. "There's far more profit and less risk in seizing rich merchant vessels."

Miles listened carefully to his brother-in-law. The once jet black hair had grayed, but it had only made him all the more distinguished. The deepset blue eyes were grave, and the passing years had etched some lines in his slender face, but he still carried himself with the youthful, insolent grace that had marked him as a leader among men and a heartbreaker among women.

Devin was as fastidious as ever in his dress. His impeccably tailored coat of blue broadcloth that matched his eyes, his waistcoat of cream corded silk, and his black twill silk breeches fastened at the knee with four buttons all revealed that although he was now in his late forties, his body was still as trim as it had been twenty years ago.

Farnefold took umbrage at Devin's statement.

"Let me tell you, Darcy," he burst out angrily, "it is no small treasure that those pirates have taken from our plantations—great quantities of money, costly jewels, silver, and many other valuables and art objects."

"Still it is nothing compared with the profit from one plump merchant ship," Devin said calmly. "I think there is more to the pirates' game than mere plunder."

"It appears you may be right," Jefferson agreed. "This may have been what Pitt's warning was about, Miles. We have received a reliable report that the pirates are being sponsored by some powerful members of the English nobility. Sowing dissent and unrest among us then becomes as important a goal for the pirates as the financial gain from their bounty."

"It is interesting," Gallatin said in the heavy French accent that he had never lost, "that not a single merchant ship flying the flag of any nation but ours has been seized. Vessels of other countries have been approached but when they have shown their colors they have been permitted to go on unmolested."

"If dissent and unrest are the pirates' goals, I would say they have been most successful," Ludlow Massey, a lanky Georgian, observed, "and they have made our navy look like fools in the bargain. If these pirates aren't scuttled soon, you will find many people wanting to abandon the idea of a United States because they believe its government has abandoned them." Massey's blunt speech caused several of the other men at the table to chime in their agreement in loud voices.

"I have a plan, gentlemen, which I think will end the pirate threat," Jefferson said over the din. "I hope you will all support it."

When he finished outlining it, everyone except Darcy enthusiastically approved. But Darcy was the key figure in the scheme, and Miles quickly realized that a major reason he had been summoned to the meetings was to convince his recalcitrant brother-in-law to go along with the proposal. When they stopped for dinner, Miles took him aside and spent several hours alone with him.

When Devin reluctantly consented, he asked Jefferson if they might speak privately before the meeting reconvened. "I don't see how I can be ready to act in less than two months," he protested.

"We don't have two months, Devin," Jefferson said. "Two weeks at the most."

"Impossible," Darcy replied.

"But you have always done the impossible," Jefferson said softly.

Miles, to his dismay, was drafted to help Darcy make the initial preparations for his mission. Fears for Chandra's safety made it most difficult for him to concentrate on anything except his brother-in-law's impatience, and Darcy took note and teased him. "At long last you know what it is to love, Miles. 'Tis said that first love is like the measles. The longer 'tis postponed, the harder the case."

Finally Miles was permitted to leave. In his anxiety over Chandra, he wore out a half-dozen horses on the road to Haughton Hall. He was desperate to reassure himself that neither of her menaces, Warfolk or her unknown stalker, had reached her in his absence.

Miles was haunted more and more frequently now by memories of that night at the London madam's and those faint terrible shrieks he had heard from the room down the hall. His blood ran cold at the thought of what Warfolk, with his insatiable appetite for vengeance, would do to Chandra should he ever succeed in getting her back. As Miles recalled their two brief experiences together and imagined Chandra's lovely sensual body laid out before that sadistic monster, he clenched his fists. He silently vowed to give his life up to the goal of protecting her and cherishing her. And making her happy, if he were ever able.

Doubts plagued him still about whether he had truly won Chandra's heart. The warmth of their parting had indicated this was true. Still she had not admitted it to him. His mind would have been much eased had he had time before his departure for that frank discussion. At some point, they would have to sweep away the accumulated misunderstandings between them.

Then there was that English coxcomb, Pembroke. He seemed to hold some attraction for her. And no doubt

Pembroke was doing his best to win Chandra's heart in her husband's absence. Miles was baffled by why Chandra enjoyed the Englishman's company so much, except for her adherence to her father's old foolish notions.

Now, as he covered the final miles to Haughton Hall, his impatience increased with his horse's pace. Finally, the red brick mansion on the knoll came into view. As he rode up, he was dismayed to see the throngs of people on the lawn. Of course, he remembered, this was the day of the Haughtons' annual barbecue.

"Damn," he muttered to himself. He had hoped to bear Chandra quickly off to Willowmere, and instead he would be forced to spend at least a couple of hours here talking politely to his neighbors while he ached desperately for her and would have to content himself with nothing more intimate than a hand upon her waist.

He dismounted and strode toward the guests, eagerly searching the crowd for his wife. But she was nowhere to be seen and apprehension tugged at his heart. Miles was suddenly chilled despite the heat of the day. He spied Martha and hurried up to her, his face betraying his concern. "Where is Chandra? Has something happened to her?"

"Of course not," Martha reassured him. "I saw her step out onto the back portico a moment ago. Perhaps she is still there."

As they walked together toward the rear of the house, Miles apologized for his casual attire. His haste and the heat of the road had caused him to abandon both coat and waistcoat, and he wore only a white shirt open at the neck and his yellow buckskins. His usually gleaming riding boots were heavily coated with dust.

"I totally forgot this was the day of your barbecue, and I was so anxious about Chandra that I came directly here without going home to change first."

"I understand, Miles. Please, you need not worry about *clothing!* Chandra has been terribly worried since you failed to return when you were supposed . . ."

Martha stopped abruptly as the rear portico came into view. Pembroke was in the swing with Chandra, clasping her hands tightly. As Martha and Miles watched, his lordship took Chandra in his arms and kissed her.

Miles froze, his face twisted in a mixture of disbelief, anger, and pain. He felt as though his heart had suddenly been shattered into tiny bits. Had Chandra been merely toying with him when he had left for Washington, setting him up for a fool?

He watched as Pembroke released his wife and rose. Although Miles could not see the expression on their faces from this distance, Chandra appeared to be enjoying a lively conversation with the Englishman. She had evidently made no move to express displeasure.

Miles saw that he was not the only interested observer of his wife's unfaithfulness. Young Jamie McNaughton and his bride were watching. Other neighbors were scattered about the lawn, and Miles wondered how many of them had witnessed the kiss. Chandra had not even had the decency to be discreet, but had flaunted her scandalous behavior! Her public humiliation of him compounded her infidelity.

Miles whirled on his heels and stalked across the lawn toward the tables. He snatched a mint julep from a passing waiter's tray and drained the tall glass as though it contained nothing more potent than water. He had already taken a second drink and had started on it when Martha reached him.

She touched his arm, her face troubled. "I don't understand. What we just saw, Miles, I'm sure there is some explanation for it."

"Pembroke obviously made the most of my absence." Miles's eyes glittered dangerously.

"Chandra refused even to see him while you were gone. She told me she found him a tedious bore and tolerated him only to make you jealous."

"She hardly looked bored just now." Miles drained his second drink. "Nor did she seem in the slightest offended by his kiss."

Kitty appeared at his side, and Miles greeted her with such warmth that, after she recovered from her surprise, she glowed. She quickly maneuvered him away from the crowd toward a giant secluded elm, but not before he claimed a third mint julep.

Martha, turning away to attend to her other guests, sighed aloud. She wondered seriously whether there was any hope at all now for the Carringtons' marriage.

Chapter 38

After a brief ten minute rest, Chandra felt sufficiently composed to leave the sanctuary of the house and rejoin the guests who by now blanketed the lawn.

As she came down the steps of the portico, she searched the crowd for familiar faces and caught sight of Kitty Keating's green jaconet gown across the lawn beneath a large elm. Kitty was engaged in an obviously intimate conversation with a man leaning casually against the tree's trunk. Her face was very close to his and her hand rested possessively on his arm.

Chandra then turned her attention to the man. The world seemed to fall away beneath her as she recognized Miles. She missed the bottom step, tripped and would have fallen had not Pembroke caught her.

Chandra was so distraught that she scarcely noticed that it was Lord William who helped her, nor did she pause to wonder how he happened to appear so suddenly at her side.

She hastened across the lawn toward her husband as though she were walking through a nightmare. For the past week, she had lived for the moment when she would see Miles again. She had dreamed of the warmth and the passion in which they would be enveloped, dreamed of holding him in her arms, dreamed of his making love to her and of her body blossoming beneath his touch. How frantic she had been when he had not returned two days ago. She had been tormented with visions of him waylaid and murdered by robbers on the road.

And now at last he was here, but he had sought out Kitty, not her. By the time Chandra reached them, her lower lip was trembling.

Miles made no attempt to meet her, but lounged against the tree with cold contempt in his eyes.

She was so shaken by his inexplicable hostility that she could only murmur reproachfully, "Miles, you might at least have let me know that you had returned. I have been worried half out of my senses by your delay."

He gave her such a hateful glare that it seemed to freeze the very marrow in her bones. "I fear, madam, I was diverted." His left hand caressed Kitty's arm possessively. "By a more pleasant companion."

Chandra stared at him, unable to believe what her ears had heard. Horror was etched on her face.

Kitty gave her a broad smile of triumph, and Chandra realized that other guests were watching them. It took every bit of her willpower to keep from fleeing in tears. Instead, she managed to say coolly, "In that case, I apologize for having disturbed you."

With her head held high, she turned and walked away, conscious of every step she took. She would not let all their neighbors see how severely Miles had wounded her or how much she cared about him.

In her anguish, she did not notice that Pembroke was walking a half step behind her. All she could think of was getting away from those hundreds of eyes staring at her. She must find a hidden spot where she could sob out her misery in solitude. She headed toward a grove of cedar and birch that bordered the far side of the lawn.

In his haste to return to Chandra, Miles had not taken time to eat all day. The three mint juleps he had consumed so hastily on an empty stomach had befuddled his mind and turned his limbs to lead. As he watched Chandra walking regally across the lawn, her head held high with Pembroke in her wake, he was convinced, with that surety one has only in a drunken haze, that the Englishman was accompanying his wife.

"To hell with her," he thought bitterly. "I've got

Kitty here, and that English coxcomb's welcome to Chandra."

Kitty stroked his arm.

Miles turned affably toward her. How nice it was to have a willing woman for a change! A woman who did not make a fool of him by advertising her faithlessness in front of his neighbors. A woman who did not prefer an English fop's kisses to his own. And one who gave her body willingly, without pretense or coy reluctance. Still, even in his inebriated state, he was confused by the anguish on Chandra's face. She had been visibly upset to see him with Kitty. But if she cared for him as much as that look indicated, why had she been kissing Pembroke on the portico swing? It made no sense, but perhaps, he sighed, when he sobered up he would be able to figure it out.

"Come, darling," Kitty whispered seductively in his ear. "Let's leave here and go to Willowmere where we can be alone. I'll have my gig brought around."

When Miles offered no protest, she hurried off, and as soon as she had gone, Martha appeared at his side with a plate of food and a steaming cup of black coffee.

"Eat this, Miles," she ordered in the same tone she used on her children. "It will help sober you up."

He did as she bid, suddenly realizing that he was famished. As he ate, Martha spoke to him quietly. "In all the years I have known you, Miles," she said, "this is the first time I have ever seen you drunk." He did not respond, but simply attacked the plate and mug with voracious interest.

By the time Kitty returned, Miles had cleaned the plate with speed and manners that would have appalled him had he been sober. His mistress looked impatient and he allowed her to lead him off.

"Where are you going?" Martha called in alarm.

"To Willowmere," Kitty proclaimed, her green eyes glowing with triumph.

Once Chandra reached the trees, she plunged into their blessed concealment and began to run. She had gone several yards before it penetrated her numb mind that someone was running after her.

Hoping it was Miles, she turned and was shocked to find herself face to face with Lord William.

"What are you doing here?" she gasped.

He seized her roughly, anger glinting in his heavily lidded eyes.

"Let go of me," she ordered.

Instead of releasing her, Pembroke pinned her against the trunk of a birch.

Chandra was suddenly afraid, but she was determined that Lord William not suspect this. "Stop it," she snapped, trying vainly to push him away.

His mouth twisted into a sneer. "You have toyed with me too long, promising me much, but giving nothing, and now I intend to collect."

"You are mad!" She tried to squirm from his grasp and, as she twisted, the tiny gun, concealed in the deep pocket of her white cambric gown, bumped against her side. Obedient to Miles's command, she had been carrying the weapon with her constantly since his departure for Washington. Now if only she could manage to extract it from her pocket!

Still holding her against the tree, he forced her chin up and clamped his mouth upon hers. The pressure of his body against hers increased and she felt as though she were being crushed between him and the tree. She tried to twist away from his mouth and his grasp but succeeded only in scraping her back painfully on the bark. She had to get him to loosen his grip on her so that she could get her hand into her pocket.

She stopped her struggling to lull him into believing that she had acquiesced to his advances. She even forced herself to return his kiss and nearly gagged as he probed her mouth roughly.

"That's better," he whispered, loosening his hold upon her so that he could slip his hand beneath the thin cambric of her low-cut bodice. He seized her breast, forcing it up roughly so that he could fasten his lips upon its pink crown. As he sucked on her noisily, she placed her hands firmly on his shoulders, braced herself against the trunk of the birch, and gave him a mighty shove.

He stumbled backward, and nearly fell, but managed to regain his balance, cursing her roundly.

"What a vixen you are," he snarled. "No wonder your husband prefers the more complacent charms of that copper-haired paramour of his."

Chandra quickly scrambled away from the tree and pulled the gun from her pocket.

Pembroke started toward her only to find himself staring down the metal barrel of her tiny gun.

"What the devil!" he exclaimed.

"If you take one more step toward me, I will shoot you."

He hesitated, then laughed derisively. "You little bitch, you haven't the slightest idea of how to use that. Unfortunately for you, I am calling your bluff."

He lunged at her, and Chandra aimed at the fleshy part of his left thigh. The ball pierced exactly where she intended. The wound would stop him but do little serious damage except to his pride.

He staggered back from the impact of the shot and unleashed a string of curses so vile that she almost wished she had another ball to put through his mouth.

To her relief, she heard Howard Haughton calling her some distance away through the trees.

"Here I am," she cried.

Haughton burst upon them. "Are you all right, Chandra? I heard a shot." He stopped dead, gaping in amazement at the still smoking gun in Chandra's hand and the spreading red stain on his lordship's breeches.

"What the devil?" Haughton exclaimed.

"I fear his lordship was bolder than he should have been and I was forced to protect myself."

"Get Martha at once," Haughton told her.

She nodded and fled toward Haughton Hall, where Martha, sighting her, dashed across the lawn to meet her.

"What happened to Lord William?" Martha asked.

"I shot him."

"You did *what?*"

"He attacked me."

"But why would you shoot him when you seemed more than willing to receive his kisses. Miles and I saw you earlier this afternoon."

"What?" The word came out as a scream of anguish. Chandra grabbed Martha's arms and her fingers cut into them. "What are you talking about?" she cried frantically. "I cannot bear Lord William. I did not willingly kiss him no matter what it looked like." Tears spilled from her eyes. No wonder Miles had turned to Kitty and glared at Chandra with such hating eyes.

"Oh, Martha," she moaned, "what shall I do? Miles must be livid with me."

" I fear he will never forgive you," Martha said bluntly.

Chandra clutched the older woman's arm and begged, "Where is he? Please send him to me."

"He has already gone back to Willowmere." Martha paused. She could not bring herself to tell Chandra that Kitty had taken him there.

Chandra turned away and fled up the back stairs to her room where she hastily pulled on her pants and riding boots. Then she rushed down to the stable where she ordered an astonished groom to saddle the fastest horse he had, a chestnut stallion. She goaded him to his fastest gallop and raced toward Willowmere.

As she rode, the ominous black clouds on the horizon moved across the sky and paused directly overhead, promising to vent their fury at any moment.

Chapter 39

By the time Miles reached his bedroom at Willowmere with Kitty, he was wondering sourly how he had ever let her maneuver him into this situation. Of course he never would have, had he not been roaring drunk. By the time they reached Willowmere, he had slept off most of the effects of the liquor, and by the time his bedroom door shut behind them, he was thinking more clearly. All he wanted to do was rid himself of Kitty so that he could go back to Haughton Hall and have a confrontation with his wife. He was determined to have it out with her once and for all. No more sparring, no more games.

Miles watched Kitty without interest or desire as she shed her clothes, fervently hoping that Chandra would not find out in whose company he had left Haughton Hall. Jealousy was not a game he cared to play, even if, as Martha had indicated, his wife did.

Kitty was down to her shift of thin white lawn. She slipped it off, dropping it on the floor where she had carelessly scattered the rest of her clothing, and stood naked before him.

Outside, the storm broke, and a great bolt of lightning exploded across the sky, filling the room with its eerie light. For an instant, Miles thought he heard a horse, but the roar of the thunder drowned out all other noise in its deafening crash.

Kitty began unbuttoning his shirt, spreading it open to expose his powerful chest. She slipped her hands

around him and pulled him tightly to her so that her
bare breasts were molded against him.

She seized his head with her hands and pulled it
down, pressing her mouth to his. He let her claim his
lips but he made no effort to return her embrace. With
his arms hanging awkwardly at his sides, he felt like a
reluctant virgin being seduced.

The thunder ceased, and Miles listened again for the
sound of a horse, but heard nothing.

But he had not been mistaken. As Chandra had approached Willowmere the storm had turned the sky to a
peculiar dark violet with little more than silhouettes
discernible in the failing light. Then a mighty bolt of
lightning split the sky into dozens of jagged fragments
and turned the dusk to day for an instant. The lightning
illuminated Kitty's gig in front of Willowmere, and
Chandra recognized it immediately. The color drained
from her face, and her eyes were as wild and violent as
the storm.

The lightning was followed by a deafening roar of
thunder that sent the chestnut rearing and plunging in
panic. Chandra battled to control the frightened animal
and retain her seat. When finally she had subdued him,
she dismounted and threw the reins to a groom who had
come to lead the gig away.

"Take my horse and leave the gig here," she ordered
him. "It will be departing very soon."

She reached into her saddlebag, pulled out her tiny
gun, and slammed into the house.

She met Sarah in the hall.

"Where are Miles and Kitty?" Chandra snapped.

Sarah stared in astonishment at the sight of Chandra
—her face furious, her gun in hand—and cast an involuntary glance toward the top of the stairs.

Chandra ran up the steps and threw open the door to
Miles's bedroom. The noise of the door cracking against
the wall caused the couple next to the bed to start and
look up.

Kitty hastily backed away from Miles, her face white
with fear, a strangled noise in her throat.

The sight of Chandra in her riding pants, her lustrous hair tumbling about her in a wild cascade, reminded him of that day he had first laid eyes on her. Her blazing eyes and the gun in her hand pointed at him vanquished what remained of Miles's drunkenness as instantly and completely as if he had been suddenly immersed in an icy creek.

Angrily he cursed Kitty for luring him here and himself for letting her. Then his anger turned on Chandra. Damn it, he was the one who had the right to be furious after the compromising scene he had witnessed between her and Pembroke. Still he had to admit that at least Chandra had had her clothes on, which was more than could be said for Kitty at the moment.

"I do not appreciate your pointing that gun at me, madam," he said stiffly.

But she cut him off, her eyes flashing. "How dare you bring this strumpet into my home and flaunt her in front of me! How dare you sleep with her in our bed!"

A slight smile tugged at the corners of his mouth at Chandra's use of the expression "our bed." But he let it pass.

He took a step toward her. "Give me the gun, Chandra," he said calmly.

"Don't come any closer or I shall blow your head off."

Miles stopped short. Never had he seen her in such a fury, and knowing her expert aim, he did not care to test the consequences should he misjudge how far her anger would spur her. Yet, damn it, she was the one who had started all this. By God, as soon as he could get that weapon away from her, he would turn her over his knee and give her a well-deserved lesson.

Chandra pointed the barrel of her gun at Kitty. "Get out of here this instant, you trollop, or you will not live to walk out. And don't let me ever catch you at Willowmere or near my husband again."

Kitty, her eyes glassy with terror, snatched hastily at her clothes and fled, leaving a trail of garments behind her. Chandra slammed the door shut after her and turned to Miles, who was watching her and struggling mightily to control his temper. Now that they were alone, both Chandra's anger and her courage failed as she faced this man who was both husband and stranger to her. She noticed to her surprise that he was still fully clothed.

He said coldly, "I would have thought you too busy with your English lover to meddle in my affairs."

Her heart sank at his words. She would never be able to convince him of the truth. How she ached to have Miles wrap her in his strong arms, but that would not happen. As soon as she surrendered her gun, Miles would order her from Willowmere as she had ordered Kitty. He would never believe how much she loved him. He would never assuage the hunger she felt for him. In her misery she hit upon a desperate gamble. She waved her gun at him and ordered bluntly, "Take off your clothes."

He stared at her dumbfounded. "What?"

"You heard me. You wanted me to plead for your attentions. Well, I want you—*now*."

"Are you ordering me to perform my husbandly duties at gunpoint?" he asked in amazement.

"I am."

He shrugged, his impassive face giving her no clue to his thoughts.

"You should know, madam, that a man's anatomy is different than a woman's. He finds it very difficult to perform when he is in fear of his life."

Despite his words, there was no trace of fear in Miles's voice, only that dry, mocking tone that both irritated and unnerved her.

"You do not seem much afraid," she said as he calmly shed his shirt.

A strange look pulled at his face as he replied in a lazy tone that belied his words, "I assure you, madam, I am terrified."

He stepped toward her.

"Don't come another step nearer," she told him nervously. "I do not trust you."

"How am I to undertake my duties as your husband if you will not let me near you?"

If only he would not look at her that way. She knew he was only keeping his fury in check until he could get his hands on her. She had led herself into this trap, and now she had no idea what to do.

"You will not hurt me?" Her soft voice trembled fearfully.

"Hurt you? Hardly, madam." He held out his hand, and his tone changed abruptly to one of steely authority. "Now give me that damn gun."

Her courage deserted her entirely, and she obeyed.

He took the weapon and set it on the bedside table. "Don't you ever point that at me again," he said harshly.

"Then stay away from your mistress," she countered. But within her, apprehension was growing.

"You impudent vixen, you want discipline," Miles said, a strange gleam in his eye. "And I have just the punishment for you."

She looked at him in alarm. His face was inscrutable.

"Oh, Miles," she cried, not out of fear for herself but in terror that her actions had forever alienated this man she wanted so desperately, "I know you are furious at me for driving Kitty off." Tears welled up in Chandra's eyes. "But if I could only make you understand how much I love you and how I felt when I saw her here with you like . . ."

Miles's hand moved toward her, and Chandra broke off, closing her eyes and steeling herself for his blow.

Instead, his fingers gently brushed the tears from her cheeks, then moved up to caress her temples and stroke her face. He fluttered kisses, as light as a butterfly's wing, on her closed eyelids, on her hair, her forehead, her nose, her cheeks, and the curve of her neck. For a moment she was frozen in confusion, then her anxiety dissolved in a pulsing excitement at this tender yet sensuous assault that left every nerve in her body tingling.

At last his kiss alighted on her lips—and stayed.

His mouth grew more demanding, and she returned

his embrace hungrily. His arms encircled her and held her against him, molding her soft body to his strong, muscular one. Then suddenly he released her. Chandra drew in her breath nervously as he picked up the little gun on the table beside them.

"Before we proceed any further, madam," he said, his voice brimming with laughter, "perhaps I would be wise to place this beyond your reach just in case my husbandly performance should fail to satisfy you."

He sniffed idly at the barrel, and the laughter fled from his face.

"This gun's already been fired," he said in surprise.

She hung her head, unable to meet his piercing gaze.

"Tell me," he joked, "have you already shot someone?"

Her mouth felt dry. "Yes," she whispered. "Lord William."

Miles's face was again expressionless. "Mortally?"

She stared down miserably at the floor and whispered, "No."

"How disappointing. I trust, however, that you did him serious damage."

She looked up in surprise at Miles's impassive face and shook her head. "I only wanted to stop his advance so I aimed at his thigh."

Miles sighed. "And I suppose that, as usual, your aim was unerring?"

"Yes."

"Too bad." Miles shrugged casually. "Had your shot been a few inches off you would have spared a few husbands beside myself some anxiety."

She blushed as she caught the meaning of his words and retorted, "I assure you that you, at least, had no cause for worry."

"Then why did you lavish so much attention on his lordship?"

"Only to make you jealous," she replied with a flash of that disarming honesty that had so delighted him aboard the *Golden Drake*.

"Was that the purpose of the kiss I witnessed this afternoon?"

"No." Her sea blue eyes were beseeching. "You told me the scene I saw between you and Kitty that night at the Honeymoon House was not at all what I thought. I swear the same was true this afternoon with Lord William."

"But you went off into the woods with him."

"I did no such thing! I was so distraught at the way you had acted toward me that I didn't realize he was following me and . . ."

"And what?" Miles pressed, his voice cool.

"And I had to shoot him for his presumption."

"I'm sure that deflated his presumption, not to mention his ardor."

Chandra stared at her husband with wonder. "You aren't angry at me for shooting Lord William?"

"I find it quite understandable. I've been sorely tempted a time or two to do it myself."

"And you're not angry about Kitty, either?"

Miles took Chandra in his arms. "My darling, why should I be angry? Here I was wondering desperately how I was going to get rid of her when you burst in and solved the problem nicely for me."

Chandra pulled back from her husband. "Then why did you bring her here?" she demanded indignantly.

"Because I was drunk and furious at you for having kissed that English coxcomb."

"I did not! He kissed me, and most distasteful it was to me, too."

Miles tilted her lips up to his. "Let me do better, my love."

He kissed her tenderly at first and then with a growing fierceness as his hands roamed over the curves of her body, kindling her desire. Their lips remained fused for a long time as they sampled the joy of each other.

Then he was stroking her face and her hair as he murmured his love for her. It was difficult for Chandra to tell which filled her with greater pleasure, his words or his hands. His fingers unfastened the buttons of her shirt and camisole, exposing her firm, full breasts to his fiery kisses. He tantalized the taut peaks with his mouth until she moaned with delight, and her body ached for him to take her.

Finally his fingers began to fumble with the buttons of her pants. In a voice husky with passion, he complained, "I have never before, my love, undressed a woman wearing men's pants, and I confess I find skirts easier."

Her chuckle was cut short by a moan as Miles's fingers, having successfully disposed of the buttons, and the trousers as well, stroked her teasingly.

Fire leaped in her veins now, and her breathing had quickened. She pushed the shirt from his shoulders and, as he shucked it off, her arms encircled him. She pulled him to her, delighting in the feel of his warm skin and the curly hair of his chest against her.

He lifted her in his powerful arms and laid her on the bed. He hovered over her, his hands exploring her slender, graceful form with the ripe, inviting breasts, the tiny waist, the flat belly and the long, lithe legs.

"You are so beautiful, my love," he whispered as he shed his breeches.

"My love," she repeated dreamily. "On your lips, those are the most beautiful words I have ever heard."

He joined her on the bed, and they both sought what they so hungered for. His lips, his tongue, his hands caressed her body until it quivered with rapture; and she, although she was untrained in the art of lovemaking, found herself instinctively seeking to write her love for him on his body. She caressed each part of him, attempting to learn all that his body had to teach her.

At last they joined. Chandra, her desire inflamed by Miles's long, skillful prelude, surged up to meet him and clutched him to her as if she could not draw him deeply enough inside her. They moved together, transported on wave after wave of passion that rose ever higher. When at last Chandra thought she could bear it no longer, the waves crested in a series of convulsive peaks that shook her to her very core. Then the waves receded and she floated down gently on a cushion of pleasure.

As their bodies separated, she suddenly reached out and clung fiercely to him. "Oh, Miles, I love you so much."

"And I you," he answered, pressing a kiss of infinite tenderness upon her lips and stroking her smooth body.

They lay there quietly, their bodies touching, their passion spent, basking in the afterglow of their love and the closeness of each other.

Sheltered in the warm shadow of his body, Chandra was suddenly wildly curious about it. She wanted to explore it as he had explored hers. Her hand stole to his chest and she ran her fingers through the thick mat of dark hair. Her hand continued its downward course as Miles cast an inquisitive eye at her.

She started as her hand reached his dormant shaft, and she felt it harden and swell beneath her touch. She thrilled at the knowledge that she could make his body respond, and she stroked it wonderingly.

"Just what do you think you are doing?" he inquired hoarsely.

"I want to know you."

"Another minute of this, my love, and you will know me most intimately again."

Their passion rose and they came together fiercely to satisfy that need they had both so long denied.

Outside the storm grew worse as jagged fingers of lightning streaked across the night sky and thunder roared. But it was a small summer squall compared to the storm of passion in which the two lovers were caught. They shattered every misunderstanding in the wonder of their newly confessed love and their two bodies became one in ecstasy.

As Miles hugged her to him, he whispered with amusement, "Then you do not find my punishment so cruel?"

"Is this what you meant?"

"With a wife like you, what else could I mean?" he asked.

"In that case, I hope you find reason to do so frequently."

It was dawn before the long suppressed fires of their passion were banked, and they fell at last into a deep, exhausted sleep, holding each other as though they would never let go.

Chapter 40

The sun was creeping toward its noon zenith when Chandra woke. Her body was nestled against Miles, and his arm was thrown protectively over her. He still slept, his dark hair curling about his face, which was relaxed in happy serenity. Her lips curled in an unconscious smile as she remembered the night that had just passed. Unable to resist, she raised her head and settled a kiss upon his cheek. "I love you," she murmured.

His eyes opened sleepily and in the husky voice of the just-awakened, he inquired, "What was that, my love?"

"I love you," she repeated.

He grinned. "I am delighted." His voice grew serious. "But I am also most curious to know what prompted you to decide at long last that I might be a worthy husband after all."

Secure in the assurance of his love, she confessed, "I knew long ago. I had decided that upon the road from the inn that morning after our wedding."

He was suddenly wide awake. "What?" he demanded incredulously.

She stroked his cheek lovingly. "I admitted then, at least to myself, the justness of your charges against my father and his silly ideas about titles and other things. It was as if the scales had fallen from my eyes, and I saw you for the first time as you really were. But I was so angry that a man who cared nothing for me and had married me only to outwit his neighbor could make me burn so for him."

"You were wrong about me. I did care for you, my sweet. I must have. For although I itched to teach your pride a lesson, I could not bring myself to leave you in the hands of your scoundrel cousin. Furthermore, nothing would have made me marry you, just as nothing would have made me marry Sally, if I had not been willing."

"What?" she gasped, her head shooting up from the pillow indignantly. "Then why were you so cold and harsh toward me?"

"My temper was sorely strained." His hand stole up to fondle one of her breasts. "I had my pride, too, and I was not going to come begging for either your hand or your body and be cruelly rebuffed for my efforts."

Chandra kissed him lightly.

"Are you sorry, then, that you married me?" she teased him.

"I've had my compensations." He kissed her, then raised his head. There was a mischievous gleam in his eye.

"Besides, I said life with you was not likely to be dull," a broad grin split Miles's face, "although I confess the past twenty-four hours have far surpassed my wildest expectations—both in and out of this bed."

He drew her to him and stroked her back and thighs. His mouth sought hers, probing it deeply. His chin was rough and unshaven but she did not mind. Nothing mattered but her love and her need for him. His hand, like his tongue, was probing now, stirring up the fires within her. Her breath came in short gasps.

They came together in a mutual urgency and gave themselves to their union with a wild abandon, glorying in the exhilaration of their love and this deepest expression of it. He knew exactly how to arouse her, and then, tantalizing, he would draw back until she thought she would faint with yearning for him. When at last she could no longer wait, she grasped him and guided him inside her where they both knew they would fulfill each other completely.

It was some time later that Miles rang for a servant

and, although by now it was more nearly dinner time, ordered breakfast trays brought to them in bed.

"But, sir," Chandra teased Miles after the servant had gone, "think how you will disrupt your household by demanding such special service."

"Vixen," he complained good-naturedly.

When the trays arrived with mounds of eggs, ham, fresh fruit and biscuits, Chandra spotted a small, dull piece of metal on Miles's. She picked up the small object and asked, "What is this?"

A broad, comprehending grin broke across Miles's face. "It's Sarah's thimble. She's paying off the bet she lost to me. Sarah has belatedly agreed that you are a worthy wife for me, and that she likes you almost as much as she does my sister Ondine." Miles squeezed Chandra's hand lovingly. "I am certain you will have no more trouble with her."

"Why are you so fond of Sarah?"

He took a sip of coffee. "For one thing, she is my aunt—or more precisely my half aunt—one of my grandfather's by-blows. Yes, the illustrious Marquess of Pelham."

Chandra choked on her tea. "How does she come to be here?"

"Her mother was not a willing receptacle of my grandfather's seed, and so she fled to America. She came to my father for help, and my mother insisted upon taking her and her daughter in."

"And Sarah has never left?"

"No. This is her home." Miles stole a side-glance at Chandra to catch her reaction to his next statement. "And it will remain so, if she wishes, as long as I am master here."

Although Chandra was still uneasy about the housekeeper, she nodded in agreement. She could not disappoint her husband. Her acquiescence brought a pleased smile from Miles's lips.

When they finished eating, he asked Chandra, "Are you still hungry, my love?"

She nodded. "But not for food."

" 'Tis the same with me. I fear, my love, you shall turn me into an idle gentleman planter, unwilling to undertake any task except the pleasuring of my bride."

"A most worthy occupation," she laughed, "and one to which I hope you will devote considerable time."

"I shall," he promised, turning to comply with her wishes.

When at last they arose, the day was well advanced, and they had scarcely dressed when Martha Haughton arrived.

Her eyes searched the Carringtons' faces apprehensively as they came down the broad staircase to greet her in the entry hall. Reassured by their obvious happiness, she gave them a delighted smile.

"I see you two have finally listened to your hearts," she told them. "I have been so worried about the foolish way you both were acting yesterday that I had to come over and assure myself everything was all right." Her eyes twinkled with sudden humor. "Sarah tells me that Kitty departed very quickly and very unexpectedly."

Chandra blushed while Miles laughed.

"Pembroke, I am afraid, is still with us," Martha went on.

Chandra gasped. "I forgot about him. How is he?"

"You wounded his pride far worse than his leg. I do hope, however, that the next time you find it necessary to shoot a man, Chandra, that you will do it on someone else's property. Lord William is far from my first choice as a houseguest."

"I suppose I am infamous now." Chandra turned worried eyes to her husband, expecting to see him furious at her.

To her surprise, Miles only grinned. "The Carrington women have always been unconventional," he shrugged. "I should have been sorely disappointed if you had been different."

Before Chandra could seek an explanation of this statement, Martha said, "You need not worry that Lord William will tell anyone how he acquired his wound."

"Embarrassed, is he?" Miles inquired.

"And enraged." Martha's face was grave. "It would be wise, Chandra, to carefully avoid his lordship in the future."

Chandra's eyes glittered with anger. "I pray I shall never have to lay eyes on him again."

After Martha had left, Miles and Chandra stood together on the portico. "I fear, my love," he said at last, "that I must devote a little time this afternoon to my neglected plantation. What will you do while I am gone?"

"Move into *our* bedroom."

With Miles gone off toward the stables, Chandra went upstairs. She was carrying an armload of shifts and petticoats through the connecting door when she heard the door from the hall open. Glancing up, she saw Sarah there.

For the first time since Chandra had met her, Sarah seemed uneasy, almost shy. She came into the room with hesitant steps, her feet barely seeming to move beneath the skirt of her black bombazine dress.

She began speaking without preamble. "I did not believe you were right for Miles or that you loved him. I wanted him to have a wife like his mother or his sister, a woman of passion and courage." Sarah bowed her head and stared down at her hands, which were twisting a white linen handkerchief nervously. "Now I know that you are very much like them, just as Miles said you were, and that I was wrong. I apologize." She paused, and Chandra knew it had cost the housekeeper a great deal to say what she had just said.

Chandra took her hands and held them firmly. "I hope, Sarah, that we may be friends and that you will help me run Willowmere so that together we can make it a home most pleasing to my husband, whom I love very much."

Sarah clung to Chandra's hands. "I am afraid I did a terrible thing that I must confess. Perhaps you will feel differently about me when I have told you."

Chandra forced her voice to remain calm. "What did you do, Sarah?" she asked.

Sarah released Chandra's hands and began haltingly. "That day you were thrown from your horse, I purposely got you to go to the house in the woods. Miles was having supper there that night with John Dunlop, but I wanted you to think it was with Kitty Keating."

"But why?"

"I thought this might spur you to a showdown that would clear the air between you and Miles." Sarah raised her eyes pleadingly to Chandra's. "I know what I did was wrong, but I swear my intentions were the best. I hoped only to bring you and Miles together."

Chandra studied the woman. "Do you have any idea who cut my saddle?" Chandra asked abruptly.

Sarah appeared shaken. "None," she murmured.

A tiny doubt gnawed at Chandra. If Sarah had not been responsible for her fall from Gray Dancer, who could it have been? If only I knew, Chandra thought with a sigh, and if only I could put all thoughts of Warfolk behind me, then my happiness would be complete.

Chapter 41

The two weeks flew by. Despite the twin menaces that hounded her, Chandra was more content than she had ever been before in her life, basking in the glow of Miles's love for her.

Her nights were filled with bliss, as Miles lavished his lovemaking skills on her. He delighted in exclamations of joy and indeed he experimented continually in order to discover new ways of provoking such reactions from her. Chandra, as eager to please him as he was to pleasure her, responded with an aptitude that left him bewitched and marveling at the wonders of love.

Her days were becoming very busy. Gradually, under Sarah's careful tutelage, she assumed the myriad duties that were a dedicated plantation mistress's lot. She supervised the household servants, oversaw the cleaning and cooking, the smokehouse and the bakehouse, the garden and the dairy, the weaving and the sewing. She displayed a knack for handling the servants with a gentle firmness that quickly won their respect and obedience.

She personally kept the household accounts, and was astounded at the scope and expenses of the plantation. But her favorite task was arranging the many bouquets of flowers that Miles loved to have about the house: bowls of thermopis, Dutch iris, viburnum sprays, and Oriental poppies; vases of pansies, sweet William and veronica; or a single giant magnolia bloom. Her artistic flair with floral arrangements brought her many compliments from her husband.

Neighbors came frequently to Willowmere now. Chandra proved herself a charming and gracious hostess, and Miles made no secret of his pride in her. Any doubts tons' marriage in the wake of the Haughtons' barbecue tons marriage in the wake of the Haughtons' barbecue were quickly erased by the obvious love that shone between them.

Chandra still carried the tiny gun with which she had shot Lord William. She had been much relieved when she had learned from Martha that his lordship had departed hastily for a Potomac River plantation after two days of recuperating at Haughton Hall. Chandra prayed he would never again return to the banks of the Rappahannock.

She knew that Miles worried about her safety, although he never mentioned the duke or her would-be killer. He did not permit her to ride unless he was with her. And whenever she walked about the plantation compound, a trusted servant was either at her side or at a discreet distance behind her, at Miles's orders.

One night as the Carringtons were sitting on the portico after supper, catching the slight breeze that had sprung up after a blistering hot, still day, a tall, thin figure in frayed pants and a coarse shirt hurried up the path through the gathering shadows of twilight toward them.

"It's Jim Spenser," Miles exclaimed, rising to greet the youth.

Jim bowed to Chandra and shook hands with Miles. As he did, Chandra noticed the back of his worn shirt was spattered with deep brownish stains.

As Miles clasped his hand, Jim blurted out, "Please, sir, can I hire on with you?" The youth's eyes pleaded desperately. "I can do most everything, and I'm a good worker. You won't be sorry."

"But your uncle . . ."

"Oh, I know he'll cause you trouble if he finds out, but if I could just lay low here for a few days, he'll be gone. You know Dana Grove was foreclosed a couple of weeks ago, but he's refused to leave. Now they say they'll evict him by force if he doesn't go peacefully by the end of the week."

Miles suddenly noticed Jim's shirt. "Jim, what's wrong with your back?" he demanded sharply. "There's blood all over!"

Jim hung his head and did not answer.

"Take off that shirt!"

Slowly Jim obeyed Miles's command, and Chandra was hit with a wave of nausea as she saw the angry red furrows ploughed by a lash across the youth's back.

Miles's eyes narrowed dangerously. "Humphreys?"

Jim nodded. "I didn't do anything, I swear." Jim's tone was puzzled rather than defensive. "I swear Uncle Fred's gone crazy, plumb crazy."

Chandra laid her hand soothingly on the boy's arm. "Come with me and let me take care of you."

She led him toward the stairs, calling for soap and water and for Sarah to bring her healing salves.

As Chandra cared for Jim's tortured back in one of the bedrooms, the youth talked quickly to keep from crying out with pain. Miles sat listening intently on a chair next to the bed. "Uncle Fred's drunk half the time, and he sits and curses the rest of the world, especially you and Chandra."

"What does he hope to gain by refusing to leave Dana Grove?" Miles asked.

Jim moaned as Chandra touched a particularly deep groove, and it was a moment before he could continue. "Uncle Fred tried desperately to betroth Sally to Sam Bernard. While Sam was eager for the match, Sally would have none of it, and neither would Sam's parents. They weren't anxious to bail out Uncle Fred."

"Has Humphreys given up his scheme then?" Miles inquired.

Jim nodded. "Now he seems to have something else in mind. He won't even tell Sally what it is, only that he's arranging a match for her that she will like. I can't figure out what's going on in that crazy mind of his, and neither can Sally, not that she much tries or even cares. She's too busy crying in her room all day long."

Chandra was applying Sarah's salve to Jim's back. "It's inhuman what your uncle has done to you," she said fiercely.

" 'Tis nothing compared with what he's doing to his slaves."

"He always treated them badly," Miles said bitterly.

"That's true," Jim said, "but it's hideous now. It's as though he has to prove he's still their master. It's worse for the poor women. He alternates between beating them and rutting on them. There's likely to be more than a few reminders of him growing up at Dana Grove in the years ahead."

Jim caught sight of Chandra's shocked face. "Beg your pardon, ma'am, but 'tis the truth."

One afternoon two weeks after Miles's return from Washington, as he and Chandra were finishing dinner, a letter from Percy arrived.

It was addressed to Miles, and much of it was illegible, written in a sprawling, childlike hand, and so splotched with ink that some whole words were blotted out.

What Miles could make out of it filled him with horror. Percy railed at him bitterly for his stinginess in refusing to pay the debt to Murchison and blamed Miles for Lord Lunt's having disinherited him.

"But I have paid you back for the trouble you have caused me," Percy wrote. "I have told the Duke of Warfolk where Chandra is, and already he has ordered his agent in America to bring her back. You will never be able to stop him."

Miles looked blankly at the ink-stained sheet in his hands, both frightened and puzzled by Percy's reference to the duke's "agent in America." Who could that be? The fact that Warfolk already had a trusted man here made the danger to Chandra all the more threatening.

Miles did not want to show Chandra the letter, but she insisted.

"You will not find its contents pleasing," he warned her.

As she read it, the color drained from her face. The letter fell from her hands and fluttered to the floor.

"I suppose," she said blankly, "that I have been nursing in the back of my mind a tiny hope that Percy would not, after all, be so despicable as to sell me to the duke." Tears trickled from her eyes. "But I was wrong."

Miles jumped up and gathered her in his arms. "I promise you, my sweet. Warfolk will never have you. I will fight for you to my dying breath."

But he could not chase the look of great fear from her eyes.

The next day a new face appeared at Willowmere. He was a nice-looking young man of about twenty-five. He wore buckskins and a gun in his belt. His name, Miles told Chandra, was Grant Horn, and he was recently mustered out of the army after distinguished service on the frontier.

"He is a crack shot, and he will be your bodyguard," Miles said. "Whenever I am not here, he will be with you. If you are inside, he will be always at the door of the room you are in; if you are outside, he will be at your side. Don't try to go anywhere without him. Promise me."

Chapter 42

Chandra was working on her household accounts in the tiny room off Miles's office which had been his mother's study. She found she was having difficulty with the column of figures before her, although there was nothing to disturb her concentration. Sarah, whose nursing skill was much sought after, had been summoned to the bedside of a sick child in the slave quarters, and the big mansion was quiet. Tired of the figures in front of her, Chandra got up and went into the hall where Grant Horn, never far from her side these days, was at his post by the door, dozing in the heat in his straight-backed chair.

Poor man, Chandra thought, it was stifling in the hall. She let him sleep and wandered out onto the portico overlooking Willowmere's gardens, hoping for a cooling breeze.

The gardens had exploded into a dazzling summer array of color: hedges of crape myrtle were crowned with white and pink flowers. Spires of foxgloves dangled their delicate yellow, blue, and lavender bells. The barest hint of a breeze wafted the sweet fragrance of the gardenia bushes about Chandra, and she breathed deeply of the perfume. How beautiful it all was, she thought. Like an enchanted paradise.

But the spell was broken by the faraway sound of someone calling her name. It was a little slave child running as fast as his short legs could carry him up the elm-lined road. She hastened down the steps and hurried to meet him. As she reached the boy, she recognized him as the son of one of Willowmere's field hands. His face glistened with sweat and his breath came in hasty gulps.

"Massa Dunlop sez yuh to come to de house in de woods. Massa Carrington done been hurt and dey took him dere."

"Hurt! What happened?"

Her frantic questions only added to the fright in his eyes, and he shook his head.

"Ah don't know. Dey just tole me to get yuh."

Chandra, her mind whirling in fear and confusion, ran to the stable where she found Tam about to un-saddle a frisky chestnut Thoroughbred that he had been exercising. Chandra grabbed the reins from the startled man and managed, despite the handicap of her long skirt and petticoats, to struggle into the saddle.

"Mr. Carrington's been hurt. I must go to him at once." As she rode off, she cried over her shoulder, "Send someone at once for a doctor and for Sarah, and have them come to the house in the woods."

As she pushed the horse to a gallop, she prayed that Miles was not badly hurt. She could not bear the thought of losing him now that their happiness together had only just begun.

The house was quiet and seemingly deserted, but so frantic was she to reach Miles that she did not pause to reflect upon it. She leaped from her mount and ran up the steps, throwing open the door and racing inside.

The house was strangely, ominously still, the silence broken only by the raucous cry of a catbird in the distance. Chandra shivered with sudden apprehension. Something was terribly wrong. Her heart seemed to stand still for an instant. Could it be that she was too late. Was Miles already dead?

With a sob, she started toward the bedroom. Suddenly she was seized from behind. Her hands were twisted behind her back in a cruel grip, and a rope was pulled around her wrists.

She struggled frantically against her unseen assailant, twisting, turning, kicking at him, but to no avail. The duke's agent, Chandra thought in terror that gave added strength to her endeavors. But with her hands bound behind her, her efforts were futile.

She managed to twist her head far enough around to see the face of her captor. She gasped at the sight of Fred Humphreys, and for a fleeting instant, she felt a flicker of something akin to relief. Surely Humphreys could not be the duke's agent. But then she saw his eyes, sparked with a wild, unearthly gleam, and her terror rose higher. She knew that she was looking into the eyes of a madman.

"Where is Miles?" she cried, her heart splitting at the thought of what this crazed man might have been capable of doing to her husband. "What have you done with him?"

"Nothing. Nothing is wrong with your husband." Humphreys tightened the ropes around her wrists so that they cut into her skin. "But I have trapped you. I have trapped the witch." He gave a wildly exuberant laugh that turned Chandra's blood to ice. "And now I shall drive the devil from you."

Humphreys jerked Chandra around to face him, and he surveyed her triumphantly with crazed eyes. "You cast a spell over Miles Carrington and bewitched him, so that he abandoned my daughter, whom he loved dearly."

"You are raving mad," Chandra cried. "Miles never loved Sally!"

"He did! She was his lawful betrothed."

"Never—except in your imagination."

"You lie," Humphreys snarled. "She would be his wife now if you had not stolen him from her by your evil craft."

"I am no witch," Chandra cried, her fear swelling. She saw that Humphreys was carrying a long ugly whip coiled beneath his left arm.

His eyes glowed with menacing intensity. "But you are. Otherwise you would have died when I cut your saddle. But the devil protected you."

Chandra gasped. So her would-be killer was Humphreys. And now she was helpless within his power. There was nothing to stop him from killing her this time, unless somehow Sarah should arrive quickly. But, even if she did, she would be no match for him.

He reached for the whip under his arm. "Now I shall drive the devil from you, and when I have done that, you will die quickly enough. Then my Sally will have her rightful husband back, and she will be mistress of Willowmere as she should have been."

"I tell you, you are wrong," Chandra cried. "Even if I were dead, Miles would never marry your daughter."

"He will," Humphreys insisted stubbornly, his weird eyes glaring at her.

Despair welled up in Chandra. There was no reasoning with this madman. Her only hope was to try to run. She turned and fled blindly toward the back of the house. But her bound hands and the yards of material in her full skirt and petticoats hampered her progress, and Humphreys was after her like a shot. She sensed his hand shooting out to grab her. Dodging into the bedroom to elude his grasp, she heard him crash into the doorway.

She ran toward the bedroom window. It was closed, but she intended to throw herself through it. She would do anything to escape. But as she ran past the bed, she tripped on her long skirts and fell headlong to the floor.

Humphreys stood gloating over her as she lay helpless. "Now, I shall drive the devil from you," he said, uncoiling his whip.

She had never seen a whip like this. It was approximately nine feet in length and as thick as a man's fist at the top. He raised it and brought it down. She heard it whistle through the air toward her hips, and then its lash sliced into her skirts. She bit her lips together, thankful for her layers of petticoats, to keep from crying out with pain.

She waited for the lash to fall again. But, instead, Humphreys pulled a knife from a sheath on his waistband.

Chandra was certain he meant to plunge it through

her heart, but she did not flinch. At least this way it would be mercifully quick.

But her heart was not his target. The blade slashed at her skirts, cutting them away so that her legs, her thighs and her belly would be exposed to the full fury of his whip.

He picked up the lash and rose to his feet, panting like an animal. He uncoiled it, and brought it down again. As the lash cut through the air toward her, Chandra writhed and twisted in a vain effort to move to one side, out of the whip's reach. This time, a tongue of fire burned its way across her belly and her thighs, and a scream of pain was torn from her lips.

Humphreys raised the whip again, and she thrashed wildly. But the whip did not fall. Looking up, she realized to her horror that the sight of her naked had excited another kind of frenzy in her insane captor. She was about to be subjected to a different torture.

Humphreys threw the whip aside and dragged her onto the bed. He shed his breeches and dropped the leather sheath containing his knife carelessly on top of them.

As he came toward her, she drew her knees up to her chest and kicked out at him as hard as she could. Her feet caught him full in the chest and sent him reeling backward.

Chandra slid from the bed and struggled to regain her feet. Somehow, even with her hands tied behind her, she succeeded, and sprinted toward the door. That brief delay, however, had given Humphreys time to recover, and he grabbed her and forced her back onto the bed. He placed one knee beside her to steady himself. "Now," he said, grinning. "Now you'll get what you deserve."

Part Six

Chapter 43

Miles and John Dunlop were riding slowly along the road to Willowmere, discussing the prospects for this year's tobacco crop, when a horse and rider, traveling at full gallop, appeared in the distance.

"What is going on?" Miles asked as the horse drew nearer and he recognized it as one of his most prized Thoroughbreds. "I permit no one to ride Tarnation like that."

"There must have been an accident," Dunlop exclaimed.

Miles waved at the speeding rider, who appeared as though he would gallop past the two men on the road without the slightest slackening of his speed.

The rider thudded to a halt. It was Bob, one of the grooms. The man's eyes seemed as though they would bulge from their sockets as he stared, unbelieving, at Miles.

"Massa Carrington!" he stuttered in astonishment.

"Where are you going in such a hurry, Bob? That's no way to treat a horse."

The groom's confusion was obvious. "Ah was tole to fetch a doctor for yuh—dat yuh'd been hurt bad and were at dat dere house in de woods."

"What?" Miles was instantly alarmed. "Who told you that?"

"Tam," the excited groom replied. "Dat's what Miz Carrington done tole him as she went dere."

Miles felt as if a fist had just been driven full force into his stomach. It had to be a trap.

"Was Mrs. Carrington by herself?"

Bob nodded.

Miles groaned aloud. "Where the devil is Grant Horn?"

Bob looked confused. "Ah don't know."

Miles cursed to himself and exchanged a look with Dunlop. He, too, understood the danger that Chandra was in.

"Who sent for Mrs. Carrington?" Miles demanded.

Bob shook his head. "Dey didn't tell me."

"Never mind, Bob. You continue on for the physician and bring him to the house in the woods." He turned away from the groom, muttering under his breath. "I hope he won't be needed."

Dunlop drew the pistol he always carried.

"Take this, Miles. You horse is faster than mine, and you may need it when you get there. I'll follow you."

Miles grabbed the weapon and urged his horse to a gallop, praying that he would be able to save Chandra. Why and how in God's name had she eluded her bodyguard?

When he reached the house, he saw a horse tethered in front but no other sign of life. He leaped from his mount and sprang up the steps. As he reached the door, he heard Chandra's scream of pain from the bedroom, and he bounded through the house toward it.

He got there just as Humphreys was forcing Chandra down upon the bed. She was trying desperately to squirm away from him.

Miles was across the room in two steps, and grabbing Humphreys, he hurled him to the floor. The astonished man sat up, his face contorted with fury, and Miles bore down on him, yanking him to his feet.

Humphreys began blubbering with terror.

Miles's fist slammed into Humphreys' mouth.

As Humphreys crumpled, Miles turned to his wife who lay on the bed, her hands still tied and the angry red welts from Humphreys' whip scarring the smooth white skin of her thighs. Miles, in his horror, turned to concentrate his attention on Chandra.

He failed to notice Humphreys inching his way slowly along the floor toward his knife, which lay atop his discarded breeches. His fingers grasped the leather case and he extracted the blade from it. Triumph spread across his face as he jumped to his feet and raised the knife.

Dunlop reached the door of the bedroom at that instant. "Watch out!" he yelled. "Miles, he's got a knife!"

Miles whirled and threw up his arm to ward off the blow. The sharp blade slid along his arm, splitting his shirt and carving a bloody red furrow down his arm. He managed to send Humphreys flying, but the crazed man lunged back again.

Miles drew his pistol and fired just as Humphreys raised his arm to strike again. The force of the shot at such short range threw Humphreys back as it pierced his heart.

"Is he dead?" Chandra asked as Miles knelt beside the body.

Miles nodded, rose, and gathered the bed cover about her. He scooped her up and carried her into the drawing room, where he laid her on a settee.

Now that she was safe in her husband's arms, Chandra's self-control dissolved and she began to sob. Grimly, Miles examined the ugly welts that marred her delicate skin, and his face grew taut. Had he not already killed Humphreys, he surely would have done so now, so sickened and outraged was he by the sight of what he had done. "Did he succeed in . . . anything else?"

"No, not that, but if you had been a minute later . . ." She shuddered, unable to bear the thought of what would have happened.

Miles gathered her tightly to him, then kissed the welts on her arms as if by doing so he could draw the pain from them. "Don't worry, my love, you are safe now."

She nodded. "He cut the saddle cinch. He told me so."

Miles stroked her hair soothingly, and she felt a warm

sticky substance dripping on her. "You're bleeding!" she cried in horror as she saw the angry gash on his arm.

At that moment, Sarah arrived and took matters into her capable hands. Quickly she bound up the deep cut that Humphreys's knife had left. Then she turned her attention to Chandra's injuries.

"I thank the Lord that Miles arrived when he did," she said fervently as she applied a soothing balm to the wounds inflicted by the whip.

There could be no doubt about the sincerity of her words, and if Chandra had any lingering doubts about the woman's loyalty and affection for her, they were banished in that instant.

"At least we have one worry out of the way," Sarah said grimly as she finished her ministrations. "Now we have only Warfolk and the pirates to concern us."

"The pirates?" Miles repeated in surprise.

"They struck the Beaumonts' plantation at the mouth of the Rappahannock last night. And now, apparently, a third ship's been added to their fleet."

Chapter 44

When the Carringtons, Dunlop and Sarah returned to Willowmere from the house in the woods, Miles immediately launched preparations to protect the mansion from the English marauders. Every musket and pistol on the plantation was brought to him, and their condition checked to make certain they were in good working order. Then trusted slaves were summoned, and these men were each given a weapon. Dunlop took the women into another room and taught them how to reload.

To Chandra's surprise, even Sarah took up one of the muskets.

"Do you think you remember how to fire it, Sarah?" Miles teased her.

"Thank the good Lord I haven't had to since the revolution ended, but I'll wager I am still a pretty good shot." She gave Chandra a sly, half-proud smile. "From what I hear, however, I am no match for your wife."

Miles handed Chandra a musket. "I hope you can handle this as well as you do a pistol. We need all the marksmen we can muster."

Miles assigned each pair of defenders to a window or other strategic location in case of an attack, and there was little doubt in Miles's mind that the pirates would strike, and soon.

Willowmere was too rich a prize for the marauders to pass up.

Pallets were spread on the floors so that the watching sentinels might sleep next to their posts. The mansion had the air of an armed fortress.

"I want large torches," Miles told Dunlop, "the largest you can manage, placed along the lawn between the house and the river. Darkness and surprise are the pirates' chief weapons. If I rob them of the former, I will also deprive them of the latter. I want two slaves assigned to see that the torches are kept burning all night. I wager the brigands will not be quite so brave when they discover they have to make a run for the house, all the while making excellent targets for us as we watch from the windows."

Miles gestured toward the roof. "Also, I want two sentinels on the portico, and another man stationed below the house where the river bends. He is to fire a warning shot the instant he sees any suspicious movement on the water."

Chandra came over and put a hand on his arm. "Why didn't the other planters prepare to defend themselves as you are doing?"

"For one thing," Dunlop answered before Miles could speak, "most of the planters would not dare trust their slaves with weapons. They'd be as likely to use them on their owners as on the pirates. The esteem in which Miles's slaves hold him is very rare."

When darkness fell that night, Willowmere's defenders took up their appointed posts. With two muskets and a brace of pistols beside him, Miles stood at a second-floor window with a commanding view of the river and the lawn that led down to it. Outside, the blazing light from the torches nearly obliterated that of the thousands of stars in the night sky. The shrinking moon was little more than a slender crescent.

Chandra came up beside her husband, and he gave her a smile so warm with love that she could not resist reaching out and stroking the dark stubble that covered his cheek. His shirt was partially unbuttoned, revealing a bit of the dark curly hair on his chest. He wore a bandage on his arm where Humphreys's knife had sliced it.

Miles reached up and took Chandra's hand in his own, pressed it to his cheek, then guided it to his lips and kissed it.

Humphreys's marks upon her were concealed beneath a sacklike gown of pink cotton, but it was the wound he had inflicted upon her spirit that was most painful to her. She felt violated despite his failure in consummating his carnal intentions. She longed to have Miles take her in his arms, carry her off to his big tester bed, and make love to her there, vanquishing her agony with his tenderness. But he could not leave his post by the window tonight.

As if reading her feelings, he put his arms around her, drew her tightly against him, and murmured, "My love, try to put from your mind what happened today. I know it isn't easy to do, but Humphreys is dead. He can't hurt you."

She was so grateful for Miles's understanding. Her arms stole around him, returning his embrace. They stood there for a long time in the shelter of each other's arms, needing no words to express the feeling between them.

Finally, Miles gave her a squeeze. "You should go to bed, my love. You need your rest after this day."

She clung to him. "I want to be with you. Besides, if the pirates come tonight, you will need anyone who can fire a gun."

She smiled and nodded at the pallet that had been spread by the window for him.

"Let me stay beside you."

"It will be most uncomfortable."

"Not nearly so uncomfortable as it is for me to lie alone without you."

He took her in his arms and kissed her, soothingly first, then passionately. Their lips fused together with the heat of their love.

The pirates did not come that night. The next morning, Chandra wandered restlessly from room to room, unable to relax. The pallets were mute reminders of the danger that hung over Willowmere.

A messenger arrived summoning Miles to a hastily

called meeting at the Stratfords' of all the planters in the neighborhood to discuss a joint defensive strategy.

"Must you go?" Chandra asked her husband. How tired he looked. The sleep he had caught in brief snatches during the night's vigil could not have totaled more than a couple of hours. And his wounded arm was bothering him.

He took her hand. "Are you afraid to have me leave you alone here, my darling?"

She shook her head, searching for the words that would express her love and her desperate need for him. With each day, she and Miles seemed to grow closer, their love so intricately entwining them that life without him now was unthinkable to her.

"Not afraid, Miles, only lonely. When you are not here it is as though the soul has deserted this house. And my heart." She clasped her hands in his. "Please, if you must go, let me ride with you to the edge of Willowmere."

Her plea brought a frown to his face.

"Is my company so displeasing to you?" she teased.

"Your company pleases me mightily, my love, but it isn't safe. We still have the duke and his mysterious agent to contend with."

"Oh please, Miles," she begged. "Grant Horn can ride with us and guard me on the way back. It is so hard to be cooped up here. I beg of you, let me go with you."

Reluctantly, Miles acquiesced to her plea, and she ran upstairs to don her shirt and riding pants. As they started out with Grant Horn a discreet distance behind them, Miles told Chandra that he had sent Jim Spenser out to see if he could learn any new information about the pirates and their activities. The more they could piece together about the imminent raid, the better.

They were still a cosiderable distance from the edge of Willowmere when Miles insisted that she and Grant leave him and go back to the house.

Reluctantly, after a long, lingering kiss, Chandra turned Gray Dancer around and rode back toward the mansion with her bodyguard beside her. Without warning, a sudden tremor of unease, a strange premonition of danger, pricked at her.

You are silly, she told herself sternly. All the watching and waiting last night has made you nervous.

She and Grant Horn rode in silence. It was another oppressively hot day, and overhead the sky was graying with the threat of rain. As they rounded a curve through the trees, Gray Dancer was suddenly skittish, and Chandra struggled to control her wayward mount. "I don't understand what's the matter," she said, turning to Grant Horn. Just as she said this, a man on a rope came swinging out of a tall oak behind them, knocking Horn out of his saddle.

As Horn fell to the ground, another man leaped from behind a thick screen of alder shrubs and brought an iron pipe down hard on the back of Horn's head.

Gray Dancer reared violently and Chandra had all she could do to keep her seat. Suddenly another horse and rider were beside her. A hand shot out, seized Gray Dancer's bridle, and forced the horse to subside.

Chandra turned toward her benefactor and found she was facing the muzzle of a large pistol. Her frightened eyes looked up to the man's face, and she gasped.

Lord William Pembroke was sneering at her.

"What do you want?" she demanded, fighting down her rising fear.

His expression made his face, with its thin, cruel lips and cold gray eyes, seem even more sinister than it was. "Now you see what it feels like to be caught at the wrong end of a gun. Get down from that horse."

Lord William's clothes were uncharacteristically rumpled and soiled, as though he had not had an opportunity to change them for some time. His boots were scuffed and mud splattered, and stubble darkened his cheeks and chin.

"I said get down," he repeated to Chandra, gesturing at her with his gun, "or I shall have no more compunction about firing at you than you had at me."

Slowly Chandra dismounted, trying desperately to retain a defiant stance and hide her fear.

The sight of Pembroke's ugly companions only intensified her anxiety. The man who had struck Horn had a seamed, battered face that gave testimony to years of hard living. His nose, flat and misshapen, appeared to have been broken several times. One of his faded blue eyes was slightly cocked, giving him a particularly untrustworthy demeanor. His greasy, gray hair was pulled back into a queue that was tied at the neck with a soiled piece of ribbon.

The man on the rope, having dispatched Horn earthward, had slid down and now stood guard near Chandra. He was taller and younger but no more handsome than his companion. His face had several small scars, as if he had been repeatedly nicked by weapons.

Both men wore wide-brimmed black hats, black neckerchiefs, and tattered calf-length, bell-bottomed trousers. Each had a pistol and a dirk stuffed in the sash that served as a belt.

Chandra stared down in concern at Horn, lying so still on the ground with a bloody gash across the back of his skull. She dropped to her knees beside him to feel his pulse, but Pembroke snapped, "Get her up."

The two men seized her arms roughly and hauled her to her feet. They stank of fish and accumulated filth.

"Grimes," Pembroke ordered the younger of the pair, handing him Gray Dancer's reins, "take this horse and the other one and tie them up well back in the brush, so they can't be seen from the road."

Grimes obeyed, leading the two horses through the underbrush out of sight.

Chandra glared up at Pembroke. "Just what are you doing here?" she demanded.

"Waiting for your return. We saw you ride by earlier with your husband and figured that you'd be back this way before long. You gave us just enough time to prepare our welcome for you."

"I would not think you would seek my company after our last meeting," Chandra scoffed.

"Under other circumstances I would not." His thin lips tightened. "But I find that I must require your presence on my return voyage to England. I dare not return there without you."

"You are mad," she cried in alarm. "I shall not return to England with you or anyone else."

"You are wrong," he said. "Don't think for a moment I would have risked all that I have to reach you today were it not imperative that you accompany me across the ocean."

Panic was swelling in Chandra now. "What are you talking about?" she demanded.

"The Duke of Warfolk is not a man to disobey, and he is most adamant about your return."

At the mention of Warfolk's name, Chandra feared her knees would buckle beneath her, but somehow she managed to stay on her feet. Except for her shallow breaths, she gave no outward sign of the terror that gripped her heart.

"I dare not fail the duke," Pembroke said, "especially not after everything else that has happened." He added more to himself than to her, "Perhaps if he gets you back, it will mitigate his anger toward me. If I am lucky, he may take all his rage out on you."

The pieces of the puzzle all came together at once. "You are the duke's agent here, aren't you?" Chandra gasped.

He bobbed his head in a mock bow. "At your service." He turned to the older of the two men and told him, "Get a rope to tie her."

As the man plunged into the brush, Chandra forced her trembling legs into motion and started to run down the road.

Pembroke called harshly, "Stop or I shall shoot you. I have no particular care that it would not be a gentlemanly thing to do."

His tone told her how absolutely serious he was, and she halted.

"Hurry up with that rope, Skinner, and you, Grimes,"

he snapped at the younger man who was emerging from the woods, "help him. Tie both her legs and her arms."

As the two men seized her and began to bind her, she spat out at Pembroke, "You are a fool to think you can return me to England. No sea captain is going to be party to a kidnapping."

Pembroke's lips curled contemptuously. "The captain of the *Black Wind* will not distress himself with the reason for your voyage. In fact, he will welcome you aboard."

"The *Black Wind*," Chandra cried, realizing the full desperateness of her plight. She could not keep her voice from trembling as she asked the men who were tying her hand and foot, "You're from that British pirate fleet?"

Skinner's cocked eye regarded her balefully, and he grumbled under his breath, "Ain't no fleet now, it ain't. The Yankee Devil seed ta that. Not a one left, save the *Black Wind*."

"And you," she cried at Pembroke, "you are with the pirates." She remembered what Fitzhugh Flynn had said to her about Pembroke that night at Devonham's ball. "That's the business you had in America. Your story about seeking a plantation to buy was a mere ruse."

"True. My interest was in plunder, not purchase." A sardonic smirk pulled at the corners of his thin mouth. "These Virginia planters gave me far more assistance in achieving my ends than ever they dreamed as they dragged out their finest treasures to impress me. And the shipowners to whom they introduced me loved to boast of the rich cargo aboard their vessels."

His lordship's smirk gave way to fury. "And just as I was succeeding beyond my expectations, that damned American struck and destroyed two of the three ships." He turned to the two sailors. "Skinner, you carry the woman to the wagon." He motioned toward Grant Horn, who was stirring slightly as he recovered consciousness. "Grimes, you drag him down by the horses. Bind him to a tree and gag him."

Skinner swept Chandra up in his arms and plunged through the woods to the spot where they had hidden a weathered farm wagon. He dumped Chandra on the straw that had been spread on the floor and then returned to the woods for a huge, splayfooted workhorse that he hitched to the wagon.

Grimes bound Horn to the trunk of a post oak. The young man's eyes were open now, but they were glazed. He looked about wildly as he tried to comprehend what was happening. Grimes tied a filthy kerchief around Horn's mouth so that he could not cry out for help.

"Hurry up, you two," Pembroke ordered the sailors. He leered down at Chandra, tied and helpless in the wagon. "We wouldn't want to keep the duke waiting any longer than he has already, would we?"

She glared up at him, defiant and furious.

"Gag her, too," Pembroke said to Skinner, who stuffed another dirty rag into Chandra's mouth. Then he forced her down on the floor of the wagon and covered her over with straw.

She heard Pembroke tell the sailors, "I will ride ahead. You two get those weapons out of your belt and hide them in the straw. I don't want anyone imagining that you aren't simple farmers on an innocent journey."

Chandra heard a horse gallop away, and the wagon lurched forward. Tears of despair formed in her eyes. She was being dragged back to the duke and a life of hell just when she had found such happiness with Miles. Where would he be now? Perhaps he would find her before she was carried aboard the *Black Wind* and out of his reach forever.

But, she remembered with aching heart, he was not likely to return from the meeting at the Stratfords' for some time. When he found her missing, he would guess immediately that the duke's agent had seized her. But he would never suspect his identity nor that she was being taken to the pirate ship. He would not know where to begin looking for her. She had faced so many perils since she had fled Sir Henry, and in each and every case, Miles had rescued her.

But he would not be here this time, and she had no one to blame but herself. She had stupidly insisted over his objections that she ride with him, and her stupidity had condemned her, for as long as she was able to survive, to Warfolk's horrors.

Chapter 45

The wagon jolted along the rough road, bouncing Chandra from side to side beneath the straw. The ropes bit into her wrists and ankles, and she felt as though she might choke on the gag. She had no idea how long they had been traveling.

She heard the one named Skinner say to the other, "Oi 'opes the *Black Wind* don't sail 'fore us get back."

"Cap'n Flint won't be sailing without 'is lordship; 'e wouldn't dare," the younger sailor said.

"Wouldn't 'e now?" Skinner snorted. "It was 'is lordship what gave the orders to sail to this bloody river. The cap'n said it'd be our undoing, and 'e was right. And the cap'n ain't anxious to wait to meet up with that American devil what took the other ships."

"But like 'is lordship sez, none of us dare go back 'ome without the lass," Grimes said.

"And you can be sure that when the choice's 'tween 'anging and England, it's England the cap'n will pick," Skinner retorted. " 'e knows if 'e stays 'ere much longer 'is neck'll be stretching from a rope. And ours, too."

Grimes groaned. "Maybe the *Black Wind*'s already left us 'ere to 'ang."

"I don't know, but if us'n ain't back soon . . ." Skinner's voice trailed off.

Chandra listened attentively to their words and to every sound about her. Although she had little hope that Miles would be able to pick up her trail, she found herself expecting the sound of a horseman, or several, coming after the wagon. But only twice did she even hear the sound of a horse galloping in the opposite direction.

Many hours later, as though in answer to her prayers, galloping horses overtook them from the rear. The pounding hooves stopped beside the wagon, and Chandra held her breath, hoping desperately that Miles was among the riders.

But to her despair, she heard Pembroke's voice.

"It's late and dark enough now that we won't be meeting travelers upon the road," the Englishman was saying. "Pull the wagon down into those trees and leave it."

Tree limbs cracked against the wagon as it left the road and bounced down a rough incline. Then the straw was pulled off Chandra and she opened her eyes.

Night had enfolded the earth in an impenetrable cloud of darkness. Skinner freed her legs of the ropes and her mouth of the gag, then jerked her to her feet. Pembroke on a fresh mount, a powerful black gelding, rode up to the wagon, leading two other horses.

"The woman will ride with me," he said. "Hand her up, and each of you take a horse."

Chandra was unceremoniously hauled up in front of Pembroke. Skinner awkwardly climbed aboard a brown and white mare that appeared to be the most docile of the pair that Pembroke was leading. Grimes looked askance at the other, a big gray.

"Oi'm a tar, not a bloody 'orseman," he complained.

"Oi'm a tar, too, but Oi ain't complainin'," Skinner said impatiently. "Oi've no stomach, Oi ain't, for being 'anged."

The three horses galloped through the black night. Clouds covered neither moon nor stars.

After about an hour they turned off the road and plunged down a narrow path through a wood heavy with underbrush that slowed their progress.

Chandra quickly discovered that whatever the discomfort of the jolting wagon, it was nothing compared to the misery of riding with Pembroke. He took great delight in pawing her. He pinched her hard on the buttocks, deliberately trying to provoke a protest from her, but she pursed her lips together to keep any sound from escaping.

He unbuttoned her shirt, ripping away one of the buttons in haste, and his sweaty hands squeezed her full breasts roughly. He was intent, she knew, upon proving to her that he was her master and she his helpless captive. She had no power to resist whatever he wished to do to her.

She gritted her teeth and wished that she had aimed her shot at him that day two feet higher.

They were riding now over a marsh, and from occasional snatches of conversation between the sailors and Pembroke, she gathered that they were trying to reach a hidden cove on the bay below the mouth of the Rappahannock where the *Black Wind* was secreted. Pembroke questioned them closely about directions and yelled at Grimes periodically about the length of time it was taking to reach their destination.

Chandra soon suspected that they were lost, a suspicion that was verified when they passed the same grotesquely shaped tree a second time.

Lord William exploded in a storm of vituperation against the two sailors whose stupidity, he charged, had placed him in this situation. He lost interest in tormenting Chandra, and she managed, after much struggling, to rebutton her shirt with her bound hands.

Finally, after more aimless wandering, Pembroke called a halt. "We might as well rest ourselves and the horses here until dawn, when we can see where we're going," he growled.

He dismounted and pulled Chandra to the ground. The two sailors swung down from their horses in great relief and sat down gingerly on a rotting log where they began a meager meal of hardtack and biscuits.

Grimes's courage seemed to have faded with daylight. "What's us to do if the American found the *Black Wind?*" he whined.

"If he has been so unlucky as to have done that,"

Pembroke snapped, "Captain Flint has already dispatched him to the bottom of the sea."

"Not bloody likely," snorted Skinner. "The American's Cap'n Devil, and Oi'll tell you there ain't a man alive what can best 'im."

Chandra started at the mention of her father's old nemesis.

"Your imagination is running away with you," Pembroke exploded. "You damn, superstitious Jack tars have woven such tales about Captain Devil that you think every captain with a bit of luck against you is him. That American cannot possibly be Captain Devil. It is said that he had abandoned the sea after the rebellion."

" 'Tis Cap'n Devil, no other, Oi tell you," Skinner insisted stubbornly. "Oi knows 'im when Oi sees 'im. Oi seed 'im twice in that war, an' 'e was the terror of the seas, 'e was."

Captain Devil. Chandra sat staring at the ground, turning the name over and over in her mind. Could the American who had decimated the trio of pirate ships truly be Captain Devil? Skinner seemed so certain, and from the terrifying picture her father had had, she was sure that once a man had seen the devil pirate, he would not soon forget him. If it were Captain Devil, then he might, indeed, destroy the *Black Wind*. She prayed for his success.

How ironic that she should put her hopes on the man who had ruined her father, the man she had always regarded as the incarnation of his nickname. Papa had said the pirate had consigned him and mama to a life of hell. But now it seemed that only Captain Devil could save her from a true life of hell at the hands of the sadistic duke.

Skinner wrenched off a bite of hardtack with his teeth and said thoughtfully, "Oi wonder if the devil's wench still be with 'im."

"Captain Devil had a woman?" Pembroke said, astounded.

"Aye, 'e did, and that she-devil was as fittin' a mate

for the likes of 'im as ever 'e could 'ave found. Oi'd as soon a tangled with 'im as with 'er, beautiful as she was."

Pembroke shook his head and rose to his feet. Picking up his bedroll, he unfolded it on one of the few dry spots to be found on the marshy ground. He leered at Chandra. "Join me, Mrs. Carrington."

She glared defiantly at him.

He laughed mockingly, strode over to her, and yanked her to her feet. Scooping her up in his arms, he dropped her roughly on his blankets and knelt above her.

"Between now and the time we reach England, you will pay me well for that wound in the leg." His impatient fingers grabbed at the buttons of her pants. "If only your husband could see me now," he laughed, "when just the sight of my kissing you was enough to send him stalking in a fury to another woman."

"You knew Miles was watching that day?" Chandra gasped.

"Of course, that's why I kissed you."

She tried to push him away with her bound hands. "You bastard," she cried, flailing helplessly at him with her legs, but he only laughed at her, enjoying the sight of her tied and struggling.

She resorted to the only weapon she had left, her tongue. "Warfolk will not be happy to learn that you have taken your fill of me first," she hissed. "You well know His Grace's temper and his terrible vengeance."

He drew back as if she had stung him, and from the look in his eyes, she saw that he feared the duke almost as much as she did. That fear would be her only protection in the days ahead.

Pembroke reached down and jerked her off his blankets, leaving her to sleep as best she could on the damp ground.

"You may think you have won," he snarled at her, "but I wager when the duke gets his hands on you, you will more than wish it were me instead of him atop you."

Sleep eluded Chandra. The prospect of what lay ahead of her in England was horrible, but it was no more torturous to her than the thought that she would never see Miles again.

She remembered how he had held her the previous night as they had watched for the pirates. How safe and utterly happy she had felt within his warm, strong arms. How desperately she loved him. And at least no man, no matter what he might do to her body or her spirit, could wrench that love from her heart.

When the first strains of dawn touched the eastern horizon, the three men were eager to be on their way again.

Chandra was so stiff and sore from her night on the damp ground that she could move only with an awkward difficulty that brought a smile to Pembroke's lips.

"You would have found my bed more comfortable," he told her as she was hauled up into the saddle in front of him. Then he turned and said to the two sailors, "I believe I know where we are. We should reach the *Black Wind* in a few hours."

But Pembroke's estimate proved optimistic. For most of the day, they stumbled through spongy marshes, distressing the night herons and the bitterns, and through swamps studded with bitternuts, red maples, and the shiny green leaves of poison sumac. They always avoided roads, for Pembroke feared that search parties might already be out looking for Chandra.

The men grew more nervous and irritable with each passing hour, while Chandra was secretly pleased at their difficulty in finding the *Black Wind*. The delay meant more time for Captain Devil to find the ship or even, although the possibility seemed remote, for Miles to track her.

Finally, however, as the sun sank in the afternoon sky, Pembroke gave a jubilant laugh. "I know the cove is just ahead."

" 'ere's 'oping the *Black Wind*'s still in it," Skinner muttered.

Chandra prayed silently that Captain Devil had found it and sent it to the bottom of the sea.

The screen of trees opened on a small semicircular beach that embraced a sparkling blue cove, and Chandra saw at once that her prayers had not been answered. There, perhaps half a mile out on the placid water, lay the *Black Wind,* a schooner that was totally black except for a red stripe between the wales.

Skinner and Grimes shouted in relief and danced a little jig on the white sand, while tears of despair glistened in Chandra's eyes.

So Captain Devil had failed her, she thought bitterly. She would be dragged back to England and a hideous fate. What was worse, she would never see her beloved husband again.

A jolly boat had been left on the beach for the latecomers. Hastily, the two tars pushed it into the water and Pembroke dragged Chandra into it. Her hands were still bound in front of her and he easily held her down on the rough seat by locking his arms around her.

The sailors scrambled into the vessel and began rowing furiously toward the tall masts of the schooner that lay at anchor in the calm cove, its canvas furled.

As they drew near to the *Black Wind,* Chandra was overwhelmed by despair. She would rather die than board this ship. She thought of the duke's gross body, of his stinking breath, and of his cruelty. Death was preferable.

As the jolly boat drew abreast of the schooner, Chandra regarded the masts and their rigging as if they were gallows—she could almost see the hangman's noose dangling. She would not permit herself to be put aboard this ship.

Suddenly she leaped up, breaking Lord William's grasp, and tried to throw herself into the water. Her hands were still bound, and she knew she would most likely drown, but nothing mattered now except escape.

Pembroke managed to grab her legs as she jumped, and they struggled, nearly capsizing the boat in the progress.

"Gorblimey, 'er'll 'ave us all in the drink, 'er will,"

Grimes shouted as he tried to steady the wildly rocking boat.

Pembroke struck Chandra hard in the stomach with his fist, knocking the air from her, and she collapsed like a deflated balloon.

"Carry her aboard," Pembroke commanded Grimes. "I'll follow you."

Grimes did as he was ordered, slinging Chandra's stunned form over his broad shoulder. Despite his burden, he clamored on board with the same agility he displayed in scampering up the rigging.

Chapter 46

Miles looked about the oak-paneled library at Rose-wood, paying little heed to the acrimonious discussion that raged about him. Instead of addressing themselves to the paramount question of how best to protect themselves in the face of the pirates' threat, the fourteen planters from along the Rappahannock were simply venting their anger. Their meeting had disintegrated into a vilification of the fledgling U.S. government and its president for failing to protect Virginia rivers from the assaults of the marauders. The meeting had been under way for more than two hours, and nothing worthwhile had yet been accomplished.

Miles's wavering attention was recaptured by the arrival of a breathless Jim Spenser. For once, the youth overcame his shyness, so intent was he on imparting his news.

"One of the pirate ships has been sunk and another captured. The third, the *Black Wind,* turned tail and fled."

Jim's announcement was greeted by a chorus of excited voices and shouts of "When?" "How?"

"It was Captain Devil. 'Tis said the way he dispatched those cutthroats and their ships was something to behold."

Wineglasses were raised in joyous toasts to the captain's success. Only Miles did not join in the general jubilation.

"You don't seem very happy about this great news, Miles," Stratford challenged him.

"It is good news, not great," Miles replied. "The *Black Wind* escaped, and it is by far the most dangerous."

Stratford snorted. "I'll wager the ship's captain knew well enough he'd met his better and is halfway back to England by now."

Miles said nothing, but he excused himself. Howard Haughton left with Miles and Jim Spenser, and the trio rode together to Willowmere.

As they came up the elm-lined drive to the mansion, Jim said, "Did you know that the English lord my uncle once hoped to marry to Sally is back in the neighborhood?"

Miles and Howard exchanged startled glances. "You don't mean Lord William Pembroke?" Howard exclaimed.

"That's the one."

"I wouldn't think he'd show his face near Willowmere again."

"As a matter of fact, he was riding in the opposite direction. I met him about fifteen miles or so before I got to Rosewood, and he was headed toward the bay. He didn't look so good, either. His clothes were all wrinkled and stained, and he hadn't shaved."

"What do you suppose he could be doing around here?" Howard asked.

Miles's face was troubled. "Whatever it is, I don't like it."

As the men rode up in front of Willowmere, Sarah hurried out onto the portico. "Where is Chandra?" she demanded in alarm.

Miles paled. "What do you mean?"

"She and Grant Horn haven't come back. I thought they must have gone on to Rosewood with you."

"Where could they be?" Howard mused.

Miles's face was ashen. "Let's ride back along the road, and see what we can find."

They turned their horses back down the drive. Howard made a few feeble attempts at conversation as they rode, but finally abandoned the effort in deference to Miles's grim silence.

As they were winding through a wood of maples, oaks and hickories, Miles abruptly reined his big bay to a stop and dismounted.

"What is it?" Howard asked as Miles studied a flattened spot in the grass by the side of the road.

"A body was lying here," he replied.

He plunged into a thicket of staghorn sumac, following the faint footprints there. A few feet in, he stopped, listening. He could hear a horse neighing some distance farther on. Quickly Miles pushed on, oblivious to the branches that reached out to grab at him.

A moment later he found Gray Dancer and Horn's horse tied to a shagbark hickory. Several feet away, he saw Horn, still firmly tied to the scaly trunk of the post oak. Horn was conscious now and trying frantically to call out over the gag in his mouth.

As Miles freed him, he noted the ugly gash, now crusted with clotted blood, on the back of his head.

"Hit you from behind, did they?" Miles asked as he worked quickly to untie Horn.

"I guess they must have," he answered vaguely, still confused from the wound. "Mrs. Carrington and I were riding along when all of a sudden everything went black."

"Did you see your attackers at all?" Miles asked as Howard and Jim came crashing through the brush.

Horn nodded. "I was coming to just as they were taking her away. There were three men. One of them looked like he could be a gentleman, although his clothes were soiled and he was wanting a shave."

"Pembroke," Miles exclaimed. "I'm sure of it. What about the other two?"

"They looked like sailors to me, and pretty rough ones at that."

"Oh, my God," Miles cried as the meaning of Horn's words began to penetrate. "The pirates."

"But why would Lord William be with them?" Howard asked.

"I don't know, unless . . ." Miles paused, "unless he has something to do with them."

"Lord William! That's nonsense," Howard protested.

"Is it? Consider the timing. The raids on the James River began just after he left there, and the raid on the Rappahannock came shortly after he departed here. And the Beaumonts, with whom he stayed, were the first victims. The pirates seemed to know a great deal about the house, too. Pembroke could have supplied that information." Miles turned to Horn. "Grant, did you hear the men say anything about where they were going?"

Horn searched his still fuzzy memory. "No . . . although the gentleman said something to Mrs. Carrington about not wanting to keep the duke waiting."

Miles felt as if his heart had stopped. He turned and walked blindly away from Horn. Many months ago, in England, Pitt had mentioned the leader of the plot to undermine the new nation—a very powerful lord close to Prinny—Warfolk! He not only had an agent in America, but a navy of plundering brigands whose real purpose was to sow dissension. That was why Pembroke was in America.

Regaining control of himself, Miles turned back to Horn. "How did they take Mrs. Carrington? Her horse is still here."

"In a farm wagon," Horn answered. "The two sailors were driving it, and the other man rode ahead on his horse."

"I passed such a wagon piled high with straw," Jim exclaimed. "It was headed toward the bay."

"They must be headed for the *Black Wind*," Miles said, breaking into a run for his horse. "Grant, you go back up to the house and have Sarah attend to that head wound. Jim and Howard will come with me."

The trio mounted and galloped in grim silence through the fading light of the day. Miles tried to think clearly, to tell himself that he would reach Chandra in time, but if he failed? At that, he simply stopped his thoughts. Night had settled by the time they reached the spot where Jim had met the wagon.

They stopped at a plantation to request lanterns and some food that they could eat as they rode.

The going was slow now. Miles and Jim walked along the road with their lanterns, searching for any sign of a wagon turning off.

Finally, long after midnight, they were rewarded by the sight of wheel indentations going down an incline. They found the wagon hidden in an alder thicket.

Miles studied the ground carefully by the light of his dim, flickering lantern. "They switched to horses here, three of them. That means Pembroke must have joined them."

"Not necessarily," Howard objected. "Chandra would need a horse, too."

"It appears from the tracks that one of the horses is burdened with two riders. Perhaps she's riding double with one of the men. Fortunately, this second mount has a distinctive shoe. It will be easy to track."

"Not in the dark of night on a road as traveled as this," Howard protested. "Why don't we rest here and start at dawn?"

Miles shook his head stubbornly. "No, you may stay here if you wish, but it will be several miles yet before they will turn off this road, and I want to get at least that far tonight."

Miles remounted and rode on, and Howard and Jim realized they would have to follow. It was well past two in the morning when they finally bedded down to try to get a little sleep before dawn.

Miles could not close his eyes. He was too tormented by the thought of Chandra in Pembroke's hands.

How often Miles had reassured Chandra that he would never let this happen, that he would keep her safe from Warfolk's long, vengeful arms! "Trust me," he had told her, and she had. He cursed himself for having ever let her out of his sight.

In the distance, the hoarse cry of a night heron disturbed the silence. How precious Chandra had become to him. How eagerly he hungered not just for her body and her kiss, but for her flashing smile, her silvery laugh, and for the contentment that her presence brought him. He could not possibly give her up—he *would* not.

At the first glimmer of light, Miles was on his feet, and the trio set out again. Not more than two miles down the road, Miles's trained eye discerned the place at which the riders had turned off the road and plunged into the trees.

He pointed to the distinctive print of one of the horses. "See, it's them all right."

"But see how thick the dew is on the tracks," Howard said. "They passed here last night. Do you suppose we have any hope of finding them before they reach that ship?"

"We have to try." Miles's face was set and determined.

After following the tracks for some hours, they stopped and stared grimly at one another. "They have to be lost," Miles said in disgust. "We are wasting time following them in circles. Our only hope of stopping them from boarding that ship, I fear, is to reach the spot where they will meet it ahead of them."

He rubbed his chin thoughtfully. "I remember once during the revolution Devin showed me the only two spots in this section of the bay where a privateer could safely conceal his vessel. If Pembroke is going to rendezvous with the *Black Wind,* it most likely is anchored in one of them."

"Are the two spots near each other?" Howard asked.

"No, several miles apart, but we'll try the larger one first." Miles pushed his horse ahead. "That seems to me the one they would most likely pick. It is nearer to the mouth of the Rappahannock, and they may have thought to use it as their base of operations while they raided the plantations along the river."

The sun was well past its zenith when they reached the cove—and found it empty. No ship was at anchor and there was no sign that their quarry had been there.

"Damn," Miles exclaimed in despair. "It must be the other. We have wasted precious time!"

He was in a frenzy by now, and he pushed through a swamp toward the second cove with utter disregard for himself, his horse or his companions.

Jim sought to comfort Miles. "Perhaps by now Captain Devil has found and seized the *Black Wind,*" he said hopefully, "and when Pembroke reaches the cove it will be empty. Then we shall be able to take them with ease."

Miles shook his head. "I pray you are right."

"Even if the ship has not yet been taken, surely Captain Devil will find it before it can escape the bay."

Miles regarded him with a panicked expression on his face. "And Chandra will be killed along with the others aboard when he sinks it."

This thought cast a pall over them, and they rode on in silence. Dusk was settling before they reached the second cove. As the screen of trees thinned in front of them, the first thing that met their eyes was the tall masts of a schooner. It lay at anchor well off shore.

"There it is," Miles cried in jubilation. "Thank God!"

But his joy was short-lived. He put his glass to his eye to get a better look at the ship, and it was then that he saw the jolly boat pulling up beside the black schooner. Chandra was seated in the boat, with Pembroke beside her.

As he watched, transfixed with horror, he saw Chandra leap up and try desperately to throw herself into the water, only to be stunned by Pembroke's blow. Then he watched helplessly as she was carried aboard the English pirate ship.

"Damn you!" he shouted, shaking his fist in impotent fury and frustration. He had lost Chandra.

He swore furiously at the ship. "I will follow you to the ends of the earth, Pembroke," he vowed, "and I shall regain my wife and kill you."

In his rage and his sorrow, Miles slumped back in his saddle. His voice was choked with tears as he cried, "Damn you, Devin, where were you when I needed you?"

Chapter 47

By the time Grimes reached the deck and dropped Chandra roughly upon the planking, she had recovered her breath and her senses. She opened her eyes to a rather dizzy world and found herself facing the captain of the *Black Wind*. To her astonishment, he did not in the slightest resemble the leader of a band of raping, plundering brigands. He was a most handsome man. Although he was of middle years with graying hair, he had an insolent, youthful grace to his slender but powerfully built body. He was impeccably dressed in a navy-blue broadcloth jacket over a red silk waistcoat embroidered with gold. His white silk breeches were spotless. But most striking of all was his face. His deep-set blue eyes were penetrating yet kindly, his nose was straight and well formed, and he had a smiling, sensitive mouth. He returned her frightened gaze with compassion.

Surely, Chandra thought, he was as distinguished looking a man as ever she had seen, and a faint flicker of hope fluttered in her heart. Surely he would not condemn her to the duke, once he had heard her story. But would any Englishman, particularly a pirate, dare to incur the disfavor of Warfolk?

From the corner of her eye, Chandra noticed another figure well back in the shadows of the companionway, watching intently, both its face and form concealed in a voluminous hooded cloak. But Chandra was too occupied wondering how best to entreat the captain to give much attention to the figure in the shadows.

The captain scanned her face searchingly. "That was

quite a fight you put up. Why were you so reluctant to board this ship and accept my hospitality?"

Chandra's reply was cut off by Lord William's shout as he climbed onto the deck and saw the captain.

"Who the blazes are you?" Pembroke demanded.

His question was not answered by the captain, but by Skinner, who had followed his lordship up the rope ladder.

"Blimey," the old sailor exclaimed as he climbed over the gunwale and regarded the ship's commander with his cockeye, " 'tis Cap'n Devil 'imself, 'tis."

The color drained from Pembroke's face. "Is that true?" he stammered at the stranger in front of him.

"Aye, Captain Devil, at your service."

Chandra stared at him in stunned disbelief. This distinguished man bore not a shred of resemblance to that hairy, hulking apelike monster in her father's picture.

"You cannot be he," she gasped. "You do not look at all like him."

He regarded her with amusement. "Quite to the contrary. I asure you that I have always looked like me."

She blushed in silent embarrassment at her foolish statement.

Lord William, blustering in a desperate attempt to recapture his courage, demanded, "What the blazes are you doing here?"

Captain Devil gave him a long, piercing look. "Awaiting the leader of the pirates who have been plundering our coast and our ships. I was assured that he would be along shortly with a woman captive, Mrs. Miles Carrington, without whom he dared not return to England. And true to reports, here you are."

"I don't know what you're talking about." Pembroke attempted to bluff his way out of his predicament. "I am no pirate leader." With a condescending sneer, he went on, "I am Lord William Pembroke, the son of the Earl of Blandshire, and unless you want to bring more trouble upon your ill-equipped nation than it can handle, you will see that I reach England safely and with dispatch."

"I have no interest in your lineage," Captain Devil said quietly. "What concerns me is the fact that you are a pirate leader and the kidnapper of this woman." He nodded at Chandra. "Piracy and kidnapping are capital crimes here."

Captain Devil's remarkable blue eyes were somber and hard as flintstones, and Pembroke's bravado broke as he realized the man was not to be intimidated or deterred. "This charge of kidnapping is absurd," he stammered. "The woman is a runaway whom I am returning to her guardian and to her protector, the Duke of Warfolk, and there is no more powerful lord in all Britain." Pembroke tried to regain a bit of his lost assurance. "I warn you, his temper shall know no bounds should he be deprived of his rightful property by an upstart American sea dog."

"He is a liar," Chandra cried. "He took me from my home and my husband."

"She is the liar," Pembroke shot back. "She is an ungrateful wench who must be returned to her guardian."

The sun was sinking rapidly now behind the horizon, and Chandra stared anxiously through the deepening gloom at Captain Devil. Would he believe her?"

"There is a most handsome reward offered for her return," Pembroke assured him.

His words struck new terror into Chandra's heart. If Captain Devil were a mercenary, a pirate, then money would speak far louder than words of protest.

Captain Devil studied them both for a long moment. Then he said, "She is the wife of an American citizen. She will be returned to her rightful place with him."

"You are a fool," Pembroke cried. "You are turning down a fortune, I tell you."

Sparks of anger flashed in the captain's eyes. "My only reward is justice, and that I shall have when you are hanged."

Pembroke wilted beneath the captain's quelling gaze, while tears of relief glistened in Chandra's eyes. "You can never know how grateful I am to you," she murmured.

Captain Devil gave her a compassionate smile and reached out, taking her small hands in his own and pressing them reassuringly. "Please regard my assistance as a tiny payment on account, Chandra, for the misery I unknowingly caused your father. I pray that now you will be able to hate me a little less."

It was a moment before she could sufficiently recover from her astonishment to speak. "How do you know my name? Where did you learn about my father?"

The captain smiled. "Let us go to my cabin and I will tell you." He nodded to the sailors who surrounded Pembroke. "Throw the esteemed earl's son in the brig. And his two associates."

With that, the captain started toward the companionway.

As he turned his back, the Englishman suddenly reached down and grabbed a dirk which was concealed in his boot. He lunged at the captain's back.

Chandra opened her mouth to scream a warning, but her cry was drowned by the noise of a shot. The dirk clattered to the floor, and Lord William stared down in agony at his shattered arm. Blood poured from it onto the deck.

The shot had come from the shadows of the companionway. The cloaked figure Chandra had noticed earlier stepped forward, the gun still smoking, and tossed back the hood of the cloak to reveal a woman with wide hazel eyes that flashed like gold against her creamy, flawless skin. Although she was tiny in stature, she was a mature woman, yet her beauty had been preserved, perhaps even enhanced over the passing years. Her hair was still dark and rich, her carriage was regal, her delicate features—the nose, the cheekbones, the chin—all had been strengthened and refined. She reminded Chandra of a magnificent cameo.

Skinner gasped. " 'Tis the devil's own wench, and not all that much changed from when Oi last seed 'er in the war."

The woman spoke, her voice soft and musical, yet with a note of authority in it that matched her husband's: "That was a most foolish thing to attempt, Your Lordship." She turned to the sailors near him on deck. "Take him to the brig and tend his wound. It will be a long time before he raises another dirk."

"No thanks to you," Pembroke snarled as he clutched his shattered arm.

"My aim is better than you give me credit for," the woman replied coolly. "Should I have desired, I would have done you much more severe damage."

As Pembroke was led away, Chandra studied the woman, puzzled. There was something so familiar about her.

Seeing her scrutiny, the woman asked, "Have I shocked you, my dear Chandra?" Her words were soft, almost apologetic, as though she sincerely regretted the possibility that Chandra might think ill of her.

Dazed, Chandra shook her head. "No, 'tis only that for some reason it seems as though I know you from somewhere. Yet I am certain I have never seen you before."

The woman smiled. "No, you have not, but I do bear a strong resemblance to my brother—your husband. I am Ondine Darcy, Miles's sister." She nodded toward Captain Devil. "And this is my husband, Devin Darcy, whom you have only known by another, less flattering name." Ondine tucked her pistol in the folds of her cloak and took both of Chandra's cold hands in her warm ones. "Miles told Devin about your father when they were in Washington. I hope you will come to realize that he is not half so bad as you were led to believe. What Devin did he did in war, and, God knows, war is rarely fair to its victims."

Chandra looked from husband to wife to husband again. "I cannot believe you are Captain Devil. When I think . . ." She broke off as they heard a shot ring out from the beach.

A voice in the rigging called out, "There are three men on the beach and one just fired a pistol at us. Could they be more English awanting a voyage home?"

Devin strode to the rail, put his glass to his eye, and

stared through the murky dusk. "If my eyes don't deceive me, that's my brother-in-law in a fury because he thinks he has lost his wife to the pirates. Show the colors, and set his mind at rest. And you, Penn," he called to his subaltern, "take that boat and go pick him up."

Howard Haughton put his hand on Miles's arm to restrain him from firing a second shot. "You're a fool, Miles. That shot only warned them that we know who and what they are, and they will flee all the faster."

"What difference does it make?" Miles's tone was laced with bitterness. "The *Black Wind* might as well be across the ocean, for all the chance we have of reaching it or getting Chandra back."

"Look," Jim cried, "they're hoisting a flag!"

The startled trio watched in amazement as the Stars and Stripes fluttered open on the stiff evening breeze.

Jim stared at the flag. "I don't understand."

But Miles did. "It's Devin," he said, slapping his leg. "I'm sure of it. He must have captured the *Black Wind* and waited here to trap Pembroke when he showed up for the rendezvous. I'll wager his lordship never even suspected anything was wrong, just as we didn't."

Miles raised his glass again as the small boat that had carried Chandra to the brig now began to head toward shore. Despite the growing darkness, Miles recognized Penn. Miles blessed his brother-in-law with all the fervor with which he had cursed him but minutes earlier. Chandra was safe.

As the boat drew to shore, Miles splashed into the water to meet it, heedless of his riding boots.

"Penn, is my wife all right?" he yelled in a frenzy, splashing water all about him.

"Your wife's none the worse for her ordeal, but your sister had to shoot that English fool 'fore he stuck a dirk in the captain's back."

"Ondine! You mean she's aboard, too?"

Penn grinned. "You don't think she'd be staying home when there's adventure to be had." Howard called from the beach: "Miles, you go aboard and join your family. Jim and I will take your horse and ride back to the Rappahannock to spread the good word that the *Black Wind* has been captured. And you can thank that brother-in-law of yours for me personally."

Miles nodded and leaped into the jolly boat. He could not sit still, but fidgeted anxiously as Penn rowed toward the *Black Wind*. Despite his assurance that Chandra was safe, he would not rest easy until he saw her with his own eyes.

"What did my sister do to Pembroke?" Miles asked Penn.

"Winged him in the arm. A nice shot, it was."

When the jolly boat reached the brig, Miles climbed eagerly up the rope ladder, scrambled over the gunwale, and swept Chandra into his arms. Their kiss of reunion was so long and passionate that finally Ondine gave a little cough. With laughter dancing in her voice, she complained, "Having not seen you for nearly two years, my dear brother, I am overwhelmed by your eager greeting. Might I have a moment of your time?"

Miles's head bobbed up and still holding Chandra tightly with his left arm he hugged Ondine to him with his right. He grinned at his sister. "Let me introduce the two most important women in my life to each other," he said.

"We've already met," Ondine said with a smile. "And I congratulate you on your choice of my sister-in-law. I am well pleased."

Still holding his wife and his sister close to him, Miles looked over their heads at his brother-in-law.

"Thank God, Devin, you got here in time. I can never tell you the despair I felt when I saw Chandra being hauled up into this wretched pirate vessel. I thought I had lost her forever."

"Pembroke will cause you no more trouble now," Devin said.

"Lord William fares most poorly at the hands of the Carrington women," Miles said, grinning at his sister.

"Chandra shot him in the leg, and now I understand you have added additional lead to his evil carcass."

Ondine frowned. "He was a fool. That's far worse than just being a pirate."

"It's time we got under way," her husband said. "We'll take you and Chandra back to the Rappahannock."

Devin barked out orders, and the deck of the ship came alive with men rushing to their stations and scampering up the rigging to unfurl the sails.

As the vessel began to move, Miles turned away from Chandra and Ondine. "What happened when you met the pirates?" he asked Devin.

His brother-in-law snorted. "The other two ships were not worth the effort it took me to outfit a vessel to go after them. I sank one and captured the other as they left the raid on the Beaumonts' plantation. This ship and its Captain Flint were more worthy. He managed to slip away and escape while I was dispatching the other two, and fled north rather than south toward the mouth of the bay as I would have expected him to do."

Devin was watching the movements of his crew with an expert eye. Satisfied that all tasks were being performed as they ought to be, he turned back to Miles.

"Fortunately, the captain of the second ship, Mondello by name, was most talkative when he thought it would save his wretched neck. He told me how Warfolk was financing the pirates. The duke's real motive, by the way, was just as Jefferson thought: to breed discontent among us and send us back into England's arms. Many innocent people suffered a great deal as a result."

Ondine, who had been standing quietly by her husband listening, slipped her arm around her husband's waist and the two exchanged the smile of a happy, long-married couple.

"Mondello also told me," Devin continued, after looking up from his wife's lovely face, "how none of them dared to return to England without Chandra. They planned to seize her when they raided Willowmere,

which would have been last night, had I not come along
to spoil their plans. I realized then that the *Black Wind*
must be sailing toward the Rappahannock in a last desperate effort to get Chandra. But Captain Flint was no
fool. He knew I'd have him trapped if he sailed up the
river, so he refused to go, and Pembroke was forced to
set out by land to abduct her. Captain Flint did not
reckon how well I knew the bay and where he was hiding in wait."

"He put up a good fight," Ondine observed.

"Aye, he did, but not good enough, and once I put
a ball through his heart, his crew surrendered quick
enough."

Miles smiled. "Has this whetted your appetite to return to the sea?"

Devin drew his wife close to him. "When the revolution ended and I bought the plantation, I admit I
thought I would miss the sea terribly. But I have not
regretted my decision. The rich land and my wife and
children about me are all I need now." He bent his head
and kissed his wife lightly. "Besides, if I went back to
sea, who would keep this lioness in hand?"

Later that night, as the *Black Wind* was skimming
across the bay, Chandra and Miles stood on the forward deck. He stood behind her, his arms enfolding her
as they looked out ahead of them at the bowsprit stabbing into the dark. Plump clouds blotted out great
patches of the glittering star fields, leaving the night as
black as ever the pirates could have wished it.

As the wind tugged at them, Miles hugged Chandra
closer. "I am delighted that you and Ondine took to
each other at once," he said. He paused and cleared his
throat. "What do you think of her husband?"

Chandra made a wry face. "Why didn't you tell me
Captain Devil was your brother-in-law?"

"After that delicious description you gave me—more
ape than man—I could not bear to disillusion you."

She blushed. "What a silly fool you must have
thought me."

He bent his head and buried his face in the lustrous waves of sable hair, kissing her lightly. "'No, only young and naive, and considerably more innocent than I had originally suspected."

She raised her hands and clasped them over his as though to make fast his embrace of her.

He nibbled at her ear and whispered, "I love you more than words can ever tell, Chandra. I was mad with grief and despair when I thought I had lost you forever to Warfolk."

She loosened his arms and turned to face him. "My darling, being dragged back to the duke was not half so cruel to me as the thought of never seeing you again."

He kissed her forehead and smiled happily. "I want to give you a wonderful homecoming present. What would you like: diamonds, pearls, sapphires to match your eyes, or perhaps an ermine cloak? Name it, my love, and it shall be yours."

"I may have whatever I choose?" she asked, an impish light shining in her sea blue eyes.

He nodded. "What, more than anything else, do you want me to give you?"

"Your son."

His lips parted in surprise and he started to speak, but she placed her fingers on his lips to silence him.

"It is the only thing that could make me happier than I am at this moment, Miles, safe in your arms and in your love."

He threw back his head and laughed in delight, then whirled her around.

"What are you doing?" she cried breathlessly, as he swept her up into his arms.

"I have an uncontrollable urge to start at once upon the gift you desire." And with that, he headed toward the companionway. As she clung to him, her love overflowed, and she knew that at last she was home.